HIS
OTHER
LIFE

BOOKS BY ANNA E. COLLINS

Her Secret Life

Love at First Spite
These Numbered Days
A Life in Bloom
Worst in Show

HIS
OTHER
LIFE

Anna E. Collins

bookouture

Published by Bookouture in 2025

An imprint of Storyfire Ltd.
Carmelite House
50 Victoria Embankment
London EC4Y 0DZ
Uniter Kingdom

www.bookouture.com

The authorised representative in the EEA is Hachette Ireland
8 Castlecourt Centre
Dublin 15 D15 XTP3
Ireland
(email: info@hbgi.ie)

ISBN: 978-1-83618-049-4
eBook ISBN: 978-1-83618-048-7

To all who have loved and lost.

ONE

ISLA

At some point in the past two years, heading to the store for a basic errand had become the equivalent of running a medieval gauntlet for Isla Gallagher. There was the dread, slithering like wet fog across her senses in the hours leading up to the main event, the suit of armor she had to don for protection, and the meticulous planning it took to chart the best path past any obstacle.

Granted, for Isla, the armor wasn't made of metal but of clothes and make-up from her old life, a practiced smile, feigned indifference. The obstacles were also less spiky clubs and glinting blades, and more the possibility of running into someone she knew and being forced to engage in chit-chat at the cash register. But whether the peril was real or not, if staying home was an option, Isla would happily pick that any day of the week.

Today was no different, except today she had no choice. She was making her husband's favorite meal for their seven-year anniversary, a Vietnamese stir-fry that required both lemongrass and chili oil, neither of which she had in the pantry.

She paused at the front door, the knob cool against her palm, and closed her eyes. The bus would arrive at the stop in eight minutes. She'd time her walk so she'd get there in five. Take a seat in the back, headphones on, let Port Townsend rush by outside the window in a gray February blur.

"It'll be fine," she whispered to herself. "Just do it."

A sharp inhale, and then she opened the door and stepped into the rain, pulling the hood of her jacket up.

The weather worked in her favor—nothing like a downpour to make people keep their heads down as they hurried from one place to the next—and after a fifteen-minute ride, she reached her destination with no close call. She'd worked herself up over nothing as usual, like Mom would say. ("You can't stop living your life, Birdie.") Isla knew she was right, and yet...

She stepped inside the large market on the other side of town and blinked at the garish fluorescent lights overhead while she scanned her surroundings. It was unusually quiet even for a Monday afternoon, which boosted her confidence. Maybe this wouldn't be so bad after all.

The rivulets running off her jacket were quickly making a puddle where she stood, so she pulled out her phone and opened the list containing the missing meal ingredients as well as a few other basics—ten items in total scribbled in order of the aisles. She should be able to get this done in under six minutes. Then all she had to do was wait for the return bus and she'd soon be back home again. She'd have dinner on the table by seven. Jonah would be proud of her.

There were two people ahead of her in line, and she allowed herself that time to browse the candy section. That was her mistake, losing focus for a moment.

"Professor Gallagher?"

The voice startled Isla from her internal debate between chocolate and sour gummies.

"I thought it was you," the girl behind the register said. "I almost didn't recognize you. I didn't know you lived here. How's your day going?"

Isla squinted at the girl. "Um, great." Normally she was good with both names and faces, but those stupid years of Zoom classes had messed everyone up.

The French Impressionism class, she thought. Maybe Addison something. She glanced at the girl's nametag. *Madison.*

Isla dug deep and found a smile. "How have you been?" She placed her items on the belt in a jumble. "Done with school?"

"For now. I'm applying for my master's. Museum studies."

"Oh wow. Very good."

"Your class was actually part of what inspired me." Madison paused her scanning.

No, don't stop. Isla nodded, her heart picking up speed.

"Yeah, I'm hoping to get into curation work." Madison gestured with a can of coconut milk in her hand. An *un*scanned can. "Preferably on the East Coast where my fiancé is from. We're getting married next year."

Isla forced her gaze from the can to Madison's face. What would she have said two years ago if one of her students made this announcement? What voice would she have used?

"Oh wonderful." She swallowed. "Congratulations."

Madison beamed at her but still didn't scan the damn can. "Thanks."

No, enough of this.

Isla pulled out her wallet. "Um, I hate to rush you, but I've got a bus to catch." She put as much warmth in her voice as she could, but when Madison's brow rose in seeming surprise, Isla second-guessed herself. Maybe this wasn't how she used to talk to her students. Was there a professional distance she'd lost since being away from the university?

"Of course," Madison said. And finally, the groceries went into Isla's canvas bag.

Isla hurried to pay but fumbled with the zipper to her purse when she went to put the wallet away again. Great, now *she* was keeping Madison waiting. She managed an apologetic grimace at the girl, who was holding the handles of the bag, waiting for Isla to take them.

"Ugh, this freaking thing," Isla muttered.

And that's when it happened. She looked up, sweat now dampening the nape of her neck, and reached for the bag, almost sensing the question before it found her ears.

Madison didn't let go. Instead, she cocked her head, intent on Isla. "Hey, Professor, are you okay?"

And what could Isla do other than yank the bag out of Madison's hand and run?

There was no way she was answering that question.

The whiskey slipped down her throat like smokey silk. One shot, then another.

Isla set the glass down on the counter then rested her palms against the marbled stone and closed her eyes. She counted to ten slowly before opening them, then she allowed her shoulders to come down from their high perch and returned to the hallway to remove her slick boots and dripping jacket. She'd have to mop the floors before she started cooking, but the tension had built further during the ride home, and her need for something to take the edge off had surpassed the need to protect the hardwood.

She didn't drink like this often. Well, perhaps a little more often in recent months than she had in the past, but if it helped, what was the harm? Two shots of whiskey and she could function again. She'd ventured far today, and for a good cause. She'd take care of the floors, unload her groceries, then maybe set the table before she started cooking. A solid plan.

She spun toward the kitchen and almost toppled headfirst over a black shadow sprinting across the floor.

"Dammit, Ulysses!"

The cat stopped in the doorway and peered at her over his shoulder. *Look where you're going*, the feline seemed to say. *Also, I'm hungry.*

Had she fed him this morning?

"Fine, I'm coming." Isla tiptoed after the cat into the kitchen, avoiding the wet boot prints (and now damp paw prints too) as best she could. Poor Ulysses. He deserved a more responsible human.

Once the floors were dry, the cat was fed, and the groceries put away, Isla turned on the TV like she always did when she was home alone. Reaching behind the DVD player, she pulled out the case with the disc of her choice and popped it in. Then she sat back on the floor and pressed play.

The first notes of Christina Perri's "A Thousand Years" played over the speakers, followed by a shaky camera shot panning over the church, the snow-covered grounds, the gathering of people in dresses and suits. They'd been so lucky. Bellingham had gotten dumped on in the days leading up to the wedding, but on the day of, the sun had shone from a blue sky, making the icy white still on the ground sparkle.

The music faded as the camera panned to Jonah, who grinned into it. "Let's get this party started already," he said. "Someone go get my bride."

Isla said the words along with him, her lips tugging into a smile. Time to get a-cooking.

The recipe was trickier than she remembered. She forgot that not getting all the chopping done before turning on the burner would have her in a bind during the fourth step, when two pans had to be combined, so her timing was off. The sound-track was reassuring though. She trimmed chicken breasts to the strings and pipes of the entry procession and was familiar enough with the video to know without looking at exactly which note the camera panned to Jonah's stunned face as he saw her coming down the aisle toward him on her dad's arm. Her two favorite men.

The knife slipped, nicking her thumb instead.

"Ouch." Isla watched as the first red bubbles oozed to the surface of her skin. Next to her, the waiting pan sizzled impatiently. *Dammit.* She stuck her finger under the tap. Behind her, the priest welcomed the congregation.

By the time she'd found a Band-Aid, put the chicken in the pan to fry, and poured herself another shot (for the pain), she and Jonah were facing each other on the screen. Isla paused at the table, silverware in hand, watching mesmerized as he lifted her veil. The room spun, and she steadied herself against the back of a chair. That *swish* when the soft mesh brushed past her hair—she could still hear it. Feel it. She'd been found.

She took a few steps closer to the TV, not wanting to miss that velvet awe in Jonah's eyes as he said, "I do."

The screen froze. Skipped a beat. Jonah's eyes were stuck half closed on a blink, his mouth stretched into an almost cartoonish smile.

"No." Isla dropped the silverware and hurried to the DVD player. She tapped it gently. "Come on."

The video skipped another jagged step forward and now Isla was in the picture, head bent on a nod.

"No," Isla said, louder this time. She pressed stop and ejected the disc. Breathed on it as if that would infuse it with life and wiped it with her shirt sleeve. She must have gotten a fingerprint on it or something. It was *not* scratched. It couldn't be.

She held her breath while navigating the chapters to the

right one. The vows. She rubbed absent-mindedly at her nose. Something was irritating it, but she ignored it while the screen filled again with her and Jonah. The veil lift, the blessing of the rings, the vows. The video played without stopping this time, and Isla exhaled. She needed to make another copy of this disc, just in case.

With her hands on her hips, Isla watched for another few seconds before Ulysses weaved past her legs with a loud meow.

"It was just a smudge," she told him. "Nothing to worry about."

The cat meowed again and ran toward the kitchen. That's when the smell of burning meat seeped fully into Isla's consciousness.

"Oh fuck!"

The chicken was salvageable once she'd cut the burned bottoms off, but the sauce looked wrong, and the garlic press was nowhere to be found, so in the end, Isla had to admit the dish only vaguely resembled what she'd intended.

She sat down at the table and lit the candle between the two plates. Poured another shot and held it up for a toast, but before she could say anything, the doorbell rang.

She froze, that one singular thought she'd held close all day rising to the surface.

Jonah?

She scrambled to her feet, almost tripped on the rug, then sprinted toward the front of the house with her heartbeat frantic against her sternum. Her mind swirled amber with whiskey, accompanied by the crowd cheering on their first dance on the TV. Etta James and mood lighting. A future of possibilities.

Please be him.

She yanked open the door with such urgency that the person on the step let out a small yelp.

"Jeez, Birdie. You scared me." Nancy, Isla's mom, walked

past her to the closet and shrugged out of her coat. "Would you believe I left my freaking purse at home?"

Isla swallowed hard and closed the door with a click. She was so stupid. Of course it wasn't Jonah. Jonah was tuxedos and vows. Snowy streets and church bells. Photographs and memories.

Jonah was forever gone. Dead. And that was her fault.

TWO

GEMMA

March, three years ago

"Cher!" Gemma lifted the pile of junk mail that was gathering on the kitchen counter then glanced into her aunt's handbag while simultaneously opening the kitchen drawer where pens and rubber bands went to die. No car keys.

"Cher!" she yelled again, aiming her call toward the bedroom at the far end of the narrow hallway in the small apartment they shared. "I need to get to work. Where the hell are the keys?"

When she still didn't receive an answer, she let out a frustrated groan and hurried to the bedroom. She knocked on the door but only for show, opening it without waiting for a response.

The room was dark, only lit by the muted morning light seeping in from behind the blinds, and the air smelled stale from cigarettes even though her aunt insisted she always smoked out the window. She was still sleeping, wrapped in both a comforter and a threadbare blanket.

"Cheryl." Gemma shook her aunt's shoulder.

"Wha...?" her aunt mumbled from the depths of the cocoon.

"Do you have my car keys? I'm running late for work, and I can't find them."

"On the counter."

"No." Gemma tried to control the irritation in her voice. "I've checked there. And in your purse. And in the drawer. Come on. Wake up." She shook her again.

Cheryl flicked down the top corner of the blankets. "Jesus, Mary, and Joseph, why can't a body get some peace around here?" Yesterday's mascara clung to the soft bags beneath her eyes as she blinked up at Gemma. "If they're not in the kitchen, then I don't know."

Gemma looked around the room, ignoring the half-full bottle of brandy that always sat on the nightstand. "What did you wear to work last night? Maybe you put them in your pocket?"

"I don't know." Cheryl closed her eyes again but waved a finger in the direction of the chair in the corner. "Maybe over there."

Gemma stepped over a pair of jeans and several mismatched shoes that littered the floor. Her aunt's jacket was slung on top of a pile of laundry. Fingers crossed, she felt around in its pockets, her shoulders easing as she clasped cool metal. There. Finally.

"Thanks. See you later," she hollered as she ran down the hallway and out the door without waiting for a response.

She would definitely be late today, and she'd promised her boss last time that it wouldn't happen again. But this was the deal she'd made with her aunt when her ex, Yuri, had taken off with that "catalogue model" and left Gemma without a place to live six months ago. She could have the spare room in Cheryl's apartment that she'd once stayed in as a teenager, and Cheryl could use Gemma's car to get to her waitressing job in the evenings. It was a good deal. Most of the time.

A silver Mercedes cut her off as she was about to merge onto the off ramp on the freeway, and without thinking, she laid on the horn. God, people were so on edge, especially with all the uncertainties around the new virus. The dental office she worked at had already cancelled most routine check-ups while awaiting further instructions, but there was still no shortage of patients who needed to be seen. Aches and pains, cracked fillings, cavities, denture care—those kinds of issues didn't go away just because state leaders had told people to minimize contact with each other.

Gemma accelerated through a yellow light then slowed to make a right at the next intersection. Her first appointment wasn't until nine thirty, so even though she was supposed to be at work by nine, if she was lucky, no one would notice.

She parked behind the building and jogged across the parking lot, taking care not to slip on the patchy ice left from the latest snowfall. Air laced with antiseptics and vinyl gloves washed over her when she opened the door.

She kept her head down as she went through the back entrance, hoping nobody else would be in the staff room but having no such luck.

"Traffic again?" Wendy, the receptionist, asked, coming out of the bathroom. She didn't say it in an unfriendly way, but Gemma still blushed.

"Something like that. Is he in yet?" By "he" she meant Dr. Richards.

"Yup. In the office."

Typical. Gemma hurried to change into her scrubs, wash up, and don the new masks and goggles they'd been provided. They gave her headaches and left deep marks across her nose, but she wasn't about to complain. After starting as a dental assistant at twenty, she had put herself through school to advance into a dental hygienist role over the past several years. Now at twenty-seven, she knew how lucky she was to have a stable, daytime job that she'd likely be able to stay and grow in for the rest of her career, especially after having seen her mom struggle when she was younger. There was no doubt in Gemma's mind that her mom working three jobs to pay the bills had been a contributing factor to the heart attack that had prematurely ended her life when Gemma was in high school.

When she was done changing, she reviewed the schedule, made sure her room was set up, and took a steadying breath. She'd talk to Cheryl after work today. They'd designate a hook by the door for the keys, and the problem would be solved.

"Ah, Gemma." Dr. Richards paused by her chair. "I didn't see you before. We might have to get you a new watch." He chuckled to himself at the joke.

She was lucky he was such an easy-going man.

"Sorry. My aunt was, um, not feeling well." It was only half a lie. She did need to talk to her about her drinking too. It was just that it was difficult to shift roles around like that. At one point, Cheryl had been the adult, the caretaker, and Gemma her ward. Now, more and more, Gemma felt like the responsible one.

"Oh no. I'm sorry to hear that," Dr. Richards said.

Gemma pretended to be busy with the tray on her counter. "It's okay."

"Ready for our nine thirty?"

"Is he here?"

"Should be any minute. You can get started and let me know when he's ready for me."

The day passed in a blur of patients, but as always, Gemma appreciated that "busy" rarely translated to "stressed" in this office. The first practice she'd worked at as a junior dental assistant had been very different. Disorganized, with strong personalities, and a high turnover. She'd only lasted a year there.

Consequently, when Gemma returned from her late lunch

and was met with the din of voices reaching the staff room, she popped her head into reception to ask what was going on.

"Oh yes, you've missed quite a hoopla. We had a walk-in," Wendy said. "Terrified, poor guy. I think he just agreed to some gas, so hopefully things will calm down."

Gemma still had another half hour until her next patient, so she sought out Dr. Richards to see if there was anything she could do, thinking her goodwill would make up for her tardiness.

She caught the doctor's attention over the walk-in, who was now settled in his chair breathing hard into the nose cone.

Dr. Richards lit up when he spotted her. "I'll be right back," he said to the patient. "We'll get you taken care of before long. Are you comfortable?"

The man nodded.

The doctor joined Gemma outside the room and lowered his voice. "I wouldn't normally ask, but we're short-staffed today. Do you have time to assist on this?" He cocked his head toward the patient. "He has a cracked tooth and needs a crown, but he's been putting it off for some time. Not a fan of the likes of me."

Gemma checked the time on the clock above them. "I have a while until my next one, so that should be okay."

"Great. You're the best at settling nerves of anyone here. Why don't you talk to him and see if you can get the anesthesia going?"

Gemma nodded. No problem. She'd done this a thousand times before.

She entered the room where the guy lay flat. "Hi there. I'm Gemma, and I'll be taking care of you today. How are we feeling?"

"Hmpf," the guy said through the nose cone.

Gemma reached for it and moved it off his face. "I understand you've got a painful tooth."

His eyes met hers, wide and soulful. He had an angular and symmetric face, straight teeth behind full lips, and thick, dark blond hair. Good-looking guy. Instinctively, she glanced at his left hand. Married. Of course.

"I'm in town for work and I haven't been able to chew for the past few days. It's starting to affect my sleep." His speech was slightly slurred from the gas, but that didn't obscure the pleasant rasp in it. "But I just hate going to the dentist." He said it with such emphasis that she had to smile.

"You and a million other people," she said, prepping the numbing gel. "I promise we'll take good care of you. I'll be here the whole time, and if at any point you want a break, you can raise your hand, like so." She demonstrated by lifting his forearm off the chair.

"Will it hurt a lot?"

"A little sting from the injection perhaps, but with the nitrous, I doubt you'll notice."

He nodded then faced the lamp again. "Okay. I trust you."

Always good to hear. "Here, take the nose cone again. A few deep breaths." She helped him then instructed him to open his mouth. "Ready?"

"Mm," he said.

Ten minutes later, he was well numbed up, and Dr. Richards got started with the tooth.

Gemma's next patient was a no-show, and since the guy in the chair had her hand clasped so tightly in his, she didn't have the heart to move. When Dr. Richards finally announced they were ready for the temporary cap, her whole arm had fallen asleep.

Cap on, bib off, chair up, and then Gemma got her first vertical look at the guy. Yup, he was as cute as she'd thought, even with a drop of spittle still stuck to his cheek.

"You've got a little something..." She pointed, handing him a tissue.

"Oh thanks." He wiped his mouth then touched the numbed-up quadrant of his face gingerly. "How long will it be like this?"

"A couple of hours at least so be careful if you eat anything. And the temporary crown might still be sore after."

He blew out a sharp breath. "That was pretty intense."

She smiled. "You did great."

"Thanks to you." He tried to reciprocate her expression, but only half of his face complied, resulting in a crooked grimace.

Before she could object to his compliment, Dr. Richards returned. "All right, Mr. Gallagher. That should do it for today. If you'll still be in town in two weeks, you should ask the front desk to get you on the schedule for the permanent crown. Any questions?"

"No, don't think so." He stood and accepted his coat when Gemma handed it to him. "Thanks, doc."

Gemma saw him out to the reception area, where she made sure he had Wendy's attention.

"Take care of that tooth," she said.

"You too." As soon as he'd spoken, his face twisted with a self-deprecating squint. "I mean, have a good evening. Yeesh."

Her smile lingered as she walked back into the clinic. Such a nice guy, Mr. Gallagher, antipathy against her profession notwithstanding.

Why oh why were the good ones always taken?

THREE

ISLA

Present day

"What on earth happened here?" Mom stopped short in the doorway to the kitchen.

Seeing through another's eyes, Isla took in the pile of dishes in the sink, the plastic produce bags discarded in a jumble among garlic peel, lemongrass stalks, scattered parsley leaves, and sticky bowls. The pan blackened with burned chicken pieces, the Band-Aid box, the open whiskey bottle.

"I was just... I wanted to..." Isla's voice trailed off as the knot in her throat swelled.

In the other room, the wedding video had now reached the point where the guests had lined up to wave goodbye as the newlyweds left the party in a rented sports car. The cheers and whoops echoed into the silence between Isla and her mom.

"Oh, Birdie." Nancy hurried into the living room and pressed a button on the remote.

The screen froze with Jonah looking back at the crowd, a jubilant grin on his face. Isla stared at him, at the face she knew so well. Two years she'd been without him. Two years more than was fair. She was the one who was supposed to be gone. She'd been the one behind the wheel.

"It's our anniversary today," she said before taking a deep breath. "I wanted to cook for him." Then, at seeing again the state of the kitchen, she chuckled darkly. "Clearly, I can't even get that right anymore."

Nancy picked up a shot glass from the coffee table and joined Isla in the kitchen. "Not surprising if you were drinking." Her voice wasn't unkind, but the message was clear: She did not approve. After putting the glass in the dishwasher, she started tidying the counter. Vegetable scraps and bags went into the garbage, dishes in the sink.

"Don't worry about it, Mom, I'll do it."

Nancy turned. "Will you now?" She reached out and pushed a strand of Isla's wispy blond hair behind her ear.

Instinctively, Isla leaned her cheek toward her mother's hand. "I'm sorry."

"I know." Nancy regarded her at length. "Come here." She pulled Isla into a hug. "I'm sorry too. I should have skipped book club tonight. I forgot what day it was."

Isla allowed herself to go limp in the embrace. If she could stay forever in that warmth and silence...

But no sooner had the thought entered her mind than Nancy cleared her throat. "Now, let's clean up this mess and have some tea, okay?"

They did, and soon the smell of burned chicken faded beneath that of a jasmine candle.

Isla wanted to go to bed. Her head was pounding, and the sooner this day was over, the better. But one of the downsides of having moved back in with her mother was that unescapable parent-and-child dynamic—as alive and well at thirty-five and sixty-eight as it had been at fifteen and forty-eight. If Nancy had things to say, Isla had better listen.

Nancy peered at her daughter over her glasses as Isla settled under a blanket. The TV was off now. Mom must have turned it off at some point. Isla stirred her tea, wishing it was something stronger.

Just as Nancy opened her mouth to speak, Isla's phone chimed. She picked it up, ignoring her mom's displeased expression. "One sec," she said. "I have to check the auction."

"What are you bidding on this time?"

"It's a small porcelain hummingbird. Nana used to have one exactly like it, but it disappeared at some point. It's a pair to the one she gave me." Isla pulled up the site. Her bid was still at the top with only one other person bidding so far. She was determined to win this one.

"Not too expensive I hope."

Isla looked up. It wasn't like Mom to talk finances.

"I worry about you," Nancy said as if reading the question on Isla's face. "Whiskey on a Monday?"

"It was a hard day."

"There's been a lot of those lately. And that video..." She shook her head. "What good does it do, Birdie? Your life is here. Now. Your back has healed, you're getting stronger. You can have your old life back."

A pang shot through Isla. "I can *never* have my old life back, and you know that." She'd raised her voice, heat flashing to her cheeks.

Her mom leaned forward to rest a hand on Isla's calf. "That's not how I meant it. But you're wasting yourself looking for answers at the bottom of a bottle of Macallan. Aren't you volunteering tomorrow? What are the people down at Meals on Wheels going to say when you show up smelling like a distillery?"

Isla pressed her lips together. Would she ever reach an age where her mother's perception didn't get under her skin?

"I want to help you, but you also have to help yourself.

This"—Nancy gestured vaguely around the room—"has to stop."

Isla's phone chimed with another notification. Someone had posted a message in her collectors' board group chat. She resisted the urge to look. It was probably Louise. She was always online at this hour.

"I am trying." Isla forced herself to meet her mom's eyes. "I went to the store today. I volunteer. I talk to people."

"Online. Not sure that counts. What about your old friends? I'm sure they'd love to hear from you."

And see the pity in their eyes? No thanks. What would be the point? "Maybe. Soon. I'm not ready yet."

Mom sighed. "I just don't think that Jonah—" She cut herself off. "Never mind."

Isla knew what she'd intended to say. That Jonah wouldn't want Isla to act like this. To drink, wallow, mourn. But what did Mom know? Maybe that's exactly what Jonah wanted. Maybe that's what Isla deserved.

"I'm gonna go to bed," she said. "I'm tired, and like you said, I have work tomorrow." She got up and kissed her mom on the cheek. "Thanks for the tea."

Nancy patted her arm. "Any time. You sleep well."

Aside from some night-time whiskey sweats, Isla did get a solid eight hours before her alarm blared her awake at seven thirty. She didn't have to be at the community center until ten, but she preferred to have plenty of time to get in the right headspace before leaving the house.

She'd volunteered for the local Meals on Wheels for nine months now, and though she'd been plenty reluctant at first when her mom dragged her there, insisting not another day could go by with Isla tucked on the couch watching daytime soaps, she'd come around to it within only a few short weeks. Delivering meals to the town's seniors wasn't like going to the store or walking through a crowd where someone might recognize her. Strangers were fine, and these were lonely people with a history, like her. Besides, her mom had been right—it did give her some small purpose. Helping the old folks was a form of penance. Like Isla, they were islands in the sea of humanity, disconnected, isolated, on indefinite stand-by, but she liked to think her visits kept her clients' spirits up by obscuring the permanence of that state. It didn't work on her, but if it helped someone else, it was a worthy cause.

At nine forty sharp, Isla opened the garage and pulled out her bike and its small, attached trailer. She used the remote to close the door, put her purse in the handlebar basket, then turned her face skyward. It had stopped raining, but the clouds still hung heavy in the Pacific Northwest sky, and her breath billowed in front of her.

Suddenly, a fluttering movement up near the eaves of the house forced her attention. For a split second, she was convinced she'd seen the iridescent green of a hummingbird's feathers, but that couldn't be. It wasn't the season.

She walked closer, but now everything was still. She blamed the ongoing auction of the hummingbird figurine for playing tricks on her imagination.

Damp earth and crisp cedar air mixed with hazelnut coffee on her tongue as she set off toward the community center where she would pick up today's deliveries. The road was mostly uphill, but Isla didn't mind—she relished the burn in her thighs and the sting in her lungs as not too long ago she'd been stuck in a back brace and limited to gentle physical therapy.

Out of breath and sweating in her fleece-lined parka, she opened the door to the center at exactly ten o'clock. It was a space forever imbued with the questionable scents of cooked carrots and latex paint, not too dissimilar from the cafeteria at her old high school, but she was never inside long. Only enough time to confirm her route and get her meals.

She made her way to Stan's office. He was the coordinator for Port Townsend—a seventy-something veteran with true passion for the charity—and the only one here who knew a little bit about Isla's background. Not that Isla had told him. No, that was all Mom. Isla had been incensed at the oversharing that first day, but Stan had never made a big deal about it—didn't look at Isla like there was something wrong with her, didn't coddle her. Consequently, most of the time, Isla could pretend he was as clueless as the rest of the people she ran into here.

A raised voice seeped into the hallway before Isla reached the half-open door.

"I'll take any other route," the woman said. "Or take me off that one stop and I'll do an *additional* route. Anything."

Stan answered in his equable voice. "We don't choose who we help."

Isla pushed open the door. "Sorry to interrupt—just letting you know I'm here."

"I can switch with her," the woman said. She was younger than Isla—mid-twenties maybe—with curly red hair and dark lipstick. "Please. He gives me the creeps. I've done this route for a month now. It's someone else's turn. I don't even care if her route is on the other side of town."

"What's going on?" Isla asked.

Stan's lips pressed into a tight line—a more emotional display than Isla had seen on him before—but then his features settled back into their normal composure. "Serene here has some... issues... with her route."

"Not the whole route," Serene added. "There's just this old guy who—"

"Gives you the creeps," Isla filled in. "I heard. What does he do?"

Serene's eyebrows rose. "Oh. Well, nothing really. It's more a vibe."

"A vibe?"

"Yeah. Like he doesn't say much, and he looks..."

Stan had followed their back-and-forth from behind his desk, but now he put a hand up. "Be that as it may, our clients all deserve our help. I'm not going to deny service on the basis of a quote unquote 'vibe.'"

"I'll quit then," Serene said. "It's either a new route or no route at all."

Nancy's words echoed in Isla's ears. How she thought Isla was doing nothing to help herself; that she was irresponsible, lazy even.

"I'll do it," Isla said. "I'll take both our routes." That would show her mom.

"Oh no, that won't be necessary," Stan said. "Serene's route is mainly outside of town, and since you don't drive, I'm afraid that wouldn't be ideal. But let's have a gander." He produced a God's honest paper map from within the depths of one of his drawers. Then, using a pencil, he outlined first Serene's route, then Isla's. "If I'm not mistaken, Mr. Zuft lives right here." He pointed to a spot north of Isla's circle, near the memorial park. "If you're willing to add one more stop, you could squeeze him in between Dolly and Mrs. Hauberman."

Isla nodded. "Sure. Whatever you need."

"Oh my God, thank you." Serene slumped back in her chair.

"Yeah, no worries." One more stop was nothing. It was the least she could do. Creepy vibes had nothing on Isla, and something told her Serene might be easily spooked. "You'll call over to let the guys know I'll need one more meal?" she asked Stan. "I'd like to get going."

"Consider it done. And thank you."

Isla raised her hand in acknowledgment and took her leave.

Once her bike trailer had been loaded up, she adjusted her scarf and set off. The sun was trying but failing to push through the clouds, so the temperature held steady right below forty, which was ideal for pulling a heavy load of food through the streets. By the time Isla reached her newest delivery client, she'd discarded her gloves and unzipped her coat. She'd worked up quite an appetite herself, so in addition to Mr. Zuft's meal, she also brought her own lunch along as she approached his apartment building. She liked to take turns eating with different clients each day she worked. It meant so much to them, and it took Isla's mind off the outside world. What better way to get to know her new "creepy" client than to break bread with him? On the off chance Serene had been right, Isla could leave.

"Weird vibes," she muttered to herself as she reached the exterior door. If Serene made time to get to know her clients the way Isla did, chances were they'd all be spared snap judgments like that.

She had just gripped the handle when the door swung open from inside, which made her nearly collide with a tower of a man wrapped in a dark parka.

"Oh, pardon me," he said, at the same time she said, "So sorry."

She went to her right and he to his left in that little dance people do when trying to pass each other in a small space.

"Oop." He shifted right then left again. "Maybe if one of us doesn't move?"

"Right." Isla clasped her parcels to her chest and stayed still. She'd never seen this guy about town before. He was so tall, she'd have remembered. Maybe he was new to the area. *Nice smile*, she thought, surprising herself. The unprompted assessment caused heat to rush to her face, so she looked down and allowed him to make a final dodge past her on the right. A pleasant whiff of clean wool trailed him.

"Have a good one," he called, pulling his collar up as he set off down the street.

"You too," she mumbled, the man already too far away to hear her, then she hurried to climb the stairs to the third floor. Once there, she shrugged off the awkward encounter, knocked on the door, and waited. It was a nice old building—tall ceilings, worn stone steps, two doors on each landing, a small elevator. The walls were painted a pale yellow with a graphic square pattern border near the ceiling.

There was no movement in the apartment.

She knocked again and stepped back. There—was that a shadow darkening the peephole?

"Meals on Wheels delivery," she called, in case the client was the anxious kind.

The lock rattled and the handle turned, but as the door opened, Isla's smile slid off her face and the greeting on her tongue disappeared like vapor.

Face to face with Mr. Zuft, Isla suddenly felt more generous in spirit toward Serene, because above the collar of his dapper shirt and cardigan, the old man before her leveled her with the piercing blue gaze of someone intent on laying bare your very soul, and the whole left side of his face was covered in intricate tattoos.

FOUR

MAVERICK

Seattle, March 13, 1952

Dear Nurse Cass,

I hope this letter finds you well and that you're not opposed to receiving it. I had my good friend Tommy (I reckon you remember him by his lousy guitar-playing) find out what field hospital they transferred you to. I've made it home, and though it ain't exactly the homecoming I imagined, I'm in one piece, much thanks to you. I will be in hospital a while longer until my legs heal properly, they say. At least the conditions are a far deal more pleasant here than in Inje.

The reason for my writing is that I never got the chance to thank you properly for saving my life that day. It wasn't until I breathed our wonderful homeland air again that I realized my mistake, and it's been eating at me ever since. You were an angel to me upon my injury, and that's not saying too much. You believed I was worth a shot, and without your faith, I'd have been a goner like those other poor boys. You brought me back from the brink, and for that I will forever be grateful. My mama is as well.

Truth be told, when I close my eyes at night, I still see your face leaning over my cot and feel the soft touch of your hand on mine. I'm sure I'm foolish and you hear this all the time, but the thought of you just won't leave me. Would you write me back I wonder? I'd be honored.

I trust you take good care and stay safe.

Sincerely,

Pvt. Maverick Zuft

FIVE
ISLA

"Where's the other gal?" Mr. Zuft asked, his voice rusted but pleasant.

Isla blinked several times, trying to reconcile the old man's unusual face with his ordinary attire. *Other gal?* She peered down at the box of food in her hands. *Oh, right. Serene.* "They changed our routes," she said, finding her voice again. "I'm here instead."

A glint in the startlingly blue depths. "Yes, I can see that." He opened the door wider. "Come in then. Kitchen's through here."

Isla trailed him through a narrow hallway where a woven runner covered the wood flooring and abundant nautical para-phernalia adorned the walls. Some of the homes she delivered to had distinct smells of aging, but not this place. Coffee and wood polish, Isla thought. It matched her initial impression of the place as tidy and clean. Not at all the kind of space where she'd have expected to find a tattooed ninety-year-old.

They entered a bright kitchen with a surprising number of

thriving green plants on the windowsill, and Isla set her load down on the table.

"I like your place," she said. "The big windows."

"Mm." The concurring sound rumbled from somewhere deep in the old man's chest. "I've seen worse."

"You've not been here long then?"

"A month or two. Say, have we met before? You look familiar."

"I'm certain I'd remember if we had." Isla smiled at him then craned her neck in search of a microwave. "Would you like me to heat up the food for you, Mr. Zuft?"

"*Maverick* please. Or *Mav* if you're so inclined." The corners of his mouth pulled upward for a split second. "But you have the advantage here, Miss...?"

"Right. Sorry." Isla wiped her hand on her jeans and extended it. "It's Gallagher. Isla Gallagher."

Mav's lips parted, then he took her hand. "Is that so? Miss Isla Gallagher."

Technically it was Mrs., but Isla let it slide.

"It's very nice to meet you." Mav pressed her hand gently in both of his once more for good measure before he let go.

On second thought, maybe Serene's judgment was hyperbolic after all. The tattoos were startling, Isla would give her that, but Mav himself seemed pleasant enough, if a bit touched by old age, and up close like this, his gaze was nothing but friendly. Warm, even, for such a cool color. Rather than finding his "vibe" creepy, she was intrigued. How did a man with gentlemanly manners, a sense of style, and such obvious care for his home come to have a face like that? Not without adventures in his past, that was for sure.

They stared at each other for a moment, then Isla nodded toward the food again. "Do you have a microwave?"

Maverick flinched. "Oh right. Yes of course. It's in the pantry closet over there."

"Great." Isla smiled at him and got to work, finding a plate in a cabinet and silverware in a drawer. The food would look more appetizing out of its plastic wrapping. "I brought a sandwich for me in case you want company," she said over her shoulder. "Some clients don't mind a little chat while they eat. What can I get you to drink?"

Mav had sat down in one of the French-style dining chairs, of which there were two at the small table. "Water is fine. You're not in a hurry then?"

"I get to take a lunch." Isla set Mav's plate and glass down in front of him. "Napkins?"

"A paper towel is good enough." Mav indicated a roll on the wall near the sink. "And put on the kettle if you don't mind. Without a spot of black coffee after a meal, I'll just nap like an old fool."

Isla opened the tap. "I don't mind a nap." Early on in her relationship with Jonah, they'd loved taking naps together. She'd used to drape herself over him on the couch as the rain marked slow Sunday afternoon minutes against the window-panes. He'd called her his "Isla-blanket."

"You will when you reach my age. I can sleep when I'm dead and gone."

Isla closed her eyes. Was that what Jonah was doing now? Sleeping?

The dark tendrils in her chest snaked upward but were soon cut off with a start when the kettle overflowed onto her hand. "Oh shoot." She shook off the water and wiped her hand on her shirt. "Wasn't paying attention," she said, throwing a tight approximation of a smile over her shoulder before turning on the burner.

She took one more minute to unfold her sandwich and open the small baggie of popcorn she'd packed as a side, before she steeled herself and sat down across from Mav. They exchanged another polite smile, then Mav dug in. Isla nibbled at her lip as she examined her food. Maybe it had been a mistake to do social time so soon after a day like yesterday.

They ate in silence for a while, Isla intent on the waxy leaves of one of the plants to her left, Mav on his meatballs.

"You didn't care for my little joke," he said suddenly.

"Huh?" Isla looked back at him. He'd already finished his meal and was leaning back in his chair, watching her. She stared at the quarter-inch-wide ink column of intricate lines that ran from his forehead down past his left eye to the middle of his cheekbone.

"About sleeping when I'm dead."

Isla blinked. "Well, I... It wasn't..." The kettle whistled, saving her from further mumbling. "Let me get that."

"You've lost someone I think," Mav said, when Isla set two mugs down on the table.

A tremor rose through Isla's body at his words, strong enough for the container of instant coffee she'd just picked up to slip from her hand and fall to the floor, where its contents billowed up and out—a brown cloud covering several square feet of the floor.

She froze, her hands perched in the air as if trying to capture the coffee granules. "Oh my God." She sidestepped the mess. "I am so sorry. I'll clean this up, I promise. I'm so clumsy." Her face flushing hot, she backed away. She was such a screwup. Now the old man would probably call Stan and complain. As he should. She spun in one spot, hands still shaking. Where were the cleaning supplies?

Mav pointed to the hallway. "If you're looking for the sweeper, it's over there. Closet on the right. And don't worry about it," he called after her. "It's only coffee."

A whole jar of it. She'd have to replace it.

"Again, I'm so sorry," she said, lugging an old, corded canister vacuum into the room. "I can't do anything right these days."

"No, no, no." Mav leaned forward in his seat. "Accidents happen."

"When I'm around."

"To all of us."

Her hand tightened on the pipe. He wouldn't say that if he knew. "I'm just going to get this taken care of." She plugged in the machine and turned it on.

The loud whirr was a blessing, blocking out some of the voices in her head screaming about being a liability, a terrible person, leaving destruction in her wake. It was a pity the vacuum was such an efficient old thing.

The coffee granules gone, Isla wiped the floor with a damp rag then returned the cleaning supplies to their closet. She'd pick up a new jar of coffee tomorrow. Maybe she should offer to have the rug cleaned too for good measure. Only one corner of it had fallen victim to the spill, and it *seemed* clean enough, but...

Mav was waiting for her when she reentered the kitchen. "Come sit down," he said, patting the table.

Not wanting to cause more tension, she complied.

Mav's eyes narrowed as she did, three rudimentary birds below his temple twitching with the creasing skin. "You're very hard on yourself," he said, resting his hands over his belly. "Why is that?"

Isla shrugged. Was she?

"Hm." Mav tapped four fingers against the table. "Do you know that I'm ninety years old?" he asked.

"I saw it in your file."

He nodded. "And how many jars of spilled coffee do you think I've accumulated over those ninety years? Let me tell you —too many to count." He made a point to seek out her gaze, a gleam of amusement livening his expression. "I may even have burned some bridges and sunk a few ships."

He had her attention now, but Isla still wanted to object. She understood what he was doing. Coffee was nothing—a trivial, everyday slip. Except when the opposite was true. Because what Isla knew, and Mav didn't, was that spilled coffee *could* be an aftershock of a mistake so enormous it suggested a fault line at the very core of the culprit. A mistake that still, two years later, she had no explanation for and no way to make right. Isla dug her nails into her palms and focused on her breathing. She would not add crying to her list of unprofessionalism today.

"You're sitting now, so tell me. Who did you lose?"

Isla's head jerked up. She had denial at the tip of her tongue, adrenaline in her thighs to spring up, but as she was about to, she spotted something in the shadow beneath Mav's ear. A tiny hummingbird in faded ink.

"That tattoo," she said, touching her own skin in the same spot. "The bird. Does it have a story?"

Mav tipped his head as if considering whether to let her avoidance of his question slide. Then he nodded once, decision made. "This one?" He pointed. "Funny, no one's ever asked about the birdie what with all of this going on." He indicated his adorned face.

"I collect them," Isla said. "Hummingbirds. Have since I was a little girl. My grandparents had a painting in their house where they were depicted as guardian angels around a little boy leaning over a stream. 'Hummingbirds appear when angels are near,' Nana used to say. I've loved them ever since. Here, look." She pulled out her phone and opened the auction site before even making a conscious decision to let Mav in on this part of her life. "I'm trying to get this one. See the details? Handmade. My grandma had one just like it."

Mav took her phone and held it away slightly to see better. "Ah yes. Wonderful." He gave her back the phone. "Mine's also handmade," he joked. "Talented sergeant in my company when I was stationed in Korea. He had a book of drawings, and I liked the look of this one."

"I didn't know you're a veteran. Thank you for your service."

Mav's eyes crinkled. "There are a lot of things we don't know about each other."

Isla regarded him across the table. There was nothing challenging about him, no demands or judgments. The next move was up to her.

She folded her hands. Paused at the sight of the gold band still on her left ring finger.

The day they had picked out their rings, nothing had run smoothly. The jeweler's daughter had gone into labor, so they'd been assigned a junior clerk instead who'd insisted gold bands were out of fashion before proceeding to show them all the other bands against their wishes. Someone else might have lost their cool, but not Jonah. He'd found a way to turn it into a joke, whispering increasingly exaggerated sales pitches in Isla's ear about the magical properties of this ring or that whenever the salesclerk disappeared into the back for another tray. Toward the end of it, Isla's sides had hurt from laughing so hard. And they *had* eventually walked out with what they wanted, three hours later, leaving a disillusioned clerk behind.

"My husband," she said. "I lost my husband two years ago. His name was Jonah."

"Jonah." Mav nodded solemnly. "I'm very sorry to hear that. Life is hardly fair, one would think, that I'm still here after all this time and others get half that."

"If it was fair, he'd still be here and I'd be gone." Isla pushed at the handle of her cup of hot water so it turned forty-five degrees.

Unlike others before him, Mav didn't protest her morose statement. "Why is that?" he asked instead.

"It was a car accident," Isla said. "I was driving."

"I see."

"So I'm the reason he's dead." Her throat tightened, but she forced herself to not look down.

"Hm." Mav pulled his lower lip up, setting his jaw in a bull-doggish underbite. "And you're unscathed, are you?" he asked finally.

"I broke my back and my right arm. Punctured a lung. I was..." *Dead. You were dead. Three minutes. But Nana sent you back.* "Everything is healed now though."

"Not all wounds leave visible scars."

She smiled a little at that. Maybe he was right. Then she stood. Time to go.

"I still have more meals to deliver," she said. "And I'm sorry again about the coffee. I'll bring a new jar tomorrow."

Mav's face lit up. "Ah, so I'll see you again after all. For a while there I thought you might flee." He followed her into the hallway and held out her coat like a gentleman so she could slide her arms into the sleeves.

"Thanks."

"Can I ask, if you don't mind..." Mav paused as he opened the door for her. "How did the accident happen?"

Isla shoved her hands into her pockets. "Well, that's just it," she said. "I don't remember."

SIX

ISLA

Present day

Maverick's last question still echoed in Isla's mind as she got ready to do her deliveries the next day. It was the same question she'd asked herself over and over these past two years.

She and Jonah had gone to Bend for their anniversary weekend. She had looked forward to getting away. Had been eager to have some quality time together out of the house after almost a year of off-and-on quarantine that had left them both climbing the walls more than all over each other. Her last memory was of him pulling the car out of their garage while she locked the house. There had been flurries in the air, and a couple had landed on her bare neck, making her hurry, shivering and laughing, to the car as he opened the passenger door from the inside. "Get inside, ice princess," he'd said. "Your ride awaits."

Next she knew, she was in a hospital in Portland with Mom at her side. She didn't remember either the drive south or the days they'd spent in Bend before the accident happened. Because her memory still hadn't returned, she'd told herself it was best not to know. That it didn't matter since nothing could bring Jonah back. The days when the dark abyss in her head took over, drew attention from her present, and shackled her to the house were her punishment, and a well-deserved one at that. Her husband couldn't move on, so why should she?

There was also that one singular flash in the dark that she'd only ever told Louise about. Her online friends were a motley crew of bird curio collectors in a social media group she'd joined as a distraction six months after the accident, and perhaps because of their varied backgrounds, the conversations tended to range from the more relevant porcelain brands and flea market finds all the way to astrology, recipes, and travel recommendations.

Do you guys believe in life after death? she'd asked a while back in the group. The responses had been varied, and eventually everyone but Louise had moved on to something else. That's how the two of them had started messaging one on one and then talking on the phone. Louise was working as a journalist for her local paper somewhere in southern Washington, a collector of owls, and, it turned out, quite the connoisseur of tarot practitioners and energy healers. She very much wanted to believe, she'd said, since she'd lost a childhood friend not long ago, and consequently that was the first time Isla had admitted to someone else that "death" had not been silent. To her relief, Louise hadn't found it the least bit odd that Isla had regained consciousness with the very clear and vibrant memory of her dead grandmother's voice ringing in her head from beyond.

As comforting as the possibility was of there being more to life than she could see, it still didn't retract a thing from that weighty unknown that Isla carried around daily. She'd tried to push it away, to accept the black hole in her mind, but its nagging was never far beneath the surface. And Mav asking the question point-blank hadn't helped. It made the second bike ride to his place feel more uphill than the day before—and it wasn't the fault of the gravy-laden meatloaf trays in her trailer.

I'll be in and out in a minute, she told herself as she unloaded his food. She'd eat her sandwich with Mrs. Hauberman today. She'd replace Mav's coffee jar, exchange a few cordial remarks, then take her leave.

"I bought cookies," Maverick said in greeting as he opened the door for her. "I figured we could try again for some coffee?"

And how could she say no? He was a lonely old man after all.

Mav had already put the kettle on, so all Isla had to do was spoon instant coffee into their cups and not spill anything. That and take charge of the conversation.

"Tell me something about you," she said, reaching for a chocolate chip cookie. "Where did you move from? Do you have family around here? And how did you get all of those?" She gestured to his tattooed face.

Mav stirred his coffee in measured circles, then he lifted his cup and peered at her over its rim. "Don't worry. I won't ask any more questions about Jonah."

Isla's mouth snapped closed, her cheeks heating.

Mav sipped the hot brew then set the cup down gently on its plate. "But if you really want to know..."

"I do." Isla shoved half a cookie into her mouth, which made her "please" come out more like a sputtered "pweash."

"I grew up in Seattle. Married late—I was fifty, she was forty-six—no kids. Lorraine and I got thirty wonderful years together." His eyes twinkled as her name crossed his lips. "Best time of my life."

"Do you have a picture?"

"I sure do." He shuffled into the other room and returned holding a silver frame. "This was taken on her seventy-fifth birthday, before she got sick."

Isla took the frame and angled it to get a good look. Lorraine was a petite woman at least a foot shorter than her husband, with a neat silver bob and a radiant smile. In the photo, they held hands, leaning into each other as if they'd just shared an inside joke, and it made something in Isla's chest squeeze tight. "It's a great picture," she said. "You look almost the same." He did, except for a slightly fuller face and thicker, darker hair back then.

"You flatter me." Maverick held out his hand for the frame. "Oh, my sweet Lorrie." He ran a fingertip over his wife's face. "Do you know what she said the first time we met? She said, 'I don't much have the patience for reading, but I quite like the story your face is telling.'" He chuckled. "How could I not marry her after that?"

Isla smiled. "Agreed. I'm so sorry for your loss."

Mav waved her off. "Don't be. I'll see her before long."

Isla had been about to put her cup to her lips. Now, she lowered it instead. "You will?"

"Don't tell me you're one of those 'this is all there is' folks." Mav set the photo down, adjusting it just so. "The hubris of the human race, thinking we know all there is to know." He reached for a cookie. "But you know better than that, I believe."

What's that supposed to mean? Isla's lips parted, ready to take the bait, but then she caught herself. Nope, she wasn't going there today. "And now you've moved here," she hurried to say instead.

Mav nodded once, not pushing it. "I needed to be by water again."

"Again?"

"After Korea, I..." Mav's lips tightened briefly into a line, then he sat back in his seat. "I took to the seas, you might say. Made a career of it working the cargo routes. There aren't many harbors around the world that I haven't seen."

He was a sailor then. A globetrotter. "The tattoos are from your travels."

"Indeed they are."

Made sense. Isla was about to ask if they held any special

meaning when her phone rang in her pocket. She pulled it out, ready to reject the call, but when she saw Western Washington University on the caller ID, she let two more signals ring out until Maverick interrupted her stupor.

"Need to get that?"

She knew what they wanted. Had already let two other calls go to voicemail. "Yeah. Sorry." She got up and stepped into the hallway. "Hello?"

"Isla, you're a tough person to get a hold of." Dean Abbot's deep voice came over the line followed by a rumbling cough courtesy of his penchant for smoking cigars.

She hadn't spoken to her boss since last summer, but now here he was in her ear. "Hi. Yes, I've had some, um, cell phone problems lately. Got to get that fixed."

"Mm."

They exchanged a few pleasantries before the dean got down to business.

"What we're all wondering over here is—how are you doing?"

How was she doing? Such a big question with all kinds of expectations tied to it. Not that she didn't understand why he had to ask. This was her second full school year on leave, and while she wasn't costing them anything, she knew it wasn't a good look when the accident had happened so close after she'd made tenure. "I'm out of the brace. PT helped a lot," she said, offering partial truths.

"That's great." *Cough, cough.* "And are you feeling, um, stronger? Generally I mean."

Stronger. She hadn't watched the wedding tape last night. Did that count?

When she didn't respond, he continued, "The reason I'm asking, of course, is that we're deep into preparations for next year. And what we're very much hoping is that you're planning on returning to us. What are your thoughts on that?"

Isla cleared her throat. *Working. Focusing. Interacting with people who knew her before.* Her skin felt suddenly clammy. "I'm thinking about it. Talking it over with my doctors. You know." She closed her eyes at the lie.

"Right, right. And do you think you might have an answer for us soon?"

Isla kept her head down. "Yes. Yup. Pretty soon."

"Great." *Cough, cough.* "Okay. Well, you know where to reach me. Let's touch base again next week or so, yes?"

"Sounds good."

They hung up, and Isla sucked in a deep breath before returning to Maverick in the kitchen.

"Everything okay?" he asked.

Isla nodded, shoving her phone back in her pocket. "Work. I mean my old work. I'm an art history professor. Or I was. They want to know if I'm coming back this fall."

"And are you?"

Isla shrugged. "It's complicated."

"Life usually is." Mav held out the plate of cookies toward her, but she declined, remaining standing.

"I'm not... solid. Not like before. How am I supposed to prepare lectures, tutor, grade, do research when all I can think about is—" Her voice broke.

Mav got up from his seat and put a gentle hand on her shoulder. "I know, I know."

"And it's not only the job. Jonah's sister, Katelyn, works there too, same department—also my fault incidentally—and I can't imagine... I mean I wouldn't want to..." A stubborn tear broke free of her lashes.

Isla was the one who'd told Katelyn about the opening in the department way back when. Ancient history now, but if she could have it undone... Her distress deepened at the ugly feeling because the truth was Katelyn had never been anything but friendly when they were both colleagues and sisters-in-law.

"There, there." Mav handed her a tissue. "I'm sorry, I shouldn't have asked."

Isla sniffled. "No, it's fine. *I'm* sorry." She wasn't simply being polite. Something about Mav halted her usual self-consciousness. Not that she wanted to burden him. He was her client after all, not the other way around. "I should probably go."

He didn't press it, instead quietly handing her her purse. "Will I see you again next week?"

Isla paused in the doorway. She could say no. The point of volunteering was to do something nice for others, not to get something out if it herself. She had no claim on that. And yet...

"Looking forward to it," she said.

And she meant it.

"Proud of you for not letting the call go to voicemail this time," Louise said over the phone that evening.

Isla had just finished telling her about the dean's call and his question while organizing her hummingbird collection. She lifted a colorful figure carved from wood and wiped it off, then moved to the next. It was better meditation than sitting cross-legged on the floor, that was for sure. "Thanks."

"But you don't know what to tell him?"

Isla turned a crystal hummingbird a few degrees so the light would catch the facets better. "I think it's still too soon."

"Well, you'd know best. But if you want some guidance, I'm happy to pull a card for you."

"That's okay." Last time Louise had pulled a Four of Cups card and told Isla it meant she was stuck. Isla hardly needed a tarot deck to know that.

"I keep telling you not to knock it."

Isla smiled and picked up the original Coalport hummingbird—the one Nana had given her for her fifth birthday. It was a green and purple beauty with its wings spread and its beak in a pale pink flower. "I checked earlier and mine is still the highest bid by the way," she said, switching topics.

"How many days left?" Louise asked, knowing instantly what Isla was referring to. The auction for this bird's sibling figurine.

"Twenty. I think the seller is hoping to build interest with this one."

"Isla?" Mom's voice cut through the house, interrupting them.

"Hold on," Isla told Louise then stuck her head into the hallway. "Yes?" She could hear Nancy's footfalls on the bottom stairs.

"I've made tea. Could you come downstairs?"

Isla checked her watch. Eight thirty. Usually, Mom was well on her way to falling asleep in front of the TV at this hour. She frowned.

"I have to go," she told Louise. "Mom needs me for something."

They said their goodbyes, and Isla placed the porcelain bird back in its spot before closing the curio cabinet.

If evening tea was unusual on its own, Isla was even more confounded when she got downstairs to find her mom waiting for her on the couch with the TV off.

"Everything okay?" she asked.

Nancy smiled and patted the seat. "Come sit. Let's chat."

Isla hesitated but then made her way around the couch. "Why do I suddenly feel like I'm fifteen again?"

"Don't be silly." Mom looked away. "Who were you talking to?"

"Louise."

"More bird stuff?"

Isla reached for the mug on her side of the table. "Mom."

She leveled her mother with a pointed stare. "What's going on? What did you want to talk about?"

Nancy brushed her shoulder-length silver waves back and adjusted her glasses. "The university called here earlier today looking for you."

"I know; I talked to Dean Abbot." Isla tried a careful sip of her chai.

"Oh." Mom's eyebrows jumped. "And?"

"And what?"

Her mother set her mug down and crossed her arms. Then she released them again and stuck both hands between her knees as she leaned forward. "Don't you think it's time, Birdie? To go back to work I mean?"

Isla took a deep breath. There must be something in the air today. "You know it's not that simple."

"But at some point, you need to start living again. Really living. You're young. You have a life ahead of you."

"Unlike Jonah."

"Oh, sweetie." Mom removed her glasses and rubbed at one eye, leaving crumbs of mascara on her cheekbone. "I know you think I'm nagging, but it's been two years. And as much as I feel for you, the Jonah I knew wouldn't want this for you. An idle life, a small life. Forsaking your career."

Everything inside Isla tightened, and she stood abruptly. "Don't tell me what he'd want. You don't know. Maybe this is exactly what I deserve and he's happy about it."

Her mom regarded her calmly for a moment. "Sit down," she said finally.

Isla huffed out another breath, still contemplating flight, but in the end, she sank back into the cushions.

"I need you to get your life back together again." Her mom spoke slowly and articulately, her gaze not wavering from Isla's.

"But, Mom—"

"No." Nancy's eyes softened. "I know you're still hurting. I know because I am too. Losing your father was the hardest thing I've ever had to deal with, and the pain is there every day. But it serves no one to hide underneath that cloak of grief."

"It's not the same. And maybe you forget I lost Dad too." Isla glanced up at the mantel where her parents' wedding photo sat front and center. He'd been dealing with emphysema for almost as long as she could remember. In and out of hospitals her whole life. When the pandemic struck, he'd been one of the first to succumb. "You weren't the cause of Dad's death. You don't have to wake up every morning and wonder what happened. Why you're here and not him."

"I know that." Nancy brushed a fleck of dust off the table. "I know that," she repeated, more quietly this time. "You lost them both, and it's not the same."

That's right, Isla thought, breathing easier with the acquiescence.

"But that still doesn't change things." Mom looked up. Her back straightened, and she squared her shoulders. "What I really wanted to talk to you about tonight is that I *need* you to find a way to move on, because come this summer you'll be on your own. I'm selling the house and moving to Arizona."

And like that, the safety net that had caught Isla when she'd fallen, that she'd counted on for two years, was gone.

SEVEN

ISLA

Isla let the mouse hover over the SEND button without clicking it. In front of her on the screen was the email she'd worked on for the past two hours—the email to Dean Abbot letting him know she was planning on returning to work this coming fall.

In the days since her mom had made her announcement, Isla had been treading water, resisting the currents wanting to drag her down. She wasn't ready for this—for living on her own, supporting herself, working—and yet, this was the new hand she'd been dealt. If only she could figure out what her next play would be.

Other than letting Isla know that workers would soon be descending on the house to repaint all the walls, Nancy had been giving her space—Isla wasn't so wrapped up in herself that she didn't notice. She wanted to tell her mom it wasn't necessary, that she wasn't angry with her, but she hadn't found the right time yet. In all honesty, Arizona sounded like a great place. The dry heat would be better for Mom's burgeoning arthritis, and she'd be making the move to the gated retirement community with two of her widowed friends. Even as Isla struggled with her own situation, Mom's choice made sense.

Isla pressed the button, the *swosh* signifying the email had been sent making her stomach drop. She had six months, give or take. Six months to somehow get her act together.

It was a gray Saturday, with a damp, forty-four-degree chill seeping through her jeans as she biked across town to the memorial park where they had a family plaque for those who had passed on. In her backpack in the basket was the candle and sleeve of Oreos she always brought with her when she visited. Oreos had been both Jonah's and her dad's favorite, and also the reason Isla and Jonah had met in the first place. They'd both reached for the last pack of double-stuffed goodies on the shelf of the local convenience store shortly after she'd moved to Bellingham.

The first thing she'd noticed about him was his hands— broad and tan and alive somehow as they entered the sliver of her vision not preoccupied by her grocery list. Their knuckles had brushed, and they'd both retreated, but her apology had caught in her throat when he'd smiled at her. Such an inordinate display of delight for a Tuesday afternoon in the cracker aisle. He'd let her have the Oreos of course, and at the register, she'd let him have her number. Their wedding cake had been a cookies-and-cream dream.

There were quite a few people milling about the large green space when she arrived, but most of them were on the far side of the pond. Isla veered left past the large stone monument to the grove of cedars that guided her to her spot. Wet footprints trailed her as she crossed the grassy expanse. She should have brought something to sit on.

After lighting the candle, she crouched down and brushed a few leaves off the plaque. Her fingertips touched the inscriptions—her grandma and grandpa's names, her dad's, then lingered on her husband's. When she'd asked to have his urn

placed here instead of in Bellingham, his family had deferred
to her.

"Hi," she said, allowing a moment's stillness before she
pulled the cookie package out of her bag. "Brought cookies."

The wrapping rustled as she opened it and helped herself to
a chocolatey bite. She chewed slowly, trying to savor the sweet
flavor on Jonah's behalf, but as usual, the treat went down no
easier than if it had been cardboard. She wiped a crumb from
the corner of her mouth and stood. There was no wind today,
no sound coming from the trees, but far away she could hear
faint voices from other visitors and beyond that traffic. The
everyday backdrop was a comfort as the silence between her
and the plaque stretched.

The first time Isla had come here, she'd had so much to say.
She'd cried, raged at life's unfairness, begged Jonah for a sign he
was okay and to forgive her. She'd told him about her physical
therapy, her progress, her nightmares. But the more time that
passed, the harder it was to remember how they'd used to talk to
each other.

"Mom's moving to Arizona," she said now. "What do you
think about that?"

She imagined his response would be something like "Good
for her," or "Nancy will like the heat," but she could be wrong.
There were moments when he'd been so deep in his own
thoughts, she'd barely gotten a reaction from him, like that time
when she'd had to take his book away to make him hear the
news that her tenure application was moving forward to its final
step. But that was marriage. You took the good with the bad.

Isla wrapped her arms around herself to protect against the
threatening shiver.

"I don't know how to do this," she whispered. Her gaze
drifted from Jonah's name to her grandmother's. "I wish you'd
tell me what to do."

Just then, a couple of crows took flight from the nearby tree,

startling her. She looked up and there, twenty feet away on the
northbound path, a figure in a dark coat and hat was walking
toward her. She blinked. Was that...?

"I thought it was you," a dapper Maverick said as he got
within speaking range. "But I didn't mean to interrupt."

"No, no. You're fine." Isla paused on the bouquet of flowers
the old man was carrying. "I wasn't expecting to see anyone I
knew, that's all. How are you doing today?"

"Not too bad, not too bad." Maverick patted the flowers.
"Visiting an old friend. You?"

Isla was about to give him the usual trite response—that she
was fine—but something in his expression stopped her. Maybe
it was because of where they were, but the curious lilt of his
question reminded Isla of her dad, and she'd never lied to
her dad.

"I've been better actually," she said, returning her attention
to the plaque.

"Oh?" Maverick stepped closer so that he, too, could read
the inscription. "'*Neil and Embeth Smith, Delwyn Smith, Jonah
Gallagher,*'" he read. "'*Loved. Missed.*'" A tremulous sigh trailed
the words. "Yes, I see."

"Cookie?" Isla held out the package.

"No thank you, dear."

Isla helped herself to one more then allowed the silence to
engulf them for several minutes.

"I told my boss I'll go back to work this fall," she said finally.

Mav burrowed his neck deeper in the collar of his coat
against the chill. "At the university?"

Isla nodded.

"And now you're wondering if you've promised too much."

Isla's gaze flew to his. "How did you know?"

"I've been there," Mav said, joining his hands behind his
back. "I was injured in Korea and sent home. It haunted me that
I was here, safe, and my friends were still there. Gave me no

rest. I enlisted with my best friend, Tommy, full of youthful bravado and naivety, and in an instance, everything we'd envisioned went to dirt when the vehicle I was in took a direct hit. He was in the one behind me and saw me die."

"Die?"

Mav put up a hand and smiled. "That's how he described it. Though he wasn't entirely wrong. I was definitely somewhere else for a while."

Isla's pulse quickened. "What do you mean?"

"The surgeon thought I was a hopeless case, but one of the nurses begged him to try to save me. When I woke up days later, I knew of their conversation even though it had taken place outside the MASH unit—that's a field hospital—I was in. No explanation." He shrugged. "It took me years to let that go and live my life."

His profile was impassive, the inked lines at rest across the soft, creased skin. Isla held her breath. Had he just told her what she thought he'd told her?

"My grandma," she said, gesturing to the plaque. "Right after the accident, when they were working on reviving me, I saw her, and she spoke to me."

"I'm not surprised." Mav's blue eyes settled on hers. "What did she say?"

Isla gave a sad little chuckle. "'Look around,'" she said. "She told me to 'look around.' But I have no idea what that means. Look around where? In the afterlife? Was I supposed to remember something about it to bring back here? Was there something I was supposed to find to save Jonah? I don't even remember what happened the night of the crash." The words spilled out of her, her spoken questions and those she still kept to herself stacking on top of each other into an insurmountable tower she couldn't get around.

Mav's hooded eyes closed, and he inhaled deeply through his nose. "Yes, that is a lot to think about," he said. "And one would much rather a whale that breaches the surface than an unknown shadow circling in the depths." He frowned. "I wonder..."

Before he could finish the question, Isla's phone chimed with a message. He gestured that it was okay for her to check it.

As soon as the screen lit up, Isla's stomach tightened. "Oh shit," she mumbled.

"Trouble?"

"He already told the department," she said. "I literally sent the email an hour ago." She opened the message and scanned the few sentences therein. "Katelyn says she's happy to hear I'll be back and could we meet for coffee sometime soon."

"Jonah's sister?"

Isla swallowed hard and put her phone away. "Yup." Why had she told Dean Abbot she'd be back? She wasn't ready. Not when the mere thought of facing her sister-in-law made her want to run away. Katelyn had her own questions, her own grief —but everything was tied to Isla.

She bent down and blew out the candle. It was time to go.

Mav didn't protest but fell into pace with her as she set course for the entrance, back the way she'd come. She scanned the lawn as they walked; nodded to people they met. One man sitting on a bench near the fountain fifty feet away stood out— perhaps because it was a chilly day to sit on a bench—and she lingered briefly on his familiar figure. A friendly smile floated past her mind's eye.

"See someone you know?" Mav asked.

Isla shook her head. "No, but I think that guy might live in your building." She tilted her head toward the fountain.

Mav peered around her. "Could be. I haven't been here long enough to know all my neighbors yet."

"Do you know any of them?" The tall man was the only other person she'd seen in his building. Then again, most people were at work when she showed up with her meals.

"There's a very nice family with a little boy living across from me." Mav nodded then gestured to his tattoos. "Kid's scared of me though. And I'm not necessarily seeking out new friends these days."

"Other than me."

Mav winked at her. "Other than you."

They continued around the final bend on the path, and when they were almost at the gate, Isla summoned up the courage to ask a more personal question. "And what about the friend you're visiting here—was he also in the war? If you don't mind my asking."

"Um..." Mav tilted his head up to the sky. "Yes."

"Did he make it back home?"

Maverick nodded, less hesitant now. "Married, had a family, and lived a long life. We lost touch, but I'd like to believe it was a happy life. Passed on around the same time my Lorraine did. Such is life at ninety."

Isla paused, her bike between them. How could he be so cavalier about it? "It doesn't weigh on you? That you're here and they're not?"

"And what purpose would that serve, Isla?" He said her name with great sympathy. "Would it bring them back? Absolve me of any of the many mistakes I've made in my long life? No."

He was right in part; her pain wouldn't bring Jonah back, but if she'd earned it, wouldn't healing from it be cheating? Not that she even knew how to attempt something like that.

Maverick placed a hand on Isla's handlebars. "I think the difference between you and me—other than my advanced age and creaky bones—is that I have very few questions left. Maybe what you need are some answers."

Answers, Isla thought as she lay in her childhood bed that night, staring at the ceiling.

Answers, she thought again upon waking. Wouldn't that be nice?

Her phone buzzed with a message from Louise. *Someone else is bidding on your bird. Just checked.*

What? Isla opened the auction app and sure enough, hers was now only the second-highest bid. Not only that, but the other bidder had upped the price by a hundred dollars.

"The heck?" Isla mumbled before increasing her bid by 105.

Thanks, she texted Louise. *What are you up to today?*

Sundays were the slowest day of the week. Mondays were for grocery shopping, Tuesdays and Wednesdays for meal delivery, Thursdays recovery time from being social, Fridays she worked on her collection, and Saturdays she visited the memorial park. But Sundays felt like placeholders where nothing could get done.

They used to be reserved for lazy mornings in bed, reading together on the couch with her feet in Jonah's lap, and dinner with his family in Ferndale, but even though they'd invited Isla many times since the accident, she'd never gone.

Watching my niece. Louise sent a photo of two tiny hands covered in flour. *We're baking cookies.*

Isla threw the phone down on her bed. Then she closed her eyes and counted backward from ten, willing the sudden blockage in her throat to resolve. It wasn't Louise's fault. She didn't know that Jonah's death had robbed Isla not only of her husband but of the one thing she'd wanted more than anything —a child. They'd decided to start trying shortly before the accident, a cruel coincidence if there ever was one. At the time, they'd decided to keep it a secret, and now it would forever stay that way.

Having steadied herself, she reached again for her phone as the auction app chimed. The other person had outbid her again.

She upped her bid once more. This wasn't one she wanted to lose.

How high are you willing to go? Louise asked when Isla told her.

And that was the crux of it, wasn't it? Another reminder that she had no income to speak of.

Mom was right: Isla couldn't go on like this. Not if she was going to be able to deliver on her promise to Dean Abbot come fall. And maybe Maverick was also right and she needed answers. But that begged yet another question. Where would she start? In the tangled ball of yarn her past had become, which end was the right one to tug at—the one that would make it all unravel?

EIGHT

GEMMA

April, three years ago

The office was dark and silent when Gemma unlocked the doors. They'd been operating with a skeleton crew for the past week—only Dr. Richards, the other dental hygienist, Fran, and Gemma. Everyone else was on furlough until further notice in accordance with CDC recommendations and they weren't doing any preventative appointments.

Fran had grumbled about having to do the work of the assistants and reception in addition to her own responsibilities, but Gemma didn't mind. She was grateful to get out of the apartment, especially now that Cheryl had been let go from her waitressing job. She hummed to herself while preparing the two rooms they would be using for the day, and then she logged in to the computer and picked an upbeat eighties playlist for the speaker system.

They would only be seeing six patients today—three crowns, two root canals, and one extraction. Gemma scanned the schedule, her eyes catching on one name. It was the nervous cracked tooth from two weeks ago—Mr. Gallagher, first name,

Jonah. And he was the second patient of the day. She'd better get the nitrous ready for chair two then.

Dr. Richards arrived twenty minutes later and Fran shortly after him. The first patient did not, however, and when Gemma called, she said she'd left a voicemail over the weekend that she was sick and couldn't make it. There had been no voicemail, but it wasn't like anyone was going to tell a sick person to come in and "open wide" under current circumstances, so Gemma wished the patient a speedy recovery then went to grab her book from the staff room. Fran was assigned Mr. Gallagher, so Gemma would be biding her time at the front desk until their first afternoon root canal arrived.

She was deeply entrenched in a historical Scottish Highlands time travel novel when the front door opened and a pair of familiar hazel eyes met hers above a black mask.

"Jonah. Hello." Gemma tried to make her smile shine through her surgical mask as best as she could. The use of his first name was intentional—a tried-and-true strategy to make patients feel more at home.

He'd paused right inside the door, gazing around the waiting room, but now he took a step toward her. "I'm here for my, um, crown."

"Right. How has the temporary one been treating you?"

"Okay. It's a little sore, but nothing I can't manage."

"We'll get that taken care of and you'll be good as new. I've got you all checked in."

"Okay." He pulled off his beanie. "Thanks."

When he didn't move, she nodded toward the chairs along the wall. "You can have a seat if you want. Fran will be right with you."

"Okay," he said again, and this time, he sat, arms crossed in front of him and one leg bouncing up and down.

Gemma shook her head as she left the reception to let the

others know he was here. She'd have to give Fran a heads-up that this one needed kid gloves.

Jonah had only been in the chair for ten minutes when Fran came outside to where Gemma was back in the world of kilts and Jacobite uprisings.

"He's asking for you," she said.

"He is?"

"Yeah. You weren't kidding about the nerves."

Gemma put her book down, a small thrill bouncing through her. A request like that was always the best compliment. "I guess I can take over. Will you mind the phones?"

"Sure, no problem. I owe you one. Got a killer headache too, so it's probably for the best."

"Take some ibuprofen. It's quiet out here. Only one call all morning so far."

Gemma hurried to wash up and put her gloves and goggles on. Then she joined Dr. Richards at Jonah's chair.

"How are we doing?" she asked.

"Okay," Jonah garbled back. "Will it hurt?"

She met the doctor's eyes, and he nodded to her, a sign that she could take the reins.

"We're going to do what we did last time, okay?" she said. "You'll breathe some nitrous, we'll get you numbed up, and then we'll fit the new crown. It'll be ten, fifteen minutes tops."

"Okay."

She reached for the nose cone but paused at the sight of his clasped hands, the grip so tight his knuckles were whitening. "Relax," she said, touching his shoulder. She needed to think of something that would distract him.

As she applied the numbing gel, she started talking. "It's weird how quiet the streets are, right? It probably didn't take you very long to drive here today. My commute has been so much better. Not that I like what's going on." She straightened his bib then sat back to let the doctor get to work. "It kind of reminds me of this one time at an old job. I worked summers at Oaks Amusement Park when I was a teenager. Do you know it? It was great—there were a bunch of us just having a good time. Well one day we showed up, and there was hardly anyone there. Which was unusual."

Jonah let out a small "uh" sound as Dr. Richards removed the temporary cap.

"Focus on me," Gemma said. She took his hand on instinct, and he relaxed again.

"Anyway," she continued. "It was me and two of my friends walking through an almost empty parking lot. The gates were open, but the place was basically deserted. Like in some kind of horror movie. It turned out there was a storm coming. Everyone had gotten the memo except us."

Jonah squeezed her hand.

Gemma looked up at Dr. Richards. "Need me to do anything?"

"No, almost done."

"So, my friends and I helped ourselves to popcorn and slushies and played a few games of whack-a-mole before the thunder rolled in and we figured things out. But that's what the city reminds me of these days. Like a storm is coming and everyone is hunkered down."

"Okay," Dr. Richards said. "Crown is in. Now, let's make sure nothing is too high. Gemma?"

She extricated her hand and reached for the articulating paper.

"We're done?" Jonah asked.

"Almost." Gemma tapped his chin to get him to open again. He had a tiny dimple in the middle of it where his stubble congregated. She could feel it prickle through her glove. "There you go."

Once the crown was polished and his bite adjusted, Gemma helped him sit up.

"How does that feel?" Dr. Richards asked. "All good?"

Jonah touched his cheek and moved his jaw around. "I think so."

"If you have any issues, give us a call, okay?"

"Thanks, doc."

"Let me grab your coat for you," Gemma said, reaching for where it hung on a hook around the corner.

"Thanks." He took it from her and put it on. When he faced her again, his expression was transformed. Gone was any apprehension, replaced instead with the self-assuredness one would presume to find in a man with his good genes. "Did you really work at an amusement park?"

The change made Gemma tongue-tied. It was like their roles had flip-flopped. No longer was her attention to him one-sided, and she wasn't used to it. "I did. Three summers in a row. Why?"

"It's so random, but I worked at the Evergreen State Fair as a teen. Similar thing. Loved it."

"Free rides, fireworks, people having fun. What's not to love?" Gemma walked through the doorway to the lobby with Jonah trailing her, but no one was at the front desk. Fran must have gone back to the staff room.

"And the smells," he said, eyes crinkling at the corners. "Buttered popcorn, elephant ears, French fries."

"Roasted nuts, hotdogs." She grinned up at him.

For a moment, a comfortable silence stretched between them, then Jonah pulled his beanie back on.

"I'm sorry you had to see me like that," he said. "Dentists are my kryptonite. Believe it or not, I'm usually a pretty laid-back guy."

Seeing him now, she believed him. "I get it. No worries. You should see me near any sort of open water."

"No way? I played water polo in college. I love the water."

"But sharks!"

"Rare in swimming pools."

They both laughed.

How long had it been since she'd made small talk with a guy like this—some simple friendly banter. An innocuous connection. Between her aunt and her ex, she'd grown used to feeling like she was in the way, so to be looked at like someone who brought value filled her with energy.

"Well, thanks again," Jonah said, reaching for the door.

She wanted to keep him talking, to extend the moment a little, but drew a blank. "Sure thing," she said instead. "Take care."

And then he was gone.

Fran called in sick the rest of the week, so Gemma and Dr. Richards were alone in the office the few hours a day they had patients scheduled. When she was home, she spent most of her time in her room reading. She would have preferred to be on the couch in the brighter living room where a large glass sliding door led to a balcony overlooking a small park, but Cheryl seemed to have taken up permanent residence in front of the TV, and Gemma found it difficult to focus on her stories with daytime talk shows as a constant backdrop.

To make up for the too-sparse amount of daylight let into her space through a small north-facing window, she'd tidied, washed the sheets, and hung up a few prints that had been sitting in a box since she'd moved in. It made the room cozy, especially when the rain pounded the pavement outside. She also made sure to go for walks every day to soak up whatever vitamin D she could, and she still hadn't given up on getting her aunt to come along.

Gemma knew she had it pretty good all things considered. Her best friend from high school, Sadie, lived down in Eugene with her family, and when Gemma told her that she'd gone through five books from her to-be-read list in seven days, her friend groaned.

"Oh my God, to be able to read even one book," she said. "With the twins home from preschool, there's no time. All I'm doing is trying to keep them quiet so Parker can work from home. I fucking hate this."

"Aww, I wish I could come rescue you for a night out," Gemma said. "But hopefully this will all be over soon, and we can get back to business as usual. I can't keep living with Cheryl forever, that's for sure, and I need to make some new friends. Can you believe all those assholes picked Yuri's side when he dumped me? Well except Ariel, but she's moving to Nevada."

"That settles it. We need to find you a new guy. How long has it been? Six months? Seven? That's just not healthy."

"It's fine."

It wasn't fine. She still hadn't been able to bring herself to unfollow Yuri on socials, telling herself she needed the reminders of what a douche he'd been. But those reminders also included the new woman—all light-blond, sun-kissed, five-foot-ten of her—so maybe Gemma wasn't so keen to hit the dating apps any time soon. What she craved was some good conversation and a few laughs. For someone to be curious about her as a person.

Before she could stop herself, she blurted, "There was a cute guy in the office last week actually."

"Oh really? Tell me everything."

Gemma faced her reflection in the mirrored closet door. *Damn you.* She tried to backtrack. "Um, there's not much to tell. He was nice, that's all."

"Nah, I don't buy it. There must be more than that if you're still thinking about him."

She was still thinking about him, Gemma realized, pathetic as it was. Was that all it took these days—a few minutes of friendly conversation and a handsome face? Not that it mattered. "He's spoken for of course."

"Ring?"

"Yes."

"But that doesn't necessarily mean anything. Did he mention her?"

"No."

"Maybe he's recently divorced. Or a widower. You don't know what you don't know. You should call him."

Gemma let out a sputtered laugh. "I can't do that."

"Why the hell not? Who knows—maybe he's sitting at home right now, all by his lonesome, wondering what you're up to. Call him."

Gemma's cheeks warmed. "That would be unethical. He's a patient."

"So call him to follow up on his dental work. Does he have any complaints? Does he want to leave a review? Make something up."

"I... I don't know."

"Shit, the little monsters are in the pantry. Gotta go. Keep me posted. Love ya."

Sadie hung up before Gemma had a chance to respond. She stared at her phone for a long moment. Was there something to what her friend was saying? She flipped onto her stomach on the bed, and as she did so, her necklace slid out from beneath her top to dangle in front of her face. Yuri had bought it for her on their three-month anniversary, and she still loved it. There could be many reasons why someone still wore jewelry after a relationship ended. Maybe the ring didn't mean what she'd assumed it to mean. Maybe she did need to find out.

Gemma was still debating the merits of Sadie's suggestion the next day in the office, but when Dr. Richards had left for the day and she was closing down the computers, she made her choice. It was common courtesy to make sure he wasn't having issues with the crown, wasn't it? She could ask, and if he was fine, that would be that. No harm done.

With shaking fingers, Gemma looked Jonah up in the patient chart and jotted down his cell-phone number on a sticky note. Then she hurried to put it in her purse. She'd drive home then call. Have one last think about it beforehand. It was only three thirty in the afternoon, so he might not even pick up. With some luck, her call would go straight to voicemail and then the ball would be in his court. If this whole thing turned out to be something resembling a game in the first place that was.

She had convinced herself of that scenario to such a degree that when after five beeps a voice croaked out a bass-y "Hello" on the other end, she didn't speak at first, expecting the shrill tone to sound indicating the start of a message.

When that didn't happen, she realized he was there, live, in her ear. "Um, hi. Um, is this Jonah?"

A lengthy coughing fit followed. "Yeah, that's me."

"Um, hi," she said again, squeezing her eyes shut. "Hi, this is Gemma from Dr. Richards' office. I'm just calling to see, um, how you're doing with that crown."

"Oh." He cleared his throat. "Sorry. Hold on a second."

She waited. Something rustled on the other end, followed by the clang of something being set down onto wood. Another coughing fit, then he returned. She could tell by his breathing.

"You sound terrible," she said. "Are you okay?"

"I've been better," he rasped. "I must have caught the stupid virus somewhere. It's knocked me out for sure."

"Oh God, I'm so sorry."

A brief silence billowed between them before he sniffled. "Oh right, the crown. That's what you asked about. Sorry, I get kind of loopy when I have a fever."

He had a fever too? "That sounds bad. Hopefully you have someone there to take care of you."

"Nope only me."

Inside Gemma's head, Sadie yelled, "Told you so."

"But yeah, the crown is good," he continued. "No issues. You guys did a good job."

"And you're not just saying that because you hate going to the dentist?"

He chuckled, which led to more coughing. "No. I promise. Nice dig though."

She smiled. "That's not how I meant it. I want you to be comfortable." She cringed. "I mean—we want all our patients to be comfortable. Satisfied and comfortable." Oh Lord, she should stop talking now.

"Well, I am. Thank you." He was quiet for a beat, and it sounded like he'd taken a sip of something.

She was gearing up to end the call when he sniffled again then asked, "So how have you been? These are weird times, right?"

Gemma stared unseeingly out the windshield of her car toward the apartment building. That wasn't a question she'd ever been asked by a patient.

"It is weird," she agreed. "But I'm good. Better off than many, I think, since I'm still working. My aunt is driving me a little nuts—I live with her right now, long story—but other than that, I can't complain." She snapped her mouth shut. He wasn't asking for an account of her life.

"That's refreshing to hear," he said. "Since complaining is becoming something of a national sport."

"I know, right? I think my aunt is going for the gold medal in the hundred-meter grumble."

"Ha!" His laugh mixed with more coughing before he managed a throaty, "Good one."

"Hey, are you really doing okay?" she asked. "Have you seen a doctor?"

"I talked to my primary yesterday and I guess I have to let it run its course as long as it's not affecting my breathing."

"Ah okay, that's good then." Time to wrap it up. She'd asked the question she'd intended, and he'd answered. "Well, if there's anything else I can do—*we* can do—don't hesitate to reach out, okay? I hope you feel better." She readied herself for his good-bye, but instead there was a pause.

Finally, he cleared his throat again. "Well actually—and this is probably going to sound pretty out there—but I'm still in my job rental since I couldn't drive home to Bellingham like this, and I don't have any food left. Is there any chance you'd be able to drop off a bag with the basics outside my door and maybe some cold meds? I'll send you money. It's just I... I'd be super grateful because I don't know anyone around here. But it's completely one hundred percent okay for you to say no."

She knew right away that she wouldn't, but she still paused to remind herself this meant nothing. She'd just happened to call him at a time when he was in a bind.

"Of course," she said. "I'd be happy to. Text me your address and a list, and I'll come by in a bit."

He let out an audible breath. "Thank you," he said. "You're a lifesaver."

NINE

ISLA

Isla sat on the floor in front of the TV again, the remote in her hand as the familiar wedding march played on the screen. The dress, the smiling faces, the vows, the confetti. The party where the videographer had made his rounds, asking people to record messages for the newlyweds between dances.

She studied the faces. Her own and Jonah's most of all. There had to be something there. A clue or at least something to jog her memory. Why they'd decided to celebrate their seventh anniversary all the way down in Bend at the rather pricey hotel where Jonah had once popped the question. Why they *hadn't* been at the hotel the night of the accident. Why Isla, who never drove, had been in the driver's seat. Why she'd had the vision of Nana. It seemed a fallacy of logic that the woman on that dance floor seven years ago was the same person sitting here on Mom's rug, still in pajamas at eleven in the morning on a regular February Monday.

A door opened somewhere behind her, Mom's keys jingling onto the small table in the hallway. Footsteps followed but stopped in the doorway to the living room. Isla knew what would come next and paused the video as Jonah lifted his own camera to capture the photographer in action.

"Not again, Birdie." Her mom entered the room, unzipping her jacket. She was in her walking clothes—warm sweats and a headband—her cheeks red from the winter air. "I thought we decided it wasn't good for you."

Isla put the remote on the table. "It's not what you think. Maverick—he's one of my clients—thinks I need to figure out what happened. I was hoping this would give me a place to start."

"Your wedding video?"

Isla shrugged. When she said it that way... "I don't know."

"And we already know what happened. It was an accident, Birdie. A terrible, awful accident. Looking for reasons that aren't there will only bring more grief." Mom slung her jacket over the couch's armrest and proceeded to lean forward for a calf stretch.

Was she right? She had a point about the video—Isla could admit that much—but would Isla really be better off leaving this alone? Wasn't that what she'd done for the past two years?

"I think you're wrong," she said. "Remember when we had that sit-down with Dad's doctors after he passed? You got to ask your questions, they walked you through his treatments and why they didn't work." Of course, they'd already known he was unlikely to make it once put on the ventilator, so in his case, the outcome had been anticipated.

Mom straightened again. "That's not something you forget."

"And do you think it helped you? Not having to wonder about his last moments?"

Mom's gaze traveled from Isla to the TV, where the video hovered on Jonah. "I take your point."

Isla's shoulders lowered. "Okay, good. But you're probably right about the video. It's got nothing to do with anything."

"What about his camera?" Mom asked, somewhere else in thought. "Did he bring it to Bend that weekend?"

A flutter of something kicked off inside Isla. She'd long since printed and organized all the photos from Jonah's laptop into a stack of albums that rested in a box in the back of her closet, but now that Mom mentioned it, she didn't actually know where his camera was. She stared at the TV, where Jonah's face was covered by the big lens. She couldn't imagine him not having brought it along, which either meant it was lost or...

"If it wasn't in the car with us, Katelyn might have it," she said. It was Jonah's sister who'd grabbed their belongings from the hotel in the aftermath. She'd dropped off Isla's things and some of Jonah's with Nancy, like his rings, watch, and phone, but Isla wasn't sure what had happened to the rest. At the time and in the grand scheme of things, it hadn't seemed important. "She texted me the other day."

Nancy dropped the arm she'd been stretching. "She did?"

"After Dean Abbot shared the news." Isla got off the floor and pushed her hair off her forehead with a tight stroke. "Crap —this means I'll have to text her back."

Nancy studied her for a minute. "You really weren't wallowing over it today, were you? You're doing something."

Isla didn't have to ask what she meant by that. She knew the idleness of her recent existence had been a source of worry for her mom. Any change, then, would signal hope.

"I'm trying." Isla gave her a tight smile, making sure it didn't promise too much.

Nancy nodded. "Well—I'm off to take a shower. You should text her now, while it's fresh in your mind."

"Yeah, yeah." She watched her mom disappear up the stairs. *Text Katelyn now.* Isla bit down on the inside of her cheek. Fine. She sighed. *Fine.*

Katelyn responded within a minute, her exclamation points

betraying her surprise at hearing from her sister-in-law. After a couple of polite back-and-forths, Isla sent the question at the forefront of her mind.

I was looking for Jonah's camera. Do you guys have it?

Her fingers shook typing her husband's name and sending it off like that. Not asking about him but about one of his belongings. Like it was in bad taste.

But Katelyn's response was free of accusations. *We do. Simon has been using it for a photography class in school.*

Isla wrinkled her nose. If her fifteen-year-old nephew had it, what were the chances of pictures from two years ago not having been deleted?

I was wondering about old photos, she texted. *If there were any on it.* Then, because she didn't quite know what she was hoping to find or how to explain it, she added a white lie. *Organizing some albums.*

*I'm not sure about that,*Katelyn wrote. *But I'll ask him when he gets home and will let you know.*

Hours. That was hours she'd have to wait for an answer. Isla sighed again. *Sounds good,* she typed back. *Thank you.*

The afternoon dragged on. Perhaps in a gesture of goodwill, Mom drove them to the grocery store, so even that provided only marginal distraction. She checked the auction and found her bid was still the highest, which she reported to Louise with three fingers-crossed emojis. When she received no response, she sent another text about the camera, too, to fill her time with something. She didn't want to read, or watch TV. Her room was tidy, laundry done, and her collection in order.

Finally, she pulled on her sneakers and went for a walk around the block. She couldn't remember the last time she'd done something like that just because, but there was something new stirring inside her. A need to move. An urgency.

She'd looped around the neighborhood twice and was walking alongside the middle-school fence when her phone rang, but it was Louise, not Katelyn.

"What do you think is on the camera?" she asked. "I've never heard you talk about it before."

Isla told her that she'd forgotten about it until Mom pointed out Jonah having it in the video. "It could be nothing. Even if he had it with him, I don't know if he was using it. But it's at least a place to start. Mav thinks I have too many questions and not enough answers."

"And if it's a dead end?"

Isla looked both ways as she crossed the last street before her mom's block, skipping over the puddles of water by the curb. "I don't know. Like I said—I'm short on answers."

Louise was quiet for a while. "You know," she said eventually, "maybe I could help. I ask questions all the time as part of my job. Maybe if you think of someone I should call or, you know... Do you have the, um, the police report?"

Isla pulled up short in front of Nancy's house. She'd read it at some point; she was certain of that. Had someone handed it to her while she was still on bedrest? There was a vague memory of lying down, struggling to hold up the pages. "I've read it," she said. "But I don't have a copy, and I feel like I would have remembered it there was anything important in it."

"You never know. I could contact the police department for you. See what I can find out. They should be able to send it to us."

"You would do that?"

"Of course."

Isla continued up the stairs and opened the door, considering this. It *was* another thread to pull at.

Louise cleared her throat. "I'd need to know what police department to contact. Do you know?"

Isla didn't. The accident had happened on a rural stretch of road south of Crescent, Oregon, but she couldn't remember if they had their own sheriff's office, and she told Louise as much. More she didn't have time for because she had another call coming through—Katelyn was finally getting back to her.

After promising Louise she'd talk to her later, Isla hung up and accepted Katelyn's call.

"Okay, yes, so there is a memory card," Katelyn said after their initial greetings.

Isla started to sweat. "Really?"

"Apparently, Simon swapped it for a bigger one when he started this class, but after digging around in his drawers, he found the old one." She paused. "I don't suppose you're planning on coming up this way soon?"

The question made Isla realize for the first time that if she was to go back to work like she'd said, she would eventually have to return to Bellingham. Find a new place to live. Start over in what had been her and Jonah's domain. The thought made her knees weak. "Not for a while," she said, forcing her voice light. "Would you be able to email me what's on it?"

"Sure. Yes. I guess I could do that. It'll be after basketball tonight though."

Isla let out a breath. "Great. Thank you. And say thanks to Simon too. How is he doing?"

The question steered the conversation to safer waters, and when Isla eventually hung up, she stared at the screen, a small smile reflected in the dark glass.

She'd been plagued by nightmares since the accident—some infused by abstract threats, others sharply outlined and painted in realistic strokes. A recurring one was ringing the doorbell at her in-laws' house and when they opened and saw it was her, their faces would twist with fury before they chased her off, shouts of "Murderer!" cutting through the air.

Now, after speaking to Katelyn, one of the many bogeymen hiding in her mental closet had retreated a few steps.

The photos arrived in her inbox a little after nine that evening. Isla had Louise on speaker, too nervous at what she might find to open the zipped file alone. The album populated with thumbnails, and Isla hovered over the first one with the mouse. Then she clicked it open.

"It's me posing in front of the hotel," she said, examining the woman in the photo—the cocked hip, raised arms, her smile. Every rational part of Isla knew it was her, but without the memory, it was like looking at a stranger. She clicked down the list, backward in time. A view of a river. Isla sipping a to-go cup of coffee. A funny sign inside a restaurant. Disappointment flooded her system and made her shoulders slump.

"Anything else?" Louise asked.

"I thought there'd be something here to make me remember. But it's only mundane stuff. Things he found interesting."

Jonah's ability to appreciate his surroundings that way had been one of the qualities she'd fallen for—that he at times saw things from different perspectives. Of course, there had also been times when she'd wished he'd put the camera down. Not every sunset needed capture—sometimes just experiencing it together in the moment was enough.

"Don't be so hard on yourself. You only just started looking."

Isla hummed a response as she continued browsing the thumbnails. There were a couple more shots from what must have been their road trip to Bend, then several studies of ice-clad branches after a particularly heavy snowfall, and a few snaps from New Year's.

Isla stared a long time at the group photo where champagne glasses and sparklers glittered and gleamed in the hands of their smiling friends. There were Katelyn and Mark without a worry in the world. Pete and Tovah had moved to Denver a year ago, but Adnan and Sudita were still in Bellingham as far as Isla knew. The guys were originally Jonah's friends from high school, but Isla had become close with Tovah and Sudita too. They'd reached out many times after the accident, but Isla had never responded. She couldn't. She didn't blame them when, eventually, the phone calls and messages stopped.

"Anything?" Louise asked.

Isla had almost forgotten she was on the phone. "No. Just holiday stuff now."

"Gotcha." Somewhere on Louise's end, a doorbell rang. "Oh, shoot, I forgot my aunt was coming over."

Probably for the best. So far, it seemed Isla had made a big deal of nothing. "You go. No worries."

"You sure?"

"We can talk later."

After disconnecting, Isla opened her text thread with Tovah instead. The last communication they'd had was ten months ago —a photo of her friend's new house. Isla hadn't even said congratulations. *Snip, snip* and her tethers to the world had been cut one at a time.

She put the phone down and returned to the computer.

Next were Christmas photos. Mom had stayed with them that holiday as it was the first one without Dad. Closeups of their gingerbread house, moody shots of golden lights illuminating Douglas Fir branches. On Christmas Eve, they'd gone over to Katelyn's house for a large family gathering. A smorgasbord of treats, wreaths, smiling kids, gifts. At some point, someone else must have gotten their hands on the camera because Jonah was in a few of them, wads of wrapping paper at his side.

Isla moved on, and soon the series turned to random snaps of festively lit cityscapes, a red bridge over an icy river, Jonah in his car, and finally, an impressive town-square Christmas tree, probably taken somewhere in Portland on Jonah's last trip there in December.

Isla's finger stiffened on the mouse. Her ears were suddenly tingling with the absence of noise in the room. She clicked through the last three pictures again. Red bridge, Jonah, tree, Jonah, red bridge, Jonah...

She stared at the familiar slant of his brow for a long moment. In the photo, he was driving, but he'd taken his eyes off the road for a moment, and a smile played on his lips. Unguarded.

"What the hell?" she mumbled.

The room spun as what she was looking at sank in. The tree and bridge were both in Portland, which meant the photo of Jonah must have also been taken there. There was only one problem—Isla hadn't been with him on that trip. And if she hadn't taken the photo, then who had?

TEN

ISLA

Present day

The photo of Jonah lingered sideways in Isla's chest as she completed her meal deliveries the following day. She was vaguely aware of Maverick making conversation, but since she'd forgotten her lunch at home, she didn't stay long. "Lots going on," was her excuse when he probed. It wasn't a complete lie. It was just that most of what was "going on" was in her head.

Could the photo have been taken by a colleague? she wondered, biking back to Mom's through town. Someone he knew well, with whom he was comfortable letting his guard down. Just because he'd never talked about co-workers didn't mean he hadn't had a few close ones, right? And he was allowed to have other people in his car. He and Isla had never needed the other to account for every moment of every day they were apart.

But even as she tried to convince herself that was the case, she knew deep down she'd stumbled upon *something*—not only because of the particular expression on his face but because of the pit it had left in her stomach. She knew she'd felt it before, but when she tried to pinpoint the sensation, it skirted away like quicksilver.

She braked and stepped off the bike to lead it across the street. All these unknowns were giving her a headache.

After making herself a sandwich in the kitchen, Isla remained standing, leaning against the counter trying but failing to recall if Jonah had ever mentioned someone he was friendly with in Portland.

Surely, he hadn't—

She cut the intruding thought short. *No.* He would never do that to her.

As if wanting to prove his faithfulness to herself, she moved into the living room where the wedding video sat tucked into its case. If she watched it again, she'd be able to laugh those ludicrous thoughts away. And maybe there was still something there that she'd missed. She eyed the case from a distance then set the plate down on the table. Mom had a dentist appointment this afternoon and wouldn't be home for a while...

Squatting, Isla opened the door to the entertainment center and picked up the case. In an instant, a whirlwind reel of the wedding flowed through her mind. There'd been nothing but joy that night—it was so tempting now as always to immerse herself in happier times.

No, she shouldn't.

Her thumb caressed the smooth plastic, so cool and inviting against her skin, then, still gripping the case, she forced herself upright and stood for a moment, staring at the black TV. If it didn't help her to watch it, maybe Mom was right, and it did the opposite. Her teeth dug into her lower lip.

Before she could change her mind, she turned and strode with determined steps into her bedroom, pulled out one of the storage boxes under the bed, and tucked the case inside. As always, Ulysses was curled up in a ball by the pillows, but at the commotion, he lifted his head and blinked yellow eyes at her.

"It's the right thing to do," Isla told him. "It's not answering any of my questions." She reached across the comforter to scratch him behind the ear and was awarded with the low revving of a feline engine. "Besides, it will make Mom happy." The purring increased in intensity. "Oh, you too, huh?" she chuckled.

Ulysses stretched and crept closer to Isla, who'd sat down. Her hand moved of its own accord across the shiny black coat as her mind churned in ever more convoluted circles. Photos, holidays, road trips, and vows. Somewhere in all of it there must be a key waiting to be found. The question was, where?

"Sorry about yesterday," Isla said, setting down Mav's meal on the counter on Wednesday. "I was a bit in my head."

Mav took a glass out of the cabinet and turned on the tap. "Anything in particular going on?"

Isla started the microwave and watched the plate spin. "I got some photos off Jonah's old camera." She fell silent as the seconds counted down on the display.

"And?" Mav sat down in his chair.

How to explain? Isla took the plate out and grabbed silverware before setting everything down in front of Mav. "And it's probably just in my head, but I can't"—she flapped her hand around her head as if chasing away a mosquito—"get it out of here."

"I see." Mav scooped up a forkful of peas and brought them close enough to his face to sniff. Then he tipped them back onto the plate. "They look so appealing, don't they?" he said. "These tiny green pearls. You'd think they'd taste a delight as well, but no. Sneaky little suckers."

Isla laughed. "You feel very strongly about your vegetables."

"I do." Mav smiled, then cut a piece of tilapia instead and chewed carefully. "I've earned the right to be picky."

"Note taken. No peas."

For a while, the only sound around them was that of chewing and the crinkle of the paper wrapped around Isla's sandwich, but when half of Mav's food was gone, he sat back and leveled his icy blues on her.

"Can I see the pictures?" he asked.

Isla hesitated, but then she pulled out her phone and opened Katelyn's email and its attachment.

"It's this one," she said, scrolling to the one of Jonah, and handing the phone to Mav. "Tell me what you see."

Mav took his time, while Isla watched him expectantly.

"You have a good eye," he said eventually. "Caught him unawares in this one."

"Right." Isla shoved her hands into the pocket of her hoodie. "Except I didn't take it, and I have no idea who did."

Mav looked up and blinked at her, "I see. Could have been anyone though, couldn't it? Coworker, client, friend."

"It would have had to have been someone who knew him well enough that they felt comfortable grabbing his camera and firing off a candid shot."

"Friend it is."

"I don't think he had any down there."

"Mm. I see how that might cause some pondering. But I'm sure there's a perfectly reasonable explanation."

As vague as that was, it still eased something within Isla. Maybe he was right.

"Are there more?" Mav asked.

"Scroll to the left." Isla pointed. "Christmas and New Year's mostly."

"Looks like a good family," he said. "Ha-ha, those kids are drowning in gifts." He kept scrolling. "Huh." He flipped back and forth between two photos.

"What?"

"I take it Jonah really didn't like Christmas?"

Isla frowned. "Why would you say that?"

Jonah had always loved Christmas. Every year, he was the first one at the Christmas tree lot the day after Thanksgiving, and he took the Gallagher cookie swap more seriously than anyone else. He also went to great lengths to spread his Christmas cheer around. The first year they'd dated, he'd made Isla an advent calendar with presents for each day of December, each more thoughtful than the next—a tradition he'd stuck to ever since—and he kept a running list of gift ideas for the people he loved in his phone throughout the year. The holiday spirit mattered to him.

Isla leaned closer to the screen to see what Mav was looking at. Several images swished by: Katelyn's kids animated with delight at various gifts, the adults laughing in the background, Isla herself holding up a sweater someone had gifted her, and Jonah, not participating.

She took the phone from Mav and swiped back and forth through the photos. He wasn't in all of them, but wherever he was, he made up an impassive void amidst everyone else's exuberance. "I don't understand," she mumbled. She'd been so stuck on the car photo that the Christmas ones had faded into the background, but now that Mav had made his observation, she couldn't unsee it. Jonah looked miserable.

In the final Christmas image, Isla had her arm around her husband's shoulders, grinning at the camera. The rest of the family crowded them on either side, some holding up gifts, others throwing up bunny ears. In this one, Jonah, too, looked at the camera, and the corners of his mouth were turned up, but instead of setting Isla at ease, the overall impression made her stomach twist.

"This makes no sense—Christmas was his favorite," she said.

"Maybe he had a bad day."

If he did, she hadn't been aware of it at the time. Everything had seemed perfectly normal to her. Hadn't it? First the candid car photo, now this. What did it all mean? The pit lodged in her stomach hollowed further, not only because she didn't understand the Jonah she was seeing, but also because it made her question her memory going back even further than the week of the accident. It made something scratch at the barred door in her mind. Something with sharp claws.

Mav watched her for a while then nudged a crooked finger toward her head. "What's going on in there?"

Isla scrunched up her face in concentration. "There's just something about these photos that makes the other ones—the albums in my closet, the framed portraits in my room, my screen saver—feel... almost like they're lies. I mean, I know they're not, but, ugh, I can't explain it. It's like—I *know* we were happy. I remember laughing, talking... arguing too, of course, but making up. And maybe the whole quarantine thing wasn't our best time, but we loved each other. You know—at the core."

"Of course you did." He put his hand on hers, urging her to lower the phone. "Isla dear, this could be nothing."

The screen went black as she shook her head. "But what if it's something? What if it's important? I don't know who took that photo of him. Who he smiled at like that. Why he *didn't* smile at Christmas." Isla scoffed. "Like I need more questions without answers. Why can't I just remember?"

Mav watched her with soft eyes for a moment. "Have you talked to someone about this? Maybe it's a block of some kind."

"I'm talking to you."

"I mean a professional."

Isla shook her head. "I had a therapist for a while, but she moved, and I didn't feel like searching for someone new. The waitlists are too long anyway." She fiddled with the corner of her phone case. Pushed it off the device then back on. "My friend Louise is contacting the police department to talk to someone about getting a copy of the accident report," she said.

"But I don't know what good that'll do. Refresh my facts, I guess."

Mav nodded slowly. "I hear you."

"But what about what's in here?" Isla tapped her temple. "What if even the things I think I remember aren't real?"

"The report can't unveil that."

"Exactly."

Mav paused for a beat; cleared his throat. "Would you go back there?" he asked. "Retrace your steps?"

Isla's eyes shot to his as her stomach lurched.

"Sometimes the only way forward is through," he continued. "No matter how impossible the journey might seem."

"I couldn't," Isla sputtered. "I don't... Where would I...? How...?"

"But you need to get to the bottom of this, Isla, dear. And I think you know that."

His gentle tone eased the turbulence within her, and she let her shoulders relax again. She inhaled slowly and let it out. He was right. She did know. Except there was one problem that would be harder to get around.

"I don't drive," she said. "Not since what happened. I don't even have a car."

A smile bloomed across Mav's face, making inky lines bend into swirls, and then he placed his hands on top of the table and leaned forward. "Well, I guess you're in luck then, because I do."

ELEVEN

MAVERICK

Seattle, June 21, 1952

Dear Cass,

How it thrilled me to find your letter on my doorstep. I had hopes but no expectations for it, so it was the best of surprises. Especially to learn you'd thought of me too.

I'm doing well, thank you kindly. I've been home in my mama's care for over a month now and can walk without much trouble if I take it nice and easy. Books are my trusty companions, and I have recently finished both Orwell's 1984, *which was one grim tale, and* A Tree Grows in Brooklyn *upon my mama's suggestion—a far more heartening story. I was just pondering what next to read when your letter arrived, and I instantly knew it would have to be Mr. Dickens'* Great Expectations. *Perhaps you thought I wasn't aware of you reading it aloud by my bedside, but I was and cherished daily your fine storytelling. I will need to start from the beginning but am truly eager to do so. Have you finished it? If you have, don't tell me how it ends.*

I was mighty impressed by your account of the work you have been doing lately in the surgery. Do you plan to continue in nursing once you're back home? (God willing, always.) It is a noble calling, what you do, and I reckon I am not the only one who owes you a debt of gratitude. As I regain my strength, I find myself contemplating what to do next. Mama wants me to return to school, but I don't know if that's for me. I used to have these big lofty goals, but now I would simply like to make a difference like you, be part of a community, and make enough to support a family of my own one day. Do you find that the war has changed your dreams too? If you don't mind my asking.

I keep an eye on the news from the front whenever possible and pray for the safe return of you and all the others over yonder. If I could, I'd go back, but since that's not in the cards, I place my trust in God to watch over you. Will you write to me again? Nothing would make me happier.

Yours sincerely,

Maverick

TWELVE
ISLA

Nancy stared at Isla across the bowls of steaming chicken soup in front of them on the table. "You're doing what?" she asked, spoon frozen in mid-air. "A road trip?"

"I'm going to go back to Bend to see if it will help me remember. Mav is taking me. You said it yourself—I need to move forward. And in this case, we think all the unknowns are stopping me."

She didn't say there was a chance Jonah had kept things from her. Barely wanted to acknowledge that to herself. But that photo of him existed, which meant somewhere out there was a person who'd made him smile when Christmas with Isla and his family hadn't. As much as she couldn't put her finger on why, these seemingly disparate points in the past conjured a constellation connected by invisible lines she'd yet to decipher.

"We?"

"Mav and me. And Louise too. She's going to help."

"So everyone's on board." Mom put the spoon down. "And by everyone, I mean these people who you barely know."

Isla's nerve wobbled. "You think it's a bad idea?"

Nancy huffed and gave a small shrug. "I didn't say that. But I'm your mother; I'm allowed to worry."

They had a few bites in silence before she spoke again. "What I don't understand is why this Maverick person would offer to do this in the first place? And he's old, isn't he?"

"He's a young ninety."

"Ninety!" Nancy balked. "How is his vision? His reflexes?"

Isla's spoon clanged against the bowl as she set it down. Those were legitimate questions and ones with the ability to make her quake if she spent too much time on them. But Mav was sharp, and she needed to do this. "I know. I have thought about that, but I think it'll be fine. We'll only drive in daylight, and only a couple of hours per day. Or do you want to take me?" Isla knew the answer to that. Between Mom's social commitments, new moving plans, and preference for her own kitchen and bed, that was never going to happen.

In the background, the song changed from a country standard to the swelling violins of the *Moulin Rouge* soundtrack.

Nancy put her spoon down. "I want to meet him."

Isla held her tongue even though she itched to point out that she wasn't seventeen anymore. "Of course. If that makes you feel better. And to answer your other question, he says he's doing this because being old is boring and it's been years since he last had an adventure."

"Ha!" Mom nodded. "Ain't that the truth." She seemed to mull this over for a minute, then she reached for her bread roll and broke it in half. "And what if you don't find what you're looking for?"

Isla knew what she meant. Would this trip to the past amplify the grief anew, make the nightmares worse, lock her down in inaction once more?

"At least I'll have tried." She reached for one of her mother's hands and squeezed it. "But, Mom, what if I do find it?"

. . .

Nancy drove them across town two days later. She had a made-from-scratch Hamburger Helper casserole in the backseat because "it was your dad's favorite and all men love hamburger helper," and a nice silk scarf around her neck as if they were going to church.

"No need to be nervous, Mom," Isla said from the passenger seat.

"Who said anything about being nervous?"

"Mm-hmm."

Nancy tapped her fingers on the steering wheel. "But I keep thinking about those tattoos, and I worry I won't be able to keep a straight face. Is he very *rough around the edges?*" She lowered her voice as she did on those rare occasions when she couldn't help but curse.

"Oh my God, Mom. He's like any old man. Just... decorated. They're from his sailor years."

"Okay." Nancy sucked in a deep breath. "Okay, I'm sure it'll be fine."

Isla smiled out the passenger window. This would be interesting.

Maverick, too, had cleaned up for the occasion. The sparse white hair on the top of his head was water combed to one side, and he wore a vest on top of his usual shirt.

"Welcome—come on in," he said, holding open the door for them. He grasped Nancy's hand in his and shook it, then turned to Isla. "So this is your mother?"

"Nancy," Mom said. She was doing her best not to stare at the tattoos, Isla could tell.

"Lovely to meet you, Nancy." He ushered them into the sitting room where Isla hadn't been before more than in passing. "I understand you have reservations about our little journey."

"Right to the point," Nancy replied, sitting down in the seat Mav indicated. "I like that. Reminds me of my late husband."

"Oh really?" Mav's eyebrows twitched. "I hope you'll accept my condolences for your loss. Isla's told me about her dad."

"Delwyn," Nancy said. "Yes, thank you."

"Delwyn." Mav nodded. "Strong name. Irish, is it?"

"His father was Welsh."

"Ah." Mav sank into a worn upholstered high-back and crossed his legs.

"We brought some food for the weekend," Isla said, holding up the casserole. "I'll put it in the fridge and write down heating instructions while you two get acquainted."

She took her time in the kitchen, moving things around in the small refrigerator to make room for the glass dish, locating pen and paper in one of the many drawers. The reason was twofold—first that she wanted Mom to make her own impression of Mav as only that would set her mind at ease, and second to allow her own nerves to settle. It wasn't that she didn't trust Mav, or that she regretted the decision she'd made to face her past head-on, but at the same time, she hadn't been able to escape the sense of being caught in an undercurrent with its own mind about where to wash her up ever since. And while she hoped it would be in a place of clarity, she was also very much aware she could end up right back where she'd started—or worse.

Mom's laugh trickled into the kitchen, pulling Isla from her thoughts. Mav must have won her over then. She capped the pen and put it away, then returned to the living room.

"Did you hear the one about the whale and the seagull?" Nancy asked her before facing Mav again. "The adventures you've lived."

"That I have." Mav nodded. "And now here's another one. Should we go see the car?" He slapped his palms onto his thighs and stood with some effort. "To assure you we're not setting off in some dirty rust bucket."

Isla and her mom looked at each other.

"Might as well," Nancy said.

The three of them fit snugly in the small elevator that took them into the basement of the building. Maverick's keys dangled from his hand, clinking together with each jolt of the mechanisms.

"This way." He turned right in the garage, and they followed past cave-like, gray concrete walls. "She's a reliable old gal this one. I normally tuck her in for the winter, but I'm sure she won't mind coming out of hibernation a little early. Here we are."

In front of them was a pristine silver-and-blue 1990s Chevy truck with a covered truck bed and sparkling hubcaps. Isla wasn't sure what she'd pictured Mav's vehicle of choice to be, but it wasn't this "old gal," of that she was certain. A beige LeSabre perhaps or a Lincoln Town Car. Something statelier. Then again, there was a lot she didn't know about Mav, and the neatness of the vehicle fit with both his person and his home.

Isla opened the passenger door to look inside at the same time Mav took a seat behind the wheel, his wrinkled hands caressing it in a gentle grip. The blue cloth bench seat was in equally good condition as the exterior and smelled vaguely of pine air freshener.

"Do you drive a lot nowadays?" Mom asked, peering in next to Mav.

"You mean on account of my advanced age?" He smiled. "A fair bit. Not to worry. I still have eyes like a hawk and reflexes like the jungle cats of the Amazon, according to my doctor."

Isla laughed, running her hands across the dash. "You do, do you?"

"More or less." Mav stuck the key in the ignition. "And worst case, you still have your license, right?" He turned the key, and the engine rumbled alive as a cold hand gripped Isla's insides.

She was about to protest, say that wasn't the deal, when the engine sputtered twice then went out with a loud bang that echoed against the concrete walls. The silence that followed went uninterrupted for several seconds as all three of them had frozen in place.

"Oh my," Nancy said finally.

"Hmm." Mav released the wheel. "She's never done *that* before."

Despite the car issues and Mom's renewed concerns, Isla spent the next few days making lists of places to visit and people to talk to so that she'd be ready when Mav was. He'd had the truck towed to a mechanic who'd ensured him it wasn't a fatal fault, so they were optimistic this setback was only of the temporary kind.

Tuesday over lunch, she laid out her route for him, something more optimistic coating the lead weight of unease lodged in her chest.

"The first day will take us to Olympia," she said. "There's a restaurant Jonah and I went to several times, but I don't know if we ate there that weekend."

"Worth a stop."

"Plus it should be easy to get hotel rooms there with short notice."

"And then?"

"Portland. Several of the photos on his camera are from Hoyt Arboretum, and Portland was part of his territory." At Mav's quizzical expression she clarified, "He was in pharmaceutical sales." She pointed to the next bullet point on her list. "The drive from there to Bend is a little on the long side—three and a half hours—but maybe we can do half in the morning, take a long break, then drive the rest late afternoon?"

"As long as I have a good night's sleep the night before, that should be doable," Mav agreed.

"And from there, we'll drive locally. The, um... spot where it happened, stores, restaurants, possibly the sheriff's office. Louise is still waiting for confirmation about them sending the report. I'm hoping we can stay at the hotel so we can talk to the staff."

She looked up and found Mav watching her, a small crease between his eyebrows, deepened by three inked dots on the left side of the bridge of his nose.

"Something wrong?" she asked.

"No." His lower lip pulled up then released. "No, it's a good plan. I suppose I'm just wondering how you're feeling. About all this, I mean. I haven't pushed you into something you're not ready for?"

There was genuine concern in his eyes—enough that Isla didn't want to dismiss it.

"I'm nervous, but I don't feel pushed," she said. "Not by you, anyway. I could back out tomorrow, but where would that leave me? Mom is still moving. I'm still going back to work in the fall. My life will change again whether I want it to or not. And I need to do *something* to get to a place where I'll be able to handle that."

"You're very strong. Not that I'm surprised."

"Ha!"

"No, I mean it. It took me many, many years to fully return to the world of the living after my brush with death. To recast my experience into something that was about more than me— *my* wounds, *my* guilt, *my* needs, *my* fears. *My* life. Disaster has a way of shrinking your world, making you look out for number one. To protect yourself. It made me selfish. But not you. You've taken what little spark you had left and shone it on others." He gestured to his delivered meal. "That's admirable."

Isla blushed. "Thanks, but that's not how I see it."

Maverick raised a forkful to his lips then paused. "Then my hope is that by the end of this you do."

Isla squirmed in her seat. For so long, the only voices she'd had in her ear were Mom's concerned one and her own scathing one. Mav's praise made her want to hide.

She took a big bite of her sandwich, chewing slowly while feigning interest in the empty street outside. March had begun with nonstop rain, but today there was a lighter aura above the clouds—a hint that there was, in fact, still a sun around which they whirled. If she leaned close to the pane, she could see the edge of the memorial park—not the west side where her family members were commemorated, but the other.

Look around. Nana's words floated up from Isla's subconscious, an echo from what now seemed like a dream. Was this what she'd meant? For Isla to go on this road trip?

With that thought, renewed urgency flooded her. That might be it. "How soon can we leave?" she asked Mav. "Did they say how many days it would take to fix the truck?"

"It depends on when they get the parts. He said I'd have it back Monday end of business at the latest. Could be sooner though."

"Then we plan on leaving Tuesday. Is mid-morning too early for you?"

Mav blinked at her. "In a hurry all of a sudden?"

Isla ignored his question. "You'll be ready? Let me know if you need help packing."

"Oh, I can manage. Tuesday it is. I'll make sure to make my other arrangements."

"For?"

"Oh you know..." Mav gestured vaguely into the air. "What about your deliveries?"

Shoot, she'd almost forgotten about that. "Yeah, I'll need to talk to Stan about someone covering those while we're gone."

It wouldn't be a problem. It was only two days a week, and she'd been flexible with the scheduling so far and had earned his goodwill. Maybe Mom would even take over for her if she asked. With that last obstacle cleared in her mind, she cleaned up the table and took leave of Mav.

Tuesday.

The road she'd been stuck on for the past two years was coming to a fork, and it was high time for a detour.

THIRTEEN

GEMMA

April, three years ago

The fever dream was the same again. It started true to reality with Gemma pushing open the door to the lobby of the building where Jonah's company kept a small condo for their employees to stay in as needed. She wore jeans and a puffer jacket, and she had a canvas tote full of food staples hooked over her arm. Her winter boots marked her walk through the lobby with dull thuds, and while this trek took longer in the dream, and the elevator bank stretched on into infinity, the gist of it was still true. She got inside and pressed the number two button. The doors closed.

It was when they opened that the dream changed.

When she'd actually gone to Jonah's place a week ago, she'd followed the carpeted hallway until she found the number of his unit. She'd contemplated leaving the bag and texting him from her car, but then she'd decided to make sure he was okay, so she'd knocked instead. He'd opened after a long minute, eyes glossy above his mask.

"Delivery," she'd said, handing him the bag. "I got what you asked for and added a few other nice-to-haves."

He'd taken the handles from her and peered inside. "Oh my gosh, I can't thank you enough."

He'd been in sweats and a thick hoodie—a far cry from the put-together version she'd met in the office. But in Jonah's case, it wasn't the clothes that made the man. That much was clear.

"How's the fever?" she'd asked.

He'd twisted away, hiding his face in the crook of his elbow as a cough rattled through him before answering. "Up and down."

"There's cough syrup in there," she'd said. "Hopefully that helps you get some rest."

He'd taken a step back. "Sorry, I don't want to get you sick."

She'd agreed, and they'd said goodbye shortly after that. Before she knew it, she'd been on her way back to the car.

Now, trapped in her own Covid daze, every time she closed her eyes and let fatigue pull her under, the elevator doors slid open, and Jonah was no longer inside the condo—he was waiting on the second-floor landing. At first his back was turned, but when he heard her, he spun around, elated to see her. In the dream, he wasn't sick at all. He took her bag from her then lifted her up in a tight hug.

"I've been waiting all day for this," he said.

And it felt so good to be wanted.

Gemma woke with a start, drenched in sweat and with her hair stuck in thick tendrils to her cheek. She rolled onto her back and kicked off her covers. The dream always stopped there or outside his place, so in other words, frustratingly short. Even in her current state, she craved knowing what would happen if they went inside.

She pushed herself up to sitting and reached for the glass of water on her nightstand. It was full, which meant Cheryl must have replaced it while she slept. Gemma's shoulders slumped. She'd told her aunt to stay away to avoid catching this. Everyone had underestimated how contagious it was. She'd only seen Jonah for a few minutes, and she'd still gotten sick. Though she supposed she could have caught it at the grocery store or work around the same time too.

Gemma put on a mask and left her room to go to the bathroom, trying not to make too much noise in case it was the middle of the night. The past few days, time had turned into an abstract concept not helped by the darkening blinds in her room. It could be midnight, ten in the morning, or five in the afternoon at any given time.

"Gem, is that you?" Cheryl called from the living room.

Gemma paused by the bathroom before continuing to the end of the hallway so she could see her aunt. "It's me."

Cheryl lifted the remote to pause her show. "What are you doing up? You look terrible."

"Thanks. What time is it?"

"Two thirty."

Afternoon. When was the last time she ate something?

"Are you hungry?" Cheryl asked as if reading her mind. "I can heat up some mac and cheese if you want."

Gemma's stomach growled. "Thank you. But put it outside my door, okay? I don't want you to get sick."

"I haven't been sick since—"

"2011, I know. I'm just saying. Why risk it?"

"Fine. How are you feeling?"

"A little better I think."

"See, it's not that bad."

Gemma turned and retraced her steps. She wasn't getting into that debate again.

She'd told the truth; she was feeling better. Good enough for a quick shower. Refreshed, she returned to her room where a tray with mac, a bag of chips, and a handful of carrot sticks waited on her bed.

"Thank you," she called out the door, but her aunt had resumed her show and didn't respond.

She'd eaten half the bowl of pasta when her phone dinged next to her pillow. Thinking it was probably Sadie, she picked it up mid-drink and almost spat out her water. It was him. Jonah.

Driving back up north today finally, he texted. *Just wanted to say thank you again for saving me from starvation and misery. I hope the flowers were delivered.*

The food somersaulted in her stomach as she stared at the words. They instantly conjured the dream version of him, smiling at her, so she shook her head and put the phone down. A large mixed bouquet had arrived at the office two days after she'd stopped by his place. The card had been addressed to the whole office as a thank you for exceptional care, and Gemma had fought hard to stop herself from reading more into the gesture, but now, his text made that fight futile.

Her phone dinged again. First with a photo from somewhere along the road—a snowcapped mountain in the distance —then, *How are things on your end? Still working?*

What should she do? He was asking a direct question so it would be rude not to answer.

Not right now, she typed. *I got sick too, but my aunt is taking care of me.*

His answer was immediate. *Oh no!!! Now I feel horrible!*

She smiled to herself at his overuse of exclamation marks. *Don't. I could have picked it up anywhere.*

But I shouldn't have asked you to bring me food when I was sick. I'm so sorry!

She scooted back on her bed and put a pillow behind her. *I'm getting better already. Don't worry about it.*

Another photo came through—this time a selfie of him with an exaggerated sad face—followed by: *Are you sure?*

Dammit if he wasn't even cuter than she remembered. Square jaw, rounded upper lip, strong nose. Kind eyes.

I'm sure, she typed. *I'll be good as new in the next few days.* She hesitated but then continued, *So what will you be doing when you get home?*

The moving dots seemed to go on forever before his response came through. *Working mostly. I can do a lot of my sales virtually, so that's what's in store.*

He hadn't mentioned his job before. *What kind of sales?*

Pharmaceuticals. A real thrill ride. Ha!

You don't like it?

It pays the bills. And I'm good at it.

She could see that being true. He'd certainly been easy for her to connect with. *And when you're not working?*

You know. This and that.

Was he being intentionally vague? She couldn't help but notice he still hadn't mentioned a wife.

I should get back on the road, he continued. *Really hope you feel better.*

Thanks.

And I'm sorry again if you got it from me. I almost feel like I should make it up to you somehow. Maybe dinner next time I'm in town?

Gemma stared at the screen. She hadn't seen that coming. *I'd be up for that. If any places are still open.* She added a fingers-crossed emoji.

If not, I'll cook. See ya.

Gemma dug her teeth into her bottom lip. "See ya," she whispered as she put her phone away.

FOURTEEN

ISLA

Present day

Mav picked Isla up shortly before noon on Tuesday, March 13.
The date seemed an omen, but Isla had yet to decide whether it
was good or bad. Mostly, she was eager to get the leaving part
over. Mav had taken longer to get on the road than planned,
which meant Mom had had more time to flutter around Isla
with well-meant advice for how to keep tabs on Mav's driving,
and how not to get her hopes up too much.

"I just don't know how much people will remember this
long after," she'd said. "I don't want you to be disappointed,
Birdie."

But Isla already knew it was a long shot and had told her
mom so repeatedly over the weekend, adding that it was also, at
this point, her only shot.

When Isla and Mav finally rolled away from the house,
Isla's bags tucked safely onto the covered truck bed, Mom
waved until they couldn't see her in the mirror anymore. Then
Isla rested her head against the headrest and closed her eyes
briefly.

"We're off," Mav said at her side. "Are you ready?"

Isla adjusted her seatbelt and glanced at him. Her driver sat straight-backed, hands at ten and two as they cleared the neighborhoods and entered the more sparsely populated outskirts of town. Traffic was light, the world around them still beneath heavy clouds.

"Yep," Isla confirmed. "The truck sounds good."

Mav patted the wheel. "Good as new."

They would take Route 101 south along Hood Canal to Olympia and planned on stopping "somewhere scenic" along the way per Mav's request. Isla had packed a thermos of coffee, several sandwiches, and a couple of Mom's cinnamon rolls. Mav had contributed a family-sized bag of hard butterscotch candy and a twelve-pack of water bottles for the road.

The radio was set to a seventies station, and as the dense woods of the Olympic peninsula engulfed them, the immersive chords of Elton John's "Goodbye Yellow Brick Road" filled the air in the cab. Mav hummed along atonally, and together with the muted evergreens passing by the wayside, this had an almost hypnotic effect on Isla. Her thoughts wandered aimlessly on the cusp of something she couldn't quite describe yet. Somewhere ahead was a plunge, but for now, she could pretend it was just the two of them and the road.

They'd been driving for a half hour when Isla's phone rang, interrupting the peace. She lowered the volume on the radio and accepted Louise's call.

"So, did you get it?" her friend asked by way of greeting.

"Get what?"

"The bird. It said the auction ended."

Isla's head whipped up. *The auction.* In the midst of getting ready for the road trip, she'd completely forgotten about it.

"Hold on." She opened the app and checked. Sure enough, at noon, the bids had been cut off and... she'd lost. "Fuck!" She dropped her hand to her lap and ground her jaws together.

Mav glanced her way. "What's going on?"

"Dammit all the way to..." Isla stared unseeingly at the green blur out the window. She hadn't seen Nana's hummingbird since she was a teenager, so losing this one was like losing the opportunity to reunite with a cherished friend.

"Hello?" Louise's faint voice coming from the phone seeped through Isla's disappointment.

She picked it up and put it to her ear. "I didn't get it. Damn." To her surprise, tears stung behind her eyelids as she pictured the delicate figurine. *It's just a thing, for God's sake.*

The truck had slowed, and now Mav pulled off the road into a rest area.

"Oh no. I'm sorry." Louise sounded genuinely upset on Isla's behalf. "I thought for sure you would have."

"Not your fault," Isla sighed. "There'll be others." She willed herself to believe it. This one had been rare, but you never knew. She pressed her lips into a tight smile. "We're on the road now," she told Louise. "I should go. Talk later?"

"Later," Louise confirmed.

Isla hung up. "You didn't have to stop," she said to Mav. "Just got some bad news."

"Anything I can do?"

"Not unless you own a Coalport porcelain hummingbird."

"Ah, the auction."

"Yeah." She opened the app again. Closed it.

"Is that why your mother calls you Birdie? Because you collect them?"

Isla turned her head fully his way and leaned back. "No actually. It was my nana's name for me for as long as I can remember. She said it was because birds were her favorites. All kinds of birds. But then she gave me one of her hummingbirds and..."

"The rest is history."

Isla nodded.

"Would you like to take a break here. Have some coffee?" Mav gestured to the bed of the truck that held all their things.

"We can drive a little farther."

"Sounds good." Mav put the truck into gear and merged back onto the road. After a few minutes, he glanced her way again. "It sounds like you were close with your grandparents growing up. That's nice."

"I was. Or at least with Nana Embeth and Pop-Pop Neil. My mom's parents lived in Illinois, so we rarely saw them. Nana and Mom worked together—they were both social workers—and that's how my parents met. Nana thought her son and Mom would get along, so she set them up."

"Ah, so Nancy knew your grandmother—Embeth—before she knew your dad?"

"Yup. No mother-in-law tropes there. Everyone liked each other."

"Sounds wonderful."

Isla smiled as the memories flooded her. "They had a big property not too far from Olympia actually, with a small lake where Pop-Pop would take me fishing in the summer. He was handy too, so we'd build huts, and pedal cars, and tons of birdhouses that I got to paint with whatever scrap paint he had in the shed. Nana was the one who'd point out and name all the animals we spotted—where they lived, what they ate. She always knew in what tree to find owls and in which birdhouse there were babies. And she had a whole wall of books in her bedroom so I spent a lot of time in the window seat in the kitchen with my nose in whatever I could find."

"You're an only child?"

Isla touched her heart. "Once my greatest sorrow. I was convinced I'd be the best big sister, and I couldn't understand why my parents would deprive me. Truth was, they were both only children and liked it like that."

Mav slowed as they closed in on a semi taking care in a particularly sharp turn. "Neither of them had siblings?"

"Nope. Unlike Jonah's family—he had so many aunts, uncles, and cousins... My first Christmas with his family, I was completely overwhelmed."

Mav chuckled. "I can see that."

The holiday joys of the past filled Isla with a warmth she'd long been estranged from, but just as quickly, the feeling dissipated, taking with it her smile as the photos from Jonah's last Christmas forced their way into her consciousness again. And then there were holidays going forward. Mom was going to be out of state. Isla hadn't considered that before.

Mav glanced at her. "Penny for your thoughts?"

"Oh, they're hardly worth paying for. Same old questions." No need to burden him with the extent of her talent at worrying.

Thankfully, Mav didn't press it.

"Lilliwaup is coming up," Isla said after a while. "I think there's a convenience store there that might have a bathroom. Coffee break?"

Mav agreed that was a good plan, and a few minutes later, they pulled off the road and into a parking space next to the old cedar-shingled building.

While Mav used the facilities, Isla dug out mugs that she balanced on the tailgate and filled with coffee. Her stomach rumbled at the scent of wheat and mustard from the sandwich bag, and it felt good to stretch tall even though they'd been traveling less than an hour and a half. It had been a long time since she'd spent more than fifteen minutes in a car.

"They've got a bit of everything in there," Mav said when he returned. "In case you've thought of something you forgot to pack."

Isla's mouth was too full of bread to respond, so she nodded and gestured for Mav to help himself to some sustenance.

The cups drained and the food gone, Mav inhaled deeply in satisfaction and rolled his shoulders back. The movement straightened his shape and gave Isla a sudden glimpse of the striking figure he must have cut in his youth. "Thank you for letting me come along," he said. "I'm already invigorated."

Isla stacked their mugs and tucked them back in their bag. "That's all it took?" she asked with a smile. "Well, you know—I literally couldn't do it without you."

"Now that's a watered-down word if I ever knew one— 'literally.'"

Isla resisted the urge to roll her eyes at how much he sounded like her teacher dad. "Okay, fine. How about I *wouldn't* have done it without you?"

"That's better." He closed the tailgate. "And yes that's all it took. I'm old."

"Ha! According to Nana, age is nothing but a number, so there... I'm going to run to the washroom too. Be right back."

"Wise woman," Mav said.

On her way back, Isla picked up a couple of chocolate bars and some sour gummies, not sharing Mav's predilection for butterscotch. She was in line to pay, browsing the shelves near the windows, when a movement outside caught her attention. A tall man with a baseball cap pulled low hurried past, toward the old gas pumps on the opposite side of the building from where Mav and the truck were waiting for her. She blinked, dumbstruck, as he disappeared from view. She could have sworn it was the guy from Mav's building again. But there was no way. Port Townsend was sixty miles away.

Someone nudged her elbow. "Excuse me—it's your turn."

Isla looked over her shoulder, and the woman behind her nodded toward the cashier.

"Oh, sorry." Isla cast another glance through the window, but the man was nowhere in sight. She paid then hurried outside.

The only vehicle by the gas pumps was a large red pickup truck with a blond woman behind the wheel. Isla frowned. Had she imagined the guy?

She returned to Mav, shrugging off the odd coincidence, and dumped her sweets on the seat between them. She looked out the windshield, to her side, behind her. A young couple in hiking gear, the woman from the store, a dad with a little boy who, judging by his squirming, also needed a restroom. No tall, dark, and handsome stranger.

"Everything okay?" Mav asked, hand resting on the key in the ignition. "Did you forget something?"

"No..." She pulled on her seatbelt. "Did you happen to see a man in a baseball cap over here when I was inside? Tall? Black coat?"

Mav's forehead creased. "No, can't say I did. Why?"

"I thought..." She gave a little shrug. Had staying at home for so long made her paranoid? That wasn't a flattering look. "Never mind."

"Bigfoot probably." Mav started the car. "Lots of sightings in the Olympics, I hear. Ready to go?"

"Bigfoot. Funny." She smiled, tension easing. "I didn't take you for a believer. Yeah, let's go."

"I think we both know there's more to this world than meets the eye, no?" He signaled then eased back into the sparse traffic.

"True. But seeing is still believing, so the skeptic in me reserves the right to doubt monsters walking among us until proven otherwise."

"That's fair."

Or to imagine seeing people in places where they shouldn't be, Isla thought. *Good grief.*

But when she glanced back in the mirror just then, her back stiffened. Because previously hidden from view in front of the red pickup was a small blue sedan, and while she watched, it too pulled back into the road.

FIFTEEN

ISLA

Present day

The first few miles after Lilliwaup, Isla was glued to the rearview, tracking the blue sedan as best as she could, while contemplating whether to involve Mav in her misgivings. Each time they drove around a curve, she held her breath waiting for the other car to show up, and when it did, the sight amplified a new, crawling sensation beneath her skin. Despite that, every time she opened her mouth to say something, she stopped herself. *I think we're being followed* sounded outrageous enough inside her head, and she didn't want Mav to think she was losing it. Besides, the car was too far behind them for her to see the driver.

When somewhere around Skokomish the blue sedan finally disappeared from view, Isla congratulated herself on her choice to stay quiet. Complete coincidence, she told herself. Naturally. Who on earth would tail someone like her? It took a few more miles, but slowly she allowed herself to relax into the seat again.

It was almost three thirty in the afternoon when they reached Olympia.

The hotel was of the standard sandy-brick chain variety, but the lobby was clean, and the rooms available even though check-in technically wasn't for another thirty minutes.

"How about a short lie-down before dinner?" Mav suggested.

He looked a little pale, Isla thought. It had been a wise choice to divide the drive into shorter legs like this. At times she forgot how old he was.

"Sounds good." She helped him with his door. "Let me know if you need anything. I'm right across the hall."

Once in the privacy of her room, Isla kicked off her shoes before opening the blinds wide. The concrete parking lot was directly below her, but in the distance, she could glimpse Capitol Lake if she made an effort. The waters lay cold and uninviting beneath the gray skies, but then again, she wasn't there for recreational purposes. They'd have a meal, go to bed early, and then continue on their way after breakfast.

It was possible she and Jonah had stopped here on their way south, but she had no way of knowing where since the photo roll was devoid of Olympia clues. Her best guess was that they'd filled up on gas and stretched their legs at the outskirts of town, but in case the stay at the Bend hotel that fateful weekend hadn't been Jonah's only nostalgic nod to their engagement getaway, Isla had made reservations for her and Mav at Caponi's, a restaurant she and Jonah had visited several times in the past.

Isla checked the time. She wanted to give Mav at least a couple of hours to rest, which meant she'd have to find a way to pass the time, and there was no way she'd be able to nap. Being out and on her way somewhere for the first time in so long was a shot of caffeine to her system. An espresso with five spoonfuls of sugar and a chaser of Red Bull. If the room wasn't so small, she'd pace it.

Forcing herself to sit down, she texted Mom that they'd arrived safely at their first stop.

How was his driving? she responded. *Any issues?*

Other than Isla's paranoia, which she under no circumstances would tell her mom about? *None at all.* Isla added a thumbs-up emoji.

They texted back and forth for a minute, then Nancy had to go—a movie to catch with a friend. Isla remained seated on the queen bed, toying with her phone. She opened a solitaire game she'd played a lot when she was on bedrest, but changed her mind and swiped it away instead.

Are you working or can you talk? she texted Louise. Her friend's workday wouldn't be over yet, but at times she could sneak away from her desk.

Gimme five, was Louise's response.

While Isla waited, she browsed her regular auction and antique sites for something to replace the lost figurine with but found nothing good on offer.

"Probably for the best," she mumbled just before the phone rang.

From the sounds of it, Louise was walking, her voice breathy and ambient sounds of traffic cushioning her greeting. "I got out early," she said. "Slow day."

"What are you working on right now?"

When Isla had first learned Louise was a journalist, she'd thought it an exciting and glamorous profession. Being out and about, meeting people, no assignment like the next. But Louise treated it like any other job and didn't like talking about it much. "I doubt you were looking forward to explaining impressionism over dinner back when you were working," she'd once said to Isla, and she'd had a point. Still, Isla liked to ask. She'd never been a strong writer, and people with that creative vein fascinated her.

"Oh, um, a local interest piece on the housing market,"

Louise said. "Pretty boring if I'm going to be honest. Are you in Olympia now?"

Isla confirmed that she was.

"I'm sorry I dropped the auction news on you like that, by the way. Maybe there's a way to find out who bought it and contact them?"

"You know there isn't," Isla sighed. *It's just a thing,* she thought again. "I'm fine. Bummed, but fine. I have more important stuff on my mind right now anyway."

"Yeah, so about that..." Somewhere on Louise's end, a door opened and closed. When she spoke again, her voice reverberated like she was in a stairwell. "First, you should be getting a copy of the police report emailed to you in the next few days. I called them again and asked what was up. And second..." The sound of footsteps stopped, replaced by a jingle of keys. "If you think it would be helpful, I might be able to come help talk to people when you're in Bend. I'm on deadline currently so I'm busy the next couple of days, but I could meet you in Bend this weekend."

"Wait, what town are you in again?"

"Longview. Only if you want me to come though. No pressure. I just thought there are a lot of stores and places to cover, and an extra body might be good. Plus, I don't know, it would be fun to meet in person maybe?"

Fun. Isla hadn't used that word about herself in a long time. And it was definitely not a good descriptor of this trip. But Louise wasn't wrong; she and Mav could use the help, and it was about time she and Louise met up after spending all this time talking. A few butterflies swirled about her belly at the thought. She wasn't great with people anymore. What if Louise didn't like real-life Isla?

"Are you sure you have time?" Isla asked. "Isn't that still a long drive?"

"I don't mind. And I have a cousin I can stay with in

Redmond, which isn't too far from Bend. I promise I won't be in the way."

That made Isla laugh. Maybe there were nerves on both sides.

But enough hedging—Louise's field of expertise brought resolve to Isla. "Of course you should come. That would be great. Plus, you'll get to meet Mav."

"Oh yay." Louise's voice instantly brightened. "Okay, let's touch base later this week."

"Sounds good."

They lapsed into a short silence, Isla clutching her phone to her ear. How odd to have made a friend this way, she thought. Especially when other friends had disappeared. *Been shut out, more like it.* Finally, she told Louise she should get going, and they hung up with a promise to talk soon.

Thirty minutes later, Isla went across the hall to knock on Mav's door. It was a little earlier than she'd intended, but hopefully, he wasn't still asleep. She needed to get on with her evening to see if the restaurant would bring back anything for her.

She raised her hand but paused as Mav's faint voice seeped through the door. Was someone with him? Her knuckles made contact with the wood. The talking stopped.

A long few seconds passed, then Mav opened the door. He'd undone the top button of his shirt and was in his sock feet, but it didn't seem like she'd interrupted a slumber.

"Oh hello." He sounded surprised to see her, but then again, she was early.

"I was getting hungry," Isla said. "Did you get some rest?"

Mav looked behind him into the room then opened the door wider. "I did, I did. Let me find my shoes here. Come on in." He left her in the small hallway.

"Were you talking to someone?" Isla called to him. "I thought I heard your voice."

Mav returned, shoes in hand, and sat down on the chair next to the closet. "Um, no. That must have been..." He forced his heel down. "Sometimes I talk to myself. Habit ever since Lorraine passed. Perhaps that's what you heard?"

It wasn't much different from her talking to Ulysses. "Makes sense," she said. But she also couldn't help but notice his cell phone sitting out on the desk.

Mav drove them downtown while Isla filled him in on Louise's plans to meet up with them in Bend.

"An extra pair of feet to pound the pavement can't hurt," he agreed.

The closer to the restaurant they came, the sparser the conversation. It was just Italian food, Isla tried to tell herself. Not an execution. Except, what if she and Jonah had eaten there that weekend? What if, in the middle of dinner, she became overwhelmed by memories and caused a scene?

"Everything is fine," Mav said quietly at her side as they entered. "I'm here."

He touched her elbow as if sensing how shaky the foundation she was stepping onto was. This was her first real revisiting of the past, and the urge to flee, to return to the safety of home marred Isla's movements and curbed her stride. To think this was only the beginning...

"Reservation for Gallagher please," Mav said to the hostess, who was wearing a red vest over a white button-down. "A table near the wall if possible. Thank you."

Isla felt better once she was holding a glass of house red in her hand. The muted lighting and garlic-infused air helped ease her worries. Her stomach growled, and she allowed herself to browse the menu. Comfort food, comfort drink, comforting company. She picked out a penne alla vodka dish, then sat back in her chair watching Mav dunk a piece of bread in olive oil and parmesan.

He studied her as he chewed. "Better now?" he asked.

She nodded and had another sip of wine. Looked around. Brass wall sconces, red, tasseled drapes, flickering candles.

"Anything coming to mind?" Mav reached for another piece of bread.

It was too soon to tell. As if the space was an old acquaintance she hadn't seen since childhood, she wasn't ready to ask the more personal questions of it yet. Not until they'd bridged the time passed.

"I don't know," she said.

"Food first?"

She nodded, grateful he understood.

Being out in public with Maverick was an interesting experience. He was warm and cordial to everyone they interacted with, but his face made people stare as if someone on a most-wanted list had walked past. Isla didn't think much of the tattoos anymore, but when she caught a mother on the other side of the room trying to stop her child from pointing, she considered the artsy lines anew.

"Why the face?" she asked after finishing the first few bites of her pasta. She remembered this flavor, had tried to recreate it at home, but the memory went further back than two years.

Mav put his knife and fork down, having finished cutting his tender chicken marsala into smaller pieces.

"Was it a sailor thing? Or did you run out of room?"

Amusement played on Mav's face. "Room, huh?" He unbuttoned one of his cuffs and rolled it up, baring pristine, paper-pale skin. So that wasn't it. "And though plenty of other folks on the sea were inked both here and there, I wouldn't say this"—he gestured to his face—"was very common."

"Then why? Or should I not ask?" She waited while Mav speared another bite of chicken, chewed, and swallowed.

He picked up his napkin and dabbed it against his lips. "For a long time, I didn't like what I saw in the mirror," he said finally.

Isla tilted her head and studied him. He was tall—or had been in his prime—with symmetrical features, broad shoulders, those ice-blue eyes. "You can't tell me you weren't handsome."

"Ha. You flatter me. But it wasn't about that. It was more..." He put a hand to his chest and repeated himself. "I didn't like what I saw."

Isla nodded, falling silent. She waited.

"These dotted lines." Mav tapped his cheekbone. "A friend in New Zealand offered to make those. That was the first one. He was going to put some on the other side too, but I decided I'd only do it on one to acknowledge I didn't share his heritage. The asymmetry would be mine. And once he was done, it was..." Mav pressed his lips together as if searching for the word. "Powerful." He touched two fingers to the spot again. "My reflection changed, the lines distracting from what I didn't wish to confront, and so I kept on adding to it until I was someone new. Or thought I was."

"What do you mean?"

Mav lifted his wine glass and held it aloft, a cheeky glint in his eye. "Well, I was young and stupid. Tattoos are only skin-deep. Obviously, they didn't make me a different person—that was wishful thinking."

"So you regret getting them?"

"Regret? Not at all. They served a purpose at that time." He lowered his voice. "Scared off some right shady characters too from time to time. Boy, do I have stories."

Isla smiled. "I believe it."

"But as I got older, especially once I met my Lorraine, I found ways to make a sort of peace with my past." He finally tipped his glass to his lips and savored a mouthful. Then he set it down. "And perhaps it's best to leave it at that."

There were so many more questions Isla wanted to ask, but Mav's expression made it clear this was as far as he'd go. She wouldn't push it. She knew of his injuries in the war, but maybe there were things he'd left out, and then who was she to force him back there? She should focus on her own past anyway. That's why they'd come all this way after all.

"Thanks for telling me." She raised her own glass.

"Thanks for not letting it scare you off."

After finishing her wine, Isla sat back, her body now pleasantly heavy with food and drink. For the first time since stepping inside the restaurant, she allowed herself to go there, to delve backward, test if the branches would hold.

Mav was watching her as if he knew what she was doing, but it didn't bother her.

"I remember coming here with Jonah way back," she said. "At least twice early in our marriage. I think we sat over there between the windows the last time. I had this pasta, and he had lasagna. We split a bottle of Cabernet." The tables were small, and their legs had tangled beneath the checkered tablecloth, their hands seeking each other out while waiting for the food to be served. They'd bickered about tiramisu or bread pudding then ordered both. Jonah had talked to the server about some indie filmmaker they discovered they both were into. He could talk to anyone. Isla smiled. "I think he'd recently been assigned Portland. We were celebrating because it was a step up."

"And what about two years ago?"

Isla's gaze trailed the path of one of the servers who was weaving between the tables, a tray resting against his shoulder. A fresh gust of herby tomato sauce reached her nostrils. She searched the nooks and crannies of her past.

"Don't ask me why, but I don't think we were here that weekend," she said, the words feeling true on more than a rational level. She might be wrong of course. Her mind could be playing tricks, but some deep part of her was certain there were no answers here. None that mattered anyway.

"Intuition is a powerful thing," Mav said. "More people should trust it."

A wave of affection welled in Isla's chest at his words and their lack of judgment and insistence. Somehow, he got her in a way that shouldn't have been possible after such a short acquaintance.

"To intuition." Isla raised her empty glass.

"And a good night's rest." Mav clinked his glass to hers. "This old man is ready to settle in." He waved at the server. "May we have the check please?"

It was still early by Isla's standards, but she didn't argue. Sleep sounded good after today. She'd made it through the first leg of their journey, and, despite a few ups and downs, she was still in one piece. When they parked back at the hotel next to not one but two blue sedans, she could even laugh a little at herself. She'd tell Mav about the imagined stalker tomorrow, and they'd have a chuckle about it.

Tomorrow, she'd be better. More rational. More determined. They were headed to Portland, where she knew she and Jonah had stopped on their trip south two years ago. To the arboretum where he'd photographed her. And maybe, just maybe, she'd remember something.

SIXTEEN

MAVERICK

Seattle, September 13, 1952

Dear Cass,

The trees are beginning to change here at home, and yesterday there was a chill in the morning air that brought me back to Seoul before the frost set in. Though I admit to occasional days of unbecoming self-pity at my remaining aches and pains, I still count my blessings daily that I have my life. That was no more true than when I read your harrowing description of the latest attacks. It pains me to hear of your terror as you sheltered with the others, and I pray the war will be over soon and you on your way home. You are truly the strongest woman I have ever met, but it is no wonder you dream of flying away. Even here, I sometimes watch the hawks and eagles up high with a pang of jealousy at their freedom. Do you know if Captain Eddings still keeps that black kite as a pet? It never sat right with me, and I think not with the poor bird either. But maybe no one is ever really free.

No, I am too morose today. Something about you brings my

guard down even from the other side of the world, and I can't help but be honest—like the thought of you reaches deep into my heart. It is just that work has been hard to come by, and so many here are blissfully ignorant of what is taking place beyond our borders. I spend too much time with myself.

But I will end on a happier note. The neighbor's dog just had a litter, and I am taking one of the pups. I will name him Pip for our favorite literary character. I hope to send you a photo of him next time.

Is it too much to say that I wish one day to be in your calming presence again? (There I go with that honesty.)

Yours truly,

Maverick

SEVENTEEN
ISLA

Present day

Isla had expected to wake up early, having gone to bed before ten, but when the sliver of light at the edge of the room-darkening curtains finally reached into her subconscious the next morning, it was already almost nine.

Mav had texted her an hour ago that he was headed down to breakfast, so she brushed her teeth and threw on some clothes, then hurried to the elevator.

He was seated by the window, a complimentary newspaper in front of him and a cup of coffee in one hand, but his gaze was lost on something beyond the windowpane. The morning sun slanted diagonally across the table, illuminating his thoughtful expression, not unlike in the Rembrandt print she used to pass daily in the hallway outside her office at the university. It made her slow her step as she navigated the path toward him, just so she could admire the composition.

He turned when she was a few yards away, his face lighting up. "Well, good morning."

"Sorry I slept in," she said. "I should have set my alarm."

"Nonsense. We're not in a hurry."

"Did you eat, I hope?"

He patted his stomach. "Bacon, hash browns, eggs. I'm waiting for a second wind so I can sample the waffles as well."

"Gotta love a buffet."

"Indeed." He nodded toward the food. "So what are you waiting for?"

Neither one of them was very talkative in the morning, so while Mav read his paper, Isla scanned her auction sites and did a crossword puzzle on her phone. Mav got seconds, then Isla did the same.

When she'd finished her coffee, Mav put the paper down and pointed out the window. "There it is again." He leaned closer to the glass.

"What is?" Isla scanned the barren shrubs and cedar-strewn lawn beyond.

"Your favorite. Over there by the planter. No, wait—now it's by that branch."

Isla followed his finger back and forth until she spotted the hummingbird's swift dance through the air.

"There were two of them earlier. Came real close to the glass. The server said they have a feeder around the corner."

The bird's movements seemed to spell out "catch me if you can," teasing the observer to follow—up in the air, down the rabbit hole, round and round—and as always, the iridescent green-and-purple plumage sent a burst of childlike joy through Isla.

"I would have thought they migrated in the winter," Mav said.

"Not the Anna's hummingbird. They look delicate, but they're basically as resilient as crows."

"So colorful."

"It must be finding insects to eat somewhere."

Mav shifted away from the glass. "What do you mean?"

"Protein makes their colors brighter. Or the male birds anyway."

"Is that so?"

"I know—not exactly useful information, is it? Why can't I remember the details of the Revolutionary War but could tell you all about the French duchess that bird is named after and how to make the perfect sugar water for it?" Isla shook her head. "Thanks, Nana."

"I do find it interesting," Mav said. "Give me a choice between wars and tiny creatures like that, and I know what my pick is any day."

As they made their way back to the elevator, Isla's head still swirled with memories of summers long ago, picking out flowers for the planters in Nana's yard, hanging the feeders from the pergola—high enough that the bears wouldn't get any ideas. A deep sense of longing filled her very core.

"Would you want to see where they lived?" she asked. "My grandparents I mean. Yelm would only be a short detour on our way, and I haven't been there in years."

Mav paused and looked at her. "Huh," he said. "Yelm?" He kept walking. "Yes, I suppose we could do that."

And who knew? Maybe something about her grandparents' old place would help shine a light on the words she'd heard during her glimpse of the other side. Surely if some essence of Nana lingered on this plane, it would be there.

"Do you believe in ghosts?" she asked Mav when they were on the road again.

"White sheets, rattling chains?" He took his eyes off the road for a moment. "No."

"But..."

"Trapped energies, connections with the beyond? Yes."

"Oh."

"Sailors are a superstitious breed, don't you know?" He

grinned. "Besides, I've seen and heard some unexplainable things myself in my day."

"Like what?"

"Oh, I don't talk about it. They don't like that."

"They?" Isla couldn't tell if he was messing with her or being serious.

"Let's just say I will never go back to Savannah, Georgia." He shivered as if merely saying the words gave him chills. "We went for our honeymoon, but even Lorraine, who was a most level-headed woman, had to admit we weren't as alone in our room as we would have liked. We were supposed to stay for a week but ended up driving down to Jacksonville instead after two days. In the end, it was a great trip."

Isla tried to picture a younger Mav and his wife hightailing it out of a haunted hotel, and again wondered if he was telling tall tales to entertain her. But it didn't matter. Something had happened to her after the accident—something she couldn't explain. Who was she to discount the possibility of there being other unknowns out there?

Yelm had grown since she'd last been there, but she still had no trouble finding her way through the sleepy town to the rural road leading to her grandparents' old place. The trees were a little taller, the buildings a little more worn, but it was still the same place she'd known so intimately as a child.

Mav pulled up near an outbuilding and turned off the engine. "Do you know who lives here now?"

"No." Isla opened her door and stepped out. There were no other cars around, and the house was dark. "Hello?" she called. "Anyone home?"

Mav stepped out too and ran a hand over his scalp.

"A quick peek, then we'll leave," Isla said.

"Let's at least knock on the door first. Lots of gun-nuts about these days."

Isla agreed.

Whoever owned the house had done a good job with the upkeep. The siding had a new layer of paint, the windows were clean, and there was a greenhouse and several raised beds organized on a neat rectangular gravel area by the garage that hadn't been there before.

"I must have run that trail a thousand times." Isla pointed to the compacted dirt trail that led through the field toward a cluster of trees in the distance. "Heck, I might have made that trail." *Dirty sneakers swishing through grass, scraped knees, ladybugs.*

"I think I hear someone." Mav turned back to the door. A second later it opened.

"Can I help you?" The middle-aged man at the door had glasses pushed up onto his head and a cell phone in his hand. Working from home maybe. When he spotted Mav's face, he did a double take.

Isla hurried to introduce them, hoping politeness would offset Mav's inevitable first impression. Then she explained that she'd spent time there as a kid. "I don't know how long you've lived here, but my grandparents built the place. I just wanted to show my friend."

"The Smiths were your grandparents?" the man asked, seemingly more at ease. "Nice people. I met them when we signed the papers. I'm Nathan by the way."

Isla lit up. "Oh, so you bought from them?"

"That's right. We've been here what... seventeen years now. Raised our boys here."

"Good place for that," Mav said.

Nathan chuckled. "Nothing like outdoor space when you have energetic kids in the house." He glanced at his phone.

"We didn't mean to bother you," Isla hurried to say. "Would it be okay if we walked around the property?"

"It's no bother. You're welcome to a peek in here too if you want. We changed things around some when we moved in, took down a wall, but the rest should be familiar. Upstairs is a mess though. My wife has been redoing the gable room since our youngest moved out."

Isla raised her eyebrows at Mav in a silent question, and he responded with a nod.

Stepping onto the wood flooring and hearing that first *creak* transported Isla back several decades. The furniture was different of course, and instead of a small galley kitchen, the space now opened into the living room.

"I like this," Isla said. She wasn't being polite—it was nice. She still missed the leather recliner that used to sit in the corner though, and the scent of beeswax candles that always lingered in the air. Pop-Pop had made his own.

"Brings back memories?" Mav asked.

"Yeah." Memories, but nothing more. No voices. Isla didn't know if that was disappointing or reassuring.

Nathan gestured to the kitchen. "There were notches in the pantry when we took over. Was that you?"

Isla smiled. "Nana used to measure me every time I came to visit even if it had only been a month since last time."

They did the rounds downstairs, Isla pointing out to Mav what things had looked like back then, and eventually they landed back in the foyer again. Isla toyed with the question in her mind. *Any odd happenings of the spiritual kind—unexplained visitations?* But no, she couldn't. It would feel silly.

They stepped onto the front porch.

"You know, it's a shame my wife isn't here right now," Nathan said. "She's big into all things genealogy and local history. I'm sure she'd love to hear some of your stories about this place."

"I'm happy to leave my number," Isla said. "I might even have a card." She dug into her purse and found one with the university's logo. "Use the cell number, not the other one. Happy to answer whatever."

Nathan held up the card. "Thanks. And feel free to walk around outside too, like I said. I have a meeting in five, so I'll head back upstairs. It was nice to meet you both."

They took their leave, and then it was just Isla and Mav again.

"This must be what Dorothy felt like after the tornado set her down," Isla said. "Whew. Did not expect a tour."

Mav nodded. "I'm happy to have seen it." He turned his face to the sky and added in a soft voice that sounded almost like a prayer, "Neil and Embeth."

Isla's heart swelled. "Neil and Embeth."

They looked out across the property, at the fallow growth and dark tree line, the sunlight deepening the shadows beneath the evergreens. Beyond that, the lake. High above, a hawk circled the meadow where Isla once upon a time had chased bunnies and staked out molehills. So long ago and yet the happiness of it still echoed in her blood. It was a comfort to know it remained here in this place regardless of where her future would take her.

"I think I'm ready to go," she said.

"Portland?" Mav asked.

"Portland," Isla confirmed.

She kept her eyes on the house as long as she could when Mav drove away, but eventually, the trees swallowed it up, and she settled into her seat. The two-lane road was straight and dry, the passing landscape offering a lulling backdrop, so it wasn't until they slowed to rejoin I-5 by Centralia that Isla stirred out of the reverie Yelm had brought about.

"Do you need a break?" she asked Mav.

"I'm doing all right." He glanced in the rearview and blind spot, then merged onto the expressway.

Out of habit, Isla did the same in her mirrors, but when the sun reflected blue a few car-lengths behind them, she whipped around to look out the back window.

She blinked, a jolt of recognition shaking her.

"What is it?" Mav asked.

Isla swallowed then forced in a deep breath. "I don't want to alarm you," she said, "but I think we're being followed."

EIGHTEEN

ISLA

Present day

"Now why on earth would someone be following us?" Mav asked while Isla kept her eyes on the blue sedan in the mirror. "Isn't it more likely that it's just a car heading in the same direction as us?"

"It was at the rest stop too."

"Could be a similar vehicle."

Isla gnawed on her cheek. Was Mav right? It did seem a ridiculous notion that someone would be following *them* of all people. There were a lot of emotions at play—she could be imagining things. Except... "I thought I saw the guy from your building when we stopped in Lilliwaup."

Mav's brows rose. "Rowan?"

Isla frowned. "Who's Rowan?"

"Oh." Mav adjusted his grip on the steering wheel. "A neighbor."

"I thought you didn't know your neighbors."

"I've met a few now." He sped up then tapped the brake a couple of times when he got too close to the car in front of him.

Isla studied him, but when it seemed as if he wasn't going to elaborate, she turned back to the mirror. The blue sedan was further away now. "Well, I don't know his name, but I mean the guy I thought was at the memorial park when we ran in to each other a few weeks ago." Of course, she couldn't be completely sure that had been the same person as the guy who'd held the door for her at Mav's building. Ugh, the more she deliberated, the more unlikely it sounded. "Never mind. I'm probably making things up. Let's forget about it."

"Hmm," Mav hummed in agreement, his lips pressed together.

They drove in silence for the next few miles with Isla keeping an eye on the rearview every so often. The nearest car behind them was now too far away to be able to tell its color. She turned on the radio.

"How long do we have to Portland?" Mav asked midway through Barbra Streisand singing about people who need people.

"A little over an hour. Need a stop?"

"No." He threw her a quick smile. "Looks like a beautiful day down here. Where would you like to go first?"

It was the question Isla needed to shift her focus to the task at hand. Olympia had been a long shot, but she knew she and Jonah had stayed in Portland on their way south, so the chance of memories being triggered was greater there.

"Let's see if we can check in to the hotel, and then I want to go to Hoyt Arboretum."

"That's where he took your picture?"

"Yes."

Isla pulled out a plastic baggie from her purse and retrieved the short stack of photos she'd had printed. She flipped to the Portland snaps—a mural somewhere in the Buckman neighborhood, a closeup of two extravagant donuts, and a wide shot of Isla looking up at the gnarled trunk of a towering redwood tree.

A shiver skated across her shoulders. In a few hours, she'd be standing in that very spot again.

Mav glanced at her. "Everything all right?"

"What if I still don't remember anything?"

"What if you do? Take heart, my dear. The sun is shining, you're 'in pursuit' as they say, and once we get to Bend, your friend will be joining us."

"I should be getting the police report too."

"There you go."

The knot in Isla's belly thawed. Mav was right—as uncertain as the trip was, she had reason to be optimistic. "Thanks, Mav." She smiled at him.

"You're very welcome. Now let's turn the music up."

Isla had never seen Mav in casuals before, but when they met up in the lobby of the hotel that afternoon, there he was in ironed blue denim and athletic shoes. Paired with his bespoke coat and hat, it was as odd an incongruity as the two different halves of his face. He must have noticed her staring because he looked down at his feet then up again.

"We're about to walk in the woods, no?"

"We are." Isla tempered a smile. "Sorry." She gestured to his legs. "I didn't expect you to come prepared."

"Once you've marched far enough in a day that your toenails fall off, you think about good shoes a different way. I may be ancient, but I'm always prepared."

"Point taken." Isla considered her own fashion sneakers. Then again, they weren't walking that far.

It was a fifteen-minute drive to the arboretum from the hotel, and with each turn, each green light, Isla's breathing grew shallower. When Mav parked, she jumped at the *clack* of the car doors unlocking. Knowingness simmered deep within her muscles and reverberated through the soles of her feet when she stepped outside. Already, this felt different than Olympia.

She pulled out the photo again. This had been a favorite spot in Portland when she and Jonah had visited in the past, so she knew where that tree was. "Let's go," she told Mav. "It's this way."

They made slow progress through the old growth, repeatedly getting passed by other hikers, but Isla didn't care. Damp moss and rich soil imbued the air with the crisp scent of living things, and even though the canopy blocked most of the sunlight, it wasn't as cold as she'd thought it would be. In a way, it was better to appreciate the stillness of nature's cathedral like they were now—one step at a time—than to rush through it. Isla was certain she'd never paid attention to the many sounds in these woods before. Woodpeckers searching for food, squirrels scurrying up the solid trunks, the rustling in the ferns off the beaten path that suggested more critters beyond what they could see.

"A little break," Mav said, after they'd made it up a slight incline. "Whew."

Was it the shade or was he paler than usual? "Is it too much for you?" Isla asked, looking around for a spot to sit. Maybe that fallen tree trunk up ahead?

"How much farther?"

"Ten minutes maybe. Come on—let's rest." She took Mav's arm and led him to the tree, then she pulled out the water bottle she'd brought from her backpack and handed it to him.

He took a deep swig. "Ah, that's better." He rested the bottle against his leg and glanced upward. "Impressive, isn't it?"

She followed his gaze then returned her attention to his face. Color was seeping back into his cheeks. "Would you rather wait here?" she asked. "I don't want you to overexert yourself."

Mav waved her off. "Nah. I'll be fine. Not used to all this fresh air. Give me another minute and I'll be good as new."

Isla walked ahead, scanning the ground. She picked up a long, straight branch and brought it back. "Here—you can use it as a walking stick."

Mav took it and stood. "Excellent." He inhaled deeply. "Okay, I'm ready."

The tree in the picture grew not far from the Redwood Deck—an overlook that was always full of both amateur and professional photographers with their posing subjects. Today was no different. A family of four posed in matching outfits on one side of the deck, while on the other, several couples were trying to find the best angles for selfies.

Isla and Mav passed them, but as they did, something stirred in Isla's chest, and she stumbled on a root stretching across the path.

Mav got hold of her jacket at the last moment. "Careful there."

Isla straightened and paused to look back. There was something about the deck...

"What are you thinking?" Mav asked next to her in a hushed voice.

"I'm not sure." Isla considered the wooden structure and the brighter drop-off beyond.

"Stay here or go on?"

Isla hesitated before turning forward again. "Let's keep going. It's up ahead."

The trail curved, and then they were there. Down a small slope, the large redwood loomed like a foundational pillar ahead of them. Isla slowed, holding up the photo to make sure, and then she homed in on the exact spot where she'd stood two years ago.

"Here, you take this." She handed the photo to Mav. "I'll be right back." Without waiting for an answer, she hurried the remaining yards and let her feet find their old prints. Then she closed her eyes and inhaled the cool, old-growth air deep into her lungs.

"I'm here," she whispered to the trees. *Tell me, tell me, tell me...*

At first, there was next to nothing. A light rustle high above her where the wind brushed the evergreen sails. The tail-end echo of a bird's trill fading between the tree trunks.

But then the *click* of a camera's shutter rebounded through time, snapping Isla's eyes open. Unseeingly, she trailed the large redwood upward, just like she had that day.

"Look up a little more," Jonah told her. "There."

Click.

She smiled at her husband. Asked him if he got the picture. He was squatting to get the right angle, eyes locked on the camera's screen. Then he raised his head, but...

The vision dissolved.

"Not yet," Isla whispered, squeezing her eyes shut. "Come on."

He raised his head, but his gaze was lost somewhere far away. For an extended beat, he looked through her, not at her. She didn't recognize the expression. Then he stood, adjusted his beanie, and smiled at her like he always did, before they walked back hand in hand.

Isla ground her feet harder into the decaying leaves beneath her feet. That was it? She turned to find Mav studying her. After one more glance at the tree, she made her way toward him.

"You remembered something," he said. It wasn't a question.

"Barely. Jonah taking the picture." Why had he looked at her like that? Had he been tired? Upset about something?

"And?" The green of the forest tinted Mav's curious eyes turquoise.

"I don't know. His expression." Isla took a few steps back toward the way they'd come.

Mav followed but didn't speak.

"You know how when you catch someone sort of spacing out—how they seem to be in a completely different place?"

"Sure."

"It was like that except"—Isla gestured around them—"it didn't fit with what he was doing." She kicked a pine cone out of the way. "But I don't know—who's to say that's even what happened? My brain isn't exactly reliable."

Mav was silent for a moment. "I think we need to operate under the assumption that if a memory comes back, attached to a place like this, then it's real. We could question everything of course, but reality is in there somewhere." He pointed to her head. "For now, let's suppose that is indeed what happened. Does it mean anything to you?"

She wanted it to. More than anything. "Not really."

"Then that's okay too. Because if nothing else, it should instill some optimism about what this trip might yield. You remembered something. It's better than nothing."

Isla let that sink in as they approached the Redwood Deck again. New visitors had arrived; new poses were being struck. Mav was right. And they had a long way to go still.

A collective gasp rose from the people on the deck, stopping Mav and Isla in their tracks. A young man had dropped to one knee and was proposing to his girlfriend.

"Will you look at that," Mav said.

The proposal before Isla morphed into a different formation.

A baptism on the deck. Dressed-up family members, a makeshift font, a robed priest. Isla tearing up because starting a family was at the forefront of her mind. Their minds.

She grasped Jonah's arm as they watched. "Beautiful place for it," she said.

"I'd prefer a church if we have kids," he responded.

Next to her, Mav clapped. "And she said 'yes.' How marvelous!"

"Huh?" Isla blinked at the hugging couple on the deck. "Oh, yes. Great."

She corrected Jonah. "You mean 'when,'" she said.

The glimpse of the past cut off there. If he'd responded, she couldn't remember with what. It had probably been a slip of the tongue, nothing more—he'd been all for their new plan to start a family when they'd talked about it a couple of weeks earlier. He'd wanted at least two kids, he'd said, reminiscing about childhood vacations and the shenanigans he and Katelyn had gotten up to. Isla had agreed. At least two.

Isla hooked her arm through Mav's as they set off toward the trailhead. She would try not to dwell on the meaning of every little flashback. Like he'd said, even a vague glimpse of illumination in the impenetrable dark of the past two years was a good sign. A very good sign even. She'd pocket the glimpses like individual puzzle pieces, obscure though they were on their own, and maybe at the end of all this, a clearer image would emerge.

"Tell me about the march and the toenails," she said as they walked on.

And Mav did.

Isla had one more stop in Portland the next day before they could continue onward to Bend—the donut shop. Or shops. The artisanal fried treat chain had four locations, and since Isla couldn't be sure which one was the site of the snapshot, they'd have to visit all of them.

Mav grumbled at the prospect at first, citing "having done enough walking for a week" the day before, but when Isla informed him only one of the locations was within walking distance, meaning they'd be driving, he was game again.

"It's been years since I had a good cruller," he said, "so I suppose it won't be a terrible hardship to go for a drive. They were Lorraine's favorite."

No hardship indeed, Isla thought, when they emerged from the third shop with yet another bag in hand.

"It would be rude to visit without making a purchase," Mav said. "Besides, we didn't try the apple fritter at the last place."

Following his lead, Isla had bought the same donuts from Jonah's photo at each place, hoping it would spark something, but so far, she'd had no such luck. The flavor on her tongue was familiar, but not unique enough to stand out against a hundred other such memories. A donut was a donut was a donut. And unlike in the arboretum, the environment would have been different two years ago—different people surrounding them, different noises.

"We still have one more spot to check," Mav said as they parked back at the hotel. "Though I must say I'm feeling a little heavy in the gut currently." He patted his belly, leaned his head against the headrest, and closed his eyes.

In the yellow tint of the garage lights, his skin took on a sallow tone that brought to mind waxy figures Isla had once seen in a London museum—lifeless imitations of people. Maybe she was pushing him too far.

"I can go by myself if you'd prefer to go upstairs and rest," she said, putting her hand on his arm. "I know this is a lot."

His pale lashes fluttered up. "What? Oh, no, no. A walk will be good for my digestion." He smiled and winked at her. "But perhaps don't let me buy more pastries."

The final shop was three blocks from the hotel. The sky threatened icy rain but held on to the wet for now. Nevertheless, they hurried as best as they could, with scarves pulled up high, hats low. It was a relief to step inside the sweet-heavy air of the shop.

Mav coughed once inside and in line, patting his fist against his chest.

"You okay?" Isla asked.

"The damp," he said. "It clogs my airways." He cleared his throat again. "I'm fine."

Isla's hand hovered over his back, but she dropped it when the line moved forward.

Are you here? she asked Jonah in her mind, like she had in each of the other stores. But again, there was no response. Maybe he'd run out to pick up donuts on his own back then. For all she knew, she hadn't even been a part of the outing.

Mav took a step to the side, drawing her attention back to the present.

"Are you sure you're not going to get anything?" she asked, her head swiveling in his direction.

Then everything happened so fast.

Mav's hand came down hard on the railing keeping the line in order, and his knees bent.

"Dizzy," he managed, before his other hand touched the floor.

Isla grappled for his jacket to prevent him from going down hard, her voice rising above the fray in a shout of alarm. "Mav, no! Someone help!"

Somewhere behind them, the bell above the door jingled and a loud baritone cut through the hubbub surrounding them. "Everyone out of the way! Let me through!"

Isla looked over her shoulder as the crowd parted, and there, pulling a small cannister out of a bag, was the guy from Maverick's building. The guy with the blue sedan.

NINETEEN

ISLA

Present day

"Someone get a chair," the guy said as he unzipped Mav's coat and reached for the top button of his shirt.

"You?" Isla sputtered.

He glanced at her, an expression of regret skimming across his face. His mouth opened, but before he could speak, a college kid appeared at Mav's feet with a chair.

"Where do you want it?"

The guy looked away from Isla. "Right there is fine. Let's get his legs up."

Together they lifted Mav's feet up onto the seat.

"Maverick." The guy fitted a mask to Mav's mouth and nose then patted his jaw. "You all right there?" He clipped a small device to one of Mav's fingertips.

Someone standing above Isla informed them that an ambulance was on its way.

Isla's eyes were locked on Mav's pale face. It was all she could do. Too many questions warred in her mind, but blanketing them all was worry so intense she couldn't formulate more than a two-word sentence. *Come on.* She should have insisted he stay back and rest. This was on her.

Mav's eyelids fluttered.

"That's it." The guy cradled a gentle hand against the side of Mav's head. "Wakey, wakey."

They know each other, Isla thought with sudden clarity. The realization startled her out of her self-pity, and she studied the guy more closely. He was about her age, with brown hair, slate-blue eyes, and an intentionally scruffy jaw. Underneath his dark parka, he wore jeans and a knitted cream sweater.

"Who are you?" she asked.

"My name is Rowan," he said. "I'm Maverick's nurse."

"Nurse?" Isla blinked at him.

"Let us through please." Two paramedics entered and joined their little grouping on the floor.

"He's anemic," Rowan told them. "From MDS. I got his oxygen up, but we should probably get him looked at."

"His name?" one paramedic asked.

"Maverick Zuft," Rowan and Isla said as one.

"Is one of you next of kin?"

Rowan raised his hand. "I have power of attorney."

"I thought you were his nurse," Isla said.

"Also an honorary nephew of sorts." Rowan leaned over Mav. "He's waking up. Maverick, there you are. You had a stumble. Everything will be okay."

At the sight of Mav opening his eyes, Isla took his hand and squeezed. *Honorary nephew?* What was that supposed to mean, and why hadn't Mav told her about Rowan before?

Rowan turned to her again. "Look—I'm happy to explain more later, but maybe we can focus on getting him into the ambulance now?"

She nodded.

"You ride with him. I'll follow," Rowan said.

And even though she didn't know this man, in that moment, she could have kissed him for taking charge.

Once the doctor had examined Mav, Rowan came to get Isla from the waiting room where she'd paced a track in the carpet in front of the vending machines.

"He's fine," Rowan said. "They'll keep him overnight for observation, but there shouldn't be a cause for worry."

"No cause for worry?" Isla stared at him. "He's clearly not well, and I had no idea."

A slight color spread across Rowan's cheeks. Then he nodded. "Yeah, I know. I'm sorry. I told him it was a bad idea."

"To travel or to lie?"

"Both." He nodded to the elevator bank. "Come on—I'll take you upstairs, and he can tell you himself. If it's any consolation, I think he feels pretty sheepish about it."

"As he should." Isla allowed herself to be herded into the elevator. There was something about Rowan that disarmed her. She'd planned on calling him out for stalking them, but he was so obviously on Mav's side that she couldn't muster the energy. "I'm Isla by the way," she said instead.

Rowan chuckled, his eyes glinting as the door slid closed. "Yes, I know."

Mav was resting when they reached his room. He had a small tube in his nose and a heartrate monitor connected to a machine next to the bed, but other than that, he looked normal. He opened his eyes when Isla took his hand.

"Hi there," he said, his lips turning up.

Rowan pulled a chair up to the bed for her, and she sat. "Hey."

"Much ado about nothing, I'm afraid," Mav said. "Sorry for making a fuss."

"Hardly nothing." She leaned closer. "Why didn't you tell me you were sick?"

"Barely sick," Mav said. "Mostly I'm just old."

"You have a nurse who travels with you. Apparently." She raised an eyebrow.

Mav eyed her, his lips pressed together. "Are you very cross?"

"You made me think I was imagining things. That's not nice. I truly thought we were being followed." She glanced at Rowan, who was leaning against the windowsill.

Mav wiggled his head sideways a few times. "Technically, I suppose we were. But there was nothing nefarious about it."

"How was I supposed to know that?"

"He asked me to stay out of sight," Rowan said. "It's my bad that I didn't do a very good job of it."

"And do you always follow his orders?" Isla's words sounded snarkier than she'd intended.

"Hey." Mav squeezed her hand. "Don't be mad at Rowan."

"Then tell me. What's going on? Why all the secrets?"

"Because if I'd told you about my little health issue, we'd still be in Port Townsend." He leveraged the full force of his cool blue gaze on her. "You know that's true, and you needed to do this."

"I could have found someone else to help."

"Could, yes. Would, doubtful. Besides, I wanted to help you. Your story... It connects." He moved one hand over his heart.

"So..." Isla hesitated. "What's going on with you?"

Mav glanced at Rowan. "I have something called myelodys-plastic syndrome. It affects my blood—the production of healthy blood cells."

"It makes him anemic, which leads to fatigue and dizzi-ness," Rowan filled in. "It can also lead to—"

"It's mild," Mav cut in. "I'm fine."

Isla gestured around the room. "Evidently."

"I'm not used to all the exercise." He patted her hand. "Like I said—I'm old. But I refuse to be committed to some home where I'll fade away into the night. I fainted. Big whoop."

Isla smiled at him. "Do you really feel okay?"

"Really, really."

She nodded then looked at Rowan. "And you have an 'honorary nephew,' whatever that means."

"Technically, he's the son of Lorraine's best friend. I've known him since he was little."

"Ah. And how did this arrangement come to be?" She pointed a finger between the two of them.

"When I received my diagnosis last year, I knew I didn't want to be in a nursing home. So I called Rowan, who I knew to be a reliable and pleasant sort of chap with the right training. And I made him an offer he couldn't refuse."

"Wasn't that great of an offer." Rowan kicked off the wall and joined them at the bed, an affectionate smile softening his expression.

Mav grinned. "Oh hush."

"But it was good enough. And I'd been wanting out of the city." Rowan shrugged. "I'm a writer—or trying to be. Working for Mav allows me to do more of that than when I worked at the hospital."

"He runs a tight ship," Mav said. "Insisted on coming along on the trip. But I couldn't very well have him in the car with us because—"

"That would give away your illness."

Mav touched his nose to indicate Isla had strung things together.

"But what I still don't understand is why you weren't upfront about your condition when we first met. Before you knew about Jonah."

Mav peered at her. "Hello, I'm Maverick Zuft, and I have

MDS? That's what you wanted me to say? Are *you* in the habit of starting new acquaintances announcing your afflictions?"

Isla shrank. "No."

"Right. Because if you do, that's all people see. And I already have 'old' and 'odd-looking' going for me." Mav had raised his head off the pillow while he spoke, but now he sank back down again. "I'm very sorry I was untruthful." He peered up at her from beneath heavy eyelids. "But now that you know, I hope you won't treat me differently. This is just a small bump in the road."

A bump? He didn't think they were going to continue the trip, did he? "But shouldn't we—"

"I'm tired now," Mav said, interrupting. "I need sleep. We'll talk when they release me in the morning."

His voice invited no recourse, so all Isla could do was nod. He was emotional about the whole situation; she could understand that. Surely he'd come to his senses after a night's rest?

"Rowan." Mav reached for him. "You see to it that Isla gets back to the hotel and take care of the charge for the additional night."

Rowan dipped his chin. "Will do."

That settled it.

As they walked back to the garage, Isla struggling to keep up with Rowan's long strides, she tried to decide what question to ask first. There were so many to choose from. Finally, she settled on, "Do you always let him boss you around like that?"

It came out more judgmental than she'd intended, but Rowan didn't seem fazed by it.

"He pays the wages, so he calls the shots," he said, unlocking his blue Corolla with a beep of the key fob. "Within reason of course." He opened the door for Isla and waited until she got in to close it.

She buckled her seatbelt and watched him fold his tall

frame into the driver's seat. "You've known him your whole life?"

Rowan waited to respond until he'd backed out of the parking spot and made it up the ramp. "More or less. We moved to the Seattle area from out of state when I was six. My grandma and Lorraine were very close and lived on the same street, so I'd see Uncle Mav and Aunt Rainie, as I called them, almost every time I visited my grandparents."

"That's nice."

"Oh no—he absolutely terrified me until I was about fifteen. Are you kidding? That face?" Rowan chuckled. "But then I had a school assignment where you had to interview a grandparent or someone of that generation, and since my grandpa had recently passed away, Mav offered. He showed me souvenirs from all over the world, told me stories from the seven seas that topped any book I'd ever read, demonstrated his knot-tying skills."

"He hasn't showed me that."

"I'd recommend you don't let him try it *on* you. It took me an hour to get out of the chair at the time. Always up to something."

"I'm starting to see that."

They made a right turn, then a left, with Rowan consulting the map app on his phone to navigate through the city. It didn't pass Isla by that he hadn't asked her which hotel. He was probably staying there too.

"So I interviewed him," Rowan continued after merging with the traffic on the expressway, "and ever since, we've been close. He may think of me as an honorary nephew, but to me he's always been a bonus grandpa."

"I'm sure he liked that, especially since he never had kids of his own."

"Right." Rowan checked his mirrors. It was rush hour, and

traffic crawled bumper to bumper, but fortunately their exit was only a mile away.

"And then eventually you became a nurse, he hired you, end of story?"

He glanced at her, that friendly smile from the first time they'd met in the doorway to Mav's building blooming across his face. "Yup that's it. That's all there is to my life."

Isla's cheeks tugged up to match his. "I didn't mean it like that."

"I know." He smirked at the road ahead.

Little bit of a wise-ass. Like his bonus grandpa.

They were approaching their exit, and while Rowan focused on not getting into any pileups, Isla sank deeper into her seat. She half expected him to ask something about her, hoped he would, so she could probe further, but when he didn't, she tucked her lingering curiosity away. No one liked a Nosy Nellie.

Finally, Rowan flipped the turn signal on and turned into the garage beneath the hotel.

They came to a squeaky stop against the smooth concrete.

Isla unbuckled and faced him in the dim light. "Thanks for the ride."

"No problem at all."

He got out of the car first, and she followed, falling into step next to him on their way to the elevator.

"Floor?" he asked as they got on.

"Five."

He hit both number five and number seven, and when the door opened on her floor, he held it open after she stepped out.

"Hey," he said, "if I didn't say so before—I'm sorry if I scared you with my inadequate stalker skills. I should have told him no." His face was half in shadow, but his gaze was clear and steady and filled with nothing but genuine remorse.

"It's okay," she said. "He is pretty darn hard to say no to."

She took a step back, getting ready to turn. The need for silence and time to process was becoming more urgent as the sky outside darkened. "I'll see you in the morning."

Rowan raised his hand. "Have a good night."

Once in the solitude of her room, Isla sank down on the end of her bed and rested her face in her hands a long while. She didn't cry—Mav would be okay after all—but she focused on her breathing until the bedlam in her head quietened down. Then she took off her shoes, scooted backward on the comforter, and collapsed against the pillows. The lamp on the desk by the TV cast an intricate yellow halo against the wall and ceiling that allowed her something to focus on while her muscles shrugged off the events of the day. Outside, the rain had started, icy droplets pattering against the window and the traffic below.

She pulled out her phone and started typing a text to her mom but erased it halfway. The trip was over, that was the logical conclusion of today, but she couldn't yet bring herself to type the words. Instead, she opened her email, more out of habit than anything else, and there it was.

The accident report.

TWENTY
MAVERICK

Seattle, December 19, 1952

Dearest Cass,

How my heart lifted at your last letter. To hear you long to see me again as well is the best gift anyone could have given me this Christmas. No, not the best one—that would be news of a ceasefire and your homecoming—but a close second. There is snow on the ground, and the city has strung garlands between the buildings downtown, but as I sit here on Mama's sofa in front of a crackling fire and a small, sweet-smelling tree that she's decorated with tinsel and lights, I don't think of the impending festivities as much as I think of you. I wonder if the Christmas spirit will reach you at all, if you will hear from your family, if there'll be Mass to attend, a celebratory meal. I wish, I wish, I wish...

Pip is doing very well, thank you for asking. He's a right little rascal who would spend his whole day eating if I let him, but his company has brought me so much joy that I happily contend with lost socks and frayed rugs. He's even won over

Mama, and that's a feat. She is not an animal-lover sort of person, and she does prefer her rugs in one piece. I hope that doesn't make her sound unfeeling—I can promise you she's not, and I reckon the two of you would get along just swell.

How odd to think we'll have a new year before this letter reaches you. Surely 1953 will see either the war or your tour end, don't you think? What are your hopes and dreams for when it's over? Tell me everything—I am as always eager for word from you.

Wishing you a most happy Christmas and a peaceful New Year!

Yours truly,

Mav

TWENTY-ONE

ISLA

Present day

"Another one please." Isla pushed her glass toward the bartender and watched as he poured the whiskey. She'd stop at two tonight, but those two would have to count. "I'll take some water too when you get a chance," she said, dragging the shot glass toward her with a hooked finger.

"I'll have the same," a voice said beside her.

She looked up ready to rebuke whoever dared invade her space, but instead of a stranger, there was Rowan. "Oh, it's you."

He gestured to the empty chair on her left. "Mind if I sit?"

Two hours had passed since they'd parted at the elevator, and in that time, the universe had seen fit to add insult to this already injurious day. Mav was in the hospital, they'd have to return home emptyhanded, and now the police report had put her face to face with the remnants of the wreck.

While the report itself had disappointed, lacking any new information that might have been helpful, there had been photos attached to the digital file that hadn't been part of the document she'd seen way back. She'd scrolled through the stark series several times already, unable to shake both the strangling echo of pressure where her seatbelt had compressed her ribs and the voyeuristic sense of partaking in someone else's trauma. A snap of the rear license plate. A dark wide-angle of the exterior of the car at the scene illuminated by spotlights. Something that looked like tire tracks in the brush off the road. The triggered airbags. A collection of items from inside the car in a plastic bin. Her eyes had blurred at the sight of the intact first aid kit Jonah had kept in the center console. Much good it had done them.

Isla clutched at her throat to stifle the lingering knot. She didn't want to go there. Maybe she'd be wise to embrace this offered distraction to help her keep a level head.

"Sure, why not?"

"Such an enthusiastic invitation." Rowan sat, an aromatic whiff of cedar and spice ruffling the air between them. He nodded a thanks to the bartender for his drink.

Isla dragged a palm across the bar top. "I'm not in a great mood."

"Ah." He twisted his glass. "I'll consider myself warned then." He sipped the Macallan then set it down. "You know, I have been told that I'm a good listener. Just putting it out there."

"I expect you'd have to be as a nurse."

He looked at her more intently. "Okay... I kind of get the feeling you want your space. I didn't mean to impose."

She was being rude. So rude. A flush of heat hit Isla's cheeks. "No. I'm sorry." She held up a finger to make him wait then finished her shot. The fiery liquid burned its way down her throat. "You're being nice and I'm..." She gave a little shrug. "Stay. Please."

"You sure?"

"Yes."

The bartender took her empty glass, and she asked him for a ginger ale. Then she turned back to Rowan. They weren't close so she had nothing to lose by telling him what was going on. It wasn't like her, but maybe changing things up would be good.

"How much do you know about me exactly?" she asked.

He blinked in a way that suggested he hadn't been prepared for such a direct question. "Um, I don't... I..."

"It's okay," she said. "I know Mav is a talker."

Rowan sighed and pulled himself together. "Fine. Then quite a lot probably."

"About Jonah, the accident, this trip?"

"Your job, your sister-in-law, your mother moving." He pressed his lips together.

"So everything basically?"

"If it makes you feel better, you can ask me whatever you want. We'll even the score."

"How tall are you?"

He sputtered out a laugh. "That's your most pressing question? I'm six foot five."

It was impossible not to smile when he smiled, and she struggled to temper it. "It was the first thing that came to mind. Don't worry—there's more."

A text message lit up Isla's phone screen. It was Louise asking if she'd received the report. Isla's smile died, and she swiped the message away. Rowan followed her movement but didn't say anything.

Isla hesitated, but then she took a deep breath and handed him the phone, where one of the photos was now displayed. "I've been waiting for the police to send me the report for the accident," she said. "I've seen it before, right after it happened, but my friend suggested I might have missed something back then. I received it today, and there were some photos attached." She indicated for him to look through them. "I know they don't really show much," she said while he did.

Rowan looked up. "I don't know. Maybe this one will help us pinpoint the location." He indicated the wide-angle one then scrolled on. He paused on the bin of glove-box sundries—napkins, pens, car manual, sunglasses, leather bracelet, flashlight, two protein bars. "Is that Morse code?" he asked, zooming in on the bracelet.

Isla's forehead wrinkled as she examined the image where small studs lined the masculine leather strap. "No idea."

"S... E..." Rowan squinted. "God, I'm so rusty. Mav taught me when I was a kid. Maybe R, then E again."

"Weird. I don't remember Jonah ever wearing anything other than a watch."

They both hunched over the screen.

"Hold on—let me look it up." Rowan pulled out his phone and found a Morse code key. "Let's see. Dash, dot—that's N. Dash, dot, dot—D. Then I, something, I. The rest isn't visible."

"Serendipity," Isla said, the letters having strung themselves together in her mind.

Rowan's gaze went up and left as if searching for confirmation somewhere on the ceiling. "You're right. *Serendipity.* Cute."

Isla nodded. It was cute, except it wasn't exactly something a guy would buy for himself, nor did it seem like a gift she would have given Jonah. She supposed she might have—it had been their anniversary after all—but knowing he didn't wear stuff like that, it seemed unlikely. So where had it come from?

Rowan flipped through the other photos one more time. "Must have been hard to see these," he said when he was done.

Isla shrugged off the bracelet question. With so much on her mind already, what good would it do to add another conundrum? For all she knew, Jonah could have found it in the street. She took the phone from him and set it down. "More than anything, it surprised me."

"What about the report?"

"Nothing new there. It has the where and when, the damage to the car, what hospital they took us to, but there were no witnesses and no other cars at the scene. We weren't speed-ing. *I* wasn't speeding," she corrected herself. "And still..." Her voice cracked.

Rowan reached out and covered her hand with his. The comforting warmth of it seeped into Isla's skin.

She pulled hers away. "Sorry. It's just that now that this trip is a no-go, I was hoping something else would come through. Instead, it feels like I'm chasing shadows."

"What do you mean it's a no-go?"

Was he joking? "Um, maybe because Mav is sick and in the hospital. We have to get him home so he can rest."

"Ha! Never gonna happen." Rowan finished his drink, his hair flopping back from his forehead to reveal a two-inch, silver scar right at his hairline. "I'm telling you right now that when we show up at the hospital tomorrow morning, he'll be dressed and pacing the hallways."

"You're not seriously suggesting I let him drive me to Bend as if today didn't take place?"

"No, of course not. I'll be driving."

Isla stared at him.

"I was going anyway," Rowan said, matter of fact. "We can all take my car."

Isla's brain churned with the need to conjure a protest, but to her surprise, none came to mind. Would she actually be able to continue the trip?

"Unless you object to having me along that is? I do take up a bit of space." He stretched his long legs out. "But you should know I've already called the hotel to say we'll be a day late, per Mav's request."

She'd still get to Bend tomorrow. Louise would join them Saturday. Rowan could help talk to people too, as well as keep an eye on Mav. And the hotel—she'd completely forgotten about that. The tension in Isla's shoulders eased. "Yeah. I mean no—I'd be fine with it."

"Really?"

Isla nodded. She meant it. Rowan may be a stranger, but so far, he'd proven himself to be nothing but pleasant company in what could have been an awfully awkward situation. Plus, she trusted Mav's judgment.

"Thank you," she said. "I was preparing myself for going home tomorrow. This changes things."

He tipped his head. "Glad to be of service."

Isla had another sip of her ginger ale then pushed her chair back. "But that probably means we should get some sleep."

"You go ahead." Rowan flashed her a quick smile as he pulled out a laptop from the satchel he'd slung over the backrest. "I have another hour in me."

"Writing?"

"Yep."

A barrage of new question immediately popped into Isla's head. "Can I ask about it tomorrow?"

"We'll have over three hours in the car."

She smiled. "You'd better prepare yourself then. I'll be taking you up on your offer."

His eyes glinted in the light from the modern glass pendants above. "I'd expect nothing less."

Rowan had been right about Mav being ready for them the next morning with one exception—Mav wasn't pacing the hallways; he was already down in the lobby having discharged himself when they arrived.

"Finally," he said. "I need coffee. What they serve here doesn't deserve the name."

Rowan had packed up Mav's bag at the hotel and found a place to park the truck. The brother of a friend of his lived in Portland and was okay with giving up a spot in his driveway for a few days. Isla didn't ask how they'd get the truck back to Port

Townsend at the end of this. That was a question for another day.

"I still think we'd have been more comfortable in the truck," Mav said when Rowan explained the plan to him. "That bench seat is more than wide enough for three."

Rowan and Isla exchanged a look. "Be that as it may, Isla and I decided the Corolla was the way to go, and that's what's parked outside so..."

Mav grumbled, but then he relented. "Fine. Whatever gets me out of here faster. Let's go."

Isla had been prepared to take the backseat, but Mav beat her to it.

"You young folks can socialize up there," he said. "I'm going to take a nap."

They headed east out of the city, and soon Highway 26 stretched out before them, flanked by tall firs and maples. Traffic was light, seventies rock played softly on the radio, and the remaining clouds from last night's showers were gradually giving way to what promised to be one of those rare sunny March days. After texting her mom the update she'd been unable to articulate the night before, Isla allowed herself to relax into the seat and let her mind go blank.

She was lost in thought about what lay ahead until Mav suddenly let out a snore from the backseat. Rowan and she both glanced back, their eyes meeting with shared amusement. That was it, she thought. Time to get some answers from him.

"Did you end up getting some sleep?" Rowan asked, beating her to it. "Or do you need a nap too? You're quiet this morning."

She swallowed the words on her tongue and rested an elbow against the door as she looked at him. "No, I'm good. I slept fine. Maybe I'm just plotting the line of questioning you invited last night."

His eyebrows jumped. "Oh really? That's what you're

doing." He glanced her way. "Well, give it your worst. I have no secrets. What you see is that you get."

"Okay." She pursed her lips, pretending to think hard. "That scar on your forehead—what's it from?"

He touched it, keeping his eyes on the road. "This one time in school, we went on a field trip to a science lab where I got bit by a radioactive spider. After that strange things started to happen."

She slapped his arm. "Funny."

He chuckled. "It is Spider-Man related though. Only I was seven, obsessed with superheroes, and thought climbing the walls couldn't be all that hard. We had a narrow hallway upstairs where I realized I could get all the way up to the ceiling if I pressed my hands onto one wall and my feet onto the other. Thing is—when you've done that a few times, your arms get tired. So I faceplanted. Twelve stitches and a concussion."

"Ouch."

"Live and learn. After that, Batman became my favorite. We had paper bats taped to every single lamp in the house for a while, and if I noticed my parents turning one on, I'd jump out from around a corner in my cape, ready for my mission."

"Cute." Isla could picture it—little Rowan dressed in black, all serious. He'd proven himself efficient and in charge when Mav collapsed, that was for sure.

He sputtered a protest. "I wasn't cute. I was vengeance!" He raised a fist in the air.

"Of course. My apologies." Isla shook her head, bemused. "So are you still into fantasy, superheroes, and stuff? Is that what you write?"

"No, no. My book is historical fiction. Kind of a war epic, family saga kind of thing. It's loosely inspired by Mav's life actually. Secrets, drama, adventure, love."

"Is it any good?"

"Ha! Ask me when it's done."

"Is it your first book?"

"My third. But the other two will never see the light of day. I'm considering them practice. This one... Mm, maybe."

"Will you let me read it?"

"Nope."

Isla laughed. Slowly, the image of Rowan was crystallizing, and the most surprising thing about the process was how straightforward it was. He wasn't giving her half-truths or saying what he thought she'd want to hear. The authenticity was there at a core level. It was refreshing.

"So final," she said. "Will you let Mav read it?"

"Maybe. But not until I know how it ends."

"That's fair, I guess."

The woods around them were getting denser as they entered Mount Hood National Forest, and for a while, Isla allowed the rush of green outside to clear her mind. When Rowan hit the gas to overtake a logging truck, Mav woke up and announced he'd like to stretch his legs, so when signs announced a pull-off coming up—a trailhead for the Pacific Crest Trail—Rowan slowed and took the exit.

Despite the cool air, they weren't alone in the large parking area. Hikers of all calibers seemed to be capitalizing on the beautiful weather, so there was a line for the restrooms. Rowan and Isla waited for Mav by the car, Rowan leaning against the trunk. He inhaled deeply and tilted his face to the sun.

"Amazing," he mumbled.

Isla shaded her eyes to look at him. "Nature lover?" she asked. "Is that why you agreed to move with Mav to Port Townsend?"

He held his pose. "What do you mean?"

"You said that when Mav recruited you, one of the reasons you said yes was that it would get you out of the city."

He pushed off the car and turned to her. "Well, there's a

certain peace to it, right?" He gestured to the abundant land-scape surrounding them. "What's not to love?"

She didn't respond, sensing he had more to say.

After a moment, he added, "But I was also living alone in a small apartment, not doing much more than eating, sleeping, working, and watching TV, and I was feeling pretty stuck. I went through a divorce a few years back, and even though it was a mutual decision, that shit takes a toll."

He'd been married? A slew of new queries popped into Isla's mind. Who was she? When did they meet? Why didn't it work out?

"I needed a change," Rowan continued. "New scenery. Maverick thinks I'm doing him a favor? No. He offered me a lifeline, and I took it."

Isla scanned the distance and spotted Mav making his way back toward them. "He seems to be good at that," she said. "Knowing what people need."

Rowan shrugged. "He's lived a life."

It was more than that, Isla thought as they got back in the car and continued. Mav had also died a death, however briefly, and she knew better than anyone the lasting effects such an experience could have. The difference between the two of them was that Mav had had time to gain perspective while Isla wasn't there yet. But maybe one day she would be.

It was dark when they reached their hotel in Bend. It was the same one she and Jonah had stayed at both two years ago and for their engagement weekend many years earlier, so Isla approached the doors with caution, as if the past might jump out at her any second.

"All good?" Mav asked, hooking his arm through hers as they entered the lobby of the old building.

Isla trained her senses on the room—how the sideboard lamps in the sitting area illuminated the wood paneling, the scent of carpet cleaner mixing with the bright notes of a candle burning on the reception desk, the way their voices rose toward the tall ceilings. Something stirred in her mind like a microburst but settled again without offering anything of substance. She tried to hold on to it, but whatever was there, hidden deep within her, slipped out of her grasp like the final wisps of a dream.

"I think so," she said. "Let's check in."

The small hotel was run by an older couple who'd converted and expanded what was once an old school into the quaint hotel now in its spot. Mr. Boyle greeted them himself and exchanged a few pleasantries with Mav before asking what name the reservation was under.

"That would be Isla Gallagher," Mav said.

As soon as he did, Mr. Boyle's head swung toward Isla, his face growing paler. "Oh," he said expelling a gust of a breath. "I thought you looked familiar. Mrs. Gallagher. Of course." He reached across the counter for her hand. "It's a real relief to see you doing so well. When all that sad business happened... Such a shock. I am very, very sorry for your loss."

Isla pulled her hand free as gently as she could and cleared her throat. "Thank you. That's very kind."

An awkward silence stretched between them until Rowan stepped in. "It's been a long day," he said. "I would love to get up to the room for a rest."

Mr. Boyle averted his attention from Isla. "Yes, of course. My apologies. I just never thought we'd..." He typed something into his computer. "It *is* good to see you, Mrs. Gallagher."

Isla forced her lips into a stiff smile, but she was the first to turn toward the stairs once they'd received their keycards. Out of the corner of her eye, she registered that Mrs. Boyle had come out from the back to join her husband, but just when she thought she was in the clear from more small talk, the woman's operatic voice called her name.

She paused, one hand on the railing, then told Mav and Rowan to continue upstairs without her. She'd catch up.

"It is you," Mrs. Boyle said when Isla reached the front desk again. "I have thought of you and your poor husband so many times over the years, and here you are."

"Here I am," Isla agreed, her mind already upstairs in a hot bath.

"I'll be right back," Mrs. Boyle said, then she scurried through the office door out of sight.

"She has something for you," Mr. Boyle said. "Hold on."

What on earth might the woman be fetching for her? Isla tried to recall if there had been any complimentary treats when they'd been here for their engagement but drew a blank.

The door opened again, and Mrs. Boyle reappeared, clutching a paper bag in her arms. "Housekeeping found it in the closet after your sister came for your things."

"Sister-in-law," Isla corrected automatically, accepting the bag.

"I tried reaching out to her, but perhaps it wasn't deemed important in the grand scheme of things. I couldn't make myself throw it away."

Throw what away?

Isla steeled herself before opening the bag and reaching inside.

Her fingers only had to graze the soft corduroy for a happier past to invade her present. A past of snowy walks, holiday shopping and cocooning bear hugs she never wanted to end.

It was the winter jacket Jonah had worn the night they first met.

TWENTY-TWO

ISLA

Present day

Isla pulled the jacket free and let the bag drop to the floor. Her hands fisted in the soft material, clutching it to her body.

"Thank you," she said, her eyes welling up. "Thank you so much. I can't believe you kept it."

Mrs. Boyle's lip quivered, but then she sniffled and drew up straight. "I'm glad I did and that it's back where it belongs."

Mr. Boyle put an arm around his wife. "We hope you'll have a pleasant stay. If there's anything else we can do for you, please let us know."

Isla assured them that she would, and then she set off up the stairs, still hugging the jacket close.

As soon as she closed the door to her room behind her, she buried her face in the bundle. Her nose chased Jonah's scent in every crease and fold but found nothing no matter how deep the inhale or how desperate the plea. Too much time had passed.

She held it out before her then spread it out onto the bed. This jacket was so inextricably linked to every winter memory she had of Jonah that she couldn't believe she'd never once thought of it since the accident. Playful snowball fights. His arm around her shoulders to keep the cold at bay on starry nights after late dinners with friends. The cool scent of his skin beneath it when he returned inside after shoveling the driveway. Katelyn must have forgotten about the closet when she gathered their belongings that weekend, and Isla had always assumed Jonah had been wearing it in the car that night. Why hadn't he? The temperature had been in the thirties.

Isla shook her head at the addition of another question.

Her phone dinged with a message from Rowan.

We're going to go get dinner in town in a few. Want to come?

She wandered over to the window and glanced out into the impenetrable dark beyond her reflection. No, she thought. She needed to be alone tonight. It wasn't just the jacket—Jonah was closer here somehow. Or maybe she was less distant.

Kind of tired, she typed. *I'll get a sandwich from downstairs and tuck in early. See you tomorrow.*

He sent her a thumbs up, and she appreciated his good sense not to probe.

This room was smaller than the one she'd been in last—she knew that from their card statements and Katelyn's account of the suite—but something familiar dwelled in the atmosphere. She couldn't be sure of course, but there was a ripple somewhere inside her at the sight of the dark floral wallpaper, the wood-frame bed, and the ink prints on the wall that was similar to what she'd experienced in the arboretum before she'd remembered Jonah snapping her picture by the tree. Like she was playing a game of hot and cold, and her hands were getting warm.

She sat down on the bed and pulled the jacket to her again.

"Am I not looking in the right places, Nana?" she whispered. "What am I not seeing?"

But the universe kept quiet, and eventually Isla had to concede that whatever simmered beneath the surface in this place would stay that way for now.

Louise in real life looked exactly like her profile picture online. Thick, wheat-blond hair, perfect winged eyeliner, and a tentative smile that grew wider the closer Isla got to her.

"Do we hug?" Louise asked when Isla reached her. "God, I've been nervous and excited all morning. Nervo-cited. Let's hug."

She was a head shorter than Isla and fine-boned like a wren, but her embrace was surprisingly forceful.

"It's great to meet you finally," Isla said after they separated. It was. Louise had been an unexpected connection to the world when Isla hadn't had the energy to maintain other friendships, and this—getting together in person—proved their rapport had been real. Not like Mom had described it, merely "anonymous, superficial chats."

They were in the parking lot of the hotel, having decided to grab a coffee just the two of them before getting Mav and Rowan and driving out to the spot where the accident took place. Isla still hadn't filled Louise in on everything that had happened in the past couple of days, so Rowan's presence especially would definitely be a surprise.

"It's kind of like a blind date almost, isn't it?" Louise said.

Isla laughed. "Yeah, I suppose. I don't remember. It's been a long time since I went on any date."

"Yeah, I got you. Same."

"But you're so..." Isla was going to say "adorable," but maybe that was patronizing since Louise was so petite? "Pretty," she said instead, though it was an inadequate word choice.

"Aww, thank you. Right back at you."

They drove into town and found a café.

"Wait, there actually was a stalker, but he was Mav's friend and a nice guy?" Louise made a "mind-blown" gesture as she stared at Isla across the table.

"Yup."

"And Mav collapsed in a donut shop?"

"Not sure the type of shop is relevant, but yes."

"So now nurse-guy is traveling with you?"

"Mm-hmm." Isla sipped her latte, taking care not to burn her lip.

Louise leaned forward. "Is he cute?"

"Um..." Isla squirmed at the direct question. Rowan wasn't not-cute, though "cute" painted too juvenile a picture. He was too steady, present, and grown-up for that word. At the same time, it would be dishonest to deny he wasn't objectively attractive. And not only looks wise.

Louise sat back again suddenly, interrupting Isla's thoughts. She covered her mouth with her fingers. "Oh my God. I can't believe I asked you that. That's not at all why we're here." She lowered her hand. "If you hadn't noticed, I tend to talk too much. Occupational hazard. Sorry. I didn't upset you, did I?"

Isla smiled to reassure her. "Don't worry about it."

"I promise I'll save my nosiness for when we talk to people in town." She mimed zipping up her lips and throwing away the key.

"No. Nosy can be good." That's why having Louise here would be helpful. She knew how to ask questions, and from the looks of things, she wasn't afraid to be too forward—a character trait no one had ever used to describe Isla.

Louise finished her drip coffee then wrinkled her brow. "So okay. If we're going to be serious, then..." She nodded toward Isla's left hand. "I imagine being here can't be easy." Her voice softened and slowed.

Isla peered down at her wedding band, glossy gold against her pale skin. She reached for it and spun it once. "It's... weird," she said. "Because I don't remember, it feels like I'm traveling in someone else's footsteps."

Louise studied her carefully. "You really don't remember anything from that night? Not where you were, what you did, what you talked about, where you were going?"

Isla shook her head. "Nothing."

"Mm." Louise's head bobbed up and down. "You know, some might say that's a blessing in disguise."

"What do you mean?"

"I guess—sometimes reality can be worse than our imagination."

Isla scoffed. "Not mine. For two years I've had to contend with imagining Jonah dying, essentially at my hand. I'm pretty sure no real scenario could top that."

"Then you're hoping you'll remember something that makes that scenario better?"

"No." Tension built inside Isla. Something spiky was trying to break out of her chest. "No, I know I was driving. You saw the police report."

"Then why put yourself through this?"

"Because." Isla huffed out a harsh breath. "How can I move on from something that isn't here?" She tapped her head. "Any time I try to think it through—that weekend, the accident, everything—I get stuck. One black hole to fall into after another. And maybe—just maybe—if I can remember... if I can tell myself the story of what happened in order, one event after the other, it will somehow make sense." She wrapped her arms around herself. "No, I'm not here because I think I can change the facts and absolve myself. I want answers so that maybe I can stop asking the questions."

Louise's eyes had rounded as Isla spoke, and now she cleared her throat and looked away. "I didn't realize," she said finally. "The pain I mean. You've never told me."

"We bonded over silly birds." Isla allowed herself a wry smile. "That was my only escape at the time."

"Hey, there's nothing silly about them."

"Fair enough."

The mood lightened, and Isla finished the last of her drink.

"Maybe it's time then," Louise said when Isla put her cup down on the table. "Are you ready to get out of here?"

Ready to go face the place where Jonah had taken his last breath? Isla wasn't sure. But as with so many other things lately, there was only one way to find out.

She stood and grabbed her coat. "Let's go get the others."

Rowan and Mav sat in the front seats and Isla and Louise in the back as they made their way south along Route 97 toward Crescent. The air outside had a raw chill, and even though the heat was on, Isla couldn't get warm. She pulled Jonah's jacket closer around her and buried her chin in its collar. It had been a last-minute decision to switch into it before they left, and Isla was glad she had. It made her feel closer to him.

"So, Louise, as a journalist, you must do a lot of writing." Rowan glanced in the rearview mirror.

"Sure. Among other things."

"Very cool. To do it professionally I mean."

A look of perplexity swept across Louise's features.

"He's writing a novel," Isla said, the corner of her mouth pulling up. "Prepare to have your brain picked."

"I'm just curious what it's like," Rowan continued. "I imagine you have stricter parameters to follow, but do you feel like it's a creative job at the same time?"

"Um..." Louise cocked her head. "Yeah, I'd say it's fairly creative. I have to think of what questions to ask in order to create the story, you know."

"Which I kind of do with my characters too."

"Right. And the word choice needs to be compelling."

Mav turned around. "If you ask me, it was better when the journalism profession was there to report facts. To objectively inform. Now it's all about who can get the most readers. No offense."

Louise smiled. "None taken. And you're not wrong."

"But maybe there's less of that in local press?" Rowan asked.

"Sure. Yeah."

"Did you always know you wanted to be a journalist?" Isla asked.

"Not really." Louise brushed something off the side of her nose. "But I always knew I wanted to work with people. The rest was more 'right place at the right time.'"

Isla nodded. She too had ended up in a job she liked and that suited her but that she hadn't originally aspired to. She'd known she wanted to do something with art ever since seventh grade art class but teaching it hadn't been on the table until college.

As the forest on either side of the road was starting to thin out, giving way for sporadic buildings, they all fell silent.

"This is Gilchrist," Rowan said. "Crescent should be up ahead."

"But we have to drive through it, right?" Mav asked.

Isla handed Mav her phone so he could show Rowan. "Yeah, the coordinates from the police report are further south." She sat back and focused on keeping her heart steady.

Once they'd passed Crescent, they drove another few miles, and Isla was just going to ask if they'd missed it when Rowan slowed and pulled to the side of the road. There was no natural place to stop, but the road was wide and straight so they should be easy enough to spot.

As they got out of the car, what struck Isla the most was how flat everything was. No hidden turns, no hills. The verge was trimmed so that the main tree line sat at least ten yards in with only scattered trees closer to the road. And yet this was where she'd lost control of the car. Of all the places for a single-vehicle accident, it seemed the most unlikely.

She scanned the growth along the road. Watched the others move closer to the trees. And she knew when Rowan found the spot by how his back straightened.

Twenty feet ahead of Isla, two tall firs stood together about four yards from the shoulder and down a small slope. She started moving toward them at the same time Rowan called, "This might be it."

Isla knew it was. She recognized the V-shaped trunk of one of the trees from the photos, and the other one had a large gash in the bark from the impact. At the sight, her stomach dropped like she was flying over a dip in the road.

"It's too high up to be from a car," Louise said when she and Mav reached them.

For a long while, they stood, eyes fixed on the tree, then Isla said, "We were airborne." She considered the road behind them, several feet higher than the spot where they were standing. When the car had gone off the road, it hadn't merely driven into the tree, it had flown. Her stomach vaulted again, recognizing the truth in the memory.

"Makes sense," Mav said. "Speed and elevation."

Louise circled the tree. "Do you remember anything else?"

Isla focused. First there was nothing. But when she looked up into the branches of the tree, a snapshot of pandemonium flared through her head. She gasped.

Rowan was at her side instantly, his hand at her elbow. "You okay?"

She nodded. "I don't know what it is. The impact maybe."

"It's starting to come back," Mav said. "That's good."

"Maybe if we walk through it?" Louise suggested. She took out a notepad and pencil from her purse.

"Are you up for it?" Rowan asked Isla.

She nodded again. "There's not much to it."

"You were driving..." Louise began, indicating for Isla to continue.

Isla walked back up the slope to the road and faced the tree. "We were driving south, Lord knows why. Or I was driving," she corrected, "which also makes no sense."

"It was dark, late," Mav filled in. "Not much traffic."

"And at some point, I lost control of the car for an unknown reason, we went off the road, flew into that tree, and my husband died." Isla forced herself to face the point of impact.

The others followed her gaze.

"Maybe an animal ran across the road?" Rowan suggested.

"Except there were no tire marks noted in the police report," Louise said. "Typically, if there's an animal, you instinctively hit the brakes before you steer."

"I don't know if that's true," Rowan said. "That might depend on if you're used to driving at night."

"What about another car?" Mav asked.

Louise lowered her hand holding the notepad. "Wouldn't they have stopped? The police weren't alerted until more than thirty minutes after it happened by a trucker heading north."

Isla shrank deeper into Jonah's jacket, fighting the impulse to put her hands to her ears and block out their voices with a "la, la, la." They could speculate all they wanted, but that's all it was. Speculation. She shoved her hands into the pockets and was about to tell the others that she wanted to leave, when her fingers met the dry friction of paper. She frowned and pulled out a folded note. Opened it.

"Do any of those scenarios sound familiar, Isla?" Louise asked from what sounded like far away.

Isla looked up from the note. "Huh?" She'd missed something—that much was clear from their expressions. "Sorry, I was..." She shifted her stance, fiddling with the paper in her hand.

"What's that?" Rowan asked, stepping closer to her.

Mav and Louise joined them.

"It's a phone message from the hotel." Isla pointed to the logo at the top of the note. "It was in Jonah's pocket."

"What does it say?" Mav asked.

Isla scanned the words again and the date in the top-right corner—the day before the accident. "'*Please call Gemma ASAP*,'" she read. She looked up at each of their faces, hoping their reactions would settle the turbulence brewing in her mind. *A random note. It doesn't mean anything.*

Instead, Rowan's jaw was tight when he took the note from her, read it, and handed it to Mav, whose blue eyes seemed to pierce the paper. He, in turn, gave it to Louise, who whispered the written words to herself as she read, her fingers tightening around the note.

They all stared at each other at length, and then, finally, Louise asked the question they were all thinking.

"Who the hell is Gemma?"

TWENTY-THREE

GEMMA

May, three years ago

Gemma didn't think she'd hear from Jonah again. He'd felt bad about her getting sick and therefore obliged to leave things on a polite note. People did that all the time. So when, a few weeks into May, she received a message that he'd be coming into town for a couple days, she first couldn't believe it. He really wanted to see her?

I believe I owe you some food, he texted.

Not "dinner," food. That could be interpreted any which way.

She weighed her response carefully, typing and erasing words until finally she settled on, *What did you have in mind?* Not too presumptuous, and it put the ball back in his court.

It took a while for him to respond—enough time that she wondered if she'd scared him away with her question. But after she'd unloaded the dishwasher and watered the half-dead spider plant Cheryl kept on the kitchen counter, her phone chimed with another message.

Are you free Thursday evening? Dinner?

Gemma's stomach somersaulted. He was actually asking her out. A nice, normal guy with a job, a sense of humor, and the ability to carry a conversation. *Sure I can make that work,* she typed. *Where do you want to meet?*

Do you know Zazu's Pizza? At 7?

Sounds good.

I know it's not very exciting, but there aren't many places that are still open and it's walking distance from my hotel.

He'd looked around then. Which meant he'd been thinking about this. A smile slipped onto Gemma's face. *It's perfect. See you then.*

She'd never been to Zazu's, but she'd heard good things about their wood-fired pies.

Cheryl entered the kitchen carrying a tub of clean laundry for folding. "What are you smiling about?"

"Nothing." Gemma put her phone down on the counter, which made her aunt frown.

"Who are you messaging?"

"No one. Fran from work. Dr. Richards is still sick so the office will be closed tomorrow too."

Cheryl eyed her for a beat, but then she seemed to accept the explanation. "All right. Well, good. Then you can help me clean tomorrow. I want to shampoo the carpets."

Gemma temporarily forgot about Jonah. "You want to what?"

"I heard the virus can linger, especially on soft surfaces."

Her aunt had made a 180 as far as precautions went after

hearing from a former colleague who'd been hospitalized. "Cher, I really don't think that's an issue in here."

"You think what you want, but I'm doing it. I'm renting a machine from the hardware store. Curbside pickup. Will you at least go get it for me?"

Gemma bit her tongue. It was a good thing that her aunt was off the couch and doing something. An improvement. She should encourage that. She picked up her phone again and moved toward her bedroom. "Sure thing. Let me know the time."

Cheryl could clean and worry about germs. Gemma had other things on her mind.

After frantic searching, Gemma found an outfit in her closet that felt right for the dinner with Jonah. It wasn't quite date garb but definitely a step up from work function, and miles above the sweats she lived in at home. Her reflection in the hallway mirror said "cute, but not trying too hard." Black jeans and a polka-dotted top.

"You going somewhere?" Cheryl asked. She was back on the couch after scrubbing the apartment top to bottom over the past few days. Her follow-through had been impressive, so as much as this new hyperfocus on germs seemed a substitute for a real purpose, Gemma wasn't complaining. Even in her aunt's bedroom, a fresh spring scent had replaced the always lingering cigarette smoke. Come to think of it, she hadn't seen Cheryl smoke in a while.

"Um, I'm meeting up with Sadie," Gemma said.

"Is that safe?"

Best to stick close to the truth. "We've both had it recently, so we're good."

"Okay." Cheryl turned her attention back to the TV. "Have fun. Just shower when you get back in case."

Gemma didn't respond to that. Instead, she grabbed her purse and headed out the door, grateful her high school acting skills could still come in handy.

Jonah was waiting outside the restaurant when she arrived. In blue jeans, suede shoes, and a lightweight gray jacket, he struck a more casual figure than when she'd seen him the first time in the office, but it was still a put-together look. He lit up when he spotted her and took a few steps her way.

"Hey," she said, fighting a smile she wasn't sure was appropriate.

"Hello." He held out a small bag. "For you."

A gift?

"It's just something small."

She took it and peered inside. Then she laughed. "Roasted nuts," she said. "Because of the—"

"Amusement park," he filled in. "Yeah, it's from this little sweet shop back home. They have the best stuff, and it made me think of our conversation."

"Thank you so much." A tender warmth spread outward from her chest. *So thoughtful.*

For a moment they simply looked at each other, a tentative current testing the air between them for purchase. Then Jonah nodded toward the restaurant.

"Are you hungry?" He put on a mask.

"Always." *Always?* Gemma followed him inside, pulling up her gaiter. *Could she sound any more eager?*

As soon as they entered, it was clear that the evening wouldn't go as planned. The dining area was barred off with a sign stating "TAKE-OUT ONLY."

"You picking up?" the guy at the counter asked.

Jonah turned to Gemma, his eyes flicking back and forth. "Um, no, we..." He faced the guy. "Give us a minute." He guided Gemma toward the door with a gentle touch to her lower back that she felt all the way up to her neck. "I didn't know," he said. "I should have called to ask. Do you want to leave?"

Gemma glanced at the sign. "Do we have a choice? They're not seating people."

"Yeah..." He frowned. "Fuck. I was looking forward to catching up."

She was too. There had to be another place that was open somewhere. Or... "We could get it to go," she said before she could change her mind. "Eat at your place?"

He stilled, eyes settling firmly on hers. "You'd be okay with that?"

She shrugged, feigning nonchalance. "Sure. We both need to eat, right? I mean, if it's okay with you."

"Yeah, yeah." He ran a hand through his hair. "Yeah, of course. Um..." He rocked back slightly on his heels. "Then let's order, I guess. What are you in the mood for?"

Soon a prosciutto, basil, and mozzarella pie to split was cooking for them in the brick oven.

Jonah was staying in a regular hotel this time.

"The condo is only for longer visits," he explained as he handed her the pizza box so he could unlock the door. "I'm heading home tomorrow."

Maybe home to his wife, the angel on Gemma's shoulder whispered. *Don't forget about that detail.*

She followed him into a small suite that immediately opened into a kitchenette slash living space smaller than her room at home. There were two doors to their left which Gemma assumed led to a bathroom and a bedroom.

"Couch or counter?" Jonah asked, gesturing toward the sitting area and the kitchen before he shrugged out of his jacket.

"Couch," Gemma said, continuing toward it.

"Couch it is. Can I take your jacket?"

She gave it to him along with the small gift bag, and he put them on one of the bar stools. Then he opened the fridge. "Water or light beer?"

"A beer is good. Thanks."

The logistics of it all disturbed the butterflies inside her that had settled earlier when they'd ordered food. Being here in this tight space alone with him was different than being out in the open. Personal. As Jonah looked through drawers and turned on side lamps, Gemma couldn't help but wonder if he felt it too and that's why he was keeping busy.

"The pizza will get cold," she said when he'd opened the fridge a third time. "Come sit."

He paused what he was doing and stood, hands on the counter facing her. Then his shoulders lowered as if he'd willed them to. "Right," he said. A half-smile flashed across his face. "I think I'm a little nervous."

His confession was unexpected, but Gemma kept a straight face as he approached. "How so?"

"This." He gestured to the food. Her on the couch. "I didn't... I'm not..." His chin slumped to his chest. "Never mind."

"Would you rather I leave?" She held her breath.

His eyebrows rose. "No," he said empathetically. "No, I don't want that at all." He took a seat on the cushion farthest from her on the couch. "This is just different than what we'd planned."

"And that's... scary?" She forced herself to have a sip from her beer bottle.

He held her gaze. "A little."

She reached for the box. "Why don't we eat? Everyone needs food. You can tell me about your job."

"You do not want to hear about my job." He chuckled, and that seemed to break the tension. When he reached for a slice, he moved with more ease again.

"Why not?"

"Because everyone is losing their freaking minds right now.

Half my team are refusing to do in-person sales calls currently, which means there's more ground to cover for those of us that do."

"So you don't mind the traveling?"

"No. I get restless easily. I'll do it as long as I can, especially since the new spike in cases might ground all of us soon. You're lucky to have a job that's deemed essential." He folded his slice in half and took a bite. "Mm." His eyes closed briefly. "So good."

She watched him chew. Yuri had devoured food with a sort of frenzied chomping, but Jonah was completely different. He was deliberate in savoring the experience, and each time he swallowed, he paused for a beat as if revering each bite.

It made Gemma slow her intake too, and he was right. The pizza was delicious.

When they'd finished, Jonah sat back on the couch and stretched his arms above his head. His off-white Henley rode up a smidge, revealing a sliver of fair skin along his abdomen. Gemma busied herself with folding up her napkin and closing the box that now only held one measly slice to avoid ogling him.

"So what about clowns?" Jonah asked out of nowhere.

A laugh bubbled up through Gemma's chest. "What?"

"You like them? You're scared of them? People usually have opinions, and you've worked at an amusement park."

"Ah, that." She scooted back and folded one leg under her. "In that case, I'm neutral. They don't scare me, but I also don't find them funny. You?"

"Love 'em. Highlight of my childhood when the circus came to town."

"A firm stance. I respect that."

"Acrobats however? Terrifying. To this day, I will not watch any sort of daredevil stunts on TV unless I know it's prerecorded, and no one will get hurt. And forget about live shows. My wife wanted to go see Cirque de—" He cut himself off and pressed his lips closed as if the W-word had registered a second too late.

Gemma focused on keeping her breath steady. Hearing him mention his wife for the first time dispersed the notion that she was somehow in the past. And if she wasn't in the past, she was real.

Jonah ran his palms down his thighs. "Anyway, I didn't go."

Gemma knew she could leave. It would be the easiest thing. But despite the initial awkwardness and this tension, tonight was still the best time she'd had in a long while.

"What's her name?" she asked, watching him carefully.

He ran a hand across his jaw. "Isla."

"That's pretty."

He leaned forward. "Look, I—"

Gemma interrupted him. "We shared a pizza. We're talking. You're not doing anything wrong."

"No?" His eyes were dark on hers in the golden lamp light.

"Do you want me to leave?" she asked again.

He hesitated, but then he shook his head.

"Okay then." She tried for a smile.

He looked down at his hands then back up. "Maybe the problem is how much I don't want you to leave."

Her stomach flipped. It wasn't all in her head after all.

"That doesn't have to mean anything," she said once she thought her voice would hold steady. "Tell me more about your travels. Is it only for work? What's the most interesting place you've been?"

Would he stay with her and let the moment pass? She waited.

"Italy," he said finally, leaning back again. "Tuscany."

Gemma relaxed. "I wish I could go."

"You'd love it. Here, I'll show you." He pulled out his phone and clicked around, then he shifted so she could see. "I like photography," he said. "I have way too many pictures on my laptop, but I keep some of my favorites in my phone."

Beautiful landscapes of rolling golden-green hills and ancient stone villas lit up the screen. Gemma could almost feel the warmth of them on her skin.

"I've never been out of the country," she said. "These make me want to go. They're beautiful."

"Thanks." He put his phone away. "If you could travel, where would you go?"

"I might have to say Tuscany now." She laughed. "No, but Paris is probably at the top of my list. Maybe it's cliché, but it's always seemed the epitome of class to me. Strolling the avenues looking at art, reading in some big park, a morning croissant at a quaint little café."

"Why don't you go?"

"By myself."

"Why not? Or take a friend."

"My best friend has kids now so that ship has sailed."

He smirked. "I'm pretty sure people still travel after they have kids. The travel industry would collapse if they didn't."

Did he have kids? For all she knew, he could have a whole brood of them back home.

"I don't think I would—at least not while they were little. It sounds so stressful when Sadie talks about it."

"That's your friend?"

Gemma nodded.

"Well." He put his hands behind his head in a stretch. "She'd know best, I suppose. All we can do is speculate."

No kids. She drew a breath of relief.

"So what made you want to work with teeth?" he asked.

She tittered. "Sounds kind of gross when you say it like that."

"You know me—I'm prejudiced against anything dental."

She told him about her start, not wanting to go to college

after high school, finding a dental assistant ad, etcetera. She talked about what she liked about it, what her challenges had been, and he, in turn, regaled her with stories from the world of doctors' offices and sales meetings.

The conversation meandered leisurely between topics, and when Gemma glanced at the clock some time later, it was already well past eleven.

She yawned, covering her mouth with her hand. "I should probably head out soon," she said, not without regret. "Or my aunt will start texting me."

Jonah glanced at the digital display on the microwave, a look of surprise coming over him. "I can't believe it's this late."

She collected her plate and bottle and brought them to the kitchen.

"Leave the rest," he said. "I'll take care of it when I get back."

She reached for her shoes. "Get back?"

"I'm obviously walking you to your car. It's the middle of the night."

"It's like five minutes away."

"Then it won't take me any time."

Gemma's chest expanded. Why weren't all guys like this?

It smelled like rain outside though the streets were dry. Maybe it was on the horizon. Spring showers and all that. Despite her jean jacket, goosebumps rose on Gemma's arms.

"I can't wait for summer," she said as they strolled down the sidewalk at a casual pace.

The streetlights painted moving shadows across Jonah's features with each step. "Is that your favorite season?"

"I don't like being cold."

"I prefer fall," he said. "When the trees are changing."

"Because it's pretty or because of your photography?"

"Both. I'm also a sucker for pumpkin spice." He sidestepped a planter and ended up in her space, his arm brushing hers.

"Are you?" She squinted up at him, only a foot or so away. "Sometimes it's hard to tell when you're being serious."

He grinned. "A good trait to have when in sales. But I haven't told you anything untrue."

"Just maybe not the whole truth." Gemma wasn't sure why the words jumped out of her, but she regretted them right away. *Way to make things serious.* Now he'd probably think she was needy or disappointed or upset or all of the above.

But contrary to her fear, he didn't take offense. Instead, he turned his attention forward and nodded to himself. "Only because we ran out of time," he said quietly.

"Sorry, I didn't mean—"

He put a hand up to stop her. "It's fine. I get it."

They walked in silence the last hundred yards to her car, where she steeled herself before meeting his gaze. "Thanks for walking me. And for dinner. I had a good time."

"Of course." He rubbed a hand across his neck. "Thank *you.* It's been great. You're very easy to talk to."

Gemma's stomach churned. This was goodbye. Had to be. It didn't matter that the impending absence already made her miss him. "Okay, well..." She pulled her lips into a small smile and went in for a hug.

He hesitated for only a beat, then he wrapped his arms around her.

It was like coming home.

With her nose buried in the cool skin beneath his ear, his scent enveloped every fiber of her. She couldn't help but inhale deeply, not caring if he noticed. He smelled like sea and rosemary, and paired with the proximity—his body heat, his hands on her back—it made heat pool low in her belly.

When he finally stepped back, one of his hands trailed down her arm until their fingers touched. At first, she thought it was accidental, but then he took hold of her hand and stayed there, watching their linked fingers.

"You should go," he said, but he still didn't release her.

"I should," she said, but she made no attempt to move.

Around them, the city lay quiet with only distant sounds of traffic suggesting they weren't completely alone in the world. The moon lined the low clouds in silver.

His foot slid forward half a step.

Hers did the same.

When he captured her other hand, she rolled her shoulders back and faced him. His lips parted as a silent understanding stretched between them. Then he let go and dragged his hands up her arms to rest on her shoulders. Still his gaze remained steady.

It was up to her, she realized. He was letting her choose.

Except it wasn't really a conscious choice.

Banishing all thoughts of reason, she wrapped her arms around his waist and lifted her face to his. As soon as her breath skated across his lips, his self-control vanished, and he met her in a soft kiss. The sensation ignited a flame behind Gemma's ribs that had lain dormant for a long time, and it made her tug at his jacket to get him closer. He deepened the kiss with a smooth stroke of his tongue as his hand trailed into her hair. She reciprocated by stroking his stubbled cheek while her blood whooshed an uneven rhythm in her ears.

When they finally parted, her lips prickled, but her heart sang.

"Now I'll go," she said. And she did.

There was no need for promises or plans. She'd see him again. As uncertain as the times they lived in were, of this one small thing, at least, she was sure.

TWENTY-FOUR

ISLA

Present day

"It's not like I don't know what it looks like," Isla said into the silence of the car. Somewhere in the back of her mind, a bracelet spelling out "serendipity" in Morse code was trying to materialize, but she kept it at bay. *Coincidences, nothing more.* "But I'm telling you—Jonah wouldn't cheat. He was a good man."

They were halfway back to Bend, and so far, no one had mentioned either this Gemma person or the note since they got back on the road.

"Of course he was," Mav said.

"Good men make mistakes too." Rowan regarded Isla in the rearview.

She knew that. And Jonah hadn't been perfect. But something like this? No.

"Hey." Louise got Isla's attention. "She could be a colleague. Don't stress about it."

The colleague theory again. But what if "Gemma" was the person who'd taken the photo of Jonah in the car? The one who'd given him the bracelet? That was hardly colleague behavior. *No, stop it!* At least now she had a name to ask about. "I'll call them Monday and find out. They're closed on weekends."

Louise nodded. "I think that will be good. In the meantime, we'll canvass the town."

Talking to people was the last thing Isla wanted to do. She needed space, silence, and time to sit with what had just transpired. The tree, the straight road, and the note—possibly also the bracelet—might be disjoined details in this story to the others, but Isla knew at a gut level that a context was being formed, and she couldn't see its pattern with all these voices around her.

As soon as they pulled into the hotel parking lot, she excused herself. "I'm going to go for a walk before we do anything else. I need a moment." She turned to Louise. "Will you be okay waiting in the lobby, or should we meet you in town later?"

"Oh, um..." Louise clicked open her phone for the time.

"I'll keep you company in the lobby," Mav said. "I could do with another coffee."

"Tea," Rowan corrected. "You've had enough coffee today."

Mav looked like he was about to argue, but then he got out of the car with a resigned, "Tea it is."

"I'm going to get some writing done," Rowan said. "Meet back in an hour?"

Isla pulled on her gloves. "Sure."

While the others went inside, Isla set a course toward the River Trail. She reached the scenic path at a quick pace, her breath billowing in front of her in the cool air. It felt good to move. Like the fog was clearing. Her legs were a pace away from breaking into a jog, but since she wasn't wearing the shoes for it, she didn't allow the transition. Instead, she set her sights on a bridge far in the distance and decided she wouldn't think a single thought until she got there.

It was a good intention, but not a realistic one. The note still burned in her pocket, so when she finally reached her goal, she stopped at a strip of railing overlooking the water and rested her elbows against it while allowing her heart to slow. *Gemma*, she thought. Louise could be right that she was a coworker, but it hadn't passed Isla by that there was no phone number on the note. Whoever she was, Jonah must have known her well enough to know how to reach her, and he'd never mentioned anyone by that name.

Was she here that weekend? The thought struck Isla with sudden force, making her push off the railing. What if she'd somehow been involved in the crash? She could be a stalker— someone who'd chased them off the road maybe.

Isla shook her head. No, she was reaching now. She would have hit the brakes before things got out of hand. She was a careful driver for God's sake. Besides, they didn't live in an action drama. They were ordinary people with ordinary lives.

But whatever the note was about, they had to get to the bottom of who Gemma was. Jonah had known her well enough not to need her number. *Well enough to smile at her like that in the car? Well enough that their meeting could be considered* serendipitous? Monday couldn't come fast enough.

Isla's phone rang. She pulled it out of her pocket and got ready to answer but then she saw the time—only fifteen minutes to get back. She spun on her heel and set off walking again, picking up her mom's call on the go.

Nancy was busy on the other end and didn't respond to Isla's, "Hello," right away.

"Ulysses, no," her mom said. "That's not for you. You stinking cat. You're getting yogurt all over the counter."

"Hello?" Isla said again. "What's going on?"

"He put his whole paw in my bowl," Mom said. "Hold on."

Isla walked as fast as she could, the phone pressed to her ear. She hated being late.

"Okay, I got it now," Mom said. "I'm not going to miss him, that's for sure."

"You are too. Or is it someone else who makes blanket nests for him on the couch when I'm not looking?"

"Fine, I'll miss him a little. Which is sort of why I'm calling. But first things first. How are you? Is everyone behaving? Mav's doing better? Did your friend make it there?"

"Whoa, Mom. Slow down. Everything is fine."

"It's just that your message described quite an eventful few days."

Now that was an understatement. "Yeah, but we're on track again."

"Oh good. Are you exercising? You sound like you're out of breath."

"I went for a walk. Now I'm heading back. We, um... went to the place where it happened today. I needed to think."

Nancy was quiet for a long while. "That must have been hard," she said.

A knot lodged itself in Isla's throat. Why did parents have that power—to hook into your most core emotion and pull it to the surface? She blinked at the blurring river then forced herself to swallow the knot down. "It was."

"Any memories?"

"A feeling in my stomach from when we went off the road, I think. Nothing else. But we're going to head into town as soon as I get back and start talking to some places we might have been."

"Do you expect people will remember?"

Isla knew her mom too well to know that wasn't an open-ended question. "I think what you're really saying is you don't think they will."

"It has been a long time, Birdie. I don't want you to be disappointed."

"I know." As Isla veered off the trail and into a park, she

slowed her stride to make conversation easier. "Hey, Mom, do you remember if Jonah ever mentioned the name Gemma when he talked about work?"

"Gemma?" The sound of a spoon meeting ceramic resounded through the line. "No, I don't think so. Why?"

"No reason." Mom didn't need to know about the note yet. She'd worry needlessly.

Isla glanced at the time again. Now she was definitely late to meet the others. "Shoot, I've got to run. Was there something else? You said something about missing Ulysses?"

"Oh right. Well... Two things. I wanted to let you know we've set a date for the move."

Isla's step faltered. Somehow, since being gone, she hadn't thought once of either Mom's Arizona move or her own return to work. Now it all came crashing back. "Oh yeah? When?"

"May 31."

She stopped altogether. "May? But that's only two months away."

"The realtor said I'll get more interest if I sell before the summer. A lot of people move over break, especially if they have kids."

"I guess. But..." *What about me?* she wanted to ask. It was too soon. "But will that give you enough time? Wouldn't it be easier to go in—I don't know—July maybe?"

Mom was silent for a beat, then she said, "We can do hard things, Birdie. Both of us."

Isla looked up, and there in the distance were Rowan and Louise. Rowan waved when he spotted her.

"I know," she said into the phone, even though she still had her doubts. "What was the other thing?"

"When do you think you'll be back? Beth and Maggie want me to fly down to Phoenix with them Thursday to meet with our realtor there, but someone needs to be home for the painters."

"I don't think that'll be a problem."

"You think or you know?"

They only had the hotel until Monday morning, then they were heading north again, so Isla saw no scenario where they wouldn't be home Wednesday night at the latest. "Go with your friends," she said. "I promise I'll be home by then." Isla waved back to Rowan. "But I've got to go now. The others are waiting."

They said goodbye, and Isla hurried to reach her friends.

"We were getting worried," Louise said when she did.

"I was on the phone with Mom. Sorry I'm late. Where's Mav?"

Rowan cocked his head in the direction of the hotel. "He was getting grumpy, so I told him to stay back and rest. Nurse's orders. We'll come back for him before dinner."

Louise pulled her shoulders up high in her red puffer jacket. "Ready to go?"

Once in the car, Rowan set course on the small downtown area where most of the shops and eateries were located.

"What exactly are we hoping to find out?" he asked.

Yes, what was she hoping for? Isla looked out the window, trying to picture another car ride along these same streets two years ago. She and Jonah had had at least twenty-four hours in town before they went to dinner at The Log House and never made it back to the hotel. Jonah must have brought his camera, and they both liked small antique shops. It was obviously unlikely anyone in town would know details of the accident, but if someone remembered her, maybe she could at least create a timeline of the events of that day and jog her memory that way.

"Anything," Isla said. "If we were shopping in town. Where we had lunch."

"If you were together," Louise chimed in.

Isla twisted toward her. That was a good point and one she hadn't considered. If they'd spent the day separately on what was supposed to be an anniversary trip, that could be damning.

Except with Gemma's name percolating in her head, Isla didn't know if she wanted an answer to that question.

"Sure, that too," she said. Something—anything—was better than nothing if she was to illuminate the black holes in her head.

Rowan parked on Bond Street, and they gathered in front of the car.

"It's not very busy today," Louise said. "Where do we start?"

Isla considered their options. There was a coffee shop and an art gallery across the street, and a clothing store next to where they were standing. "Split up?" she asked.

"You'll have to send us a picture then," Rowan said. "Of you and Jonah, I mean, so we have something to show."

"Right." Isla pulled out her phone and scrolled through her feed. She selected one of the two of them together and one of Jonah. In it he was grinning at the camera, posing in front of a firepit in Katelyn's backyard a couple of years before the accident. The flames warmed his face and glinted in his eyes, and he was wearing the jacket currently wrapped around Isla's shoulders. *Back when he was happy.* A shiver pricked her neck at the thought, which was there before she could prepare for it, because didn't that imply that there had been a time when he wasn't? Or had she meant "happy" as opposed to "dead"? Yes, she'd probably mis-thought, she decided and pressed SEND.

Rowan's and Louise's phones dinged simultaneously.

"Got 'em," Rowan said.

Louise opened the images and stared at the screen, her hand going to her sternum as she let out a long sigh through her nose. "You've never showed me a picture of you two before," she said. "It makes everything more real somehow." Her eyes fluttered closed for an extended beat, as if she was trying to contain herself. "I'm so sorry, but this whole thing is so tragic."

The genuine emotion in her voice hit Isla square in the

chest. Her old friends from college and work had been at her side in the beginning, visiting her in the hospital and even making the drive to Mom's once she'd been well enough to move in there. But one after the other they'd carried on with their lives, and when Isla couldn't keep up, she'd absolved them of remembering her and her sorrow. She'd pulled up the drawbridge and made the moat fertile ground for her demons, both to keep herself in and others out. To have people in her life now who empathized and recognized that for Isla grief wasn't a temporary state but a new skin, and who didn't shy away from its ever-shifting shades, meant everything.

"Come here." She pulled Louise into a tight hug. "If I haven't said so before, thank you for being here." She let go and faced Rowan, who was watching them with soft eyes. "Both of you."

Rowan cleared his throat and swung his head away from her gaze, rubbing his fingers across his lips. "Of course," he mumbled in a voice that was thicker than usual.

Isla took a steeling breath of the cool air. "Okay. So. Louise, you take the clothing store; Rowan, you take that café; and I'll stop in at the gallery. Ask if they remember hearing about an accident two years ago." As she said it aloud, the futility of their mission once again imposed, but no, she wasn't going to let that deter them. She pressed on. "You can show the photos, see if they remember us. Any little detail could help jog my memory."

The other two nodded, and then she and Rowan crossed the street.

Ten minutes later, they met up by the car again, none of them with anything to report.

"It was only the first place, and there's a ton to go. Let's continue," Rowan said, and Isla fought the impulse to hug him too.

They worked their way down the block through a sweet shop, another few clothing stores, and a New Age crystal place where the owner offered to do a palm reading for Isla to aid her quest, which she politely declined to Louise's great disappointment.

"It can't hurt," Louise said. "We should explore all avenues, and I can't tell you how many times the cards have guided me right."

"Tarot," Isla explained to Rowan, who looked like he was having a hard time following their conversation.

"Oh. You're into that?"

"I am. She's not," Louise said. Then to Isla: "Think about it, okay?"

Isla said she would.

The afternoon was getting late, and most of the stores were closing, so when they'd talked to staff in both the Mexican restaurant on the block and a second coffee shop, Isla called it a day. There were only so many times she could hear "No, sorry" in one afternoon. Besides, they had tomorrow too.

Later that evening, they had reservations at the same steakhouse where Jonah and Isla had eaten the night of the crash. Unlike in Olympia, here Isla knew she was walking into the place where Jonah had most likely last been seen alive, making the doors feel heavier than they should have when she pushed them open.

The first thing that hit her was the scent of grilled meat and smoke from the sunken fireplace centered in the room. Then the press of laughter and animated conversations. The place was packed as usual, with every table taken and more people waiting at the bar. The Log House had the best honeydew Martinis Isla had ever tried, and the waiters shook them at the table then left the shaker there for a refill. Her mouth watered at the thought. She hadn't had a drink since Portland.

"Looks like there's a wait," Rowan said.

Isla pushed through a group of people crowding the foyer. "Not when you have reservations."

They were seated in a booth along one of the walls, and because of the high backs, it was like entering a small private room that muted the outside noise. Two sconces and a metal-caged pendant lit up the space.

"It's very fancy," Louise said, undoing the fan shape of her white napkin and placing it in her lap. "But still kind of cozy. I like the fireplace."

"Isn't it nice?" Isla asked. "Just prepare for your hair to smell of smoke when you get home."

The smoke smell had swathed her in the cold air that night.

Before her mind's eye, she saw herself push open the door of the restaurant and step outside into the darkness, the warm inside air behind her billowing at her back as if giving her a shove. But where was Jonah in this memory?

She returned to the present and reached for her water glass. When she'd finished drinking, Mav was watching her from across the table. He raised his eyebrows in question, and she gave a small nod. Yes, there were memories here.

Louise and Rowan hadn't noticed. They were busy reading over the menu. Isla picked hers up too and followed their lead.

"What are you having?" Rowan asked on her left. "The filet medallion sounds amazing. Do you know if it's any good?" He pointed to it on her menu.

Isla smiled. "That's what Jonah always ordered. With a side of scallop potatoes and Béarnaise sauce."

"A man of good taste then." Rowan looked up, and because he was right next to her, their eyes met with a proximity she wasn't used to.

They both looked away at the same time, but not before a wave of some long-absent tide rolled through Isla, making her grasp onto the menu as if it was a lifesaving buoy. Thank goodness their server showed up right then.

"I was thinking," Louise said once they'd been served their drinks, "I know you're going to call Jonah's work and everything, but are there other places we should put on the list to contact in case that doesn't pan out? You said he traveled for work. Do you know where he stayed? Hotels keep records."

"He usually stayed in the company condo," Isla said. "Unless it was only for a few nights or someone else was using it." She took a big gulp of her Martini.

"What else would he have done when he was on the road?" Louise asked. "Any hobbies? Did he work out? Maybe a gym membership? Think of places where he would have met other people."

As in places where he might have met this Gemma... Isla drank again.

"How long was he usually gone for? Did he typically talk about his trips when he got home?"

"Hey now." Mav turned to Louise. "That's enough questions. Let the girl enjoy her meal." His voice was sharper than Isla was used to hearing it.

"Maverick..." Rowan spoke with an edge.

Louise sat back, her expression pinched. "Sorry. I didn't mean... Sorry. Of course."

Isla looked from Louise to Mav. His lips were set in a tight line, and he was currently locked in a silent argument with Rowan. Finally, he huffed, reached for his wine glass, and muttered something that sounded like "It's hard enough for her as it is."

He was being protective of her, she realized. Always watching out for her. And as much as she didn't need him to protect her from Louise, she still reached for his hand across the table and squeezed it. "I'm fine," she said. "Promise."

Then she turned to Louise and reassured her too. "No worries. I know you're trying to help."

Louise let out a breath. "Are you sure? I know I can get a little overeager at times."

"Yeah, we're good."

"And here's the food right on time," Rowan said, indicating the server.

As they dug in, Mav asked Louise about her meal, no doubt to make amends, and while they talked, Isla leaned closer to Rowan. "What was that about?" she whispered. "Mav's not usually testy with people."

Rowan tipped his head toward her. "Oh, he can be."

His breath was warm with pepper and plum courtesy of his glass of Syrah. It reminded Isla of the sangria her dad used to make every Thanksgiving. She fought the impulse to inhale deeper.

Rowan leaned closer still, facing the back of the booth so he could whisper the rest. "But he told me she was asking a bunch of questions of him when you were on your walk too. I believe the word he used was 'nosy.' Which, I mean, what journalist isn't? That's why I suggested he stay back when we went into town earlier. He's just looking out for you. And they seem to be fine again. I'll talk to him later if you want."

Isla agreed and returned to her steak frites, and gradually, her full belly and the addition of a second Martini relaxed her enough that she was able to enjoy the rest of the evening. She was leaning back against the wood partition after they'd paid the bill, waiting for Rowan and Mav to return from the restroom, when Louise smiled at her from the other side of the table.

"Thanks for letting me come along tonight," she said. "I learned some new stuff. Did you know Mav can fold a sailboat out of a napkin?"

"I didn't. He showed you?"

"Yeah, you were busy talking to Rowan." She moved the silverware on her plate into a neat line. Hesitated. "You two seem to get along really well."

"What do you mean?"

"I mean like maybe he likes you."

Isla sputtered out a few consonants. "No, he doesn't."

Louise shrugged. "Okay. If you say so." She smirked. "Would it be so bad if he did?"

Isla bit down on the inside of her cheek. *Would it be bad?* She shrugged the thought away. No, Louise was wrong about this one. Rowan was just being friendly.

And speak of the devil, there he was with Mav across the room now.

Louise started pulling on her jacket. "Oh, I took the liberty of showing Jonah's picture to the staff when I went to the bathroom earlier by the way. I hope you don't mind."

"And?"

"Nothing. The hostess said hardly anyone who worked here two years ago is still on staff. Which makes sense. So many places had to downsize because of the pandemic."

"Right." Isla tried to brush off this information, but the weight of futility lodged itself anew in her stomach. If not even this place where she and Jonah had definitely dined could remember him, what were the chances that any other place would?

"Are we ready to go?" Rowan took his coat when Isla handed it to him.

"Yup, all ready."

Isla trailed the others out the door, but her step faltered when the cold outside air hit her skin, the sense of déjà vu stopping her in her tracks. The gateway between the comforting warmth inside and the harsh night was a before and after etched in her cells, and with it a warning. Something was wrong.

Rowan noticed her lingering first and returned, concern stamped on his features.

"I got this pit in my stomach," she said before he could ask.

"Is it the food?"

"No, I think I'm remembering something. But I can't..." She frowned as she tried to capture the flimsy shreds of the feeling.

"Is there anything I can do?"

She concentrated for another few moments then gave up. "No. It does what it wants. Stupid memory."

They proceeded to where Mav and Louise were waiting.

"False alarm," Isla said. "Again."

"Okay, well... I'm going to head up to Redmond," Louise said. "Thanks so much for today. It honestly doesn't feel like I just met you all." She hugged them each in turn.

"I'll walk you to your car," Isla said.

"Meet back in town around ten tomorrow?" Louise asked when they reached it. She dug around in her purse for the keys and unlocked the door.

"Ten, ten thirty." Isla took hold of the top of the door as Louise got into the driver's seat. "I'll text you when everyone's awake and done with breakfast."

"Sounds good." Louise went to grab the door handle.

"Wait. Your scarf." Isla leaned down to pull the end of her friend's knitted scarf off the ground and handed it to her. But as she squatted at Louise's side, the sense of déjà vu returned, stronger this time. She stood, staring at her friend but seeing Jonah instead.

Louise didn't notice. "Okay, see you tomorrow." She pulled the door closed at the same time Isla pushed it shut from the outside.

And there in the smooth, chilly metal against her palm was the memory.

Isla stayed at the table to pay the bill, but Jonah didn't wait. He needed fresh air, he said. He wasn't feeling well.

No, Isla thought now. It wasn't that he'd said he was feeling sick. He'd just seemed off, so it had made sense to her that he needed air.

She lifted her hand off Louise's car and stepped back.

He was looking for the car keys in his pockets when she reached him, even though he'd handed them to her to keep in her purse when they'd arrived like he always did.

"God, I'm such a screw-up," he said. "I've lost the damn keys."

And it was the way he slurred each S that finally made her realize he was drunk. She helped him into the passenger seat. Crouched down to lift his feet into the car. Closed his door and paused, her hand against the metal and her mind against an equally solid wall of confusion because her husband rarely drank. He'd only had one glass of wine with dinner. But he'd also gone to the restroom several times during the meal. Had he stopped at the bar? Without telling her?

Louise pulled out of her parking space and waved. Isla waved back, though the movement was subconscious, disconnected from the images moving behind her eyes.

Yes, she'd tucked her husband into the passenger seat that night. And then?

Then she'd gotten into the driver's seat and started the car.

TWENTY-FIVE

MAVERICK

Seattle, March 27, 1953

My darling Cass,

Such joyous news! Oh, the relief I felt hearing that you will soon return home to our good ol' US of A. Please do everything in your power to stay safe until then. (I write this knowing it is possible you may leave Korea before this letter reaches its destination. How about that? I might see you sooner than it takes the post to travel!)

But I could scarcely believe that you've willingly stayed this long and could have been home many months now if not for volunteering extra time. I admit I was at once rattled and proud upon reading your words. Selfishly, I wish you safe on this side of the big blue pond, and yet you still being there is also a testament to your character beyond any other I have met. Your care for your fellow man truly knows no bounds.

It makes sense that your parents will want you home with them for a bit once you are back. If they are at all like Mama, this has surely been an ordeal for them. Allow them to pamper you for a spell and don't fret about finding work straight away. I understand the urgency you express and the desire to move forward, but I reckon a woman of your caliber will have her choice of a job once you and they are ready. Will they object to me calling on you, do you think? I sure hope not. It is the thing most presently on my mind when I am not at work.

Yes, I have found a job and one with mighty fine prospects to boot. Thanks to a friend of my uncle's, I am learning the ropes in car sales and hope to pocket my first commission soon. Perhaps I'll use it to treat you to dinner at the swankiest place Tacoma's got. Now wouldn't that be a dream come true?

Please let me know the moment you receive your date of travel, by mail, telegram, or telephone. I have included Mama's number below and will be counting the days.

With love,

Mav (and Pip)

TWENTY-SIX

ISLA

Present day

Sunday was their last day in Bend, so they made the most of it, splitting up four ways to talk to anyone and everyone they encountered in town. Unfortunately, Isla's fears were confirmed and not a single person could say with certainty that they remembered either Isla or Jonah, or someone named Gemma for that matter. Halfway through the afternoon, Isla had started including her in her line of questions out of sheer desperation.

"Now will you do the palm reading?" Louise asked when they met up by the car with all avenues exhausted. "It can't hurt."

Isla looked toward the crystal shop. "I don't know. What could she possibly tell me about Jonah from the lines in my hand?"

"It's not about that. It's about perspective and new ways of seeing things."

Isla hedged. On the one hand, Nana had told her to look around, and Isla supposed that could be interpreted as not closing down any lines of inquiry, no matter how farfetched. On the other, she couldn't say she believed that her palms hid any deep truths about her other than how much manual labor she might have done and the quality of her moisturizer.

"Please." Louise pulled at Isla's arm. "I've always wanted to see a reading, and remember—she said it was free."

Isla caved. "Fine. For you. Because I'm grateful you're here, okay?"

Louise clapped her hands together. "Yay."

"I think I'll sit this one out," Rowan said. "Mav and I will be across the street when you're ready."

"What are you on about?" Mav asked. "I want to see the palm reading."

The two men stared at each other, then Rowan put his palms forward. "Okay then. *I* will be across the street. You guys enjoy."

"Such a skeptic that one," Mav said as they entered the shop.

It was warm inside, the air infused with the herbal smoke of burning incense.

The woman at the counter lit up when she saw them. "I knew you'd be back," she said. "Any luck with your search?"

"Not really," Isla responded.

"Will you still do a reading for her?" Louise asked. "Like you offered yesterday?"

"Of course." The woman pulled her sleeves up and with them several charm bracelets. "And who is this?" She faced Mav. "You, sir, have an unusually vivid aura, if you don't mind my saying so."

Mav's eyes widened with amusement. He extended a hand, and the woman took it. "Maverick Zuft at your service."

"Very interesting," she said. "Is that an Unalome on your cheek?"

"Good eye. It certainly is."

She flipped his hand over and let a finger trail his palm

briefly before she released him. "Like I thought," she said. Then she turned to Isla. "Right through here, my dear. We'll go in the back. Your friends can come too."

They trailed her into a kitchenette where a small round table sat centered on a hand-woven rug.

"You two can sit over there." She pointed to a bench along the wall and waited until Mav and Louise were settled. "Now." She waved Isla forward. "That chair is for you. Get comfortable. I'm going to light the candles."

"Do they help with the reading?" Louise asked.

"No, they just smell good," the palm reader said. "Let's get started."

There was something about the space that removed whatever qualms Isla had felt walking in, and to her surprise, she didn't hesitate before presenting her hands to the woman.

"I take it it's your first time?" the woman asked. Her grip was steady and warm.

Isla glanced at Louise then back. "Yes."

"And you wouldn't have except your sister made you."

Isla startled. "My sister?"

The woman looked up from Isla's hands. "Not sisters?" she asked, toward where Louise and Mav sat. "Huh... But there is a bond there. Good friends then. You're lucky." She returned her attention to Isla, tracing one of the lines in her palm. "Makes sense. You have strong lines of influence. People who care about you very much and whose advice you trust."

Clearly, Isla thought. Two of them were in the room right now.

The woman extended Isla's fingers. "Long fingers suggest you approach life with careful thought, and this here—the mount of Venus—indicates a love for beauty and the arts. Do you paint perhaps?"

"I'm an art history professor."

"Yes, I can see that."

Isla fought the urge to roll her eyes. So far this wasn't exactly blowing her away.

"But you haven't worked in a while," the woman said, and Isla's thought was cut short. "See here. Your fate line." She pointed. "See where it fades and almost disappears. A loss of purpose, floundering. When there's a small breach with one line ending and another taking over, I usually see a career change or a move, but this is different to me. The good news is it picks up right here." She touched a pink nail to the middle of Isla's palm. "And then it gets stronger again. You'll find your way back to your path."

Isla met Louise's gaze and mimed, "Did you tell her that?" Maybe Louise had let Isla's situation slip the day before when they were canvassing.

Louise shook her head.

"Your life line is also broken in several places," the woman continued. "That can mean a rich life, full of experiences and adventures, but also one ripe with challenges. I do find it interesting that..." She paused to examine both of Isla's palms.

"What?" Isla leaned in closer.

"This overlap is unusual. It's an abrupt cut-off, but when you examine it closely, the continued line seems knotted to the broken one." She spun around in her chair. "Mr. Zuft was it? May I see your right hand again?"

Mav extended his arm to her. "Go right ahead."

"Yes," the woman said. "See, the same overlap. Tell me, Mr. Zuft—you've been to the other side, have you not?"

Mav hesitated, but then he nodded.

The woman let go of him. "Yes, I could tell as soon as you walked into the store. I wonder..." She spun back to Isla. Traced the life line again. "You as well?" she asked. "A second chance?" She let out a small laugh before Isla could respond. "I've read about this, but I've never actually come across it in a reading before. And now, in two of you, life so persistent that a new one knots itself to an ending old one."

Isla swallowed. All this was in her palm?

The palm reader gripped Isla's hand tighter. "But your new beginning hasn't been free of challenge. These small intersecting lines—little stumbles if you will."

"I lost my husband," Isla said, her voice more solid than she felt inside.

"I'm very sorry." The woman folded Isla's hand closed and set it down on the table. "But a straighter path is ahead. You will move forward, and the fork in the heart line means so will your heart." She watched Isla with soft eyes. "Just pay attention to the world. Look around. We're all connected, and you never know who'll cross your path."

Isla flinched, not sure she'd heard right. "What did you say?"

"To pay attention? Don't let the past prevent you from seeing the present."

"No, the other thing." Isla looked at Mav. "You heard it too, right?"

He inclined his head "Yes, but..."

"You said to 'look around,'" Isla told the woman, her heart going from trot to gallop inside her chest. "That's what my grandmother said to me when I was flatlining. Do you connect with the other side? Did she tell you to say it?"

"Um..." The palm reader's gaze skated from Isla to Mav and Louise and back. "It was just a recommendation. I don't..."

"Isla." Mav had risen and approached the table. He gave her a discreet shake of the head. "Let's wrap up and get going. Rowan will be waiting."

"But I—" Isla paused, taking in the expressions on the other faces in the room. Kindness and sympathy tinted by concern. Isla deflated. "Okay. Sorry." She thanked the woman and allowed Mav to escort her back to the store.

"She was only giving you advice," he said under his breath. "She doesn't know your grandmother."

"But it feels like she might," she whispered back.

"Because you want it to be so."

Isla stopped. "No. And don't tell me you suddenly believe that would be impossible when you're the one who assured me my experience was real and mattered."

"Guys." Louise touched Isla's arm.

"That's not what I meant," Mav said. "Only that it's a common phrase and this lovely lady here"—he nodded at the woman—"is a palm reader, not a medium."

"I read energies though," the woman said. "And I once dreamed that my aunt was in pain, and when I woke up, I found out she'd gone into labor."

"Not helping," Mav muttered.

The feeling of something more being at play still lingered for Isla as they left the store, but embraced by the sobering evening chill, she let go of the weird hunch. As an academic, she knew better than to rely on feelings—fleeting and ripe for misinterpretation—over facts when drawing conclusions. With that in mind, it made logical sense that the woman had only offered generic advice. She wasn't making claims to communicate with the dead—she was trying to be helpful.

"How was it?" Rowan asked when he joined them soon after. He brought with him a whiff of ground coffee beans and cinnamon. "All questions answered?"

"Don't be rude," Mav said.

"It's fine." Isla pulled Jonah's jacket tighter around her. There was a damp wind coming off the river this evening. "Pretty much a waste of time."

"I wouldn't say that." Louise was bouncing in place and blowing into her hands. "She was optimistic about your future— the possibility of falling in love again, moving on. Right?"

Isla chuckled. "She can hardly tell people the opposite. Not many return customers that way."

Rowan smiled. "Someone's joined me in the skeptic corner, I hear."

"I'm a realist," Isla corrected. "And can we please go somewhere? I'm freezing."

They ended up at a sports bar in the middle of town known for their burgers and brews, but they'd only just ordered when Isla's phone rang. It was a Bellingham area code, so she picked up, thinking it might be someone she knew.

She covered her other ear with her hand and hunched down in the booth. "Hello?"

"Um yes, hello. I'm calling for Isla Gallagher."

The female voice wasn't familiar, but Isla still responded. "This is she."

"Oh hi. My name is Kim Campbell. You met my husband Nathan a few days ago. We're the ones who bought your grandparents' house in Yelm."

"Oh. Right. Hi. Hold on one second." Isla gestured to the others that she was going to take the call in the foyer and wiggled out of the seat. "What can I do for you?" she asked when she reached a quieter spot.

"I was sad I missed you when you stopped by. Your grandparents were such lovely people, and Nathan said you shared some stories about the house. I find that stuff so fascinating, so I finally said to myself, *give her a call.*"

"Yes, he told us you were interested in its history."

"Very much so."

Isla glanced into the restaurant, and her stomach growled. "I'd love to answer all your questions, but it might have to be at a different time. I was about to have dinner."

"Oh, I'm so sorry."

"I should be back home in a few days. Could I give you a call?"

"Of course, but there's one more thing. I'm renovating one of the rooms upstairs right now and—do you remember the hatch on the wall in the gable room by chance?"

"Sure. I used to make my dad put a chair in front of it so no monsters could come in."

"Well, it's a ventilation hatch from what I understand, but when I took down the drywall that blocks off that tiny crawl-space a couple of months ago, I found an old shoebox inside. At first, I thought it belonged to my son since it was his room, but after looking inside, I think it must have been your grandma's."

"Really?" Isla turned her back on the busy restaurant and paced to the window overlooking the parking lot. "What's inside?"

"From what I can tell, mostly knick-knacks, souvenirs, a few photographs, things like that. I didn't dig any deeper—it's not my place. I haven't had it in me to get rid of it, and now it makes sense why. Maybe you'd like to have it?"

A time capsule, Isla thought. *Nana's treasures*. A thrill of excitement coursed through her. "Oh definitely. That's so cool."

"I'm happy to ship it to you if you give me your address."

She could do one better. "No need. We'll start driving back north tomorrow so I can stop by in a couple of days if that's okay. That way I can answer any questions you might have about the house too."

"You'd do that?" Kim's voice tilted up.

They wrapped up the call while Isla tried to imagine what treasures Nana might have stowed away. She pictured dried flowers, ticket stubs, photos of Nana and Pop-Pop in their youth. Nana had always said it was a whirlwind courtship, which Isla had thought sounded like the epitome of romance when she was a teenager.

"You guys will never guess who just called," she said when she returned to the table. She relayed Kim's message and watched the others' jaws drop.

"Ooh, that's so exciting!" Louise said. "I wish I could come along."

"I buried a time capsule at every house I lived in growing up," Rowan said. "I still wonder if anyone's found them."

"Then there's also the possibility that she didn't mean for it to be found," Mav said, his tone more restrained. "I'm an old man with a long story. If you peek in my drawers, you'll see hints of the plot, but only hints. I would hope when I'm gone, no one except the people who knew me well in life fashions themselves qualified to tell the tale."

"But Isla was close with her grandma," Louise said.

"Mm." Mav nodded once then reached for his water glass.

A small laugh bubbled up Isla's throat. "How odd would it be if that's what Nana wanted me to 'look around' for all along. What if it had nothing at all to do with Jonah?"

As soon as her husband's name crossed her smiling lips, Isla was knocked back in her seat by the impossibility of the moment. She stared at her hand, with its golden band, then at the motley crew around the table.

"What is it?" Louise asked. "You look like you've seen a ghost."

Isla shook her head. "No, it's just... I don't think I've said his name like that before."

Rowan cocked his head across from her. "How?"

"Like there's light at the end of the tunnel," Mav supplied. "No pun intended."

"Yeah."

Isla lowered her chin and intertwined her fingers on the table as she sat with that. She wasn't done yet, but maybe at the end of this journey, there was hope for her after all. While she still didn't have answers, she did know more now than she had a week ago. Jonah had acted a little off in Portland on their drive down, possibly even further back around Christmas. He hadn't been as happy as usual, and he'd been uncharacteristically drunk the night of the accident, which had made Isla the driver by necessity.

Then of course there was the call from Gemma and the bracelet. Something had been bothering Jonah, that was for certain, but he'd also been the one to book the weekend away for their anniversary, so he must have wanted to celebrate. That's why an affair made no sense. And other than to explain why Isla had been driving, none of these discoveries shed any light on the accident as such. If anything, new questions had been added to the pile of old ones. It was all so confusing.

When they were done eating, they said goodnight to Louise and got in Rowan's car to head back to the hotel for one more night. In the morning, Isla had several important phone calls to make to Jonah's job and the places he'd stayed when traveling. Hopefully they'd get some leads before returning to Portland.

They'd been on the road for ten minutes when Rowan read a road sign out loud and hit the brakes.

"What is it?" Isla asked.

"Is there a golf club on the way to the hotel?"

Isla scanned their dark surroundings as if that would tell her anything. "Not sure."

Rowan pulled out his phone to consult the map. "It was the third roundabout," he said. "I should have taken the first exit, not the second."

"Or used the map to begin with," Mav said from the backseat.

"No harm done," Rowan said as he did a U-turn on the empty stretch of road. "Just a few more minutes in your uplifting company." He rolled his eyes so only Isla could see.

Soon they were on the right track again, and as they pulled into the hotel parking lot, Rowan cracked a joke about the evening's sightseeing being complete. Isla undid her seatbelt and got out to help Mav out of the low car, but as he was unbuckling and gathering his hat and gloves, he suddenly paused and looked up at her, his face a muddy yellow in the streetlight above.

"Didn't you say you don't know how you ended up south of town in the opposite direction of the hotel that night?" he asked.

"Yeah." Isla extended a hand for him to take.

The very next moment, she realized what he was insinuating and that she now had another discovery to add to her list.

She pulled him out of the car as they said in chorus, "The roundabouts."

TWENTY-SEVEN

ISLA

Present day

Isla was on the phone with the regional office for the pharma company Jonah had worked for at 8 AM sharp on Monday. Once connected to HR, she explained who she was and asked if her husband had been working with someone named Gemma in the year before he passed.

"You don't have a last name?" the HR rep asked. "Emma is a common name."

"No, it's Gemma," Isla clarified. "With a G."

"Ah. That should make it easier. Let's see..."

Isla waited, listening to the clickety-clack of keyboard strokes on the other side of the line.

"Okay, are you there, miss? It doesn't look like there are any Gemmas in our employee register. There's a Gena in our Salt Lake region. Could that be your gal?"

Isla read the note on the desk in front of her. It definitely said Gemma. "Gena" sounded nothing like it. "No, I don't think so," she sighed.

"Sorry about that. Anything else I can help with?"

"No that's it." *Unfortunately.* "Have a good one."

With heavy steps, she made her way to the small dining room for breakfast. Rowan and Mav were already seated and engaged in animated conversation, but they looked up when she pulled her chair out.

"No Gemma at his work," she said, slumping into the chair and tossing her room key on the table. "Damn. I really thought that would be it. Now what?"

"Some coffee?" Rowan asked, gesturing to a carafe on the table.

"Sure—thanks." She held out her mug, and he poured. "I'm going to call the apartment building where he usually stayed after I have something to eat, but I can't say I'm hopeful."

"You never know," Mav said, hunched over a crossword puzzle.

Rowan thought for a while, stirring sweetener into his refilled mug. "What about asking for an expense report?"

Isla relished the dark brew seeping into her cells and waking up her senses. "How would that help?"

Rowan hesitated. "Look, I know you don't think he would have cheated, but—and I'm not saying he did—if that's the case, there may be dinners, gifts, unusual hotel stays, flowers... And who knows? Something like that might lead us to her."

Jonah's expense reports. If nothing else, they would probably give her the names of the other hotels he'd used. "I suppose I could ask."

"It's public information," Rowan said. "They can't say no."

"Okay." Isla stood again. "Can you order me some avocado toast? I'll be right back."

Ten minutes later, she was back at the table, triumphant. She'd spoken to the same HR rep again, and the report was on its way. "I should have it in my email within the hour," Isla told the others. "Now let's eat."

Before Isla had finished one half of the toast, her phone

dinged with a notification. She had a sip of coffee then wiped her mouth before clicking open the email. "Let's see this thing."

There were two attachments to the email—one spreadsheet report for the year prior to Jonah's death and the other smaller file that he'd submitted in the months prior to the accident. Isla opened that first, but a quick scan told her she'd find nothing of interest. He hadn't traveled at all those first two months of the year, so aside from his work phone, gas, and some stationary, there was nothing there.

The year-long report was a different story. The expenses were in chronological order by month, but within each month everything was jumbled—gas, hotel, meals, office items, phone apps, etc.

"Can you sort by type?" Rowan asked.

Isla frowned. "I wish I had my laptop for this." Still, she was able to enlarge the file enough to be able to see the commands, and then she changed the "sort by" field so the expenses were instead listed by type.

"Great. Now we can address the ones you might have questions about."

"Okay. Accommodations." Isla scrolled to A. There were two hotels listed in Portland in addition to the corporate rental. Isla highlighted their names as places to call.

Next was "Meals." Most of the line items were for less than thirty dollars, but there were a few that stood out as obvious multi-person events.

"But there's no way of knowing if it was a work meeting or not," Isla said.

Rowan was scrolling on his phone. He showed her the calendar on his phone then pointed to a line on hers. "This one is a Saturday night. Do you know if he usually entertained business contacts on weekends?"

Isla shrugged. She wanted to say yes, but the truth was, she didn't know. She hadn't been that interested in the ins and outs of his day-to-day business. At least not any more than he'd been interested in hers. They'd compared notes at the end of the day —high points and low points mostly. But everything in between? Not so much. What married couple did? Especially that last year when they'd been home and up in each other's business ninety percent of the time.

Mav put his crossword puzzle away and joined their little conference. "If there's no way to find out time of day and who he was with, we'll only ever be able to speculate. It's not like we're going to visit every restaurant, right? I think we're better off focusing on things that stand out. One-off expenses."

Isla nodded and went back to the top of the list. Cell phone, Internet, member fees, a printing expense, multiple lines for mileage and parking, a new mouse for his laptop. Everything seemed to be in order. She got to the bottom of the list where the final category was marked "X."

"What does that stand for?" she asked.

Rowan looked. "I think it's expenses that weren't approved."

"'Office,'" Isla read. "I remember he wanted to expense our home office during quarantine but couldn't. Something about that being part of the job description."

"What's that one?" Rowan pointed.

"'Dr. Richards, DDS,'" Isla read.

"DDS?" Mav frowned. "He tried to expense a dentist visit?"

"It was stupid," Isla agreed. "But he cracked his tooth on something during a meal with a client, so he thought he'd give it a shot."

"It's out of the ordinary," Rowan said. "You should highlight it."

Isla did. "I think that's it," she said. "I'm going to go upstairs and pack and call the apartment building in Portland, then we can head out. Is an hour enough time? I'll need to let Louise know when we'll be in Redmond. I promised I'd ride with her to the city."

"Abandoning us, are you?" Mav asked.

"Temporarily."

"Whatever will we do?" Rowan's lips pulled into a cheeky smile.

Isla met his gaze, struck again by the way it made her insides dip. She slapped him lightly on the shoulder, which only made his eyes sparkle more, then she left the table.

Packing took less than half an hour. After that, Isla punched in the number to the apartment building and let the call connect. But while she did get someone on the line, he refused to answer questions over the phone, stating that would be "against our policy." If Isla wanted answers, she'd have to come in and prove she was who she said she was.

Fine, she thought. They had to stop in the city for one night anyway to break up the drive, visit the hotels, and pick up Mav's truck.

It was a sunny day—the first in a while—and the abundant birdsong coming from the trees surrounding the parking lot promised an imminent spring. Isla turned her face to the sun before she got in the car, relishing the warm rays caressing her skin. When she opened her eyes again, Rowan was watching her.

"What?" she asked.

"Nothing," he said. "The look on your face made me think of John Muir."

Isla pursed her lips. "I look like an old-timey explorer?"

"Smooth," Mav said to Rowan as he folded himself into the backseat. "Aren't you supposed to be good with words?"

"No," Rowan hurried to say. "I meant a quote of his. 'In every walk with nature one receives far more than he seeks.' What I meant was—you looked peaceful. Like the life beneath your skin was rejoicing in reaching toward the sky, connecting with its source, relaxing into it."

"Wow." Isla stared at him, then she turned to Mav. "I think he *is* good with words."

"Make fun all you want," Rowan said. "It was just an observation. An expression I hadn't seen on you before."

They both got in the car and buckled, but when Rowan didn't say anything else, Isla let his words take root. For such a long time now, being in the world had caused her nothing but pain, like a blurring filter had obscured the beauty of the backdrop to her life story. But since setting out on this journey, colors had become more vivid, shapes were beginning to crystallize, and she could once again take in more than just the insular physical space she inhabited. And Rowan was right—that was more than she'd sought. But how curious that he'd spotted it in her before anyone else. She wasn't used to being seen that way.

"You're not wrong," Isla said, facing him. "Sorry for teasing."

"No worries." He glanced at her as he slowed for a traffic light. "And for the record, I don't think you look anything like John Muir."

"Ha. I'll take that."

Bend, too, was different beneath a blue sky. Awake and full of promise. Isla might have gotten from it what she could for now, but at least she was leaving with a less bleak image of the town than her mind had conjured over the past two years. She'd had good memories here at one point, and the sun seemed to want to remind her of that.

Thirty minutes later, they pulled up in front of Louise's cousin's house to find her waiting outside the door. Her wide-legged pants and oversized sunglasses made her resemble a displaced hippie, and Isla half expected Rowan to comment on it, but he kept quiet, instead focusing on helping Mav into the front seat Isla had vacated.

"So, what's the plan?" Louise asked.

Isla told her what the apartment manager had said and added that they also needed to stop at the two hotels. "I doubt it will lead anywhere with how many people come and go in a year, let alone two, but I need to at least ask."

"How about Mav and I take the hotels, and you guys take the corporate condo?" Rowan asked. "Then we can decide next steps from there. It'll probably be almost dinner time by then."

"And I'll have to say goodbye." Louise pouted. "It's an early night for me with work tomorrow."

"You'll come up and visit me soon though, right?" Isla said. "We're not that far if you think about it."

Louise's face flushed with emotion. "I'd love that."

Mav stuck his head out the car window. "Are we going to hit the road soon or what?"

"Okay." Isla slapped her palms against her jeans. "Rowan—when we get to Portland, you and Mav show the pictures, ask if they'll share records... Anything that might give us more information."

"Aye aye, captain." Rowan saluted her and rounded the car back to the driver's side. "Are we following you or...?"

Isla threw a smirk over her shoulder as she and Louise reached Louise's white sedan. "I know you probably miss stalking me, but let's drive at our own speeds and touch base when we get there."

Rowan laughed. "Or you can stalk us for a change. See you in Portland."

"He's very cheerful today," Louise said as they got in the car. "Did something happen?"

"Not really." Isla smiled to herself. Maybe there was something in the air.

. . .

They reached Portland in the middle of a conversation about Louise's latest owl find—a woven tapestry, nabbed for a steal—courtesy of another member of their online group who was tapped into the vintage quilt community.

"I'm going to put it in Josie's room," she said after describing it in detail.

"Your niece?"

Louise stopped behind a bus letting out passengers. "Yeah, she'll love it."

"Your sister doesn't mind?"

"Oh. Um, no. She prefers not to spend money on stuff like that."

Isla looked at her friend. "That's so nice of you. You're like everyone's dream aunt."

Louise's cheeks turned pink, but she didn't respond.

They were approaching the city center, so Isla pulled up her phone for directions. "Take a left at the next light, then it's two more blocks and a right."

"Got it." Louise made the first turn. "Did you ever find a replacement for that hummingbird?"

"No." Isla shifted in her seat. They'd stopped only once on the drive north for a bathroom break, and now her legs were getting stiff. "I'd kind of forgotten about it if I'm going to be honest. I might look into it when I get back." There it was again, that feeling of new priorities replacing old ones. Had she really been heartbroken over a porcelain figurine a mere week ago?

"I'll keep an eye out. Oh, there's the building."

Just as they parked, Rowan sent a text saying that they'd gotten nowhere with the first hotel and were heading to the second.

Did you drive straight here? Isla asked. How were they so far ahead?

Mav fell asleep so figured I would. Where are you at?

Just got here. Heading inside.

We'll come meet you when we're done.

The administrative office for Jonah's corporate lodgings was located in a glassed-in space in a corner of the lobby. No one else was around, so Isla went straight up to the door and knocked. The man inside looked up with a start as if he wasn't used to visitors.

"Hi," Isla said, sticking her head inside. "I called earlier today asking about records of my husband's stays here."

"Yes, I remember." The man, whose nametag said "Tom," approached them.

"Here's my driver's license," Isla said, holding it out.

"For...?"

"You said I'd need to prove who I was. I'm Isla Gallagher, and my husband, Jonah Gallagher, used to stay here as one of Rozer & Rozer's employees. I'm particularly interested in any records you might have of visitors."

Tom took the license and glanced at it before handing it back. "Yeah, I don't think that will matter. I checked with the boss, and we don't give out information on our residents."

Isla's stomach sank. "But on the phone you said..."

"That we couldn't give out information over the phone. We also can't give it out in person. That would infringe on the tenant's privacy."

"But her husband is dead." Louise's voice was harder than Isla's. "So there is no privacy to invade."

Tom looked at her. "And you are?"

"A friend," Louise said.

Isla had an idea. "Give us a moment," she said, pulling Louise to the side. When they were out of earshot from Tom, she whispered. "What if you flash him your press badge? We could say you're writing a story and promise him that you won't reveal your source."

Louise blinked at her. "But I... I don't carry that with me." Her gaze flashed to Tom, who was making a poor attempt at pretending not to be watching them. "I don't know. That feels kind of shady."

"It's just asking questions. He could still choose not to respond." She pleaded silently with her friend.

"Fine. But I'll do the talking."

They returned to Tom.

Louise squared her diminutive shoulders and cleared her throat. "I'll level with you, Tom," she said. "I'm a journalist for *Columbia Valley Daily* and we're currently profiling important contributors to the community who were lost prematurely to Covid. But because Mr. Gallagher didn't reside here permanently, we need to confirm the number of days he was here to make sure he meets the cut-off to still be considered a resident and that he wasn't going against company policy by having guests stay."

Isla had to force her jaw not to drop. Every word Louise said was delivered with such authority and conviction that, for a second, she believed the story too.

"All we're asking is to see his records," Louise continued. "No harm, no foul. The dates won't be in the article, and neither will your name. Please. As you can see, it would mean a lot to his widow to have him honored in this way."

Tom turned to meet Isla's eyes, and she nodded in solemn agreement.

"I don't know." Tom scratched his cheek and glanced over his shoulder at the computer on his desk.

"Jonah Gallagher," Isla said. "If you could go three years back. Please?"

Tom huffed. "And my name won't be in the article?"

Louise smiled. "No mention whatsoever."

"Okay, give me one minute."

Louise bumped Isla's hand discreetly in victory as Tom went to print the record.

"That was amazing," Isla said. "You're a very good liar."

"Thanks," Louise whispered back. "Though I'm not sure that's a compliment."

"I don't know how helpful this is going to be, but here you go." Tom handed Isla a sheet of paper from the printer. "That's all I have. Don't make me regret it."

Isla folded it, thanked him profusely, and then she followed Louise out onto the sidewalk. As soon as they were out of Tom's sight, they hunched over the print-out. Isla skimmed the printed rows with her fingertip. When she got to the end, she let her hand drop to her side and looked up.

"Nothing," she said.

Louise scrunched up her nose. "Not nothing. It has the dates on it."

"But that's not what we need. There's no mention of a Gemma or any other visitors for that matter."

"Chances are they don't keep track of that."

"Then what are we here for?" Isla fought the urge to stomp her foot. "I'll be right back."

She shoved the door open again and returned inside, this time entering Tom's office without knocking. She held up her phone with Jonah's picture centered on the screen. "Do you remember him?" she asked, adrenaline fizzing in her veins. "He was a little taller than you, friendly. Pharmaceutical sales rep. The last time he was here was before Christmas a little over two years ago."

"Um..." Tom looked at the picture then up at Isla with rounded eyes. "I've only been working here for fourteen months, ma'am. I'm sorry."

"Oh." Isla deflated. What was she doing? None of this was Tom's fault. "Sorry." She started backing away. "I'm just...

Sorry," she said again, then she spun on her heel and returned outside with flaming cheeks.

To her surprise, Mav and Rowan had joined Louise on the sidewalk. The sun was setting but had warmed the day enough that Rowan had shed his coat, and Mav had unbuttoned his like they'd been out for a spring stroll.

"Anything at the hotel?" Isla asked.

"No." Rowan gestured to the building. "Not here either I hear."

Isla shook her head. "Fuck."

For a long while, none of them spoke, and Isla was about to suggest they go get Mav's car and call it a day when Rowan asked to see the expense report again. Isla pulled it up and handed him her phone.

"What are you thinking?" she asked.

"There was that dentist visit too," Rowan said. "Might as well cross all the Ts."

"Want me to give them a call?" Louise asked, pulling her phone out. "What was the place called again?"

But Rowan was already tapping in something on his screen. "I've got it," he said, putting it up to his ear.

They waited while it connected.

"Yes, hi," Rowan said. "I'm new to the area and wanted to make an appointment for a cleaning." He listened and answered a few questions with, "Mm-hmm. No. Yes earliest possible, and"—he met Isla's gaze—"my friend recommended I see Gemma?" His voice tilted up at the end as if asking a question.

Isla held her breath.

Then Rowan reached out for her shoulder. "Mm-hmm. Mm-hmm. She does have availability? That's great!" A grin spread on his face. "Oh, hold on, you're cutting out. Hello?" He hung up.

"Well, how about that?" Mav asked.

Isla stared at them in disbelief. "There's really a Gemma working there?" If that's where Jonah had met her, it didn't bode well. No way would a dental hygienist call a client at his hotel for tooth-related reasons. Come to think of it, why would anyone who knew him call the hotel? Wouldn't they have had his cell number?

"Where's the office located?" Louise asked.

Rowan checked his phone. "Vancouver, across the river. We could stop by tomorrow morning on our way north."

Despite the many lingering unknowns, Isla allowed herself to be swept up in the general excitement at this new development and agreed that was a good idea. At least they now had a lead.

TWENTY-EIGHT

GEMMA

July, three years ago

It was hot outside. For two weeks straight, temperatures had climbed into the nineties during the day, and to keep bills down, Cheryl refused to set the air conditioning lower than seventy-eight degrees in the apartment. This meant that on a day like today when Gemma was off work, she parked herself on the couch in front of a fan and moved as little as possible.

Cheryl didn't seem as bothered by the heat. She had a new pep in her step since landing a job at the school district food service, distributing meals to families who were taking advantage of the extended summer service. Daytime hours and a purpose had vastly improved her mood, and thereby Gemma's.

On this Monday afternoon, Gemma was on her laptop, having just ended an instant message chat with Jonah, when her aunt's keys jingled in the lock. Jonah hadn't been back since May due to his company putting a temporary halt on travel, and while the kiss had played on repeat in Gemma's mind for weeks after it happened, now so much time had passed that she sometimes wondered if she'd imagined it. That's why these conversations online were so important.

She stared at the last line he'd sent: Can't wait to see you again. Hoping soon.

As Cheryl opened the door, Gemma snapped the laptop shut and put it aside.

"You haven't moved since this morning?" her aunt asked. "It's beautiful outside. If you stay in the shade, it's not bad."

"No thanks." Gemma stretched. "How was work?"

"Busy. Margot's daughter had her baby."

"I don't know who Margot is."

Cheryl ignored her, set her purse on the counter, and disappeared into the bathroom for her daily shower.

Gemma sighed and opened the laptop again. *Soon,* Jonah had said. It couldn't be soon enough. Right now, life was utterly predictable. Dr. Richards had opted to keep his whole staff employed by rotating them on fewer hours, which meant Gemma worked between twenty and twenty-five hours per week, always with Mondays off, and because everything was closed, when she was off, she was at home.

She'd tried getting into running, but the summer heat was less than ideal for such exertion. She'd attempted a sourdough starter and making her own bread but found it too messy—not to mention she kept forgetting to feed the thing. She did read still. Cheryl had bought her the *Bridgerton* series for her birthday a few weeks ago, and she'd devoured them, one after the other. The only problem was that they made her long even more for Jonah's return.

She typed in his name in the search bar as she had so many times before. He wasn't that active on social media, so the results were sparse, but there were a handful of images linked to conferences and the like that at least let her see his face. In one of the photos, he was with *her.* Isla.

Gemma enlarged the image and studied the lanky blonde.

She looked cold, but in a beautiful, Scandinavian kind of way. Big eyes, well-defined eyebrows, a prominent cupid's bow. Jonah had said she was a professor. At the mere thought, Gemma shrank into the couch cushions. To look like that and be smart? Not fair.

Before she could change her mind, she typed in another search, this time for *Isla Gallagher*. She'd resisted it all this time, perhaps sensing the quicksand that would mean stepping onto, but this time curiosity won out. And Isla was much more active online than Jonah. There were several social media accounts (all private), her university profile page, images from conferences where she'd been a speaker, and a couple of podcast episodes she'd been on—one about Degas and one on the very niche topic of figurine collecting. Gemma also found photos other people had tagged her in (that weren't private), published research papers, and even links to old high school and college volleyball stats. It was interesting that Jonah wasn't featured in any of the photos. Did that mean he'd chosen not to go to those events, or had he been the photographer? Or in plainer words—did it say something about Jonah's marriage or not?

Gemma pressed her fingertips into the soft tissue beneath her ribs to stop the roiling inside. Ugh, this was exactly why she'd told herself not to go down this rabbit hole in the first place.

She was considering a new search to find out more when the messenger window popped open at the bottom of the page again. Jonah was back.

You still there? the message read.

Gemma hurried to close the page with Isla's search results as if he'd caught her red-handed. Yes, she typed.

I just got word. I'll be down there a week from Wednesday. Will you be free?

Finally, Gemma thought. Like a bird, she responded. Or I'll have work, but my evenings are open.

Keep them like that, was his response.

Gemma flushed hot at the sound of a cabinet door slamming shut in the bathroom, followed by a curse, and then Cheryl opened the door and stuck her head out. "I left the groceries in the car. Can you run down and get them before everything is ruined? I still need to moisturize."

Gemma glanced at the screen, but it seemed like Jonah was gone again.

"Fine." She set the laptop on the coffee table.

"Thanks. Keys are in my purse."

Jonah's words flashed before her the whole way down to the sauna-like garage and the whole way up again. He was coming back. He longed for her. No matter what uncertainties she had about him and his wife, that had to count for something. People fell out of love, marriages ended—that was a fact of life.

"Put stuff in the fridge too," Cheryl said when Gemma returned. She was walking around barely clothed with a towel still on her head, fanning herself. "God, it's hot."

"I keep telling you." Gemma raised her brow and nodded toward the couch. "Use the fan."

After she'd stuffed the fridge with milk, cheese, and lunch meat that was likely questionable after spending almost an hour in the hot car, she folded up the grocery bag and put it under the sink.

"Want some water?" she asked her aunt.

"Um, sure." Cheryl looked up from Gemma's laptop, which was still open on the table. "What's this?"

"What's what?" Gemma brought two full glasses over to the couch.

"You're still talking to him?"

Gemma froze. Of all the bad decisions she'd made in her life, one of the worst ones must have been telling Cheryl about

Jonah. They'd shared a bottle of wine one night, and Gemma had asked her aunt if she ever missed being in a relationship. Cheryl had never remarried after her husband Herb, Gemma's mom's brother, drank himself to an early death sixteen years ago. Before Gemma knew it, she'd admitted that she'd met someone but that it was complicated. And her aunt had guessed why right away.

"You're seeing him next week?" Cheryl asked now.

Gemma scrambled to come up with a response, but the only one that appeared was the not entirely truthful one, "It's not what you think."

"'My evenings are open.' 'Keep them like that,'" Cheryl read aloud. "Sounds like it's exactly what I think. You're fawning over another woman's man like some love-sick puppy who doesn't know her place."

Gemma pressed her lips together. She wasn't fawning. They had a good time together.

"What happens when he leaves again?" her aunt asked, her voice creeping up in pitch. "When he goes home to his wife? Are you going to be sitting here on the couch on standby? And that's without me even mentioning what this says about his character."

"There's nothing wrong with his character," Gemma snapped. "We enjoy each other's company, that's all."

"Yeah, I bet you do," Cheryl huffed. "For fuck's sake, Gem. Have some self-respect. Don't be like your mother and let a man walk all over you."

Gemma cocked her chin up, the insult shutting down reason. "What's that supposed to mean? She left my dad. She did the right thing."

"After how many years of putting up with his crap? How much of her money going to bail for him? Of our money? God knows Herb could never say no to her." Her expression softened. "After how many black eyes?"

Gemma looked down. She knew the stories, remembered the fights, but thanks to her mother leaving with Gemma when she was four, the violence had never physically touched her. "That's not the same thing and you know it. She did the best she could."

"I'm not saying any of it was her fault." Cheryl adjusted the fluffy pink towel on her head. "I'm saying don't pick the wrong kind of guy when you have a choice."

"Jonah and my dad have nothing in common. Can't you be happy for me that I've met someone I like. Who likes me?"

"Not when it'll end in heartbreak."

"You don't know that."

"I know men."

"He's not like—"

"Not like other men? Ha! Keep telling yourself that." Cheryl stood and ripped the towel from her hair. "But whatever. I'm only your aunt. What do I know? See him, don't see him..." She raised her hands in front of her. "Just... be careful. And whatever you do, don't fall in love with him." She marched off.

Love. Gemma's stomach somersaulted, but she forced it to settle. Who'd said anything about love? She closed her laptop and ran her palm over the smooth cover. Of course she wouldn't fall in love with Jonah. She wasn't stupid, and surely she had more self-control than that. They'd get together, talk, have fun. That was it.

Cheryl didn't have to worry, and when things calmed down tonight, Gemma would tell her as much.

Or better yet, she'd show her.

They met up in a park off the river nine days later after work. The late afternoon meant peak temperatures, but the worst of the heatwave had passed, and Gemma was comfortable in a light-yellow sundress as long as she stayed mostly in the shade. Walking those last hundred yards to where Jonah was waiting for her made her feel like a soda bottle that had been shaken before opening. What would she say? What would he say? Would it feel the same?

He sat on a bench, focused on his phone, but when she was twenty yards away, he raised his head and a bright line of pearly whites stretched across his tan face. His hair was lighter, sun-kissed and messy, and already her fingers itched to run through it. Yes, seeing him set off the same kind of joyous resonance deep within her as it had before. So far so good.

He struck a clean-cut figure in blue shorts and a light gray T-shirt that stretched across his broad shoulders as he stood. "Hello," he said, tucking his phone away as she approached.

She slowed a few yards away, not sure if she should go in for a hug or not. As much as they'd talked online, it had been two months since they'd seen each other in person, and who was to say they'd be able to pick up where they'd left off? Gemma wanted to—that much she was sure of—but what did Jonah want?

"You look gorgeous," he said, letting his eyes skim over her. "Like a sunbeam."

Oh, to hell with it. She walked into his space and reached up, and to her great relief, he welcomed her into his embrace without hesitation. He held her for a long while, and when he finally let go, he met her gaze straight on, hazel eyes made gold by the late afternoon light.

"Hi," she said, trying to make her voice drown out her heartbeat.

He touched her jaw almost like an afterthought then let his hand drop to hers. "It's been too long."

She nodded. His lips were a foot away. All she had to do was bridge it and she'd be home again. But when two joggers passed them, she pushed the impulse away, chastised by the reminder that there were people around.

"Go for a walk?" she asked, tugging on his hand. "I've been in the office all day."

He agreed, and they set off along the river.

"How long are you here for?" Gemma asked.

"Four nights. The company would prefer us to do all our meetings online, but it doesn't work that way. I need to see my docs occasionally or they forget I exist. But it's why I haven't been back sooner. I wanted to." His voice was sincere. "You should know that."

"You made no promises," she said. "And I understand. The whole world is upside down right now anyway."

They walked in silence for a minute to a backdrop of children playing on a nearby play structure.

"Ah," Jonah sighed. "I miss traveling. I don't know how people do it—staying in the same place day in and day out. It makes me want to rip my hair out."

"Would be a shame on such great hair."

That won her another toothy grin. "Was that a compliment?"

"Yes." She stopped and reached up to run her fingers through the strands at his temple. Soft and silky, like she'd known they'd be. "Very touchable."

"Thank you." He dug his front teeth into his lower lip and swung their clasped hands forward so he could kiss the back of hers.

His breath across her skin sent a ripple of excitement up Gemma's spine. She started walking again. "So work is no good?" she asked.

He shrugged. "It's fine. I mean, I always worked from home to a certain extent, but now that I know I have no choice, it's much harder to contend with. Maybe it's because Isla works from home too, so we share the space."

Gemma forced herself not to flinch at the mention of Jonah's wife so he'd continue.

"It used to be just my cat Ulysses and me, so I could sit wherever, but now we have to plan each day down to the hour almost. Who has a meeting when? Who gets the office? Who needs complete silence to grade papers?"

"I think I know the answer to that last one," Gemma said, making her voice light.

"Yeah. I know I shouldn't complain, but there's definitely a difference between spending five hours together in the evening versus all waking hours."

His words struck an elated chord inside Gemma. They shouldn't; she didn't want him to be miserable. But what he was expressing made it easier for her to picture a world where he got his happiness from her and no one else. Not that she was about to admit that aloud.

"That's probably normal," she said. "Maybe eventually you get into a routine. My aunt and I get on each other's nerves quite a bit. Did I tell you she's taken to cleaning the groceries? She literally puts them in the bathtub to wipe them down with a homemade cleaning solution, and then she cleans the tub."

Jonah's eyes widened. "Isla does too. Well, not the bathtub part, but she's been stock-piling antiseptic wipes and cleans everything we bring home. I don't get it."

Another silence stretched. They'd made a loop around the playground and were now headed back toward the parking lot.

"I'm glad you were able to get away," Gemma said eventually. Then she mustered up some courage and added, "For you and for me."

He stopped and pulled her closer. "Are you?" he asked, voice low.

She did a quick scan of their surroundings. There were still people about but no one close enough to make her feel watched. She tilted her face up to his. "Mm-hmm," she said.

He kissed her like he was parched and she was water, his hands sliding up her bare arms, leaving goosebumps in their wake. She clutched his shirt for purchase and parted her lips to allow him in, and when he accepted her invite, the world spun. With the pressure of his lips, the lush strokes of his tongue, his entangled caress through her hair, Gemma was launched into freefall, only staying upright but for her hold on him. His scent cocooned her and spiked the air like a potion designed to incite craving, and it was only with the greatest willpower she finally allowed him to retreat enough that they could again breathe separately.

Jonah's gaze was wild and his lips flushed as he stared down at her. "You're so beautiful," he said, this time wrapping a finger around a lock of her hair and releasing it against her chest. Something pained swept across his face. "I want you so much," he whispered with a puff of air. "I know I shouldn't, but I do."

She kissed him again, softer this time, resting her palm against his cheek. "Then have me," she whispered back.

It was inevitable, this thing she felt for him. Fate.

And as they rode the elevator up to his hotel room a little later, she knew that even if, right then, someone would have told her he'd never truly be hers, she wouldn't get off. She would take what she could get, whatever was on offer, and she would cherish it. And right now, the offer was paradise.

TWENTY-NINE
MAVERICK

Spokane, October 1, 1953

Darling Cass,

It has been three months to the day since that first afternoon in the park. I think about it daily—how you walked toward me in your polka-dotted dress, shining brighter than the sun itself. That was the best day of my life, and saying goodbye five weeks ago was the worst. But don't you fret. It's a temporary hitch, and it warms my heart to know you are waiting for me to return.

I am still on the lookout for a new job back in Seattle, but so far I've had little luck. Thank goodness Mama didn't mind one bit keeping Pip with her. Now that I know sales is not my cup of tea, my options are somewhat more limited. In the meantime, I will cruise around our beautiful state in this delivery truck, thinking of you no matter where I am, and trying to count my blessings. Sad to say many of the returned veterans are worse off. But I am darn proud that you've already snagged a job at the hospital—just like I foresaw. Well done, my darling!

I knew it would pain me to be away from you but not how much. Believe me when I say this past summer with you was the time of my life. When I close my eyes, I see those baby blues of yours looking up at me, those rosy cheeks and witty lips, and in the hush of the night, it is your sweet voice I hear. I dream often of your soft embrace. Cass—you have stirred something in me and made me a new man. I've got to get back west. I've just got to!

Writing those words now, I am overcome with emotion. Were we not separated by half the world for too long? And here I am and there you are. It ain't right.

No, I hereby solemnly swear that I will be back in the city before the snow seals off the passes. I will take whatever job comes my way and once more be in your arms. We'll make Christmas outshine summer with our love. Yes, I said it. I love you. And I cannot wait to see you again.

My heart is yours,

Mav

THIRTY

ISLA

Present day

Good luck today and let me know how it goes, Louise texted Isla in the morning.

Isla sent her a thumbs up. Her friend had left them after dinner the night before since she had to go home and back to work, but it was good to know she was still thinking of them. Isla certainly hadn't done much else for most of the night. Short bouts of shallow sleep had been interspersed by longer intervals of rumination, and at first light, she'd given up and taken a long shower.

Breakfast? she texted Rowan at seven thirty, not expecting a response, but to her surprise, he texted back after only a few minutes that he'd meet her downstairs in ten.

"Mav is still getting ready," he said when he sat down at her table. "He's surprisingly particular about his morning routine." He nodded *yes* to the server offering coffee then sat back in his chair. "Did you get any sleep?"

"I'll take a refill please," Isla told the server. To Rowan she said, "Second cup in ten minutes. Does that answer your question?"

"That bad, huh?"

Isla stirred sweetener into her cup. "I'm just nervous. What if it's her? What if it isn't her? If it is her, what does that mean? What do I say?"

"Mm." Rowan brought his cup to his lips and blew on the dark surface. "When you and Mav decided to go on this trip, Gemma wasn't on your radar at all, right?"

"Right."

"What were you hoping this would lead to?" He gestured around them. "I mean, I know you wanted to find out how it happened, but... Eyewitnesses? Someone to blame? Returning memories?"

"Can I pick all of the above?" Isla asked. "Or any one of them. Anything is better than nothing."

When she thought back to the weeks and months leading up to meeting Mav, the image most deeply ingrained in her mind was a snapshot of her on the living room floor watching the wedding video and Mom turning it off. The wedding march then a black screen. The bouquet toss then a black screen. Almost like they'd been playing a game where no one could win. The worst outcome of this trip would be if she went home and rolled that die again.

She lifted her cup, then changed her mind and set it back down. "When I was eight, I was afraid of the dark. I still don't know why, but every night I would obsess about what might be in my closet or under my bed or outside the window, and for a full year, my parents had to sit with me until I fell asleep. My drawings had monsters, my stories had perilous situations, and the more they told me not to think about that stuff, the more I did. But then that summer, my parents went on a trip with friends for a week while I stayed with my grandparents, and

Nana had no patience for spending hours at my bedside every night. She had her shows and whatnot.

"So my second evening there, she and Pop-Pop announced we were going on an adventure to catch moonlight for night cookies, and it required going into the woods. I protested at first, but they put fairy lights in jars to lead the way and made it sound so magical that eventually I gave in. Plus, I had a soft spot for cookies." Isla smiled. "We walked across the field and past the tree line, and every so often, one of them would direct my attention to a rock or a plant or an animal print and ask me questions about how the dark made them different or the same as during the day. And by the end of it, I was running ahead and pointing out things to them."

"What about the cookies?"

"We baked them by candlelight when we got back. Nana pretended to have caught some moonlight in a jar—I'm sure it was just sugar with decorative glitter mixed in—and we ate them on the porch while listening to the rustling of animals in the growth around the house and guessing what they were. After that night, I wasn't scared of the dark anymore because I'd gotten to know it well enough to be able to set it aside and focus on other things." Isla paused to have a sip of her coffee then tucked her hands between her legs. "But with Jonah's death, there's been nothing concrete for me to confront. Like you said—no eyewitness accounts to offer facts, no culprits to hold responsible other than myself, no memories to explain all the things that made no sense."

"Nothing to let you know it enough to be able to set it aside."

Isla nodded. "And I'm sure eventually I'd have outgrown my fear of the dark even if that evening had never happened, just like time heals wounds when we lose someone, but in this case, I don't want to wait any longer. I can't. I have a job to get back to. I need to move and be able to live alone."

"You need to live. Period."

The tension in Isla's shoulders from tossing all night eased at Rowan's earnest perception of her. "Yes." She sighed. "I need to live. So all that to say—I was hoping this would lead to night cookies. I wanted to walk into the dark of my mind and light things up, find them, examine them, understand them. And then I wanted to tuck them away."

"But you do know more now. You know you were driving because Jonah was drunk and that you probably took a wrong turn at a roundabout, which led you to end up far south."

The dining room was starting to fill up, so Isla waited to respond until an older couple had passed by their table farther into the space.

"That only means I've made it halfway across the trail through the field. But what about behind the big oak tree or under the large rock? What about in the closet?"

"There are still questions that keep you stuck," Rowan guessed. He shifted in his seat and crossed one long leg over the other. "That's why this Gemma person feels high stakes. But where does she fit into your story? Is she a monster or a jar of fairy lights? She can't help you remember, so it's either she's to blame or she knows something. Or neither, I suppose."

The coffee sloshed like a frothy swell inside Isla's stomach, so when the server passed, she asked for an order of the home-made scones. "Do you want anything?" she asked Rowan.

"I'll have the same," he said. "Thanks."

Isla looked at her watch. Still only barely past eight. The dentist's office didn't open until nine thirty.

"I'm not sure how she fits," she said. "In an ideal world, going to Bend would have triggered everything to come back. Just *whoosh*." She swept her hands past her head. "Since it didn't, the second best would be if someone talked to Jonah or me that weekend. I know I didn't call or text anyone. I still have my phone, and we've interviewed all of freaking Bend. So that leaves Jonah. If Gemma knew him—or if she was there—I want to know."

Rowan adjusted the knife next to his napkin with his forefinger. "And if he had an affair with her?"

Isla had pictured a whole future with Jonah. Sunday morning mimosas, quoting cheesy movie lines to each other well into old age, one day traveling to Greece, Scotland, maybe Australia even. She'd wanted him to be the father of her future children and knew he'd have made a great one. They had loved each other—she knew that as certain as day follows night. But no marriage was perfect, and quarantine had been an odd time for everyone. "Like I said, at this point, any information is better than no information. I just want the dark to make sense again. At least an affair would be something concrete to work through."

Rowan moved his napkin off the table to allow the server to place a plate in front of him. "Maybe you're right."

Isla did the same and dug into her first scone as soon as the server left. It was still warm from the oven.

"Ah, there's Mav." Rowan waved. Then he pulled out the chair next to him. "All snazzed up for the ladies now?" he asked when Mav reached them.

"Very funny." Mav sat and placed his napkin in his lap. "Nothing wrong with looking presentable." He wore a gray V-neck sweater over a collared dress shirt, and dark slacks. His chin was impeccably shaven and his sparse white hair combed neatly at his temples. "How are we this morning?" He patted Isla's hand across the table.

"Better now." Isla exchanged a private look with Rowan. Deep diving into her childhood had helped clarify today's stakes for her. The worst thing that could happen would not be to find out Jonah had cheated but that Gemma knew nothing.

. . .

"Are you sure you're okay to drive again?" Isla asked Mav on their way to the parking lot after checking out.

Rowan had needed gas for his car so he'd already left but would meet up with them outside the dentist's office.

"Mm-hmm, yes." Mav hoisted his bag over the curb. "I drove it back from Rowan's friend's house, didn't I?"

"Because we have quite a distance to cover today with the stops in Vancouver and Yelm." They'd stay another night in Olympia like they had on the way down, but since Mav's incident, Isla hadn't made the mistake of forgetting his age. "If you need more rest..."

"Oh hush." Mav shot her a heavy glare as they approached the truck. He unlocked it, and they put their bags on the flatbed.

But after he'd stuck the key in the ignition, he paused instead of reaching for his seatbelt.

"What is it?" Isla asked. "Do you need directions? I have them here." She held up her phone.

"You know," Mav said, "maybe I am feeling a little light-headed after all."

"You are?"

"Yes. I think so." He blinked at her, the glint in his eyes countering what he was saying.

Isla studied him. "Should I call Rowan? Do you think you need a doctor?"

"Oh no, this is an age thing. Ninety years of walking makes a body tired."

"Okay..." Breakfast had run longer than she'd intended so by her internal clock, they were already behind schedule. The dentist's office would be opening in a few minutes, and it was a thirty-minute drive give or take depending on traffic. "Maybe I'll let him know we'll be running late then?"

"Or..." Mav rolled his fingers against the steering wheel. "Maybe you could drive?" He turned to face her.

"Me?"

"It's not that far. And if I feel better in a minute, we could pull over and switch."

Isla fought against the protest inside her. She couldn't drive. She had decided many months ago that she'd never again get behind the wheel. Then again, it would be the fastest way to get to Vancouver. To get the truth.

"Do you feel like it might pass soon?" she asked.

Mav put a finger up to his chin as if thinking. "Hard to say. Could be five minutes. Could be the whole morning."

The whole morning?

Mav sucked in air in his cheeks and blew it out. "I suppose we could ask Rowan to come pick us up, but then we'd have to return for the truck later, and that might mean not getting to Olympia until after dark. Plus, I believe it's supposed to rain this afternoon. I'm not sure I'd feel comfortable driving under such conditions. Hmm. What to do? What to do?"

Isla bit down on her lip. Studied the map on her phone. Their destination was a straight shot north on I-5. If she stayed in the right lane, maybe she'd be okay? As far as comfort zones went, she *was* already testing its borders.

"Okay," Isla said.

Mav's eyebrows twitched. "Okay?"

"I'll do it. Let's switch."

Before she could change her mind, she unbuckled and got out. Mav was slower, but soon they'd swapped seats, and Isla put her hands on a steering wheel for the first time in two years, one month, and one day. The cool plastic felt foreign to her palms.

Sensing Mav was watching her, she turned the key, and the engine rumbled to life. She could do this. *Nothing to it.* Gas, brake, signal. At least it was nothing like the sleek crossover she'd driven last. She forced her grip to relax a tad, then she checked her mirrors, put the truck in reverse, and backed out of the parking space.

Rowan was waiting for them when Isla pulled into the lot in front of the strip mall where Dr. Richards' office was located. The drive had been uncomplicated, traffic not too bad, and after a few miles, Isla had even asked Mav to put on some music. But after she'd parked and turned off the engine, a wave of heat still rolled through her as the knot between her shoulder blades released. She'd done it—this thing that a week ago had seemed as impossible as taking flight. She'd really done it.

Rowan opened the door for her, which was good since her hand was trembling.

"You drove?" he asked, bafflement etched on his face. "That's fantastic."

She jumped out. "Mav was a little dizzy, so I didn't have much of a choice."

"Dizzy?" Rowan watched Mav's head become visible over the roof of the car.

Mav smiled. "Nothing to worry about."

"Is that so?"

"Feeling much better now."

Rowan chuckled then mumbled something under his breath that sounded like, "I bet you do."

Isla was too caught up in her own thoughts to analyze their exchange, because here they were. Here *she* was, about to meet Gemma.

"I think I want to go in alone," she said. "Do you mind?"

"We'll wait here," Mav said. "Take your time."

No time like the present.

Isla approached the building as if zombies might come pouring out of it, scanning past a daycare center, a drycleaner, and a greeting card store before her eyes fixed on the black lettering in the dentist's window that announced that walk-ins were welcome to get "The smile you always wanted."

She took a deep breath and went inside.

The waiting room was small but neat with several blue

chairs and an upholstered window seat. The woman at the counter finished what she was typing on the computer before addressing Isla.

"Can I help you?"

Isla stepped closer. "Um, hi." She looked around, pausing on a built-in aquarium in one wall. "I was..." She shifted her stance. "Hi. I'm here for, um, Gemma."

"Okay." The woman adjusted her screen. "Do you have an appointment?"

"No. Not today. My husband did. I just had a question. If she's here." Isla forced herself to smile even though all the blood in her body felt like it was stuck in her feet. She might actually have to sit down.

"Oh, okay." The receptionist's chipper tone dragged a little. "Let me go check, all right? One moment."

Isla grabbed on to the counter. This was it.

The fish swam round and round in their tank—their fluttering fins mirrored in Isla's stomach. The second hand on the wall clock slowed.

Then, finally, footsteps approached on the other side of the door.

THIRTY-ONE

GEMMA

September, two and a half years ago

Gemma had always considered herself a patient person. Growing up, she and her mom had lived hand to mouth for many years after leaving her dad, with her mom often working multiple jobs, so Gemma had grown used to waiting. Waiting for her mom to come home. Waiting for money saved up so she could get that pair of jeans she wanted. Waiting to be picked up from soccer and theater rehearsals. Waiting for bureaucracy to work itself out so they could get subsidized housing. Waiting to be old enough to make her own decisions.

To her credit, her mom had kept the cogs of their lives moving steadily until she passed, which did result in a predictable, forward motion. But with rusted gears, progress was often slow, and for a long time, that was all Gemma had known. Consequently, she'd honed the trait of patience, and many times in her life, it had served her well.

But with Jonah she'd come undone.

This stupid pandemic, she thought as she moved laundry from the washer to the drier, flinging wet socks around her in her haste to be done. Not that she had more pressing things to do. It was Saturday and she had no plans. Again.

His stupid company.

She'd known when she'd left his bed in July that it might be a while before he could come back, but two months?

At first, she'd been fine. They'd texted and spoken on the phone when they could, and in late July, his wife had left to go on vacation to Eastern Washington with friends for a week, so they'd been able to do video calls too. Gemma had toyed with the idea of driving up there, but in the end, she hadn't even brought it up for fear of seeming clingy. This was hard for him. She could tell. And she hadn't wanted to make it worse.

It was a small consolation that Jonah expressed similar frustration about being stuck at home.

"We barely talk," he'd said last night, referring to his wife. "We coexist and each day is the same. Like Groundhog Day. It's no one's fault, but it doesn't feel like living. I'm losing my mind."

His confession hadn't landed as softly inside Gemma as she might have expected—almost like she'd been told a secret she had no business knowing about an old friend she'd once cared about. She'd opened the window and let the evening soothe the odd sensation, reminding herself relationships were messy and no one was perfect. Then she'd told him what she'd do to mix things up when she saw him again, and when they'd hung up, she'd had to take an extra-long, cold shower.

Not that it had helped. She was still pent up and distracted as she punched the buttons to turn on the drier. She swore under her breath when she closed the folding door to the closet that held the laundry machines in their bathroom.

"Got any plans tonight?" Cheryl asked from the couch in the living room.

"Does anyone have plans anymore?" Gemma snapped.

"Well, I'm meeting up with Cindy and Barb from work.

We're doing driveway happy hour at Barb's house since it's nice out. Bring your own lawn chair—that sort of thing."

"Good for you," Gemma muttered.

Cheryl stared at her from across the room. "Did something crawl up your behind today?"

"No." Gemma opened the fridge and considered her options. Still water or sparkling water. When she closed the door again, her aunt was right there on the other side. "Ah!" Gemma jumped.

"Sorry, didn't mean to scare you." Cheryl leaned against the counter and crossed her arms. "What about the apps?" she asked.

Gemma opened her seltzer. "Apps?"

"For dating."

"Cher, come on." Gemma rounded the peninsula and continued into the living room.

Her aunt followed. "No, I will not 'come on.' You're twenty-seven, you have a good job, you're beautiful, and kind, and smart. You're a catch."

Despite her mood, there was a slight thawing inside Gemma at her aunt's praise.

"So why the hell are you wasting yourself on a married man? Nothing good can come of this."

The thaw froze again, and Gemma suppressed a growl as she spun around in front of the balcony door. "You don't know that. And you don't know Jonah."

"Once a cheater, always a cheater." Cheryl sat back down in her spot.

"No." It wasn't like that. The feelings were real. But how could she get her aunt to understand?

Gemma scanned the room, landing on a studio portrait of her and her mother from when she was about five that she'd snuck in between Cheryl's wedding portrait and a picture of Cheryl, Herb, and the dog they'd had when Gemma was little.

"So no matter if it's the wrong match, you think people should stay with their partner then? Seems hypocritical when you've said you think my mom should have left my dad sooner."

Cheryl sighed. "Of course not. But there's a right way to go about it and a wrong way. And this isn't right." She paused briefly. "Which you know."

Gemma did. But she was pretty good at not thinking about it most of the time, and it helped that she wasn't the one committing the transgression. Whatever Jonah's reasons were, who was she to judge? She wanted him to be happy, and he'd been happy when they were together.

"He's not going to leave her," Cheryl mumbled.

Gemma cocked her chin up. "He might."

"And you'll get hurt." Her aunt's eyes softened with all the affection of a surrogate parent. "You deserve better. But if you can't see that, I can't help you."

That wave of frustration that barely allowed itself to be contained these days washed over Gemma again. "I don't need your help. I need your support."

"Of course I support you. But we have different ways of defining what that means right now."

Gemma threw her hands in the air and stomped off. "I'm going for a walk," she said.

Cheryl's voice trailed her out the door. "Enjoy the fresh air."

Ugh, it was so annoying, this pragmatic, healthy, sociable version of her aunt. Where was the discontented, night-dwelling commiserator when she needed her?

As soon as the thought had crossed her mind, Gemma's cheeks heated. She wasn't being fair, and she *was* happy Cheryl had turned things around in this way. She pulled out her phone and sent her a quick, *Sorry.*

I know, Gem, was her aunt's response, which lodged a thick knot in Gemma's throat.

She walked to the park two blocks away and found a bench to sit on as the afternoon wore on. Jonah had to come soon, she told herself, that unfamiliar impatience bubbling hot through her veins. There would be no other remedy to her state of mind.

I miss you, she texted him.

I miss you more, he texted her the next day.

And then, as if the words had been an incantation, on Monday they finally received the news they'd been waiting for.

She'd got him for three weeks this time.

Jonah's company had put off training new sales reps for the past six months, but now they had several openings to fill since many people had quit or moved during quarantine. Jonah had volunteered to lead six small in-person training sessions on sales techniques at the regional offices to complement the virtual modules that covered product knowledge.

The first evening he was back, Gemma stood outside the door to his corporate condo, the hallway stretching empty in both directions and the air trembling with suspended anticipation. She smoothed down her hair, adjusted the neckline of her top, closed her eyes for a beat, then knocked.

He opened wearing a navy Henley, gray sweats, and a smile that reflected the same relief coursing through Gemma. She flung herself around his neck, and he held on, kicking the door closed with his foot before he carried her inside.

Because it was a work night, she didn't stay over, and she went home to sleep the two following nights too, but on the fourth night, when the credits for the movie they'd been watching rolled, he hugged her close on the couch, her back to his chest, and nuzzled into her neck.

"I want you to stay tonight," he said. "Will you? We can have breakfast together."

His lips teased the skin beneath her ear, sending fiery

tendrils down her arm and back, and making her giggle. She twisted in his arms to look at him. He was wearing a pair of black-rimmed glasses that he claimed to only need for movies and the like, but now she lifted them off his nose and raised her chin for a kiss.

He was quick to oblige, his hand finding the sensitive skin in the gap between her jeans and top as he worked her lips.

"Yeah, I'll stay," she murmured against him. "But I don't think we'll be getting much sleep."

"Is that so?" He scooted down and helped her turn with a steady grip on her hips so that she came to lie on top of him.

She lifted her head and looked down at him, her arms supporting her on his broad chest. Right then, in that moment, it was just the two of them. No one else between them. How did she get so lucky?

She rolled her hips against his and nodded. "Does that scare you?" she asked.

"Scare me?" He laughed, eyes flashing hot. "I can sleep when I'm old. Bring it on."

She only went home to get the mail and a change of clothes for the next two weeks. During the days, they both worked of course, but once she was out of her scrubs, she drove through changing autumn foliage not to a quiet room in her aunt's apartment but to dinners, movies, walks, and delicious nights with a man she was rapidly falling for. Their time was limited, she knew that, but it also didn't seem to be ending, and that gave her hope. Yes, he'd have to go back to Bellingham this time, but maybe, possibly, some day in the future...

One of Jonah's last nights there, they lay wrapped in his sheets, her bare leg slung over his, her hand drawing lazy circles across his chest.

"You always smell so good," he said, bringing a lock of her hair to his nose. "Like apples and vanilla cupcakes."

She tilted her head up and smiled at him. "I would have

thought I'd smell like you right now. In your bed, wrapped in you." She pulled her arm tighter around him.

"No, I mean it. It's mouthwatering." He rolled over onto his side, so they were facing each other.

"You must be hungry," she said, reaching for his cheek and letting one finger trace the stubble along his jaw.

He closed his eyes, which made her bolder, painting patterns all across his features. He was so beautiful like this. Open, vulnerable, hers.

"Jonah," she said, her heart thrumming.

"Mm-hmm." His eyelids fluttered, but he didn't open them.

She bit her lip. "What happens next?"

"Oh, you'll have to give me a little longer," he said, a devilish smile tugging at his lips. "I'm still spent."

Her hand stilled. "No, I mean after you leave."

His eyes opened, dark wells in the pale moonlight falling through the window. He reached up and covered her hand with his, then brought her fingers to his lips. "Then we'll talk on the phone again. And I'll be back at some point."

She gave a little nod and swallowed against the tightness in her throat. "I wish you didn't have to go," she whispered. "I think I'm falling—"

He kissed her, a soft, warm brushing that ended with a gentle tug on her bottom lip. "Don't say it."

"Even if it's true?"

He kissed her again—only a peck this time. A brush of his nose against hers. His breath smelled faintly of the chocolate cheesecake they'd shared earlier. "You know it's not that simple. No one plans for this kind of thing to happen. And you know I have more than myself to worry about." He rushed through the last sentence.

Gemma knew she should stop. Take a hint. But Pandora's box had already been opened. "Do you not have feelings for me?"

"Gemma..." He rolled onto his back and brought one hand to his forehead. Then he tipped his head to face her again. "Of course I do. You're amazing. More than amazing. I can't remember the last time I felt this... content." He found her hand and squeezed it. "And I don't want talking about it to break the magic. Don't you see? There's a lot of stuff I need to... figure out. You know."

She didn't know. He hadn't told her, so how could she? But when he looked at her like this, she knew he was telling the truth. He wanted to be with her. So maybe if she gave him space, he'd come to the right conclusion and leave Isla. Gemma would be able to tell Cheryl "I told you so," and she and Jonah would live happily ever after.

And Isla? her conscience asked silently. Gemma's chest tightened, but she forced in a breath. Isla would be better off free, she thought. Their marriage was clearly not good, so maybe Isla was moving on at this very moment, too. Wasn't that likely even? That Jonah *and* Isla had "stuff to figure out"? Who knew—if they were on the same page, that probably wouldn't take very long.

"Yeah, I get it," Gemma said, snuggling closer.

"Yeah?" He swept the hair off her forehead and brushed his lips across it. "Don't worry. I'm sure regular travel will start up again soon and you'll be sick of me, you'll see me so much."

"Not possible." She tugged at his side to pull him on top of her. Maybe he was right and there were better things they could spend their limited time on than talking. "Now"—she scooted her hips to get comfortable beneath his weight—"how's that stamina of yours? Still spent?"

He dove down to press a string of kisses across her collarbone. "Something tells me you're about to find out."

THIRTY-TWO

ISLA

Present day

Isla held her breath as the door to the inner sanctum of the dentist's office opened, and the receptionist returned. She had her introduction ready, her expression set to neutral, and she was ready to face whoever this woman turned out to be.

What she wasn't ready for was the receptionist to appear alone.

"Sorry, I'm temping so I had to double-check," she said. "Unfortunately, Gemma doesn't work Tuesdays and Wednesdays. But I can take a message and have her get back to you on Thursday?"

Isla's tongue lodged itself against the roof of her mouth. Her gaze flicked to the closed door. "Are you sure?" she asked.

The receptionist gave a small laugh. "Yes, quite sure." She paused for a beat. "Um, what's this about? Did you want to schedule an appointment?"

"No."

The small blue fish was lapping the bigger yellow one as if

teasing it, and when it reacted, the small one scurried off behind the plastic shipwreck. Just out of reach...

I know how you feel, yellow fish.

"I guess I'll call back," Isla said. "Thanks."

She hurried outside to where Rowan and Mav were waiting, and when she reached them, her legs gave out, and she crouched by the side of Rowan's car to make the world stop spinning.

"What happened?" Mav asked somewhere above her.

Rowan squatted beside her and put his hand on her arm. "Are you okay?"

Isla held a hand out in front of her to watch it tremble. "Fuck," she whispered. She looked up. "She wasn't there."

"What?" Mav frowned.

"She doesn't work Tuesdays and Wednesdays. And I promised Mom I'd be home by Wednesday night." She rolled back on her heels and sat down on the ground. The asphalt was dry but cold, the chill seeping through her jeans in an instant. She didn't care.

Rowan shook his head. "I can't believe this."

Isla leaned back against the car. "And yet it's true."

A subdued silence settled between them, with steady traffic on the road next to the parking lot contributing a never-ending backdrop of braking and accelerating as the traffic lights changed and changed again.

Finally, Rowan stuck his hand out to Isla. "You should get off the ground."

She considered it for a second before she accepted his offer and was hoisted to her feet. Then she brushed her hands off on her jeans and rolled her neck.

"Oh well," she said. "I've done what Nana said. I've looked around. But at this point it kind of feels like the universe doesn't want me to find this woman."

"Right now," Mav said. "We can return some other time. Make an appointment."

Isla scoffed. "I guess."

"Or..." Rowan held up a finger. "What about Louise? She could come back Thursday."

Isla stared at him. *Of course. Louise!* How could she have forgotten her friend already? Hope sprouted anew inside Isla. "I'll call her right now. All she has to do is ask questions, and we know she's good at that."

Louise picked up after the second beep. "Hello?"

At the sound of her friend's voice, Isla hurried to explain the situation. "So I'm not sure how far from Vancouver you are, but is there any chance you could get here on Thursday and see if you can talk to her? I know you have work and everything, but you're literally my last chance."

Louise was silent for a moment. "Thursday... Let me check."

Isla's toes tapped the sidewalk. *Come on.*

"Um, yeah. I should be able to do that," Louise said. "It shouldn't be a problem."

Isla showed Mav and Rowan a thumbs up. "I need to know if it's her. The Gemma from the note. Did she know Jonah? And if so, how, and what does she know about that weekend?"

"Can she take a picture?" Rowan whispered. "If it's her I mean. You might want to know."

Isla nodded to him and said into the phone, "And try to get a picture if it's her."

"Picture. Got it."

"Thank you," Isla said. "So much."

"Of course. And sorry today was a bust. I take it you're heading home then?"

"Yeah," Isla said. "Or to Olympia at least. But first we're swinging by Yelm again for Nana's box."

After a few more minutes of talking, they hung up with a

promise to be in touch soon. Isla tucked her phone away and faced Mav and Rowan. "I guess that's it then. Louise has this covered, and as far as I can see, that's the only stone left unturned."

"Ready to go home?" Mav asked.

"I wish I could say I got what I came for, but..." Isla shrugged. "At least I tried."

"I'm very proud of you." Mav patted her shoulder.

"And it's not over," Rowan reminded them. "Who knows what Louise will find come Thursday? It's an intermission."

"Nice try." Isla smiled at him. "But I'm not going to get my hopes up. If anything, maybe what I need to do is learn to live with not knowing, as impossible as that seems.

"One day at a time, right?" Mav held out his hand. "I should be okay to drive now if you prefer."

Rowan chuckled. "Oh, you feel fine now, do you?"

"Are you sure?" Isla pulled the keys from her pocket.

"Actually"—Rowan looked from Mav to Isla—"as the medical professional of the group, I'm going to make the executive decision that Isla drives. Let's not risk it when we don't have to. You had no problem driving here, right?"

Isla met his slate-blue gaze, knowing exactly what they were doing. Neither one of them masked the intentionality behind their innocent expressions well. But while she knew she could say no, she could also tell that their plotting was well-meant. And maybe they were right—it was time for her to get back up in the proverbial saddle. She let out a breath. "Sure, I'll drive. If that's what's best for you, Mav."

"Hm." Mav made a small popping noise with his lips. "Yes, I suppose it is. If Rowan says so."

Rowan slapped his hands together. "Then let's get going, shall we?"

. . .

Isla made it to Nana and Pop-Pop's house without incident. Her back was stiff, and her brain felt scrambled from focusing hard on the road, but she'd done it.

"Thank you," she told Mav after turning the car off.

"For?"

"I know you weren't dizzy. You wanted me to drive."

Mav's eyes creased at the corners. "I'm sure I don't know what you're talking about, my dear."

"Okay." She bit down on a smile. "I'm going to hug you anyway." She reached across the bench seat with her left arm and pulled him to her. "Thank you," she said again.

"Oh." He blinked several times. "But I'm the one who should thank you."

"We'll agree to disagree," Isla said, then she opened the door, because Kim had just stepped out onto the front porch.

"Hello." Kim waved. She was a short woman with curly red hair that popped against her forest-green turtleneck. "How was the drive?"

Isla introduced herself, then Maverick and Rowan.

"Come on in," Kim said. "Nathan is in a meeting but said to say hi. I'm so glad this worked out."

They accepted an offer of coffee, and while Rowan and Mav got comfortable in the kitchen, Kim took Isla on a tour upstairs.

"As you can see, I'm keeping the layout the same as it always was," she said. "Just refreshing some of the drywall, taking down wallpaper, that sort of thing. The bathroom also needed an overhaul."

"Don't tell me you kept the pink toilet all these years?"

Kim laughed. "How could we not?"

They continued into the gable room, which had been Isla's whenever she visited in childhood. Back then, it had been a girly dream with a tall, white-framed bed covered in a crocheted throw beneath the window, dried flowers in homemade vases in the bookcase, and a rolltop desk in the corner. A woven pink, blue, and green rug had covered most of the wooden floor. Right now, it was a jumble of old wallpaper, drywall dust, and paint supplies, but the light was the same, as was the view.

"Gosh, this brings back memories," Isla said. She walked over to the window. "Are there still owls in the big maple?" If there were, she should take a picture for Louise.

"There used to be, but not for a few years now."

Bummer.

"We have hawks though. And tons of hummingbirds in the spring and summer."

"Nana and I would name them. She taught me to tell them apart."

"That's more than I can do. But we do put feeders up."

"That's good." Isla continued her visual tour, but there wasn't much else to see. She paused at the space under the eaves that had been walled in last time she was up here.

"Yeah, that's where I found it," Kim said. "Tucked in through the hatch. It's out here. Follow me."

She walked to a closet off the stair landing and opened the door.

"That was my favorite hiding space when Pop-Pop and I played hide-and-seek," Isla said. "I'm sure he always knew I was in there, but he'd pretend to search forever, and since Nana kept her crafting supplies and photo albums in there, I always found something new to get into. It felt like a life-size treasure chest back then."

"For us it's winter clothes and extra bedding." Kim retreated from the small space with a box in her arms. "Not as exciting perhaps, but our boys played outside most of the time. Out of necessity," she added. "I've loved raising a family here, but the house could at times feel on the small side for our rambunctious brood." She held the box out to Isla. "Anyway, here it is."

While the size of a shoebox, on closer inspection, the

stamped Christmas tree on top of the faded red cardboard suggested the original use had been for gifting. Isla had never seen it before. She ran her fingers over the grainy lid and around the dented corners before gripping the box in both hands. The weight of it was no more substantial than a couple of books.

"You can use the desk over there if you want to open it." Kim pointed to the corner by the bookcase.

Isla hesitated. Part of her wanted to be alone when she opened it to make the matter about Nana, but another part had to know right now. "Maybe a quick peek," she said.

As she set the box down, penciled markings along the side of the lid drew her attention. "Happy Christmas, Embeth. Dec 1949," it said.

Definitely Nana's then. Isla lifted the lid.

A palm-sized tin trinket box sat on top, next to a two-colored paper heart ornament. Isla opened it to find a lock of hair and a note with "Delwyn" written in cursive. "It's my dad's," she said. "Aww."

She moved the heart aside and pulled out a small parcel wrapped in an embroidered handkerchief. Holding it carefully in one palm, she folded back the corners to uncover what was inside, and when the treasure revealed itself, she gasped.

"What is it?" Kim asked.

Isla stared at the delicately painted porcelain as if expecting the hummingbird to breathe in life and take flight any moment. It was Nana's original figurine. The one Isla had tried to buy a copy of at auction. But that also meant Nana must have revisited the box over the years, because this little birdie Isla had seen many times before.

"I've got to show the others," she said, grabbing the box off the desk before hurrying down the stairs.

"You forgot the lid," Kim called after her.

Isla set the box down on the kitchen table between Mav and Rowan. Then she held up the hummingbird. "This is the one," she said, a disbelieving laugh pealing out of her. "The pair to my figurine."

"What are we talking about?" Rowan, who hadn't been privy to the auction drama, asked.

"The same one?" Mav asked.

"Not the one I lost in the auction. This is Nana's actual one. I always assumed she got rid of it when they moved. But I'm not sure why she tucked it away in this box instead of keeping it. Or even giving it to me. Or why she didn't bring the box with her."

"Maybe she forgot she put it there?" Rowan suggested. "I think it's pretty common for older people to tuck things away 'for safekeeping' and then forget. My grandmother did that a lot her last few years."

Isla considered this. "You're probably right. She was starting to show some signs of being confused at the time." Isla glanced at Mav to see what his thoughts might be, but he was intent on the jumble of mementos in the box rather than following the conversation.

"What else is in there?" he asked, pointing with a crooked finger.

Isla lifted the paper heart and the trinket box and peered deeper. "Um... some notebooks and photos mostly."

"You don't want to check?" Mav raised an eyebrow.

"Tonight. I want to take my time with it. After all, this might be what she wanted me to look for."

"Take as much time as you need," Kim said. "I don't mind."

Mav nodded. "See, she doesn't mind."

Isla turned to Kim. "Thank you, but that's okay. But if you have more questions about the house before we go, I'm happy to answer them." As curious as she was about Nana's things, this was still a stranger's home. Kim seemed nice enough, but she hadn't known Nana and didn't know Isla. The box was personal.

After a quick walk around the property where Isla shared

some of her most precious memories of the place, they took their leave.

Isla put the box on the bench seat between Mav and her to keep it safe, and the knowledge that it was there—the subconscious attention it demanded—helped distract Isla enough from the fact that she was driving that she was almost able to relax behind the wheel. Instead of awareness heightening at every bump in the road and every vehicle overtaking them, she imagined telling Nana about the box, thanking her for the hummingbird, and asking her about the hatch and the hiding place.

They reached Olympia late afternoon, and at the first sight of the city, Isla reached over to touch Mav's arm. "Time to wake up. Almost there."

"I wasn't sleeping," he said.

She slowed as traffic grew denser and glanced at him. "You weren't? But you haven't said a peep since Yelm."

"I can be awake and not speak," Mav said. "More people should try that." He looked out the window away from her.

Isla frowned. There was a glumness to his voice she wasn't used to hearing. "Are you feeling all right? Should I call Rowan?"

It took him a moment to react, but then he shook his head, his lips stretching into a thin smile that didn't reach his eyes. "I'm fine. A little tired perhaps, but fine. Got a few things on my mind, that's all. Not to worry."

Traffic picked up again, so Isla was forced to shift her attention away from him after that. She'd talk to Rowan whether Mav liked it or not, she decided. After what happened in Portland, they couldn't be too cautious, and there was something off about her friend.

She pulled Rowan aside as soon as they'd parked at the hotel and shared her observations. "Maybe you can check him out after we get our rooms. And I don't think we should go out to dinner. I could run out and pick up a pizza if you want. Give you time to... do whatever you do as a nurse. And maybe you two should share a room tonight too."

Rowan agreed that was a good plan.

Mav barely seemed to register that Rowan changed his reservation to a double occupancy at the front desk, which further deepened Isla's concern. Only the fact that she knew he was in good hands with Rowan allowed her enough peace of mind to leave the hotel to get food.

Since Mav and Rowan had a suite, she brought the pizza there after stopping in her room to get Nana's box. It might cheer Mav up, since he'd been curious about it, she reasoned.

"Who's hungry?" she called after Rowan let her in.

Mav was on a small couch watching a documentary about the French Revolution but turned down the sound at the sight of her. "Very much so," he said. "Thank you, thank you. What did you get?"

As Mav helped himself to a slice, Isla posed a silent question to Rowan with a pointed nod toward Mav's back. The responding thumbs up made her breathe easier. Mav was okay.

Between the three of them, they finished almost the whole pizza while Rowan entertained them with stories of a misfortune-filled road trip in college that had ended with him barefoot in the Arizona desert.

"Needless to say, I never go anywhere without an extra pair of shoes or two with me since then. In fact, I keep a pair of flip-flops in my car at all times."

"You do not." Isla wiped her hands on a paper towel.

"He does," Mav said. "In the trunk."

Rowan got up and disappeared into the bedroom. When he returned, he had a beat-up pair of running shoes in his hands. "Spare-pair number two in case you still don't believe me." He sat back down and placed the shoes on the floor, then he put one foot on top of the opposite knee. "These puppies will forever be protected against the elements as long as I have something to say about it. Always ready. Always prepared." He grinned.

"Such a boy scout," Isla said, laughing, but though she was teasing, she also recognized the truth in his assessment of himself. He was always prepared. Maybe that's why his company was so comfortable—a steady presence, free of the unpredictable. And for the first time, she wondered when, if at all, she'd see him again once they were back home. It would be such a shame if she didn't.

After clearing the napkins they'd used as plates off the table, she grabbed Nana's box from the stool by the front door.

"Speaking of shoes, but not really since it's not actually a shoebox." She set it down in the middle of the table.

"I thought you wanted to go through it alone," Mav said, sitting back in his chair.

Isla shrugged and lifted the lid. "You seemed curious, and I don't mind you guys watching. I just didn't want to do it in front of someone I don't know."

Mav inclined his head toward Rowan. "Do we have time? I believe you said you were hoping to make it an early night."

"Not this early. Let's see what we've got."

Out came the paper heart, the wrapped figurine, and the trinket box again. "This has my dad's hair in it." Isla lifted the small lid to show them. "See. Delwyn."

Mav leaned forward. "It's so dark." He looked up. "I expected it to be blond like yours and your grandparents'."

"Nope, he was the outlier in the family. He was very proud of it too. Not happy with his graying temples once that set in."

One by one, Isla removed the assortment of items from within. Local news clippings of her dad's achievements in academics and sports, pretty shells and marbles, photos of Nana and some friends on a beach, a silver rattle with a blue bow, a prayer book and rosary that suggested she might have grown up Catholic even though Isla had never known her as such, a medal, a rolled-up length of lace, several gold pins with snake-and-wing motifs.

"Hey, I've got one of those too," Rowan said, picking one up.

Mav cleared his throat. "Is that it?"

"Some notebooks." Isla opened one and flipped through the pages. "Looks like she used these to keep track of expenses. Nothing but a bunch of numbers." She put it down and reached for another one, but when her fingertips touched something hard and smooth underneath, she pulled the box closer and peered into it. "Huh, there's something else..."

She handed Rowan two more notebooks then extracted a wooden case, about eight by four inches, from the bottom of the box. The lid was decorated with engraved flowers and the letters "E.M.C." Isla traced them before opening the lid with a soft "pop."

"It's a stack of letters," she said, pulling out the bundle.

Mav stood. "If you could excuse me for a moment. I need to take my pills."

"Now?" Isla had already untied the string that kept the letters together and had the first envelope in her hand. This was where the real treasure was at. The whole box may be a time capsule, but letters meant real voices from the past. "Can't it wait five minutes?"

Mav shifted his stance as he looked at Rowan. Then he sat back down, an odd expression playing across his face.

Isla pulled a folded page out of the envelope and opened it. She started to read.

THIRTY-THREE

ISLA

Present day

"'*Seattle, March 22, 1954*,'" Isla read. "'*Dear Cass, I must have started writing this letter half a dozen times by now, but whatever words I come up with sound too trite to reflect the truth and then I give up. But I know I owe you an explanation, so since time is running out, here goes.*'"

Cass? Isla flipped over the envelope she was holding and found it to be addressed to Miss Embeth Cassidy. Nana's maiden name rang a faint bell, so she'd probably heard it at some point and then forgotten.

"Sorry, I had to check. I never knew her to go by that nickname," Isla said to Mav and Rowan, who were as intent on her as she was on the letter. "Where was I?"

She found the spot and continued.

"'*I want you to know that I did get both of your last letters. Pretending otherwise would be downright false, and I have never lied to you. Even during our last days together over the holidays, I meant every word I said. I have never felt about anyone the way I*'" *feel about you.'"* Isla swallowed. She hadn't expected the content to be so personal. So... raw.

"*'But things have not exactly been going my way. That job at Bon Marche I had high hopes for? Well, it didn't pan out. And since I got the boot from trucking back in February, I've been scraping by on odd jobs, hoping for a break. I didn't tell you because I was embarrassed. Still am if I'm honest. And I only tell you now so you might understand what my situation was like when you wrote to tell me your news.'"*

What news? Isla thought. A cold pit deepened in her stomach.

"*'At first, I planned to turn things around before responding. With your old man already thinking poorly of me, it felt like the right thing to do. And when that didn't happen, I didn't know what to say. But the truth is over the past few months, reality has swept our grand dreams aside leaving nothing but wishful thinking. I can't support you (or a child for that matter) on love alone, and if we tried, I fear you'd be trapped in a sorry state with me. I couldn't do that to you when you deserve so much better.'"*

Isla looked up when she reached the bottom of the page, the implications of the words settling in. Her poor nana.

"You should continue," Mav said, clasping his hands in his lap.

Isla nodded and turned the page.

"*'So as much as it hurts, this has to be the end of the line for us. When I said I'm out of time, it is because I've signed on as a seaman on a freight ship that will set out tomorrow for Japan. After that, who knows where they'll send me, when or if I'll be back. The best thing you can do is forget about me.'"*

"Oh no." Isla let out a heavy sigh. "*'I have included the last of my paycheck here. For what it's worth, I am truly sorry. Though I don't expect it, I hope one day you will forgive me. Sincerely...'"* Her eyes snagged on the final word on the page, and her head jerked up. "What? '*Sincerely, Maverick?*' Is this a joke?" Her gaze cut from Mav to Rowan and back. When neither of them spoke right away, Isla scanned the last paragraph of the letter again. The writer had gone to sea. The writer whose name was Maverick.

Isla stood up abruptly and paced away from the table before spinning back. She must be missing something. "Why is there a letter from you to my grandmother in this box? That makes no sense."

Mav leaned forward in his chair, his complexion ghostly. "I can explain," he said. "I want to explain. I didn't mean for you to find out like this. Would you sit down?"

"Did one of you tamper with the box? This is a practical joke, right?" Isla could hear her voice rising in pitch, but she had no control over it. It was following the tension surging within her.

"Want me to leave?" Rowan asked Mav.

"No, no. Stay."

"You're both in on it?" Isla grabbed the backrest of her chair and locked them both in her sights. "It's not funny."

"Could you sit?" Mav asked again.

"I don't know. Can I?" Isla shifted from one foot to the other.

Mav placed both palms on the table, his hands trembling. "Please?"

Isla's mind had gone blank because what had Mav said a moment ago? That he didn't mean for her to find out "like this"? That meant there was something to find out. It wasn't a joke.

"Did you send her this letter?" she asked after sitting back down, stabbing at the paper with her index finger.

"I did." Mav's shoulders slumped. "And I'm guessing the others in that stack may well be from me too."

"But... how? Why? You knew her?"

"We met in Korea."

Isla sat back and crossed her arms over her chest. "You're telling me Nana fought in the Korean War? She was a social worker."

"She was a nurse first. And a damn fine one. She saved my life."

Isla's jaws snapped closed. *The nurse who'd convinced the surgeon to give Mav a chance was Nana?*

"And I—" Mav's voice broke. "I loved her."

Rowan put a hand on Mav's shoulder.

Mav patted it. "No, I'm fine." He pulled a handkerchief from his pocket and dabbed at his eyes and nose. Then he addressed Isla again. "I told you I've made many mistakes. Well, here is the biggest one." He gestured to the letter. "I was a coward and a loser, and it's haunted me my whole life."

"But why didn't you tell me?" Isla tried to get him to look at her, but he was intent on the stack of letters. "When you realized who I was and..."

"I knew." He nodded slowly to himself a few times before finally facing her. "I knew when I moved to Port Townsend. It's why I moved there. I signed up for the meal service because I knew you volunteered. I couldn't control your routes though, but I was perhaps a little ornerier with the other delivery girl, hoping that would eventually lead you to me. The fact that you got my account so quickly was a fortuitous turn of events. If you believe in such a thing."

He'd known all along? "You sought me out? And also you owe Serene an apology."

"Fair. But as we've established, I'm old." Mav's shoulders slumped. "I never stopped thinking about Cass and your dad, and I didn't want to go into the hereafter without atonement. But since Delwyn had passed..." Mav dabbed his nose again. "Oh, I was too late for him."

"Dad?" Isla shook her head. "What...?"

Mav reached for the letter. "May I?"

Isla pushed it toward him.

He held the paper carefully as if afraid it would crumble in his hands. "Oof," he sighed. "Such youthful folly."

Isla waited, her mind still churning to try and make sense of what was unfolding.

"Cass and I had spent the holidays together," Mav said. "I'd been doing lumber hauls in Eastern Washington that fall, but I missed her something terrible, so I came home and tried to make it work with a different job and such without much luck. I went back to trucking while pursuing a few other leads, but when she wrote me to say she was expecting, I had just been let go from that job too. I was across the state, had only a few dollars to my name, and was barely turned twenty-one. I wanted it to work out. Trust me, I did. But it wasn't to be."

Isla didn't want to believe her ears. "You abandoned her? She was alone and pregnant, and your answer was to leave the country?"

"Not alone. She had friends and her family, who didn't like me by the way."

Isla scoffed. "I wonder why?"

"Hey now." Rowan got Isla's attention. "It was a long time ago."

Isla glared at him. "You don't seem very surprised by this. You knew too?"

The muscles in Rowan's jaw tightened. "He asked for my help to find out where you'd gone after Bellingham."

"But why?"

"Because you're my granddaughter," Mav said, dropping one hand on the table with a *thwack*. The sound rang out into an otherwise silent room. "That's what I've been trying to explain. Delwyn may have grown up thinking Neil was his father, but the dates don't lie." He pointed to the heading on the letter. "If I'm not mistaken, your dad was born in September of this same year, no?"

September 20 to be exact. Isla leaned her head into her hands and closed her eyes. Neil wasn't her real grandpa? Nana had been pregnant already when they married? Mav was her grandfather?

"How long have you known about me?" she asked after a while.

"Since you were born, my dear. Like I said, your family was never far from my mind."

"And were you ever planning on telling me?"

Mav hesitated. "I hadn't decided. I always aimed to be of help somehow. To make up for what I did."

"Unbelievable," Isla muttered. "As if driving me to Bend would absolve you of that. For all I know, you couldn't care less about what I'm actually trying to do here."

Rowan cocked his head. "Come on, Isla—you don't believe that."

"Of course I care," Mav said, putting more force behind his words. "I care deeply. From the moment you stepped into my apartment, I could feel a kinship. Even before you said your name and confirmed that my eyes weren't lying to me. We've both loved and lost, we've both been at death's door, and we both have ghosts haunting the hallways of our past. I can't help but think Cass wanted us to meet."

"No!" Isla let her objection echo against the walls, then she started putting the items spread on the table back in the box. "You were a coward back then, and you're still a coward now. And a liar. I thought I could trust you. Both of you." She got up and hoisted the box under her arm. "And her name was Embeth."

With that, she stormed out into the hallway where she paused only to get her bearings before jogging to the other end of the floor and her room.

Mav and Rowan had conspired against her. They'd gotten close, had let Isla think she'd found good people who were on her side, had listened to Isla share the most personal part of her life, and all the while they'd kept this secret like a shield between them.

Angry tears stung her eyes as she slumped down on her bed.

As soon as she'd stepped into Mav's apartment that first day, he should have told her the truth, but instead he'd inserted himself into her life to appease his own guilt. How lucky for him that she'd been so broken. He'd made her mystery his mission but not for her sake—for his own—and he'd probably thanked his lucky stars for her misery every day since. What had he been thinking? That he could sweep in and save the day? That she'd be grateful?

Well, he could rethink that. She didn't ever want to see him again.

Isla wiped her cheeks on her sleeve, and as she did, she spotted Mav's car keys on the TV bench. Her bag was still on the floor, unopened. Two seconds later, she'd made her decision and was out the door. There was no way she was going to spend two hours or even fifteen minutes in the same car as either of them tomorrow, and it wasn't that late. Now that she was driving again, she might as well get this last leg over with.

The thought of home, of Mom, of her own bed spurred her on through the dark parking lot past slumbering sedans and SUVs. She'd text Rowan when she got there and let him know. He could come get the truck when they returned. Not that she wanted to see him either—he'd lied too. But some small concession in her mind allowed for the fact that Mav employed him, which gave him less of a choice. Plus, as far as she knew, he'd never abandoned a pregnant girlfriend, which made him marginally better.

There was a moment, right as Isla started the car, when a small voice in her head piped up to point out that this here—her in the driver's seat—couldn't have happened without Mav. It made her tip her forehead against the wheel and let the rumble of the engine transfer to her scalp and neck. Then she glanced at the hotel with its lit-up windows, sucked in a breath, and put the truck in reverse.

THIRTY-FOUR

ISLA

Present day

It was close to midnight when Isla parked Mav's truck in the driveway of Mom's house. Her shoulders ached, and her eyes felt dry and grainy from staying alert during the drive. Traffic hadn't been bad, but there was something about the darkness and the road winding through dense woods that had made her question more than once her decision to leave the others behind.

But now it was over, and she'd made it.

She unlocked the front door as quietly as she could, allowing the familiar scent of jute rug and spring showers fabric softener wash over her, but when a black shadow came for her legs, she let out a small yelp and steadied herself on an entryway table.

"Ulysses," she hissed before she squatted to scoop up the feline. "I missed you too, but we have to be quiet so we don't wake up—"

Light flooded the hallway as Mom flipped the light switch and came storming out, a Louisville slugger at the ready.

"Who's there?" As soon as she saw Isla, she dropped the base-ball bat to her side. "Birdie?"

"Hi, Mom."

"What are you doing here?"

Isla's shoulders slumped. The running and chasing were over. All she wanted was a hug and her bed. She walked into her mom's arms. "I came home early," she said, voice muffled against Mom's robe.

Nancy hugged her tight then held her by the shoulders at arm's-length. "Is everything all right?"

"Can I tell you about it in the morning? I'm really tired."

Her mom let go of her and shuffled over to the hallway window to peer outside. "Where are the others?"

"Still in Olympia."

Mom spun. "You drove?"

Isla nodded. "Ta-da." She let out a wry chuckle. "But seri-ously—can it wait until tomorrow?"

"I guess." Nancy pulled her robe tighter around her. "If you're sure you're okay."

Isla swallowed. *Maybe with a liberal definition of "okay."* "I just need to sleep. I didn't mean to wake you up."

"Do you need anything? Food? Are you hungry?"

Isla needed a lot of things. Her memory to return. To find Gemma. People not to lie to her. But since that was outside the realm of maternal magic, she settled for, "I'll grab something. You go back to bed."

Mom gave Isla's shoulder a tight squeeze, and then she left.

Isla turned the light back off and walked into the dark kitchen with Ulysses meowing at her feet. She shushed him as she tapped the light switch above the stove. The clock on the microwave said 00:08. It was Wednesday. She should probably let Rowan know she'd defected.

After digging through the fridge and finding some hummus and baby carrots, she sat down at the kitchen table, and ate, while staring unseeingly into the murky living room. The emptiness inside her matched the shadows climbing the corners and seeping into the still-life furniture. An emptiness she thought she'd filled with new friends, new meaning, purpose.

"Ow." Isla swatted at her thigh as Ulysses dug his claws into her leg. "What did you do that for?"

Soulful, yellow eyes stared up at her from the floor. "Meow."

"You want a carrot?" Isla asked.

"Meow."

She bit off a piece and put it at the cat's feet. "There you go."

Her introspection interrupted, she pulled out her phone and opened a new message for Rowan. *I'm back home. Took Mav's truck so he'll have to ride with you. FYI.*

She didn't expect him to respond, but within thirty seconds, her phone rattled against the table. *You're joking, right?*

She rolled her eyes. *Hardly in the mood for jokes.* She snapped a picture of Ulysses and sent it.

That could have been taken at any other time.

Was he serious? After what had transpired at the hotel only a few hours earlier, he thought she was sitting here making up stories for fun?

I'll leave the keys on the visor so you can come get it once you're back. Don't bother knocking.

His response was instant. *You're that upset?*

Any normal human would be.

He just wanted to do something nice for you. He didn't know how to tell you.

And you? What's your excuse?

When the response was delayed, Isla texted again. *Thought so. Goodnight.* Then she turned off her phone. She'd done her part and told him where the truck was. It would have to do.

It was either the light or the voices slipping into Isla's room the following day that woke her up. At first, she thought Mom had the TV on, but then she recognized Rowan's baritone and buried herself deeper under her comforter. It was the right thing to do because a minute later, her door opened.

"Birdie?"

The word was muffled by layers of fabric, but Isla could picture her mom's head peeking into the room.

"Are you awake?"

Isla held her breath, listening for footsteps. To her relief, the door closed instead, and a few minutes later, Mav's truck rumbled alive outside.

When she was certain the coast was clear, Isla wrapped herself in an oversized cardigan and made her way to the kitchen. Sun beamed through the windows at an odd angle, which was explained when she spotted the time. Almost 2:30 PM. She'd slept over twelve hours.

She'd just reached for a mug when Nancy rounded the corner from the hallway and pulled up short.

"Oh, you're alive."

Isla filled the mug with water and put it in the microwave. No fancy coffee today. "Just woke up."

"You missed Rowan. He said he'd call later. What a nice guy."

Isla ignored her comment and dug through a drawer for the instant brew. The microwave dinged, and she retrieved the now-steaming mug.

"Birdie?" Her mom leaned a hip against the counter.

Isla stirred the brown powder into the water and watched it dissolve.

"Look at me please."

"What?" Isla put the spoon down and turned, bringing the coffee to her lips. *Too hot.*

Mom tilted her head like a curious puppy. "Don't play me for a fool here. Clearly something happened on the trip. Talk to me."

"Fine," Isla sighed. "Let's sit."

"Does it have to do with Jonah and the crash? Last we talked you said something about the feeling of going off the road. Did you remember something else?"

Isla had deliberately not mentioned Gemma to Mom in case nothing came of that lead. She knew how it looked—Jonah getting a phone message from another woman while on a weekend getaway with his wife—and since he wasn't here to defend himself, that didn't seem fair. "No there's nothing new there," Isla said. "Not really."

"Then what?"

On the wall above the TV was her parents' wedding photo. Bright lighting, bright smiles. In true 1980s' style, her mom's dress had puffed sleeves, and she wore a veil attached to a white floral headband. Her dad was in a black tux and bowtie, and his dark hair skimmed his shoulders in a sleek, feathered style. She tried to see Mav in his features, but aside from his coloring, Dad had always resembled Nana.

"I found something out about Dad and Pop-Pop," Isla began. Then she launched into what the letters in the box had revealed and Mav's deception.

When she finished, Nancy took off her glasses and rubbed

the bridge of her nose. "Neil wasn't Del's dad?" she asked. "All those years I worked alongside Embeth, and never once did she even hint at something like this in her past. Are you sure?"

"I can show you the letters."

"So then Maverick is your grandfather by blood. That's... that's something."

"Yeah," Isla scoffed.

"But"—Mom frowned—"that all happened an awfully long time ago. Both Neil and your dad are gone. And your nana lived a long and happy life."

Isla had a sip of her now drinkable coffee. "Your point being?"

"You're very upset."

"Because they lied."

"Mm, by omission maybe."

Isla put her mug down with a clang. "Whose side are you on? Don't you think Mav, if anyone, should have understood the implications of keeping me in the dark, knowing how I've struggled with not knowing, not remembering? This trip was a quest for answers, and instead he deliberately withheld something this big. Fuck that."

"Language." Mom pursed her lips. "I get it, I do, but maybe if you talk to him, and—"

"No. I don't want to talk to either one of them right now. I want to be left alone." She got up from the table and put her mug away. "I know you mean well, but I'm going back to bed. I've got to call Louise." Her friend was the only one left that she could count on, and tomorrow Gemma would be back in the office. She couldn't let this stuff with Mav distract from that.

"Okay." Mom held up her palms, capitulating. "You have a right to your feelings. I won't interfere."

"Thank you."

Isla reached the doorway and had one foot in the foyer when Nancy spoke again. A timid little "But..."

Isla paused. She should have known that wasn't the end of it. "Yes?"

"I'd advise you not to forget that Maverick is ninety years old. He won't be around forever. And that's all I'll say about that."

Isla bit down on her tongue. *Dammit.*

Back in her room, she texted Louise to see if she could talk, but it seemed work was busy, so eventually she dropped the news in a text. *So Mav and I aren't on speaking terms right now,* she wrote. *Wanted you to know.*

I'm sorry, Louise responded. *That's a lot.*

Finally, someone who understood.

Louise excused herself shortly after that. She had a deadline, and then she would be watching her niece after work, but she promised to call as soon as she'd been to the dentist's office in the morning. Isla would have to make do with that.

As much as she wanted to crawl back under the covers again, she wasn't tired enough for sleep to make sense, but after unpacking her bag, showering, and failing at several attempts to escape into a book, she still ended up on her back across the covers, staring at the ceiling.

Outside the window, the treetops swayed in a coordinated pattern with a hawk circling above, looking for prey. It would be spring soon—a time of rebirth and change that this year, by necessity, included Isla herself. She thought of helping Mom pack up the house, finding a place to live, preparing for the courses she'd have to teach. If she went back to Bellingham as was currently the plan, she'd basically be on the doorstep of Jonah's family. She'd run in to old friends, frequent shops and restaurants that had once been part of a happier life. People would ask questions. So many questions. And she still didn't have the answers she needed to face the past. Everything depended on tomorrow and Gemma knowing something.

That or a miracle that gave Isla her memory back.

But the universe wasn't in a generous mood that week.

Louise called at 9:15 the following morning. Isla answered with a breathless, "Was she there?"

Traffic sounded in the background as if Louise had stepped outside. "Yes." Loud honking came over the line. "Hold on one second." Shuffled footsteps, then the noise muted. Louise coughed. "Um, she was. I talked to her."

"And?" Isla's fingers dug into her phone.

"Isla, I..." Louise paused. "I'm so sorry. She didn't know anyone named Jonah, and she didn't recognize his picture. I wish I had better news."

Isla closed her eyes. Not until then had she realized just how much she'd counted on this for closure. She'd been so sure. Mav had convinced her there was meaning in taking action, Rowan had boosted her spirits, she'd thought Louise would be able to dig behind the scenes, and now it turned out it had all been in vain, and two of her companions had ultimately added insult to injury instead of making things better. What was the point?

Isla hung up and sat for a moment, staring at the phone. Then she climbed back under the covers.

Perhaps that was the problem—there was no point. This was what you got when you killed your husband.

THIRTY-FIVE

GEMMA

December, two years ago

There were flurries in the air on December 15 when Gemma drove home from the mall. She'd long since finished shopping for Cheryl, Sadie and her kid, and her coworkers, but Jonah was coming for the weekend, so today's shopping spree had been all about him.

His long stay in the fall had sustained them for a while. Not that Gemma had enjoyed the separation for even one day, but she'd at least felt secure in his affection despite the distance between them in a way she hadn't before. That feeling had been solidified by near-daily phone conversations since his wife had gone back to working from her office at the university a month ago. On the days Gemma wasn't working, they could be on the phone for two hours straight, and even when she was in the office, she'd call him on her breaks, or they'd text. She wasn't oblivious to the dynamics of this shift in time allotment. More time for her meant less time for his wife. He had a finite number of hours at his disposal after all. Late at night, on more than one occasion, it had stirred up something that she tried very hard not to look too closely at. A general inkling of violating that old sisters-before-misters clause perhaps.

Granted, for the past couple of weeks, their talks had been somewhat shorter, which eased her conscience a little. Jonah had explained that he was always swamped in December in order to meet his "sales quota" or something like that, and since he was driving to Portland on Thursday, he had things to get done. Gemma had done her best not to take it personally, to not be too needy. His work was important to him, and maybe it was good that they got to miss each other a little more for a few days before reuniting.

Shopping for him had helped boost her mood. She'd found him a book by a photographer she knew he admired, a knitted sweater she could picture him wearing while they were snuggled up together watching a movie, and a unique leather-strap bracelet with the word "serendipity" spelled out in metal-stud Morse code. Because how else could she better describe their meeting? What had been the chances of him walking into *her* office of all the ones available in the area?

She'd also bought herself some nice underwear that could reasonably count as another gift for him, and with that mental picture in her mind, she navigated the snow-dusted street home.

Cheryl didn't comment when Gemma brought out wrapping paper and ribbon to wrap the gifts. She had long since given up her fretting, or, as Gemma liked to interpret it, realized her niece was happy and that Jonah was none of her business. This time, when Gemma had told her she'd not be home the coming weekend, Cheryl had merely shaken her head with a muttered, "Your life."

And it was Gemma's life. No one was steering it forward but her. She picked the road. The year was drawing to a close, and considering it had started with heartbreak and quarantine, she thought she'd done pretty well for herself. She was still working, her aunt was in a better place mentally and physically, she'd all but forgotten about Yuri, and she had a wonderful man in her life. Yes, okay—maybe her actions weren't completely innocent, but she trusted Jonah to know what he was doing. And if this continued, next year had the potential to become her best year yet.

The thought made her stomach bounce and loop like the pretty ribbon in her hand, and who would willingly give up a feeling like that?

Jonah ended up getting in late Thursday, which meant Gemma had to mentally adjust to having him to herself for only three nights instead of four. A disappointment, but he'd had a meeting change, and if not for his wife having plans with friends in Seattle for the weekend, he might not have been able to stay even that long. Everything was still good, she told herself, driving to his hotel after work on Friday. That night, they'd make up for lost time, and tomorrow she'd made reservations for them at a nice restaurant as a precursor to exchanging gifts in what she'd coined their "mini-Christmas."

She smiled at the decorated shop windows she passed. The frostbitten trees sparkled in the cool setting sun, and soon she'd be in his arms again. Yes, everything was still better than good.

She stepped harder on the gas pedal to avoid getting stuck at a red light.

He was waiting for her when she got off the elevator and rounded the corner on the third floor. His mussed head stuck out a doorway three rooms down, and as soon as she saw him, she had to resist breaking into a sprint.

Jonah's expression wavered for a split second, but then the creases by his eyes deepened, and his cheeks bunched into that cheeky expression she loved so much. Just seeing him made her blush like she was some kind of innocent Victorian maiden.

"Hi." He held the door open for her as she reached him.

She slipped by him and turned to watch him close the door. Then she flung herself around his neck and buried her face against his shoulder. "Hi."

His hands splayed low on her back as he buried his nose in her hair. She smiled against him then tipped her head back so she could see him.

"I missed you so much," she said, rising on her toes for a kiss.

He didn't immediately take advantage, but when she let her thumb trace his jaw, and her other hand slide into the hair at his nape, something flickered on behind his eyes, and he dove for her lips.

Gemma's favorite ride when she'd worked at the amusement park had been the pirate ship, where, at the top of each swing, gravity ceased to matter. Kissing Jonah did the same thing to her—it suspended her somewhere in the air above herself where she was free to look down, but earthly rules no longer applied. She was flying, unencumbered and light, connected to her physical self only through his hands, his chest, his mouth.

He spun her up against the closet door with a needy gasp, but once she was there, the coolness of the mirror bringing goosebumps to her back, he paused.

Their breaths came in short, synchronized bursts as he loosened his tight grip on her waist and leaned his forehead against hers.

"Let's maybe slow things down a little," he said, voice husky. "I haven't seen you for so long."

Because he was still touching her, Gemma didn't take it as a snub. If anything, the fact that he wanted more than a quick fuck spoke to how serious he was about her.

"I keep thinking it'll be easier, but then you're here and you're so..." His teeth dug into his bottom lip.

Gemma fought a frown, her hands steady, grasping his sides. "That what will be easier?"

He looked away. "To resist? I don't know."

Even as the word hooked a barb through Gemma's heart, she cordoned it off, refusing to give it meaning, and laughed instead. He was here, wasn't he? "So you think I'm irresistible?"

"Hmm." He tugged her closer again. "Very much so." His hands slid down to her hips and pressed them to him.

She let out a low groan. "Not a great move if you want to slow down."

He caught hold of one of her hands and pulled it up above her head, then the other. "Maybe I don't know what I want." He captured her lips again.

"Well I do," she murmured, tugging her hands free so she could push him backward toward the bed.

He didn't put up a fight.

The second day he had a client lunch even though it was a Saturday, which Gemma hadn't expected. Of course, she understood—his work was what brought him down here in the first place—but she did wish he'd mentioned it beforehand.

"It must have slipped my mind," he said when he saw her to her car before heading out. "I'm sorry. Things have been so hectic lately."

Since they decided to meet up again at a coffee shop downtown as soon as he was done, Gemma tried to see it as more time to get ready for their evening. She'd planned on swinging by the apartment to change and pick up his Christmas presents anyway—now she might even have time for a mani-pedi and a blow-out. She didn't indulge like that often, but once in a while, it was worth it.

Judging by Jonah's reaction when he picked her up later, this was absolutely one of those times.

"Your hair," he said, eyes wide with appreciation as he moved his camera bag off the passenger seat. "It looks amazing."

She flicked it a little extra for his benefit as she got in and buckled, glad she'd left a good tip for the stylist. "Thanks. How was your lunch?"

"Oh, you know..." He handed her the bag, put the car in drive, and pulled away from the curb.

"I don't. Tell me about it."

He glanced at her. "You want to know about my boring work meeting?"

"I want to know everything." Gemma cringed. *Overeager much?*

"Everything, huh?" There was amusement in his voice as he leaned forward to survey the intersection before turning left. "It's not interesting. This one was just a catch-up with one of our main clients here. We chit-chat about the holidays, talk about his practice, any new needs he might have coming up—that sort of thing. Kind of a drag."

His blasé attitude didn't sit right with Gemma. This was a meeting that had been more important to Jonah than spending the day with her, but he made it sound like something that could have taken place over the phone.

"Maybe you should have cancelled it," she said before she could stop herself, keeping her focus on the street outside. The snow had melted, leaving streams of water rushing along the curb. Her hands worried the clasp of the camera bag while she waited for his response.

"I wish," he said, coming to a stop. "But while I'm here, I might as well, right?"

Gemma ran a finger across her newly done nails while she tried to agree with him. What did she know about sales? Maybe he really didn't have a choice.

They drove in silence for another few blocks, but then Jonah reached over the console and put his hand on her knee. "I'm starving. Thanks for making reservations."

As always, his smile overshadowed any uncertainty in

Gemma's head. She was sad that they didn't have more time together, but that wasn't his fault. Those were the circumstances under which they'd met. And deep down she was grateful to have even a small slice of him. Did she want more? Yes. But she'd never been an all-or-nothing sort of person.

The twinkle in his eye when he turned her way at the next light helped her shrug off her ire. That expression just for her—she wanted it preserved. Her hands retrieved his camera without thinking.

"Did you find anything to shoot today?" she asked as she found the right grip and put her eye to the viewfinder.

"What are you doing?" Jonah's voice was lighter now.

"Just looking." She aimed it at him.

"Come on..." He cocked his head and glanced her way. A smile played at the corner of his mouth. "I'm the one *behind* the camera, remember."

She leaned back when he tried to reach for it, a happy fizz bubbling up inside her. This playfulness was exactly what they needed. "No, no. You're driving. Focus please."

As they approached a big intersection, he had no choice but to do just that, and she took her chance. Aim, focus... "Jonah," she called in a singsong voice.

"Yes, Gem."

She snapped the image and looked at the screen. It was perfect—a composition of blurry traffic out the window behind him, the streetlights illuminating his features, and that cheeky raised right brow adding indulgence to the flash of a smile he'd thrown her way at the exact right moment. "You'll have to send me a copy of this. It needs to be framed," she said.

He laughed—her favorite sound—then managed a grip on the lens. "Come on," he said again. "Put it away. We're almost there."

And this time she did as he asked.

As lovely as the meal was, Gemma couldn't wait to get back

to the hotel so they could exchange gifts. Jonah wasn't in as much of a hurry and ordered a dessert cocktail after they'd finished the bottle of Malbec he'd ordered. She wasn't used to seeing him tipsy, but then again, they were celebrating early Christmas. At least she'd stopped at two glasses of wine since it seemed she'd have to drive them home.

"You're so sweet," Jonah said, slightly slurring his Ss when they reached the car. "So, so sweet. And I like you so much. Maybe even more than... than you like me."

"Is that so?" She opened the door for him and waited until he'd buckled. He might be under the influence, but she didn't mind the way he looked at her one bit.

"Mm-hmm." Jonah rested his head against the seat and swung it toward her, his eyes glossy and adoring. "I do need some coffee though."

Gemma laughed. "Yeah, you do."

"Some coffee and a hug." He took her hand.

"We'll get you both. But I'm going to need my hand to drive."

"Right." He let go and closed his eyes. "Going to rest for a few."

Gemma went through a drive-thru for two lattes on their way, making Jonah's a double shot, and by the time they pulled into the hotel parking lot twenty minutes later, he'd already lost the chatty, excitable wooziness and settled into a more temperate state.

"Are you ready for some presents?" Gemma asked on their way upstairs. "And maybe that hug you requested earlier?" She ran her fingers down his arm and gave him her best doe eyes.

"Always." He pulled her close and kissed her on the forehead. "Let me hit the bathroom first. I've gotta piss like a racehorse after all that."

How romantic, Gemma thought, but then she brushed his

comment off. It meant he felt comfortable enough with her to not censor himself. That was a good thing.

While he was indisposed, she lit a couple of candles she'd brought and placed his presents on the small ottoman that served as a table by the couch. She also set her phone to play Christmas music, adjusted her blouse to flatter her cleavage, and reapplied a tiny dab of perfume to her collarbone.

"Whoa." Jonah stopped short outside the bathroom door to take in the scene.

Gemma beamed at him from the couch. "Merry early Christmas."

"What is this?" He approached slowly, taking in the stack of presents before him.

"We said we'd exchange presents."

"Yeah, but... Hold on." He disappeared into the short hallway and opened the closet. Then he returned with a cellophane-wrapped spa basket in his hands. "I only got you one."

Gemma forced the smile on her face not to dwindle at the sight of the generic mall-branded products even though they'd punctured the Christmas bubble she'd tried to create. She sucked in her gut to alleviate the sudden hollowness therein.

"I wasn't sure what kind you liked, but they said this was their most popular scent," Jonah said.

Not everyone was a good gift-giver. Gemma knew that. And yet she'd hoped—expected even—that he'd spend more thought on her than two minutes in and out of a store.

The thought was there before she could stop it: *What am I doing here?*

When she didn't immediately respond, Jonah scrunched up his nose. "Do you hate it? I can take it back."

The concern in his voice made her tuck the doubt back in its dark corner and snap out of it. "No, don't do that. It's great." She pulled the basket closer and undid the plastic. Then she pretended to examine each item with curiosity. "It's a very nice basket," she said. "Thank you."

It worked. Jonah puffed back up and finally sat down next to her.

"Your turn," Gemma said, setting the basket down on the floor where she didn't have to look at it.

Jonah rubbed his hands together. "Don't mind if I do."

Gemma had always liked watching other people open her gifts, and Jonah was no exception. He was like a kid on Christmas morning, which helped her forget her upset.

"Ah, this is so awesome," Jonah said, flipping through the photography book. "Did you know that he stayed with the Bedouins for six months while shooting these. Now that's commitment." He flipped the book over in his hands. "But this is hard to find. It's been out of print since he stopped working a few years ago."

Gemma shrugged. "I have my contacts." She didn't—they'd had it at Powell's.

The bracelet and the sweater were equally well received, and when all the gifts had been opened, Gemma collected the discarded wrapping paper and bundled it into the trash.

"I was thinking we could go ice skating tomorrow," she said as Jonah splayed the sweater across his lap. "Wear it then."

"Yeah..." He caressed the knitted fabric with several short strokes before putting it aside. "I'm just gonna..." He got up from the couch and made a beeline for the minifridge, from which he pulled a beer. After opening it, he took a deep swig then set the bottle down on the desk. "I actually, um, I have to go back tomorrow."

Gemma stopped what she was doing and stared at him. "What? But you were supposed to be here until Monday night."

"Yeah well, my Monday meeting was cancelled." His gaze flicked to hers and away again. "Which means I have no excuse to not be home."

Despite Gemma's resolution not to be needy, this news made white-hot color rise to her cheeks. "I wish you'd told me that sooner. First you got in late Thursday, now this?" She slumped back down on the couch. "We already have so little time."

"You know I don't have much say in that."

She leaned forward and rested her head in her hands. "I know. But..."

"There's something else too." Jonah's words came out rushed. "My territory might be changing in the new year. To Eastern Washington. I'll know more after the holidays."

Gemma's lips parted, but it took a few moments before she could string her words together. "What are you saying? I might not see you anymore?"

"No, that's not it." He ran a hand over his head. "I don't have all the facts yet, and I don't know what it would mean." He paced toward the bed and turned. "But it's also like... I'm married. And this"—he gestured between them—"I mean, we're great. You're great. But I'm not going to..."

Gemma felt like someone had punched her. "You're not going to leave her."

He flung his arms open. "Not right now at least. You think this is easy for me? Any of it? Things have been better at home lately with her back in the office. I want to have a family at some point. I can't just..." He made a motion with his hands to indicate something blowing up.

Gemma fought the impulse to cover her ears. This wasn't how tonight was supposed to go. But despite her best efforts, her eyes welled up. She looked into the dark outside the window and imagined it closing in to envelop her like the comforting blanket she'd used when she was little to block out her parents fighting in the room next to hers.

The couch cushion shifted with Jonah sitting down. "Hey, don't be upset." He placed a gentle hand on her forearm. "I'm sorry about this weekend. I didn't know how to tell you. I feel like I'm disappointing everyone."

Gemma was still fighting the swelling emotion in her throat and kept her eyes averted. *He'll never be yours*, a voice said inside her head. Maybe it was Cheryl's; maybe it came from some other place.

"Hey," Jonah said again, nudging her chin with his fingers so she'd look at him. His hazel eyes sought hers in a soft chase for her attention. "I'm here now, right? I'm here, you're here."

She pressed her lips together and tried to force at least one side up. He *was* here. That must count for something. She had to have faith. "We're here," she agreed.

"Yeah." He let the back of his fingers graze her cheek.

Her eyelids lowered.

"I'm sorry," he whispered again right before his lips made contact with her temple. "I'm sorry." Another kiss on her cheek. "I'm sorry." The corner of her mouth.

Gemma caved and twisted into his arms, clinging to him.

He pulled her into his lap so that she straddled him and rose to meet her in a fervent kiss that Gemma was certain said more than his words. He wanted her, that much was clear. She had to accept that there were complicating factors to their being together, but no relationship was perfect. He'd come around. He had to. And why would she ruin the few hours she did get with him over vague future threats that may never come to pass?

She sat back and unbuttoned the top two buttons of her blouse and pulled it down over one shoulder so the red strap of her bra became visible.

Jonah's pupils dilated. "What's this?" He stroked the satin with his thumb.

"Another present." Gemma took hold of his hand and brought it to the remaining buttons. "Merry Christmas."

"I'll say." Jonah flipped her onto her back on the couch and nuzzled his way up her neck until he reached her lips. He gave her a soft kiss then retreated. "You're amazing, you know that? I don't deserve you."

She wanted to protest, but before she could, he kissed her again, and this time, his roaming hands soon distracted her from any thought not directly connected to his breath on her skin, her rushing blood, the weight of his body, and the exhilarating rush of being adored.

THIRTY-SIX

ISLA

Present day

Day and night slipped into each other. Isla kept her blinds drawn, her phone off, and only rummaged through the kitchen for food when she thought her mom was out. Her comforter was her friend, and the silence of her room a boon. Somewhere out there, the world was still revolving around a life-giving star, but why that mattered, Isla had forgotten. Without a next step to take, without someone pointing out a direction, she may as well stay where she was. Wasn't that the thing with fate? It would find you?

Well, here I am, Isla thought. *Come get me.*

Mom had other ideas. When five days had passed since the news about Gemma, Nancy stormed into Isla's room, snapped the curtains open, and pulled the comforter from Isla's prone body with a forceful "swish."

"Enough," she said. "It's Tuesday. You have a job to do."

Isla curled into a ball and groaned. "Tell them I'm sick."

"But you're not, are you? Come on. Get up."

Isla pried open one eye and took in her mother's shape at

the side of the bed. Straight back, crossed arms. It brought back memories from high school. "Fine."

"Good." Mom nodded. "And open the window. It smells like a moth-eaten closet in here." She turned on her heel and disappeared.

Isla sat up and yawned. *Work.* Mom wasn't wrong—it was a commitment. If she didn't show up, one of the other delivery people would have to take on a heavier load, and that wouldn't be right. No, she'd go, do her job, and then she could come back here. She'd have to talk to Stan first though, because there was no way she'd keep Mav on her route.

"I made you some coffee." Mom nodded toward the table when Isla emerged from her den minutes later. "And I don't need the car today so if you'd prefer to drive over biking..."

The protest was on Isla's tongue. *I don't drive.* But then she remembered that had changed. Despite herself, this instantly made the prospect of working less of a burden.

"Thanks," she said.

Mom crossed the kitchen and kissed her on the forehead. "You're welcome."

Stan was in his office as usual when Isla arrived, and he brightened at the sight of her. "How was your trip?" he asked. "Nice vacation?"

"Um." Isla took a seat across from him. "Sure."

"Very good. Well, we're glad to have you back. Ready to roll?"

There was no easy way to say it, so Isla blurted, "I'll need to make a change to my route first."

"Oh?"

"I won't be delivering to Maverick Zuft anymore. You're going to have to put someone else on him." She forced herself to look straight at Stan.

He frowned. "You too? What's with this guy? Did something happen?"

Turns out he's my lying, cheating grandfather... "No, just a, um, personality clash. I'm happy to swap with someone."

Stan seemed satisfied with her answer and started scanning his client file on the computer. "Huh," he said. "Looks like Mr. Zuft cancelled his service anyway."

Isla startled. "He did? Why?"

Stan shrugged. "Maybe the personality clash was mutual?"

Isla seethed. It was one thing for her to drop Mav, but she hadn't been prepared for him to drop her. What if he was leaving? The thought left a bitter taste on her tongue.

"Anyway, that means you can keep your route and skip his place. Easy-peasy. The boxes should be ready in the back as usual."

Driving cut down the time her route took by almost half, and Isla was back home again early afternoon. Mom was nowhere to be seen, and Ulysses didn't budge from his spot on the couch even when she called his name. A beam of sunlight that had broken through the cloud cover illuminated him like a spotlight where he slept, and she supposed she could relate to that. Her bed was her next destination.

Or so she thought. But when she changed into sweats and was about to pull down her blinds, her stomach growled. And after she'd eaten, she decided to do a load of laundry. And after she'd put the laundry in the washer, she wasn't tired anymore. She stood for a while in the middle of the living room, listening to the purring snores of her cat while pondering what to do next. She could check her messages, clean her room, watch a movie...

A movie. Isla's reflection in the dark TV screen was distant and distorted. Before she could change her mind, she went for the storage box under her bed where she'd hidden the wedding tape weeks ago. Like an addict returning to her vice, there was a calm associated with holding it in her hands—the angular case, the click it made when she opened it. It made it easier to breathe.

Rushing as if afraid someone would walk in on her, she turned the TV on and inserted the disc, then she scooted back on the floor and hit play.

For the past two years, this had been her happy place. With the tape playing, she'd escaped into the past, lulled by the impervious state of her younger self and the hopefulness she knew she'd once possessed. After what had happened last week, she yearned to go there again.

As the disc loaded, Isla readied herself for the relief she knew would come with the first chord of the wedding march. Her posture eased in anticipation the same way favorite foods could make one salivate, only this time, the melodic first morsel came and went without satisfaction.

There was Jonah on the screen, seeing her at the altar. Isla leaned forward, willing the poignancy of the moment to settle at her core the way it had so many other times.

Who's Gemma? her mind asked instead. *Please tell me.*

And there was her dad, and Nana and Pop-Pop, but instead of a happy trio, she now saw a wider picture with Mav looming somewhere off camera. Too many secrets.

Isla didn't even make it to the vows before she turned the video off. She rubbed her face and glared at the TV. Behind her on the couch, Ulysses stretched, his paws prodding against her shoulder as if to ask what she'd do now.

"Back in the box with you," she muttered, ejecting the disc.

With nothing else calling for her attention, Isla ended up back in bed after all. She wanted to sleep, not because she was tired, but because it demanded less of her than being awake, but when you'd already had ten plus hours of snooze, dreamland didn't come easy.

After trying for a solid thirty minutes, Isla flipped over on her side with a groan, her eyes landing on Nana's box on her desk. The worn cardboard looked even older next to her laptop and metal organizers.

Might as well, she thought, flinging the comforter aside.

The seven letters were light in her hand as she spread them across her bed. She took each folded paper out of its envelope and arranged them by date. The first one was from March 1952 and Isla's hand trembled as she picked it up. *Dear Nurse Cass*, she read. *You were an angel to me... stay safe.*

With each line of text, the picture solidified further—how Nana and Mav had found kinship in their shared experience in Korea, in their love of books, in future dreams, and how their feelings had budded and bloomed into more than a distant connection. Granted, she only had Mav's side, but there were hints at what Nana's sentiments might have been hidden within his words.

Isla did a double take at the name Mav had given his dog—Pip—because Nana had named one of their cats the same thing years later. Clearly, Nana hadn't forgotten Mav, but it made no sense to Isla why she'd deliberately invited in the memory like that. What purpose would that serve other than to worry the scab?

Isla picked up the hummingbird figurine and ran her fingertips over its delicate wings.

"I'm worried I'll hurt her," she'd said to Nana the first time she was allowed to hold the delicate thing.

But Nana had reassured her. "They look fragile, and they can be, especially when they're made of porcelain, but did you know hummingbirds are also fierce and resilient? They travel long distances alone, and they protect their home and families like warriors."

That had been the start of Isla's obsession.

Now, she brought the bird to the curio cabinet where she kept her collection and placed it next to its mate. The shape of one fit beneath the wing of the other. The symmetry finally settled Isla more than the wedding video had managed. How odd to think that if not for Mav encouraging her to go on the road trip, she would never have found her way to the box.

"Were you not angry with him after what he did?" she whispered. "Did you want us to meet?"

But as with so many of her other questions, this one, too, lacked an answer.

THIRTY-SEVEN

GEMMA

January, two years ago

A new year always meant a clean slate, and one that Gemma historically had considered with optimism. Twelve months sprawled out before her for her to do with what she wanted, four seasons waiting for her to spread her arms and welcome what each had to offer. She usually made resolutions—eat more fruit, try a new hobby, add a work certification—and some years she'd even stuck to them.

But this year, she'd woken up on January 1 and gone back to sleep. Jonah hadn't even texted at midnight, and how hard was it to send a text? Since then, they'd talked on the phone only a handful of times. Something had shifted between them—something Gemma increasingly struggled to pretend didn't matter. He was still sweet and curious and thinking of her, or so he said —except it was harder to find time to connect. He'd yet to find out if his territory would be changing, and in the meantime, they were keeping him in Washington. No trips south planned in the near future.

Gemma was glad work was picking up again, so she at least

had that distraction on the daily. When she was with patients, she gave them her full attention, asked them about their lives, talked about travel, news, music—anything to be as present as she could because once she got home, there was only Jonah. She'd even started going to bed earlier to cut down on ruminating, and thankfully it seemed her body needed the rest. Every day she woke feeling like a freight train had struck her.

"You look like shit," Cheryl said on the last Sunday of the month when snow tumbled like downy feathers outside the window. "You should take some probiotics."

Supplements were her aunt's latest obsession. The ladies working food service for the school district had formed a self-help book club after one of them had needed a pacemaker back in October, and this month's topic was natural health remedies. "Every system in your body relies on the gut," Cheryl said. "I'll ask Margot for a recommendation."

Gemma poured herself some coffee and grabbed an English muffin from the plastic sleeve on the counter. "That's not necessary," she said. "I'm just tired. I've been working a lot."

Her aunt tsked. "Not just tired. You're sad. Don't think I didn't notice."

Gemma didn't respond, focusing instead on buttering her bread.

"He's not worth it," Cheryl said.

Gemma's shoulders slumped. She didn't want to get into it, but the sharpness in her aunt's voice begged for a rebuttal. "You don't know what you're talking about. He has a lot on his plate. Work stuff. Once we know more, we're going to make a plan, and things will be better. All relationships have their ups and downs—everyone knows that."

Cheryl was quiet for a beat. "All I know as far as this goes is that you're unhappy and he's the reason."

"His absence, not him."

Cheryl threw her hands in the air. "Same difference. Plus guilt weighs a ton."

Gemma picked up her plate and mug. "I don't need this right now." She stalked off toward her room.

"But maybe you should think about what you *do* need," her aunt called after her. "Because he sure isn't."

Gemma slammed her door shut with her foot and set her food down on her desk. The coffee sloshed onto her hand as she did, so she wiped it on her pajama pants, cursing silently to herself. When the worst sting subsided, she pushed yesterday's clothes off her chair and sat down. She reached over and pulled up the blinds, then blinked at the snowy daylight on the other side of the pane. Once she was used to it, she took in her room. There were clothes on the floor—not only here by the chair but over by the closet too—the plant in her window was beyond thirsty, and the top of the dresser sported a layer of dust that would never have had time to settle six months ago.

Maybe her aunt had a point. She wasn't at her best. She needed... something. She needed Jonah.

She picked up the phone and texted him. *Talk today?* While she waited for a response and for her coffee to cool off, she nibbled at the muffin, not caring that it lacked flavor.

She'd almost given up and was contemplating going back to bed when her phone finally dinged.

I'll call you tonight.

This was it, Gemma decided. She'd explain to him how important it was for her that they see each other at least once every other month if not more often. He'd understand. And if he couldn't come down here, maybe she could drive up to him. They could meet in Seattle for the day. Surely he'd be able to get away from home for that. From Isla...

Her aunt's words echoed inside her head: *Guilt weighs a ton.*

To lighten that load, Gemma spent the rest of the afternoon cleaning and doing laundry. As an extra bonus, she got to show Cheryl that there was nothing wrong with her. Some days you were down in the dumps; others you were productive and full of hope. That's what it meant to be human, didn't she know?

Jonah called shortly after eight, but instead of starting the call like he always did by telling her how much he missed her and how annoyed he was with his job, he opened with, "I don't have long. I had to say I was running out to get gas."

The thrill that had coursed through Gemma when his name had lit up the screen fizzled. "Oh."

"But I'm glad you texted. I'd been meaning to call you anyway."

Phew. He was thinking of her then. She tugged a pillow behind her and scooted back on her bed. "It's good to hear your voice."

He was silent for a beat as if there was a delay on the line. "Yeah, you too."

Why did he sound so strange? Gemma suddenly couldn't think of any of the words she'd prepared, so she settled for: "How are you?"

"You know. Busy."

"Any news on the job?"

Another delay. "Not yet."

"Because I was thinking," Gemma said, at the same time Jonah said, "So, listen, I..."

They both chuckled, then Jonah said, "You first."

Gemma hesitated. What if he was about to tell her he was coming to see her soon? Then her points would be moot. "No, you go."

"Okay." Jonah cleared his throat. "So, something's come up.

Um, I haven't been sure how to tell you, which is my bad, but the thing is..."

He's being transferred, Gemma thought. *He'll no longer have a work reason to come to the Portland area.* It was a blow for sure, but because she'd already come up with the idea for her to drive north, the prospect of hearing him say it out loud wasn't as devastating as it might have been before she pulled herself together. She could take it.

"I've decided to tell Isla about us."

His words were so far off what she'd expected that it took a moment before they sank in. Goosebumps broke out across her arms as that old, wily hope snagged her breath. "What?" The word floated out on an exhale.

He was telling his wife. Was he leaving her? Maybe Gemma had been wrong, and his recent distance hadn't signaled a cooling of feelings but of bracing for change. He *had* told her he had more than himself to consider, so that was probably what he'd spent time doing. It made sense. And without the secret hanging over them, they'd be free. A fresh start out of the shadows, and—

Jonah cleared his throat. "Like I said, things have been getting better between us lately, and, well, we're talking about trying for a baby."

The technicolor vision came to an abrupt stop. One second passed, two, three.

"A baby," Gemma repeated, as a void opened beneath her. A jet-black one with teeth. She pressed her palm against her chest. "You're going to—" Her voice broke.

"Hey." Jonah's voice softened. "Hey, don't. We always knew this couldn't last forever, right?"

For some reason, the image that rose from the depths of Gemma's mind right then was the gift basket he'd given her for Christmas. That uninspired semblance of thoughtfulness. His words now hooked into that image and made sense. Some part of her *had* known, as much as she'd refused to acknowledge it. A naïve, starry-eyed part. Shame washed over her as the truth emerged, stark and naked: Someone else had owned his heart first. She was an intruder.

"Gemma? Say something?"

She swallowed. Found resolve to center herself. Willed her voice to carry. "No, yeah. It's good. I'm good. I was just surprised because, um, what I was going to say is that I've actually been thinking that we should probably break things off. That it's time. You know." Her voice reached her ears from someplace far away, thin and impotent. When he didn't immediately respond, she continued. "We've had some good times together, but you're married." She let out a sad chuckle. "I always knew that."

He blew out a long breath. "Phew. That was unexpected. You're not upset then? You know it doesn't mean I don't care about you, right?"

His relief was another blow, but one that solidified her choice and dried her threatening tears. "I know."

Silence stretched on the line, the distance never so great between them as those long, unraveling seconds.

"What are you thinking?" he asked finally.

What was she thinking? That she'd be alone again now. Or maybe that she always had been, even during her time with Jonah, since he was never hers to begin with. That she'd been the other woman, the mistress, the side piece, and not questioned it. That Isla would soon know and hate her. Would she come after Gemma? Or was the vengeful wife as much of a myth as a happily ever after begun in infidelity? "I guess I don't understand why your wife needs to know," she said. "Couldn't we just move on?"

"You can, but not me. I've thought about it a lot since Christmas, and it's what I need to do so she and I can start fresh."

Gemma bit down so hard on her cheek that she tasted blood. Steeled herself. "When?"

"Soon. Our anniversary weekend in Bend is coming up. It'll be a good time to recommit, and I'm hoping she'll see it that way too."

A seed of hope cut through the dark. She couldn't help it. "And if she doesn't?"

A dinging sound came over the line as if Jonah had opened his car door. "I think she will. If I'm completely honest with her, she'll understand. She has to." The dinging stopped.

He was trying to convince himself, Gemma realized. Same as she had about him. How sad was that? Cheryl had been right all along.

"I'm sorry," Jonah said. "I hate this." To his credit, his voice got thick. "I want you to know that I think you're amazing. Always have. Someday you'll find someone else, and whoever he is, he'll be the luckiest guy in the world."

Gemma scoffed. She didn't want someone else. Not any time soon anyway. "So I guess this is it then," she said.

He sniffled. Was he crying? No, that was probably wishful thinking.

"Yeah, I think it would be best if we didn't talk again," he said. "Easier."

"A clean break."

They agreed. Going forward they were to have no contact at all.

And that should have meant it was over.

But a week later, Gemma got out of the shower after work, and suddenly, staring at her reflection in the mirror, she knew with stark clarity that no matter what she'd promised, no matter how strong the reason for their decision, she was going to do everything she could to get a hold of Jonah again before he could tell his wife.

Because Gemma was late.

Time-to-pee-on-a-stick late.

THIRTY-EIGHT

ISLA

Present day

On Mom's insistence, Isla picked up more shifts at Meals on Wheels that week.

"You're distressing Ulysses wandering about the house like a restless spirit at all hours," she said. "It'll be good for him to have some space."

What she really meant was, "Get over yourself and be a productive human being already," and Isla couldn't fault her. Even she was getting tired of her own behavior. March was coming to an end, and spring was around the corner, so while Isla still woke up most nights with her mind already mid-hypothetical argument with Mav, or Rowan, or even Jonah, she didn't put much effort into protesting Mom's firm "guidance."

She had yet to have any contact with Mav, but after she finished her rounds that Thursday, she had three missed calls from Rowan. He'd texted her a couple of times to check in, to which she hadn't responded, but this was the first time he'd called her.

She was about to listen to his voicemail when he called again. Whatever was going on, it must be urgent.

"Finally," he said when she answered. "Why didn't you pick up?"

"Why didn't I..." Isla huffed. "Maybe because I'm still upset with you. I was also working if you must know. Why did Mav cancel his service?"

"He did? He didn't tell me that."

Isla frowned. She'd assumed Rowan had taken over meals. "How is he getting food then?"

"Grocery delivery maybe, I don't know. But can we talk about this later? As glad as I am that you're not hanging up on me, I have an actual reason for reaching out. Mav is in the hospital again."

Isla had been on her way to get into Mom's car, which she was borrowing on the regular these days, but now she froze in the open doorway instead. "Is he okay?"

"He fainted again, and he needs blood, but he's stable. Do you know what blood type you are?"

"Is he conscious? Or is it worse this time?"

"About the same. Did you hear my question?"

"Yeah, B I think. Why?"

"B positive or negative?"

"I don't remember. Does it matter?"

"Mav is B negative. The hospital doesn't have much stock of that. But you're related..."

A gust of wind forced its way into Isla's collar, making her shiver. She tugged it closed with her free hand. He wanted her to go donate blood to Mav because on paper she was his grand-daughter? That felt made up.

"Not that I'm against donating, but I'm pretty sure that's not how blood types work. They always have O negative and that's a universal donor. I know because I needed some after the accident."

"Yes, but it's better with an exact match. Look, you don't have to see him. I mean, he wants to, but he'd never force you. I know you're mad and rightly so. We didn't tell you the truth, and maybe we should have."

"Maybe?"

"Okay, we should have. But can't you try to see it from Mav's point of view? Everyone makes mistakes. Yes, leaving your grandmother was a big one, but it's not like he moved on and forgot all about it. It's never left him. And he's not expecting your forgiveness. All he wanted was to do something kind for you in Embeth's place, and if you ask me, it takes a lot of courage to wade back into what he did and face its consequences."

"Me being the consequence?"

"I think you know what I mean." Rowan was silent for a beat then added, "He's really old, Isla, and despite appearances not very well. Please come."

The way he said her name made his voice reach deep. She did know what he meant. And somewhere beneath the hurt, she missed Mav. In the flowerbed next to the parking lot, a tiny crocus had broken though the dirt. The yellow petals settled something within Isla. Flowers meant new life—Nana had taught her that. She tilted her head back and inhaled through her nose. "Okay," she said.

"Really? Okay, great. We're at Jefferson. I'll text you the floor. How soon can you be here?"

"I might not be a match though."

"It won't matter to him. He'll just be happy to see you." The hope in his voice was contagious.

"I'm leaving work now. Give me thirty minutes."

Rowan met her at the hospital entrance. "Easier this way," he said. "Didn't want you to get lost."

"Or chicken out?" She glanced at him as they walked.

"Are you kidding? You're the bravest person I've met."

"Right."

Rowan stopped in front of the elevators. "No, I'm serious. The stuff you confronted in Bend—that takes a lot of guts. Most people would be happy to forget, but not you. You crave truth no matter if it's good or bad."

Isla blushed. She'd never heard that compliment before. She'd also never thought of it that way.

He pressed the button, and they waited in silence. Once inside, Rowan turned to her. "Will you let them test you? In case you're a match I mean."

Isla nodded. "I want to see Mav first though."

"Of course."

Rowan led her through a corridor to a different set of elevators, and then finally they were on the right floor. "It's possible he's sleeping. He's very tired."

"And a transfusion will help?"

"Yeah. For a bit at least."

But Mav wasn't sleeping. He was sitting up in his bed, his skin the same color as the sheets, eyes locked on the door. "Isla," he said when she entered. "You came."

"You didn't believe me?" Rowan asked, pulling a chair up to the bedside for Isla like he had in Portland.

"I hoped, but I'm also aware I'm not owed anything." He patted the side of his bed. "Thank you for seeing me. Please sit."

Isla did, and on instinct, she took Mav's hand. It was cool and the skin paper-thin, but he gripped hers right back. "How are you?" she asked. "I'm sorry, I—"

"No, *I'm* sorry." As frail as his figure was, his eyes were no less piercing than they'd been the first day they'd met. "I know it doesn't mean much, but you were right. I should have told you upfront no matter how uncomfortable that would have been."

Isla forced herself to not look away. "Thank you," she said. "I've been... working through some feelings about it."

"As you should. It means Nancy and Delwyn raised you right."

Delwyn, his son. Isla pulled her hand away but did so gently. "I have questions," she said. "If you don't mind?"

"I'll tell you anything."

Reading Nana's letters had sparked so much curiosity, but where would she start? After a moment's hesitation, she let the first one that came to mind spill out. "Did you know she kept the baby?" Out the corner of her eye, she noted Rowan stirring from his phone.

"Not right away. But it was the fifties, so one could assume."

"And that didn't bother you?"

Something flashed dark behind his blue irises. "Of course it did," he said with emphasis. "To walk away from your flesh and blood? You and Jonah may have never had the chance to fulfil your dream of having a child, but I think you can imagine it."

Isla nodded, but then her movement stalled as what he'd said sank in. *Your dream of a child.* How did Mav know about that?

"I didn't make much," he continued before she could ask, "but that first year away, whenever I had a few extra dollars, I sent them to her."

Isla pushed away the disconcerting hum inside her sparked by his stray comment. "That's something at least," she said. Maybe he'd guessed about the baby plans.

"Yeah. But the third time, the letter came back marked 'return to sender.' It could have been her or it could have been her father—that I'll never know. I still thought of her wherever I was. Of them. Imagining. Was it a boy or a girl? Were they healthy? Did her parents forgive her?"

Mav fixated on something out the window past Isla while

his fingers worried the blanket. He was lost somewhere else, and not until Isla touched the back of his hand did he come back.

"Oops, sorry about that. Sometimes, it's as if I can hear her again. 'In a word, I was too cowardly to do what I knew to be right, as I had been too cowardly to avoid doing what I knew to be wrong.' Charles Dickens—*Great Expectations*. She always saw me clearer than I did myself." His fingers went to the faded hummingbird tattoo on his neck. "I didn't return to Seattle for four years. My mother took ill, so I was granted leave for the summer, and I decided it was a sign I was meant to set things right. I wasn't the same person anymore, and I knew I'd have no peace until I did right by my Cass. Or Embeth I mean."

Isla leaned forward, hanging on his words. "What happened?"

"I went to her parents' house. Her father answered the door, and harsh words were spoken that don't need repeating. I didn't even get a chance to ask about her before he closed it in my face, which"—Mav pinched the bridge of his nose, his features scrunched together in self-deprecation—"I can't say I blame him for. After that, I went to the hospital where she'd worked, and as I sat in the park outside building myself up, lo and behold, there she was, on the other side of the park. I almost missed her. I'd pictured her in her nurse's uniform, but she was in a green dress with a white belt. I remember it clear as day. She was illuminated through the branches above like the sun had made her its purpose. Except... she wasn't alone."

"She was with Pop-Pop."

Mav nodded. "Yes, she was walking with Neil and a little boy of about the right age. She was happy." He closed his eyes. "I got close enough to hear her laugh, and that was all I needed. I had no right to ask for more. I'd told her to forget about me, and she had."

"Or so you thought." Isla pulled a leg up under her in the chair. "Did you ever see her again?"

"No. But I became very good at my job. Rose in the ranks. Life at sea was a good distraction. And then I met Lorraine."

"Did she know?"

"No." Mav looked at Rowan. "No one did until I told him."

Isla smoothed out a crease in the sheet. "And now I know. And my mom."

"What did Nancy say?"

Isla let out a small chuckle. "Let's just say she's more pragmatic than me. She thinks I'm overreacting. That it was a long time ago."

A knock fell on the door, and a nurse came inside. After exchanging greetings, she spoke to Isla. "Are you the granddaughter?"

It was odd to hear the word in someone else's mouth. "I guess so. Yes."

"We're ready for you, if you want to come with me."

To her surprise, the urge to stay in the room was stronger than not to, but still, Isla got up.

"You'll be back?" Mav asked.

Isla promised, and then she followed the nurse out of the room.

"Have you donated blood before?" she asked. Her nametag said Jessica.

"No."

"Have you eaten today?"

"Yes."

"Jump up here." She indicated a chair.

"You're not going to see if I'm a match first?"

Jessica paused. "Did you only want to donate to your grandfather? Because even if you're not a match for him, we always need blood. There's a national shortage."

Isla considered this, but it wasn't a difficult decision. "Sure, I'll donate either way."

Jessica lit up. "Great. I have some paperwork for you to fill out while I get things ready."

Isla took the clipboard she was handed and scribbled her information, but at the bottom of the last page, she stopped. "Thank you for saving lives," it said.

For so long she'd thought of herself as doing the opposite that the words looked foreign. "Saving lives," she mumbled. It was a new possibility.

"What was that?" Jessica returned with her equipment.

"Nothing." Isla rolled up her left sleeve.

"Left it is," Jessica said with a smile. "Sit back and relax. It'll be ten minutes at most." She inserted the needle and checked the line. "Good flow. You're a natural." She nodded, satisfied. "You should do this more often. We need it. It saves lives."

There it was again.

Isla hummed something noncommittal before she closed her eyes and said a prayer she'd be a match for Mav.

After a cup of orange juice and a snack bar, Isla was allowed to return to Mav's room. He was sleeping, but Rowan was still in his chair on his phone.

"How is he doing?" Isla asked.

"Okay. He's glad you came."

"How long will they keep him?"

"We'll see in the morning."

Isla took in Mav's still form. "Let me know?"

Rowan's eyebrow arched, but if he was surprised, he didn't say so. "Of course." He stood up and tucked his phone in his pocket. "Actually, if you're heading out, would you be able to give me a ride home? I went with him in the ambulance, and I need to get him a few things for the night."

Isla agreed, and after Rowan instructed the nurse to tell Mav where he'd gone, they left.

When they'd driven for a few minutes, Rowan turned to her. "Now that we're talking again—can I ask what happened with Gemma? Did you find her?"

A week had passed since Louise's futile visit to the dentist's office, but it still hurt Isla to have had that door closed in her face, and she must have grimaced at his question because he apologized immediately.

"You don't have to say if you don't want to. It's just been on my mind." The restless bay behind him framed his face with brooding waters.

"No, it's fine." Isla slowed behind a truck turning into the ferry terminal. "It wasn't her."

"Oh damn."

"I know. I had high hopes."

After a moment, Rowan asked the question Isla knew was bound to follow. "What's the next step?"

Isla lifted one shoulder and let it drop. "I'm not sure there is one."

"And you're okay with that?"

"I didn't say that." She made a left into a quaint neighborhood lined with older homes. "I don't know. Maybe I have to reconcile the fact that I'll never know for sure, but I..." The suspicions she'd carried since finding the note solidified into a single thesis as she spoke them out loud. "I think he had an affair. That's what makes the most sense. The year before the accident had been a little rocky with quarantine and everything, and I've remembered enough to know something was weighing on him. But how, or if, that's linked to the accident, I have no idea."

"Yeah. Sorry." Rowan was quiet for a bit. "I just think it's so weird. As someone who's been married—when things got rocky with us, I would have never even thought of making future plans as if nothing was amiss."

"What do you mean?"

"Weren't you guys trying for a baby? I would say that speaks against him cheating."

Him too? The disquiet raised earlier by Mav's comment bobbed back up to the surface.

"We were going to, but"—Isla squinted as the road signs blurred ahead—"how do you know that?"

"You probably told me."

Had she? She searched her mind. "No, I definitely didn't. It's not something I talk about."

"Hm..." Rowan's fingers tapped against his seatbelt, then he lifted his elbow up against the door. "Oh, I know—I think Louise mentioned it when we were at the hotel. You know—when you went for a walk? Yeah, that was it. Sorry. Was I not supposed to know?"

No one was supposed to know. She and Jonah had only had a few tentative conversations about it, and while they'd both decided it was something they wanted to pursue, they'd agreed not to tell anyone. Make it a surprise. It had brought them closer.

This made no sense. Louise and Isla had never even talked about babies, so there was no reason she'd have guessed it and presented it as fact to Mav and Rowan. But if Isla hadn't told anyone—and she was certain that she hadn't—then how did Louise know? Unless...

The passing sidewalk rippled like the waves on the bay, and Isla clutched the steering wheel tighter.

Louise couldn't know unless Jonah had told her.

"Hey," Rowan said next to her.

Images of Louise spun like a kaleidoscope before Isla's eyes. How they'd met, how she'd listened, how she seemed to understand Isla's grief so well. The way she'd volunteered to help on the ground in Bend and with—Isla gasped—locating Gemma.

"Hey, watch where you're..."

Rowan's voice came from somewhere far away, but Isla

blocked it out as the truth hit her upside the head. Louise had known Jonah. She'd known him and kept it a secret. Louise hadn't gone to see Gemma that day. Louise *was* Gemma.

"Isla, for fuck's sake. Stop!" Rowan grabbed the steering wheel, jerking them back into their lane, away from the pedestrians they'd been heading toward.

And with that one jolting move, Rowan turned into Jonah, doing the exact same thing but in a different time and place, and Isla's memories came flooding back.

THIRTY-NINE

ISLA

The night of the crash

"Anything else I can get you?" The waitress offered the practiced smile of someone whose late shift was coming to an end. *It's been a pleasure to serve you*, it said, *but please get out of here now.*

"I think that should do it," Isla said. She glanced at her husband across the table from her, but he didn't look up. His gaze was lodged on his hand, which was resting against the base of his empty wine glass. "Jonah?"

"Huh?" He raised his chin. "Yeah, yeah. We're good."

The waitress produced the folder with their check. "Whenever you're ready."

As she left, Jonah sighed from someplace deep within and sat back in his seat.

"You okay?" Isla asked for the umpteenth time that night.

He'd gone to the bathroom several times during their meal, taking forever to return, but, "I'm fine," was the only response she'd received. She'd assumed this getaway would be different than the past few months of halting communication between them. They were here to celebrate after all—both their anniversary and their renewed commitment to each other and their future. They'd start a family, and she felt certain that with the weight of quarantine lifting, the two of them would get back to the ease that had been between them before. Their situation was hardly unique. She knew so many others who'd felt the toll of the pandemic on their relationships. Humans weren't made for long periods of virtual isolation.

Besides, Jonah had been eager for this trip, going out of his way to plan and book it. It was true he'd been unusually pensive on the drive down yesterday, but she'd chalked that up to him planning some sort of surprise, so she hadn't asked. And he'd seemed fine earlier today, just not tonight.

"I actually need some fresh air," Jonah said, pushing his chair back. "Sorry. Can you do the, um..." He gestured haphazardly toward the check and huffed out another breath.

"Sure."

"Thanks."

She watched him make his way through the restaurant, his hands skirting the backs of chairs as if he needed them to guide him out. Was he drunk? Isla's eyes returned to his empty wine glass. She could have sworn he'd only had one.

After she paid, she shrugged on her coat and followed his footsteps outside. The cool air engulfed her as she opened the door to the dark evening, a shiver skirting up her spine. Despite a few bunches of optimistic daffodils in the flowerbeds around the hotel, spring was still far away.

Jonah stood behind their car, digging through his pockets. "God, I'm such a screw-up," he said when he spotted her. "I've lost the damn keys."

Yes, he was definitely drunk, judging by how he slurred his Ss. How the hell had he managed that?

"I have the keys," Isla said, reaching into her purse. "You gave them to me like you always do, remember?"

"Oh." His head bobbed slightly.

Correction: He was wasted. She told him as much.

"I only had a few," he said as she unlocked the car. "I needed... something."

"So you snuck off to the bar?"

When he didn't move, she walked past him and opened the passenger door. No way was he driving tonight.

He followed, but before he got in, he turned around, his back to the opening. "You're mad." The night cast deep shadows below his brow.

Isla resisted the urge to roll her eyes. "I'm confused. It's not the same thing. Can you get in please?"

He looked like he was about to object, but then he folded himself backward into a seated position.

"We can talk about it tomorrow," Isla said, squatting to help him lift his legs into the car. "Okay?"

"Okay."

She closed the door but didn't immediately move. Her hand rested against the chilled metal as the situation sank in. Why hadn't he just ordered drinks at the table? Why pretend to need the restroom? And why drink so much in the first place? That wasn't like Jonah at all. She'd have to get to the bottom of this in the morning when he'd slept it off.

Isla got in and buckled, but before she turned the key in the ignition, she looked over at her husband's slack form. His head was tilted back and his eyes closed, but his colorless lips were moving, mumbling something she couldn't quite make out. Her eyes landed on a tangle of his hair that stood straight up. Her impulse was to smooth it down, but he was somewhere else in that moment. What if she reached out and couldn't find him?

She swallowed against the tightness in her throat and started the car, then she backed out of the parking space.

As she started driving, Jonah stopped mumbling, but Isla's mind filled the silence with convoluted chatter. She kept replaying the day, asking herself what had caused the shift in Jonah. They'd had a lovely afternoon browsing stores and whiling away hours at a local coffee shop. He'd come up behind her as she'd changed her earrings in the mirror earlier this evening, his soft lips against her neck making promises for how the night would go. And then they'd arrived at the restaurant...

She'd turned the events every which way in her mind several times when it dawned on her that it was taking longer to reach the part of the town where their hotel was located than it should have.

"Great," she muttered, realizing she must have made a wrong turn somewhere. She hadn't been paying attention and now Bend was disappearing in the rearview mirror. She'd have to find a place to turn around.

"Isla?"

Isla startled. She'd thought Jonah was asleep. "Yeah?" She glanced at him but couldn't make out much more than the glint of his eyes in the light from the dashboard.

"You know I love you, right?"

Isla blinked at the compact darkness ahead of them. What kind of question was that? "Of course." She took her hand off the wheel and placed it on his leg. "I love you too."

He made a small noise, a mix between a gasp and a groan, that made her look at him again, and when she did, he covered her hand with his.

"I've had an affair," he blurted, his voice disproportionately loud in the small space.

She knew at once he was telling the truth; could feel the impact on her heart as the words first sucked the air out of her then engulfed her like a fiery backdraft that shoved her into the backrest.

Her grip around the wheel loosened, and her arms went slack as the car sped on. Her husband—her *person*—had cheated on her. Then a moment of clarity: There would be no baby.

"Isla, watch it!" Jonah yelled.

Her head jerked up to see them careening left just as Jonah grabbed the steering wheel to correct the swerve.

We're still driving, she thought in surprise. The world hadn't stopped with Jonah's confession. *How odd.*

As she felt the hard plastic of the wheel spin against her palm, her next thought was that he'd yanked it too hard. And that the trees shouldn't be right in front of them.

After that, a brief stomach drop before any other thought was overwhelmed by chaos assaulting her every sense. The world screamed against her eardrums as the car compacted against the trunks. Acrid fumes, copper on her tongue, engulfing pain.

Then darkness.

FORTY

ISLA

Isla slammed on the brake and came to a screeching stop with the right front tire against the curb. "I remember," she gasped while willing the mayhem in her head to settle. Colors and voices and the sharp, bitter scent of burned rubber muddled the past and the present together into an untidy mess that brought tears to Isla's eyes. "I remember everything."

The memories poured out of her in a rush while Rowan listened.

"I swerved," she said. "His confession—it felt like he'd struck me, and I went limp."

Rowan stared at her, his gaze inscrutable. "And you went off the road."

Isla tested the restored memory and found that it held. "Yes, but that's not how it happened."

Again, the next few seconds of that fateful night played in slow motion before her inner eye.

"I swerved left into the oncoming lane, but then Jonah

grabbed the wheel, like you did now, only he was drunk so he overcorrected."

The horror from that moment clashed with the release of the knot she'd hogtied herself with to prevent any forward motion ever since. She let out a shaky breath as warm tears welled and spilled down her cheeks.

"Next I knew, I woke up in the hospital with Nana's voice ringing in my ears."

Rowan put his hand over hers. "You're shaking."

Isla looked down at where they touched. "Am I?" A sob forced its way up her throat but morphed into a laugh. "I can't believe it," she said. "I actually remember." Half laughing, half crying, she leaned into Rowan as he opened his arms for her.

Over the next several minutes, a maelstrom of contradicting emotions washed over her, flushing her feverishly warm one second and freezing cold the next, but she allowed it to be what it was and waited it out. Relief and sorrow melded together. On the one hand, Jonah's death hadn't been her fault. On the other, he'd been unfaithful. She should be enraged, but all the realization added was a new shade to her grief. The handsome SOB hadn't just died on her, he'd done so as a consequence of admitting his betrayal. What a waste.

"You're scaring me a little," Rowan said somewhere above her head, as he patted her back. "But I think you're okay, right?"

"Mm-hmm." Isla buried her nose in the comforting scent of his flannel and wiped her cheek. "Just a little longer."

He chuckled, his chest bouncing against her. "Take as long as you need."

When she finally felt steady enough to release him, she sat back and blinked at their mundane surroundings. Everything looked exactly as it had ten minutes ago and yet she was more than she had been, her hollow core now filled with material reality once more.

"Sorry about the..." She moved her hands to mimic swerving. "Thanks for intervening."

As she said it, the second truth came rushing back. In the onslaught of recollections, she'd all but forgotten the other party to Jonah's infidelity. She needed to get a hold of Louise or whoever she was. Now.

"I don't think I should drive," she said to Rowan, already opening her door. "Would you mind?"

"Good thinking."

She was on her phone, texting, before he'd even pulled away from the curb.

I need to talk to you. Call me.

"Screw it," she muttered, then she dialed Louise's number instead.

Voicemail.

"Who are you trying to reach?" Rowan asked.

"Louise." Isla forced her voice to remain steady. "She'll want to know my memory came back."

She wouldn't tell him her suspicions until she'd confirmed it. He'd already seen her come unhinged once today. No need to fuel that fire if she was wrong.

Louise had never taken this long to respond to a message before. Her read receipts were on, so Isla knew her friend had seen the texts, and yet nothing. All afternoon she paced the house, alternating between texting and calling. Mom had taken the ferry over to Whidbey for the day with a friend, so there was no one there to tell her to calm down.

Why wasn't she answering?

Isla even went on the bird curio forum to see if she was online, but not only was she not, it seemed she'd left the group.

Please call me, she texted a little before nine. *You knew him, right? I need to know.*

And then, finally, a response. Two words only. *I'm sorry.*

"No!" Isla called out. That wasn't enough. She was so close, but this part of the story still lay in the shadows.

She sat down on the couch and stared at her phone, her thumbs perched to type.

If you were ever my friend, you'll tell me the truth.

Nothing.

"Please," she said as she called one more time, but this time it went straight to voicemail without a single ring.

She threw her phone onto the table and collapsed back onto the cushions, and that's where Mom must have found her when she got home.

As soon as Isla woke up the next morning, neck sore from sleeping on the couch, she knew what she had to do. It was eight o'clock, and in Nancy's bedroom, the sound machine was still whirring, so Isla rushed back and forth between her room and the kitchen as quietly as she could while getting ready. Before she headed out the door, she wrote her mom a note.

Driving south this time was nothing like it had been when she and Mav set out two and a half weeks ago. There was no reluctance and no dejection, urgency and determination having taken their place. She would find Louise or Gemma or whatever her name was, and then she'd finally know. If she was right, Louise was the woman Jonah had had an affair with. Louise who had been her friend through some of the darkest times. The duplicity coated Isla's senses, but in the wake of the Mav situation, it was as if her ability to truly take it in was already saturated. If she tried to picture Louise and Jonah together, it played like a bad movie she'd watched too long ago to remember why she didn't like it. The movie may be real, but its impact was limited.

Rowan had texted when she stopped to stretch her legs in Olympia. Mav would be allowed to go home tomorrow and was doing better after the transfusion. *Feel free to stop by if you want. He'd be happy to see you.*

Isla didn't respond. She was still figuring out what she wanted her future relationship with Mav to look like.

It was a little after one in the afternoon when Isla reached Vancouver and the dentist's office where, if she was right, Louise worked. She'd had time on the way there to wonder if her friend had been hiding inside the office all along when Isla stopped by the week before and had instructed the receptionist not to say anything. Today she wouldn't make that mistake.

Instead, she parked where she had a clear view of the door and prepared for a long wait. She'd bought food on the way and had nothing but time on her hands. This was it. According to their website, the office closed at five, but Isla would stay vigilant, she vowed. This time, Louise/Gemma wouldn't slip away.

Made it to Vancouver, she texted Mom. *Hopefully you didn't need the car today.*

She'd explained the situation as best as she could in her note, and since her phone hadn't blown up earlier, she assumed Mom had understood the importance of this trip.

She was right. Minutes later Nancy texted back. *Good luck. Love you.*

"Thanks, Mom," Isla whispered. She was going to need it.

The clock turned 5 PM, 5:05, 5:10. Two other people had left the building, but still no sign of Louise. For the first time since leaving home that morning, Isla second-guessed her plan. What if Louise wasn't at work today? Then this would have all been for nothing.

A car honked in the intersection at the corner of the parking lot, diverting Isla's attention, and when she looked back, there was her target in blue scrub pants and a familiar red puffer jacket, hurrying away.

Isla jumped out of the car and locked it over her shoulder as she strode with resolute steps after her friend.

"Hey!" she called. "Gemma!"

Louise stopped and whipped round. Isla's steps faltered. She'd been right. Until that moment, there had at least been a possibility of another explanation, but that was now gone.

As soon as Louise-slash-Gemma saw who'd called her, her expression went from open and agreeable to wary. She took a small step backward. "You're here."

Isla continued toward her until only a few yards remained. "And so are you—Gemma or Louise or whatever the hell I should call you."

Gemma bit her lip. It made her look much younger than "Louise the journalist."

"It's Gemma. Was always Gemma." She raised her hands as if she wanted to reach out but dropped them again. "I'm really sorry. You have to believe me, I—"

Isla lifted her chin. "I don't think I have to do anything. I can't believe it was you all along. You and Jonah? How could you—? Why didn't you—?" Her throat tightened around the elusive words. "I thought you were my friend."

"I was!" Gemma stepped closer. "I am. I just..."

Isla scoffed. "Some friend. You've lied to me for months. All this time when I was searching for answers, you knew!"

"But I didn't." Gemma shook her head. "Not about what happened. I wanted to find out too." She fiddled with the slim wristwatch on her arm.

"Am I inconveniencing you?" Isla asked. "You've got things to do more important than talking to me right now? The wife of the man you tried to steal? The friend you double-crossed?" The anger she'd found hard to conjure toward her dead husband saw no such impairment when presented with a living culprit.

"It wasn't like that," Gemma said.

"Then tell me." Isla opened her arms to encompass the world at large. "What was it like? The truth this time."

"I will, but"—Gemma looked over her shoulder—"I'm in a bit of a hurry right now."

"You're kidding, right?" The nerve of this woman.

"No." She gestured toward the daycare sign at the end of the strip mall. "I have to pick up Josie. They charge if I'm late."

Isla frowned. Why would daycare fines for her niece be Gemma's problem? "You do a lot for your sister," she said. "I hope she appreciates it. But I have questions, and I'm not leaving until I get some answers."

Gemma seemed to consider this, but finally she nodded as if she'd made a decision. "Fine. Come on. I'll get her, then we'll talk." When they reached the door, she told Isla to wait outside.

"And you're not going to slip away through a different exit or anything?" Isla asked.

"Don't worry. It's time," was Gemma's cryptic answer.

Ten minutes later, she returned to the front with a bundled-up kid in her arms. She avoided eye contact as she pushed open the door with her hip, but once she was outside, she faced Isla. She hesitated for a beat, then turned so Isla could see the little girl.

The toddler who'd buried her face against Gemma's shoulder lifted her head, and in that split second, Isla's whole world came to a stop. Blond hair, hazel eyes, a dip in the chin.

Isla's gaze cut from the child to Gemma and back, trying to make sense of what she was seeing.

"This is Josie," Gemma said. "My daughter. Say hi, baby."

Isla gasped as another piece of the puzzle clicked into place. "She's Jonah's."

Gemma nodded. "She is." She hoisted the little girl higher

on her hip. "Look, I'll tell you everything you want to know, but she's tired right now and probably hungry. I'm only a few blocks away. Why don't you come home with us and we can talk?"

"You live here? I thought you were in Longview."

"I used to be. That's where my aunt is. I moved when Josie was born. Will you come? You can leave your car here."

Isla's mouth opened and closed. The initial bolts of fury she'd been ready to hurl at Gemma for her role in Jonah's infidelity had slipped out of her hands at the sight of Josie, and now her fists clutched only emptiness at her side. "Okay," she said, unable to think of a different response.

"Okay, good. The stroller is over here."

Gemma's apartment was a small two-bedroom box in a beige 1980s building, but she'd given it personality by adding a wallpapered accent wall and quirky art in mismatched frames.

"Can I get you some coffee or tea?" Gemma put Josie in her highchair and went into the kitchen.

"Either is fine." Isla couldn't take her eyes off the little girl who was flipping the pages of a cardboard book back and forth. She sat down at the table and pointed to one of the pages. "Is that a cat?"

Josie peered up at her through dark eyelashes. Then she nodded once.

"And what does the cat do?"

"Cat," Josie said.

Isla smiled. The little girl was a spitting image of Jonah, but the shape of her brow and her mouth were Gemma's, no mistake about it.

"That's right, it's a cat. Meow," Isla said.

Josie's eyes widened as she giggled, the sound enveloping Isla's heart like a compression blanket.

Jonah had a daughter. A daughter that wasn't hers.

Gemma joined them and set a mug down in front of Isla and a cup of yogurt and some sliced strawberries in front of Josie. "Snack time," Gemma said. "You can have your book back later."

Once Josie started eating, Gemma stirred her coffee and sat back in her chair. "Thanks for not yelling," she said. "You must be furious."

Isla took stock. She had been, but was she now? The yogurt smeared around Josie's mouth made adverse emotions difficult to access. There were still pain and hurt somewhere deep within—and a voice reminding her that this was what she'd wanted. Jonah's child. At the same time, that pain stretched to incorporate the fact that Jonah would never know this sweet little person he'd created. "Furious" wasn't the right word for either of those emotions.

"I take it you were never a journalist," Isla said instead of responding directly.

"No. Always a dental hygienist. That's how I met Jonah."

"When he needed that crown."

Gemma nodded.

"Why don't you start from the beginning?"

While Josie ate, Gemma did exactly that. She told Isla about how she and Jonah had met, how she'd helped him when he had Covid, how they'd stayed in touch.

"I think I justified it by telling myself you couldn't possibly be right for him," she said, after picking up a wayward piece of fruit from the floor.

"Did he say that?" Isla wasn't sure she wanted to know the answer, but she asked anyway. Her husband had cheated on her —it was time to take off the rose-colored glasses.

"No. We didn't talk much about you. It was something I needed to believe because..." Gemma looked away. "I was falling in love with him. Or I thought I was."

Gemma's words brought Isla back to when she and Jonah

had first met. The flowers, the compliments, how he'd swept her off her feet. How his attention had intoxicated her. She knew all too well what falling in love with him had felt like. "Did he tell you he was going to leave me?" She held her breath.

"Never." Gemma glanced at her daughter. "That was a big ol' 'told you so' for my aunt."

"She knew?"

"Hard to keep a secret when you're living together."

Isla wasn't so sure of that. Jonah had managed this secret fine under their shared roof. She took a sip of coffee, her eyes drawn to the lit-up windows across the courtyard where other families were going about their evenings. Her stomach tightened as the bitter brew reached it.

"The photo of him in the car and the bracelet—I take it that was you?"

Gemma confirmed it was.

Isla nodded. *Not so serendipitous after all.* "And then what happened? Why did you call him at the hotel? Were you there?"

Gemma wiped Josie's mouth. "No. We'd ended it. He said you guys wanted to start a family, so he had to come clean. I finally got it. It was the right thing to do."

"That's how I knew, by the way," Isla said. "You told Mav and Rowan about us trying for a baby, but no one else knew about that."

Gemma's mouth formed a silent O. "I was wondering what gave it away." She ran a finger across the tabletop. "He was planning on telling you in Bend, so when I found out I was pregnant a week before, I tried to reach him."

"You hoped he'd change his mind?"

"No." The word rang out between them, plain and earnest. "I thought if he was going to come clean about *everything*, he should know about that too. But he must have blocked my number, so my last shot was calling the hotel and getting through to him that way. All the hotels actually because I didn't know which one you were staying at."

"Did he call you back?"

Gemma shook her head. "And now we know that was by choice since he did get the note."

A wave of relief swept over Isla, as if it made a difference that he'd been loyal in the end.

"I didn't find out about the accident until several months later," Gemma continued. "I was getting big and uncomfortable and in a moment of weakness, I called his company. They're the ones who told me." She crossed her arms over her stomach. "If I hadn't had my baby to think about, I don't know what I would have done."

Isla nodded. "I know that despair."

For a while, the only sound in the room was that of Josie's plastic spoon tapping the table, then Gemma asked if Isla wanted more coffee. "Or I have stuff for sandwiches. Are you hungry?"

Isla accepted the offer, and while Gemma retrieved things from the kitchen, she asked about Rowan and Mav. Isla filled her in on Mav's health.

"But you have talked to him since...?"

"Since I found out that he's my grandfather? Yes."

"That's good. I swear I sensed there was something he was keeping to himself, but I couldn't put my finger on it."

Isla cocked her head. "You did not."

Gemma put peanut butter and jelly on the table, along with a loaf of homemade bread. "I one hundred percent did. Cross my heart."

"And you didn't say anything?"

"Who was I to call out someone else's secrecy? Karma can be a bitch."

"Fair."

Their exchange had been the closest to how things had been

between them before all this had happened, and with that sudden lightness surrounding them, they set about preparing sandwiches.

"Buh-buh," Josie grunted, pointing to the peanut butter.

Without missing a beat, Gemma smeared some on a slice of bread and put it in front of her.

"Do you like being a mom?" Isla asked before she could stop herself.

A grin burst forth on Gemma's face. "I love it. I mean, it's hard too, but—best thing I've ever done."

They both watched Josie dig her thumbs into the bread, then Isla took a deep breath.

"So Jonah had died, you'd had Josie, and I assume you were working and figuring out life for the two of you. Why pretend you were someone else and sneak your way into my life?"

Gemma finished chewing, watching Isla as if gauging how honest to be. "I couldn't believe he was gone. And at first, I, um... I thought maybe you'd had something to do with his death."

"That he'd told me about you, and I'd—"

"Killed him. Yes, sorry. I'm not proud of it. I blame a lack of sleep."

"You forget I was convinced of the same until yesterday."

Gemma's eyes flicked up. "What happened yesterday?"

"I remembered what happened. I'll tell you later."

"But you—"

"No, you first. You owe me at least that."

Gemma seemed to deliberate, but then she gave in. "I found you online. One of your public posts on social media tagged the auction site, and I kind of just followed that trail. It wasn't that hard since you had your somewhat unusual first name in your user ID. Next thing I knew, I'd joined the group. I just wanted to know more. What happened to him? Did you know about us? That sort of thing. But then we started talking, and you were so... broken. And I knew how you felt.

"After a few months, I realized I liked you and I wanted to come clean, but there never seemed to be a perfect moment. At the same time, Josie was getting older, and I'd see these dads dropping off and picking up at daycare. She'll never know her dad, and I don't have any family to speak of to offer her. I thought maybe if we became friends one day, I could ask you for something of his. Something to make him real for Josie. A photo, anything. And believe me, I hear how ludicrous this sounds now, but I know what it's like to grow up without a dad. Mine was a petty criminal who forced my mom and me to flee our home when I was little."

"Oh, I'm so sorry."

"Yeah, well. Thanks. The point is, my dad didn't care about me, and I guess I want better for Josie, so if that meant becoming your friend and biding my time, I had to do it. I mean, I wanted to—I liked you—but it was also for Josie. I want her to know, or at least to feel like, her dad loved her. Because I think he would have." Her voice caught on the last word, and she averted her gaze to her hands, which were resting on the table.

Isla leaned forward and let her fingers touch Gemma's. "He absolutely would have. I don't doubt it."

A tear spilled over and rolled down Gemma's cheek, which in turn made Isla's throat tighten. Only Josie was blissfully unaware of what was taking place before her.

"You're being too nice," Gemma said, pulling her hand away and wiping her cheek. "I don't deserve it."

Isla pushed a piece of bread closer to Josie. "Maybe, maybe not."

"But I hurt your marriage."

It was true that Gemma could have said no, Isla thought, but what was to say Jonah wouldn't have found someone else if she had? Looking at the woman across from her at the table, it was obvious she was no femme fatale, no serial home wrecker, no vow breaker. She'd made a mistake by falling for the wrong guy and it had turned her life upside down. Her husband on the other hand...

"Jonah hurt our marriage. It was his choice to let you in." As she said so, Isla's shoulders tightened with an unexpected urge to punch, but it passed as soon as it appeared, because its target wasn't there. It was Jonah she should be mad at, not Gemma. Yes, Gemma had lied to her, but for a reason, while Jonah had left them both behind to pick up the pieces left by his actions.

Her words had had an edge to them though, and that got Josie's attention. The toddler startled and looked up from the messy crumbs on the table, her lower lip starting to tremble.

"Oh no, no, baby," Gemma cooed, trying to nip whatever was coming in the bud. "Here, you want your book again?" Without any concern for stains, she placed the book in front of Josie.

"Sorry," Isla said. "I didn't mean to scare her."

"You're fine."

While they'd been talking, evening had fallen outside, further shrinking the apartment into a cozy cave. Isla could see her reflection in the window across the living room. "Auntie Isla," Katelyn's kids had once called her. Was it possible Josie might one day call her that too?

The little girl shoved the book onto the floor and banged her hands on the table.

"Okay, I think you're done, sweetie." Gemma lifted Josie out of the chair and into her lap. "Is that better? Or you want your stuffies?"

Josie squirmed, and Gemma set her down on the floor. Ten seconds later, Josie had emptied a small hamper full of plush animals onto the floor.

"That works." Gemma faced Isla again. "Where were we?"

Isla watched as Josie lined up her toys in a circle. That

seemed advanced for eighteen months, didn't it? "I don't remember."

"Do you want to talk about how we go forward?"

Isla blinked and turned back to Gemma. For the first time since she'd left home that morning, she realized she hadn't thought of the "after." First and foremost, what she'd do after talking to Gemma, but also *after* she got home, *after* she could put her unknowns to rest, *after* this whole journey came to an end.

"What's the closest hotel to here?" she asked. "I probably shouldn't drive home tonight."

Gemma studied her for a moment. "You can take Josie's room if you want. There's a sleeper chair in there. Cheryl says it's comfortable."

Stay over here? Was that pushing it? "I don't know."

"Listen"—Gemma put her elbows on the table—"I know this is a weird situation, and you should absolutely do whatever feels best for you, but you need to know that while I lied about my name and my job, the rest was true. The deeper stuff. Even my love for owls. I'd like to think that's what made us friends. If you want that to be over, I completely understand, and I will leave you alone, but if it was up to me, I'd like to stay in touch."

Isla tried to picture what that would be like. On the one hand, she didn't have many friends left from before the accident, on the other, their beginning might be too odd for it to be well advised.

"Not just for me," Gemma added. "For Josie too. Like it or not, you're her best connection to her dad."

Connections...

Across the room, Josie was spoon-feeding a stuffed elephant imaginary food, oblivious to the turbulence in the universe around her.

"*Look around,*" Nana whispered.

Isla had thought she'd looked already, but considering how much she'd missed, that couldn't be true.

She sat up straighter and let the boundaries of the room dissolve to see beyond the space she occupied, outside herself. And with that eagle-eye perspective, a bigger context materialized. The truth was that Isla wasn't the closest link between Josie and Jonah. There was a whole set of aunts, uncles, cousins, and grandparents on that side who would never know Josie unless Isla connected them. Wasn't Josie an innocent who deserved to know she was wanted and loved no matter the circumstances of her birth? Then again, was Isla strong enough to move forward with the reminders of Jonah's betrayal in her life? Her head spun.

"I need to think about it," she said. "I want to say yes, but this is all a bit overwhelming."

"Whatever you need. I get it. We'll be here. But please stay the night. It's the least I can do."

And Isla did. As uncertain as she was whether Gemma's and her paths were meant to merge or merely intersect, getting on the road that evening wasn't going to help her arrive at a decision. That could only come with time.

EPILOGUE

Two months later

The sun streaked golden green through the foliage in Memorial Park as Isla strolled toward her family's spot the day of her move back to Bellingham.

Her life was once again in boxes, but this time she was on her way *to* something, not away, and on the whole, the process hadn't been as painful as she'd thought it would be. Mom had helped sort through Jonah's belongings to decide what Isla should keep and donate, Rowan had dismantled furniture and was waiting in the moving truck at the park entrance to drive her, and Mav had overseen the process from his seat on the couch with Ulysses purring in his lap. On the Bellingham side, Katelyn would have food ready for everyone when they arrived, and she'd assured Isla the whole Gallagher family was excited to once again have her in their midst.

The grass around the plaque was green and lush, welcoming Isla as she sat down. She pulled a tuft off its edge and wiped off the inscription, the embossed letters translating her loved ones' names into her skin. She'd been back only once before since everything had unfolded, but that time she hadn't been able to formulate into words what she wanted to say, so this time she'd taken a leaf from Mav's book and written a letter. With only birdsong accompanying her, she pulled the note out of her pocket, and started to read.

"*Dear Jonah. It's time to move on.*'" Her hand dropped to her knee as the sentiment reverberated through her, but then she forged on. "'*For a long time, I didn't think this day would come. I thought your death was my fault and that I should be punished, so I hid myself away from the world and retreated to a place where your memory was the only life-giving source. I could see no meaning in my job or my friends or anything else that had previously sustained me, and I was convinced I was, and deserved to be, alone.*

"'*Now I know better. I know we're all connected, and that meaning can be found wherever you look for it. If you don't believe me, ask my new grandfather, who set out to right a wrong in his life and ended up setting in motion events that led to me righting mine. Or ask Gemma for that matter. We're still in touch, and your daughter, Josie, will come to know you through both of us. Funny how things work out. I'm so sorry you didn't get to meet her.*'"

Isla paused and tilted her face skyward. She and Gemma had texted regularly since Isla had confronted her, and Isla had put together a photo album and a box containing a few of Jonah's things for Josie, but they hadn't yet met in person again. Isla told herself it was because she'd been busy planning her move, but the truth was she still didn't know if the unorthodox friendship was sensible. Even though there were days when she missed talking to her friend, and she longed to watch Josie babble through her make-believe with traits so reminiscent of the man Isla had once loved, something still held her back from bridging that final gap that would invite the two more solidly into her life.

A light breeze ruffled the note in her hand and swept her hair into her face. She tucked it behind her ear and continued reading.

"'I'd like to imagine that if you'd had the chance, you would have apologized to me for what you did and found ways to make amends. Your actions were dishonorable and beneath you, and I wish more than anything that you'd made a better choice. That said, I'm not interested in living a bitter life, so the last thing I want to say is, I forgive you. Your judgment lapsed, and ultimately, that's what caused the accident. Knowing this doesn't make it less tragic, and it doesn't make me miss what we had before any less, but it's eased the burden of blame I thought I had to carry enough to let me live again. Maybe I'll even live for both of us. Love, Isla.'"

"Oh, and say hi to Nana for me," she said as she folded the paper up. "Although something tells me she's been watching this unfold the whole time."

As the trees whispered their assent, Isla stood and brushed off her cropped jeans. There was probably more she could say, but if she allowed that to keep her here, to keep her from getting back in that moving truck, then the lessons she'd learned would have been in vain.

She backed away a step, then another.

"Goodbye," she whispered. "Wish me luck."

Three hours later, Rowan and Isla pulled to a stop outside the small townhome she'd rented in Bellingham with Katelyn as her proxy. Mom had volunteered to drive Mav in her car even though she was busy orchestrating her own move to Arizona in a few days. They'd decided that would be a more comfortable ride for him than the moving truck.

"I'm really doing this, huh?" Isla mumbled to herself.

"You'll be fine. I'll make sure of it." Rowan's reassuring voice matched her tone.

The front door of the house opened, and one of Isla's nephews stuck his head out. "They're here," he shouted into the house.

"Until you go back tomorrow," Isla said to Rowan, scratching at a new mosquito bite on her arm. Her in-laws would soon spill out into the driveway, so if she was going to ask the question that had been on her mind this past week, she had to do it now. "What do you think Mav would say if I asked him to move here? Is he set on staying in Port Townsend?"

Rowan's eyebrows drew up. "You'd want him to?"

Isla nodded. "I'm kind of attached to the old guy now."

"He only moved there because of you, you know. I think if you ask him, you'll make his day. Do it when they get here. It would be another thing to celebrate."

"And you?" Isla searched Rowan's face. "Would you come with him?"

They'd spent more time together over the past two months, caring for Mav, planning this move, enjoying spring on the Olympic Peninsula, and while it was too soon to say for sure, there were times when Isla watched him across a room, and he turned as if he'd felt it. Times when her stomach flipped when he said her name.

Jonah's dad stepped outside, waving to them. "Hello there!"

Isla returned the greeting through the window, getting ready to open the door.

"I would," Rowan said, and the cadence of his voice made Isla pause with her hand on the door handle. Their eyes met, his glinting with promise in the afternoon light.

Isla's lips tugged into a smile. "Good," she said. Then she got out of the truck.

It was a happy reunion, and with everyone pitching in, they unloaded the truck in no time, leaving plenty for catching up. Nancy and Mav arrived at the tail-end of the truck being emptied, and as soon as Isla saw them, she pulled Mav aside.

"You want me to move here?" Mav asked in response to her query. "To be near you?"

Isla took his hand. "If you're up for it."

Mav's chin began to tremble. "Nothing would bring me greater joy," he said. Then he pulled her into a tight hug.

"I take it we're moving again?" Rowan had joined them while they embraced, and now he clasped Mav's shoulder in a friendly squeeze.

"It would seem that way." There was no mistaking the gloss in Mav's blue eyes. He let out a little laugh. "I believe I'm getting sappy in my old age."

"Don't worry. We won't tell," Rowan said, exchanging an arch look with Isla.

Isla had forgotten what a raucous bunch Jonah's family could be, but it was exactly what she needed to kick off this new phase of her life. Furniture was assembled, the grill fired up, and many superlatives expressed as to how happy they were to have her back.

"Why do you have those on your face?" Ben, Katelyn's eight-year-old, asked Mav while they were eating.

"Do you like them?" Mav asked.

"A lot."

"Don't get any ideas," Katelyn warned. "No tattoos until you're a grown-up."

"You're not scared of him?" Rowan asked Ben.

"Ha! No. He looks cool. Old, but cool."

"Oh, Ben." Katelyn pursed her lips.

Mav put a hand up. "It's quite all right. I am old." He turned to Ben. "But to answer your question, I have them to remember. Each one marks a place or person or event that made me who I am. Does that make sense?"

The eight-year-old squirmed in his seat. "I guess. Would you forget if they weren't there?"

Mav stared at him, something pensive sweeping across his face. "No," he said with a small chuckle. "No, I suppose I wouldn't. What really matters tends to get etched beyond skin depth. Good point, son. Let's say I have them to look cool then." He winked.

"Okay." Ben tugged at his dad's shirt. "Dad, can we do s'mores now?"

"That's a great idea," Isla said, sensing Mav could use a break from the attention. "Rowan, why don't you get that going?"

"Will do." He rounded up the kids and headed outside.

The other adults followed, and when only Mav and Isla remained inside, she paused as she was clearing paper plates off the table and pointed to the tattoo on Mav's neck.

"I don't think I ever asked you. Did you get that hummingbird because of Nana?"

"I did."

"I think she would have liked it."

Mav looked at her a long moment. "Thank you," he said. "That means more than you know."

Isla dumped the trash in the garbage, then she held her hand out to him. "Come on. Let's go have some sweets."

The May evening had cooled off, but as they all sat huddled around the newly fanned flames in the round grill, the chill was kept at bay not only by the fire but also with sweaters around their shoulders, full stomachs, and lively conversation. Isla listened more than she spoke, content to be included, to be part of something bigger beyond her small inner world once more. These people had also lost Jonah, and they'd moved on by leaning on each other. There was strength in that togetherness. No longer would she run away from those connections and perceive them as threats. Never again.

Isla watched Jonah's mom's face as she allowed her grandson to feed her a puffed-up marshmallow; saw how her eyes crinkled with laughter as the white goop stuck to her nose. She watched Jonah's dad help Katelyn pull her jacket onto her shoulders when it slipped down; heard the low murmur of thanks drift through the air. And suddenly the question she'd kept at bay these past two months was no longer a question. Of course Josie was to be part of this family. The Gallaghers had made new room for Isla despite everything that had happened, and despite the fact that her legal claim to them was no more, so who was she to keep them from their blood? From Jonah's daughter?

Rowan brushed her arm. "You seem far away. What's up?"

She looked down at the tingling spot where he'd touched her then met his gaze. "I just realized there's something I need to do," she said in a hushed voice.

"Oh?"

She stood. "I'll tell you later. Save my seat?"

"Always."

The word held that same promise as his look had in the car earlier, and that made her brave, so as she rounded his chair, she let her hand skim across his back. There would be time for them soon, but first she had to call Gemma. Now that the decision had been made, she couldn't wait another minute.

Isla hurried through the empty house to the front step, where she sat down and clicked open a video call with shaking fingers. Gemma answered on the second ring, but the video was blurry.

"Hold on, I'm putting Josie in her PJs," she said. "One second... Almost there... Phew." Two flushed faces came into view. "Hi."

"Hi." Isla smiled.

"What's going on? Aren't you moving today?"

"I am, but..." Isla cradled the screen in both hands. "I

needed to tell you—I want you and Josie to meet Jonah's family. I want to try. All cards on the table. The wife, the mistress, the tragic death, the child. A new beginning. Maybe that's what we all need. I'm tired of living in the past."

"Duck," Josie said, holding up a yellow rubber ducky.

"I like your duck," Isla said.

"Holy cow," Gemma said. "That was unexpected."

"I'm sorry it's taken me this long."

"Are you sure?" Gemma asked.

"I'm sure-sure."

"Bird," Josie said, leaning closer to the camera while pulling at her nightgown.

Isla squinted. Was that...?

"Baby, can you let Mommy talk?" Gemma said to Josie. Then to Isla, "Sorry, it's been a long day."

"No worries. I just wanted to let you know."

"Thank you. So much." Gemma's video feed bounced as Josie climbed into her lap. "I'm... I don't know what else to say."

"Maybe we can talk tomorrow. Make plans?"

"I'd like that."

Josie was rubbing her eyes.

"Aw, she's so tired," Isla said. "And I love her nightgown." She moved her phone closer, so she could better see the hummingbird print on the front. "Your mom has good taste, Josie. Did you get that for my benefit?" she asked Gemma.

"You'd think." Gemma brought a stuffed animal into the picture that Josie immediately hugged close. "But this is actually the only piece of clothing she's inherited from me."

"I love that." Seeing the bird settled it for Isla once and for all. This was meant to be. She'd made the right call.

"Yeah, it has quite a story too. According to my mom, we showed up at the shelter when we left my dad with only the clothes on our backs and her guitar, but the nice social worker lady assigned to us gave us a duffel bag full of stuff and told me this T-shirt was special and would protect me. And it did, so I kept it. Works as a nightgown too." Gemma smiled and poked a finger into Josie's chest, making her laugh.

The light was fading fast, the clouds on the horizon now more purple than orange, and around Isla a deep stillness settled in.

"Okay, baby, should we say goodnight?" Gemma ruffled her daughter's hair.

"Night-night," Josie said.

Isla blew her a kiss as Gemma called out, "I'll talk to you tomorrow."

The screen went dark, but Isla kept staring at it, an odd stirring billowing inside her—little sparks lighting up the obscured corners of her mind like fireflies, one here, one there, tempting her to follow. A social worker with a hummingbird shirt...

No, it couldn't be, could it?

Just then, a rapid flutter caught Isla's eye in the light spilling out from the upstairs window where later that night she'd settle in to sleep.

The bird was there one moment.

And then it was gone.

A LETTER FROM ANNA

Dear Reader,

Thank you so much for reading *His Other Life*. With thousands of books to choose from, it means the world to me that you chose mine. If you found it an enjoyable escape and want to keep up to date with all my latest releases, just sign up at the following link. Your email will never be shared, and you can unsubscribe at any time.

www.bookouture.com/anna-e-collins

For me, each book I write is a new adventure. I may have an idea of the inner journey I want my characters to take before I start, but most often the exact path they take reveals itself along the way. Because of the complicated interplay between the characters through a span of many decades, this was never truer than when writing *His Other Life*. That said, the challenge was a real thrill, and I hope you felt the same as you discovered the hope and connectedness obscured by Isla's grief and loneliness.

My favorite thing about being a writer is hearing from readers, so if you loved this story, it would make my day if you'd leave a short review or get in touch through my social media or website.

Again, thank you so much for your support.

Anna

www.aecollinsbooks.com

 instagram.com/AECcreates
facebook.com/aecollinsbooks

ACKNOWLEDGEMENTS

This book is all about the interconnectedness of people, and I'm fortunate to have in my "web of life" some really stellar ones without whom I could neither put fictional characters through the wringer nor get out of bed every morning. Every one of these people deserves credit for making my life richer and more colorful on the daily.

To my agent, Kimberley Cameron, without whom there would be no books—I am, as always, deeply grateful for your staunch belief in me and my work.

To my whole incredible team at Bookouture—working with you continues to be a delight through every step of the process. Special shout-out to Claire Simmonds and Ruth Jones, whose joint editing effort has seen this book come to life. Working with editors who "get" your stories and characters truly fuels a writer's creative fire, and you both have certainly done that for me.

To my wonderful critique partners, friends, and fellow wordsmiths Megan McGee and Melissa Wiesner—your feedback on this book was invaluable and extra appreciated for its quick turnaround with deadlines looming. Your constructive honesty and willingness to invest your time are always cherished, but more than anything, I'm thankful for your friendship!

When authors tiptoe into domains outside their expertise, getting professional input makes all the difference, so a big thank you to Joyce Burback for sharing her industry know-how when I realized I knew nothing about working in a dental office.

And thank you also for keeping my smile bright. I hope you enjoy retirement!

To my husband, Brian, thanks for listening to my convoluted explanations of the various plot strings for this book until I was finally able to tie them together, and for sharing my excitement when I did. You are my anchor and my constant inspiration for all the good guys in my stories. To my kids, thank you for making me a better person, for cheering me on, and for understanding when I need to escape into my writing cave. You are my whole heart and my greatest joy.

Thank you also to my street team for your enthusiastic support, and to so many other people—friends, family, strangers—who at any point have taken an interest in, talked up, cheered for, posted about, reviewed, and recommended my books. It means more than you know.

And as always, last but not least, thank you to my readers, whether you've just found me or you've been on this journey with me since it started. My favorite part of getting to write books is when I connect with you all over these made-up worlds that still somehow matter. Thank you for reading, and thank you for letting me make up new stories again and again.

PUBLISHING TEAM

Turning a manuscript into a book requires the efforts of many people. The publishing team at Bookouture would like to acknowledge everyone who contributed to this publication.

Commercial
Lauren Morrissette
Hannah Richmond
Imogen Allport

Cover design
Emma Graves

Data and analysis
Mark Alder
Mohamed Bussuri

Editorial
Ruth Jones
Sinead O'Connor

Copyeditor
Laura Kincaid

Proofreader
Liz Hurst

Printed in Great Britain
by Amazon

58616618R00202